Crave

Gibson Boys Series, Book #3

Adriana Locke

UMBRELLA
PUBLISHING INC.

Books by Adriana Locke

My Amazon Store

Signed Copies

Brewer Family Series

The Proposal | The Arrangement | The Invitation | The Merger | The Situation

Carmichael Family Series

Flirt | Fling | Fluke | Flaunt | Flame

Landry Family Series

Sway | Swing | Switch | Swear | Swink | Sweet

Landry Family Security Series

Pulse

Gibson Boys Series

Crank | Craft | Cross | Crave | Crazy

The Mason Family Series

Restraint | The Relationship Pact | Reputation | Reckless | Relentless | Resolution

The Marshall Family Series

More Than I Could | This Much Is True

The Exception Series

The Exception | The Perception

Dogwood Lane Series

Tumble | Tangle | Trouble

Standalone Novels

**Sacrifice | Wherever It Leads | Written in the Scars | Lucky
Number Eleven | Like You Love Me | The Sweet Spot |
Nothing But It All | Between Now and Forever**

For a complete reading order and more information, visit
www.adrianalocke.com.

Chapter 1

Hadley

"This is the best idea I've ever had," I say to myself. "Or it might be the worst."

I park my car along the curb a few spaces down from Crave. The bar sits in front of me with its crooked 'a' hanging sideways on the sign. Some of the red tube lights used to form the letters are bright, while others are dim, and I wonder if I should just re-start my car and go back home.

"No," I say aloud. "You have to do this."

The sun hovers over the horizon. The sky is spectacular with bright oranges and deep purples. Sunsets are one of my favorite things in the world, but I can't enjoy this one. There are too many distractions.

Like how I didn't tell my brother, Cross, I was coming to visit a night early.

And how I forgot my toothbrush and cell phone charger back at my apartment.

And how the underwire in the push-up bra that's supposed to make me confident is actually poking a hole in the side of my boob.

Distractions abound, and I haven't even made it to the biggest distraction of all—the one with deep chocolate brown eyes and a smirk I usually want to punch off his handsome face.

Machlan Gibson. The man I'm here to convince myself I can live without.

He might tie up my insides without trying. He might've been my first kiss and my first unofficial date—the first boy I snuck out of the house to meet in the middle of the night. He might know more about me than anyone in the world and be the one person with whom I hold the most secrets.

But it doesn't matter. Not to him. And it can't to me anymore.

Every time I come back to Linton, Illinois, I hope it's the visit I stay for good. That Machlan will see what we can be, wrap me up in his arms, and ask me to work things out.

I've had that hope for years. That ends now.

This time, I'm over him. Or I will be before I leave. Somehow.

Taking a deep breath, I look back at the sign hanging askew. "You can do this," I prep myself. "Just go in, lay some groundwork, and get out before you get in over your head."

My sneakers hit the asphalt before I can rethink this entire thing. My stomach squeezes so hard I think I might have to sit back down.

Straightening my shirt, I pull a deep, steadying breath. The only indication of how wobbly I am on the inside is the way the little four-leaf clover necklace vibrates on my chest. "I've got this."

"You got what?"

I spin around, hand covering my heart, and find Peck leaning on the hood of my car. My friend since the day I met him, he's also Machlan's cousin. Ridiculously charming with his blond hair poking out the sides of his baseball cap, he has a smile that could end a world war.

"I got your number, that's what I got," I say with a laugh. "What are you doing, troublemaker?"

"Oh, just seeing what this cute little redhead was doing talking to herself. Then I realized it was you and I was like, 'Eh, I don't really need a trip to the ER tonight.'"

I know what he's getting at. Machlan *is* at Crave.

I pop him in the shoulder. He winces, humoring me, before shoving off the car and following me as I head down the sidewalk.

"What brought you back to town?" Peck asks. "Haven't seen you in a while."

I gaze at the horizon and the way the sun is barely visible over the tree line. I wish I were on Bluebird Hill watching it go down.

"Do you remember that tire swing we put up on Bluebird Hill?" I ignore his question and ask one of my own. "Is it still there?"

"I think so." He takes off his hat emblazoned with a machinery company's logo and runs a hand over his head. "I haven't been up there in a while. The last time ended up with my truck being buried up to the axle in mud and me having to call Machlan to come get it out at two in the morning." He grins sheepishly. "I'll let you guess how that call went."

My feet stop moving, so Peck halts too. We stand a few feet from the doors to Crave. His eyes search mine in a way only capable someone you've known for a long time can.

"He's in there," he says, motioning toward the door with his head.

"I hope so."

Peck's brow furrows. "Not the answer I was expecting."

"Why else would I show up here?"

"Don't you guys usually try to do this behind closed doors?" Peck asks.

"Do what?"

He runs his tongue along his bottom lip before biting down to withhold a grin. It doesn't work. I roll my eyes at both his question and reaction and head toward the door.

Whatever happens once I'm inside Crave will be fine. Either he'll serve me a drink or he'll be a major ass—either option I can work with in my plan to get over Machlan Gibson.

"Are you ignoring me?" Peck asks.

"I just want a drink," I lie.

"And what do you drink these days?" he prods, seeing through my lie. I've never been much of a drinker, and I'm definitely not the kind of girl to just stop by a bar for a drink—this bar, no less.

My mind races to come up with a drink I've heard my friends order, all the while trying not to let Peck see how hard my heart is racing and the sweat glistening on my palms. "I'm drinking a tequila and Coke."

Peck chuckles behind me. "Can I give you one quick tip?"

"No."

With a deep breath, I step into the building. Antique lanterns on the ceilings and various Christmas lights strung around the building illuminate the bar. I hold my breath before allowing the scent to hit me. It's the smell of desperation and sweat, of a thousand spilled beers and even more bad decisions. It's like perfume on your man that isn't yours: repulsive.

"Fine then," Peck says. "But when Machlan laughs his ass off because no one has ever, in the history of the universe, ordered a tequila and Coke, don't say I didn't warn you."

My cheeks burn. "Oh."

"Rum and Coke or tequila shots. Not tequila and Coke, Had." He shoves his hands in the pockets of his worn jeans as he eyes me with amusement. "But do the rum and Coke. You'd be a mess on tequila, and while I'd pay a lot of money to watch Machlan lose his shit over that, I'm not sure he'll even serve it to you."

"He has to if I order it," I say.

Peck leans back and releases a full-belly laugh. "You tell him that."

"I will." Looking him in his bright, blue eyes, I almost lose my courage and tell him to get me the hell out of here. He would. He'd take me to Goodman's, buy me a sweet tea, and drive me around as I spilled my guts. But I can't do that to him. Or me.

This wasn't a spur-of-the-moment decision. It's been a long time coming, and I finally broke down last week and realized it had to be done. I have to figure out how to move on with my life. I can't put roots down somewhere else and allow myself to fall in love or really start a life when my heart is still here. With Machlan.

Peck's face breaks into a sympathetic smile. "Take my advice and order the rum and Coke. You have a shot at getting that. Though it's a small one, it's better than your tequila chances, which are negative sixteen hundred."

"I don't understand why you don't think he'll serve me."

"Rhubarb moonshine mean anything to you?" He makes a face reminiscent of someone dying before heading toward the bar.

I stand next to the bulletin boards lining the front wall, thinking about the night with the moonshine. How Mach and I got into a huge fight and I didn't realize what moonshine was. And how he picked me up and took me home and stayed with me all night to make sure I didn't pass out in my own vomit.

Besides the people playing pool in the back, the only other patrons drinking are seated near the old jukebox. As my gaze runs across a pair of pink panties pinned to the top of one of the bulletin boards, it settles on Peck. He waves at me to join him.

His merriment at my situation is written all over his face. I hope confidence masks the fear on mine. No matter how I get to the end result, this is going to hurt.

No, this is going to be hell.

I make my way over the cement floors. A man wearing a sleeve of tattoos and an undeniable invitation tickling his lips passes me. He turns around and whistles as he walks backward to the door.

This helps.

My confidence slightly bolstered, I look back at the bar.

This *doesn't* help.

My feet shuffle, nearly tripping over an invisible boulder in my way as Machlan's lips form a thin, hard line. His arms cross his thick chest.

Even with the cool reception, my cheeks still heat.

Machlan sure knows how to make hell feel like home.

Chapter 2

Machlan

"I was wrong."

Nora slides the cash register drawer closed. "What about?"

My teeth grind together, flexing my jaw all the way to my ear. "About what I said earlier about the day not able to get worse. It could."

"What's happening—*oh* ..." Her voice trails off as she steps next to me. Her hand clamps on my shoulder and gives it a gentle squeeze. "I'll be in the back if you need me."

"Chicken," Peck calls after her.

Nora's retort and Peck's heckles fall to the wayside as Hadley gets closer.

Freckles splash across her face like they always do at the end of summer. Pieces of her hair are bleached by the sun, and her body is curvier than I remember and hot. As. Hell.

The day may look worse, but she's never looked better.

My fingers dig into the wooden bar as her muscled, tanned legs carry her my way. The white blouse almost hides the tops of her breasts, and it takes every fucking bit of self-restraint I have not to hop over the bar, pick her up, and carry her right out of here. When her brows raise in a "Got a problem?" kind of way, I hear Peck cackle. And as my hand falls to the crotch of my pants to adjust myself, I realize I don't have one problem. I most definitely have two.

Hadley's eyes meet mine, and she lifts her chin. I don't flinch. I flinched once years ago. That's what started this bullshit situation I can't win.

"Front row seats," Peck says, leaning toward me. "How'd I get so lucky?"

"Ask yourself that in thirty seconds."

"What's in thirty seconds?"

"I'm gonna split your lip." I fire a glare his way. "You didn't have anything to do with this, did you?"

"Uh, no. I want a beer. Not dead."

"Just makin' sure," I grumble.

Hadley struts across the room as though she owns the damn place. It's impossible not to watch her. Most people would buy the confident game she's playing, but most people aren't me.

Her chin is lifted too high. Her lipstick too red. Her walk too practiced to mean anything other than she's nervous as hell.

"Hey," she says. Her words are breathy as though she's just run a mile. "Can I get a ..." She glances at Peck as she sits beside him. "A rum and Coke?"

The corner of my lip is all that moves. "*You* want a rum and Coke?"

"That's what I said."

Her eyes, the same color as Nana's butterscotch pie, stare into mine. I keep searching until I find the flecks of jade that pop when she's worked up about something. The first time I saw them, I offered her a ride home from school. The second time, I was kissing her by the payphone at Goodman's. The third time, I was sinking into her next to a campfire on Bluebird Hill. This isn't the fourth time I've seen them, but it still causes the same fire to rocket through my body.

Damn her.

Customers buzz around us, unaware that I can barely breathe.

Billiard balls crack, rock music plays, and voices laugh—enough diversions to disrupt my attention. Yet all I can focus on is the spark between me and this beautiful girl who makes me want to rip my hair out.

Nora bumps my shoulder as she slides Peck a beer. "Hey, Hadley."

"Hey, Nora."

"Is everything okay?" Nora asks.

"Yeah." Hadley shrugs, the tiny little clover I won for her at the Water Festival all those years ago moving until it tucks between her breasts. "I just thought I'd come in for a drink before I head over to Cross's."

Nora glances at me out of the corner of her eye. A grin stretches across her cheeks as she looks back at Hadley. "Good luck with that."

"Right?" Hadley laughs. "Don't get me wrong. Cross and Kallie are perfect for each other, and I'm happy they're together. But staying there while they're in this honeymoon phase of their relationship should be fun."

She makes a face that I just want to kiss off her. I want to reach across the bar and grip the back of her silky sun-kissed reddish hair and pull her to me until there's nothing but a bunch of memories we're better off to forget between the two of us.

Instead, I grip the bar harder. The laminate top cracks. Peck must notice because he chokes on his beer.

"I meant good luck getting that drink, but good luck with Cross too," Nora says with a laugh. "I gotta check on the hoodlums in the back. It was good to see you, Had."

"You too." Hadley lifts the clover and toys with it in the air. Our gazes lock. "So ...?"

Blood rushes back to my fingers as I release the counter. I search for any hint as to why she's sitting in my bar because *she doesn't sit in my bar*. Not even when things are semi-reasonable between us.

"What are you doing here?" I ask.

Her chin drops at the harshness of the question. "It's good to see you, too, asshole." Her gaze chills and lingers on my skin for what feels like an eternity before she rips it away. Despite the frigidity, I'm irritated when her attention lands on Peck. "What's going on in your life, anyway, Peck?"

Peck takes a drink. "Oh, same old, same old. Working at Crank with Walker and keeping my tab here active."

"I feel for you," she says. "You work with Machlan's brother all day and then hang out with Machlan all night. How do you cope?"

"Well, Walker gives me money, and I turn around and give it to Machlan. They have a good system, if you think about it."

"Would be brilliant if you actually paid all your tab." I try to ignore Hadley, but that lasts two seconds. "What's going on in your life?"

"On vacation," she says quickly. "No girlfriend, Peck?"

"Nah, Molly hasn't come around yet." He tears at the corner of his beer label. "She will, though."

"You deserve better than her," Hadley insists. "I have this friend who I think you'd love. She—"

"Leave Peck alone. He's a big boy. He can handle his own shit." I grab a rag from beneath the counter and wipe an invisible spot between them so I don't have to see the enjoyment in Peck's eyes that I'm actually working my way into their conversation.

Peck tips his beer my way. "Is that a vote of confidence I hear?"

"Nah, more like if you want to hate yourself and go after Molly, then go for it."

"Better than ending up like you."

My head snaps up. A giant smirk is plastered on his face. The only thing that keeps me from going down that road is that Hadley is sitting a few feet away.

I toss the rag on the counter. "Hear that, Peck?"

"Hear what?"

"That. It's your thirty seconds is winding down ..."

Peck lifts off the stool. "I gotta go ... do somethin'. Find me if you somehow score a drink and need a ride home, Had." He stops short of leaving. "How long you gonna be in town?"

"I'm not sure. I had some vacation saved at my old job and don't start my new one until the first. I'm just going with the flow for a few days."

"Well, if you wanna head up to Bluebird, find me. We can go tear some shit up," Peck says.

The end of their conversation is blurred by the white noise strumming past my eardrums as I watch the two of them make plans that don't involve me. I have half a notion to interject, to take control like I usually do, and just call the shots. But I don't.

Hadley left town because of me. She moved away from her brother and her friends because I'm a jackass.

The longer she's gone, the deeper the guilt gets. There's no way to fix it, though. The things I've done, the hurt I've caused this sweet girl, are things I can't pretend she should forgive me for.

I've seen her a few times since the morning over a year ago when mascara-laced tears rolled down her cheeks, but I can't shake that vision. Her hair a tousled mess from my hands being in it the night before. Her lip quivering as she waited for me to change my mind. There was hope in her eyes that I didn't mean to put there, but I suppose I did. I did it a couple of times too many already. It's why I can't do it again.

Peck knocks on the bar top as he leaves, as if he's doing me a solid and bringing me back to the present.

"I came for a drink," she says.

"Yeah, that would work except you don't drink."

"Maybe I started."

I lift a brow. If she's fucking with me, and I'm ninety-percent sure she is, she's doing a damn good job. My blood heats as it rolls through my veins, and I have to force out the thought of her drinking with people who aren't, well, *me.* As the devil on my shoulder offers up *other* things she might be doing with people who aren't me, the vein in my temple throbs.

"I asked for a rum and Coke," she says, pressing her lips together.

"I heard."

"Damn it, Machlan. Why does everything have to be so difficult with you?"

"How am I being difficult? I'm just standing here."

Her lips part as though she's on the cusp of firing back one of her typical smartass retorts, but she surprises me: she closes her mouth.

The good thing is she shuts up. The bad thing is I can't tear my eyes way from the way her pucker plumps in a pout that sends a shockwave straight to my cock.

Fucking hell.

"Does your brother know you're home?" I ask.

Because if he didn't warn me, I'm gonna kick his ass.

"No. He thinks I'm coming in tomorrow."

The stool next to her rattles as a man who was just here sidles up beside her. "Beer," he demands and stretches his tattooed arms out too close to her for comfort.

Feet planted in place, right arm twitching to launch a shot at his weak-ass chin, I grit my teeth. Hadley flips her gaze my way before angling her body toward the douchebag.

"Didn't you just leave?" she asks him with a grin that I'm fairly sure is more for my benefit than his.

"Yeah but I couldn't stop thinking about you, so I figured I'd come back and say a proper hello."

"Isn't that sweet. What's your name?" she asks.

"Logan. Can I buy you a beer?"

"I'm Hadley, and yes, that would be great."

Logan turns to me and rests his elbow on the bar. "Make that two, bartender."

"Fresh outta beer," I deadpan.

"What the fuck you talkin' about?"

I stare at him so hard he leans away. Unbeknownst to him, he's not out of reach. My right hand could still smash his face before he realized I twitched.

"Did I stutter?" I ask.

Hadley sighs, brushing a strand of hair out of her eyes. "Come on, Mach. Stop it."

"What? I can't help I just sold my last beer to Peck."

She rolls her eyes.

Logan gives me a curious look before turning to Hadley. "Want to head outta here and find a drink somewhere else?"

Roughing a hand over my jaw, I take in Hadley. She's nervous as fuck, literally sitting on the edge of her seat. She has every reason to be. We've been in this position before. She knows how this can end. Unfortunately for the douchebag, he does not.

Hadley sighs. "Can you give me a second, Logan?"

"You don't need a second to tell him it's not happening," I say.

"This is none of your business, Machlan. Stop it."

I couldn't care less that I don't have a leg to stand on. Hadley is not my girl. She's a grown ass woman who can do what she pleases. Mostly.

I'm not about to sit in my bar and watch her walk out of here with someone else, least of all this punk ass who was in here last weekend getting a blowjob by Megan McCarter. He's the worst every night, and Hadley's all kinds of trouble tonight.

"I'd rethink this," I warn her.

"Come on," Logan says, getting off the stool. "Let's go, Hadley."

"Don't even think about it," I growl, my eyes pinned on hers.

She throws her arms up. "Why do you do this?"

"Because I can."

"Can you really?"

"Oh, Had. I assure you I can."

She ignores Logan as he suggests a bar a couple of towns over. The way she looks at me—half as if I'm a barbarian who disgusts her and the other half as if she hopes I'll scoop her up like a caveman and carry her out of here—is satisfying. She's going nowhere with him, and we both know it.

"You from around here?" Peck asks Logan as Hadley and I continue our standoff.

"Not really."

"Well, there's this place in the town next door called Peaches. Best fucking breaded tenderloins I've ever had. Takes three buns to cover the whole thing unless you break it into pieces and stack it," Peck says.

"Sounds good." Logan gets off his stool. "Thanks for the tip." He takes a couple of steps back, putting distance between himself and the rest of us.

Peck just carries on. "No problem. You should check them out. Get it with pickles and cheese and then add some salt. But here's the kicker—you know what you need to eat them with?"

Logan doesn't answer. Peck's clearly leading him, and he's waiting on the shoe to drop.

"Teeth," Peck says. "And if you don't get outta here soon, you won't be leaving with yours."

"Stop it, Peck." Hadley's eyes narrow as she sighs, returning her attention to me. "I hate you sometimes."

"Not all the time?" I ask. "Must be losing my touch."

"You know what, Logan? You better go without me. I ... It's ... Yeah." She crosses her arms over her chest and doesn't bother facing the douchebag. "Sorry about the way they acted."

I'm not. I might be sorry for a lot of things, but getting this asshole out of here without her isn't one of them.

Logan shrugs, eyeing us warily, before heading for the door. I watch him go until he's out of sight.

The burn of Hadley's stare sears my cheek. If I could stand here all damn night with her glaring at me, I would. That would mean we're in the same room, and when I'm not factoring what's best for her, that seems preferable to not being together at all.

"He seemed like a perfectly nice guy," Hadley says, breaking the silence. Her tone is fire and wit again, and I'd smile if it wouldn't instigate her further. "You had no right to run him off like that."

I scoff. "Oh, I can see how that conversation goes. 'Yeah, Cross, I don't know where your sister is. Yeah, she was in here last night and left with some asshat I threw out of here last weekend, but I figured it was okay because she said so.'"

"That's true," Peck says, sliding across the two seats between him and Hadley. "Even if that was the only reason Machlan just acted like an asshole, that excuse is true."

"Oh, don't you even act like you're innocent." Hadley pokes him in the chest. "I expected more from you, Peck."

"You do that. But don't parlay that into thinking I'm gonna help you get laid by some cartoon character."

His comment makes Hadley laugh. I can't latch onto the humorous part because I'm stuck at the "get laid" section. It's all I can do to breathe deep and not rush to the street to make sure the dickhead is gone.

The thought of her with someone else makes me crazy. It always has. I'm willing to bet it always will. But I'll be damned if I'm gonna watch it happen.

"I'll have you both know your little show isn't what dissuaded me from going with him." She flips me a look of annoyance. As it melts off her pretty face, a tempting smile replaces it. "I didn't go because I'm not wearing my pretty panties."

I can't stop my jaw from dropping. My cock swells so fast it presses against the rough fabric of my jeans and threatens to burst the seams. Memories of her tanned skin beneath white lace splayed across my sheets doesn't help. Nor does the grin toying on her lips.

She hops off the stool. Tugging at the hemline of her shirt, the fabric adjusting over the swells of her breasts, she shrugs. "Better go see Cross. Good night, guys." And before I can say anything else—before I can get my wits together or come up with a quick retort—she's gone.

And I am too.

"Hey, Peck," I say as I head toward the back of the bar.

"Yeah?"

"Help Nora lock up tonight."

"Are we taking money off my tab for that?" he shouts back.

"I don't give a flying fuck."

Storming toward the door, my entire body tight, I don't even look Nora's way.

"Where are you going?" Nora asks as I blow by her.

"Probably to hell." My palms hit the door.

Chapter 3

Hadley

"Oh my God." A rush of wind escapes my lungs as the evening air ushers me away from the bar. I'm intoxicated, and I didn't even drink. That good-looking bastard does this to me every time.

I bend down to tie my shoe. My fingers fumble with the laces, a hold-over from the adrenaline that's starting to taper off. With each second that passes, I feel a little better about my first interaction with Mach.

There was no real fighting. No bloodshed. No tears.

No sex.

"No," I groan as I stand. "I'm not going there. That is not a part of the plan."

"So there was a plan?" Machlan stands, hands tucked in his front pockets, forearms flexing a few feet in front of me. It's a casual posture that any bystander would read as a guy having an easygoing conversation with a woman. That person would be wrong.

The way his deep brown eyes are almost black and the way the little lines form between them tell me all I need to know. There's nothing casual about this.

My heart skips a beat as the scent of him rides the breeze and tortures me. It wasn't as noticeable in the bar. Out here, he's picking me apart without even trying, using his stupid cologne to unlock me like a puzzle.

His body this close to me is the equivalent of drinking three glasses of wine. I'm hot. Bothered. And the struggle to remember I have a brain and am responsible for my behavior is a real thing.

"Why did you follow me?" My words are smooth, void of emotion, and for that, I'm glad. I don't know which emotion would come through if any were attached. I want to tease him, fall into the banter we do so well, but that's not going to help the point of this visit. That's not going to help me become less attached.

"It's okay for you to pop in Crave, but it's weird for me to follow-up?"

"There's nothing to follow-up."

"I beg to differ." He starts to smile but catches it before it really breaks. "Why are you here, Had?"

"I'm not. I'm leaving."

"Will you stop fucking with me?"

"I'm not fucking with you." I move deliberately in hopes it exudes a confidence I don't own. He stands between me and the handle. "Will you move, please?"

"No."

"You know what?" I say, wedging myself against him and the door. "You're making this easier than I thought it would be." Gripping the handle, I lift. It opens, but there's not enough room to pull it wide because he. Won't. Move.

I don't look at him. I'm way too close for a move that dangerous. Instead, I tug again. The metal edge digs into his side, burying itself in the fabric of his black T-shirt, but it's not enough to make him step away.

"What is it you're trying to do?" he asks.

"Right now, it's open a door."

His chest bounces around with a deep chuckle. "Fine." He makes an exaggerated step to the side. It's just enough room for me to pull open the door. "I'm telling you—if I hear you met up with that asshole—"

"Oh, no," I say, turning around. "Don't start your shit with me."

"It's not shit, sweetheart."

Despite knowing the term of endearment wasn't used with any endearing wishes, my heart flutters. I bite the inside of my cheek to keep focus.

"And I didn't start it," he continues. "You're the one who came into Crave. I didn't come looking for you."

"I didn't come looking for you either."

It's a lie, and we both know it.

He doesn't try to quell his shit-eating grin. It stretches across his cheeks plain as day. "Nah, you did. I just can't figure out why." His lips falter. "Everything's all right, isn't it?"

"Everything is fine," I huff. "I'm not in trouble and coming back here like some damsel in distress. Although I'm sure you'd like that, wouldn't you?"

He shrugs. "You know me—Mr. Nice Guy. Always ready to lend a helping hand."

"That's such a crock of shit."

"Oh, like your little claim that you didn't come looking for me? You did, Had. Why?"

Instead of getting in the car and putting some distance between the two of us—as any reasonable, logical person would do—I lean against the door. My lungs fill with air, my senses picking up the hint of mint on his breath as he blows out a lungful of air of his own.

My body stills, my mind slows, as I'm settled by Machlan's proximity. His eyes soften, the lines in his forehead smoothen, and the tender part of him that makes my life so complicated wraps itself around my heart.

"You want to know why I'm here?" I ask, finding my resolve. "I'm here to hate you."

His laugh is immediate. "Don't you already hate me?"

"Not enough."

His laughter trickles away. He takes me in, searching my face for some answer to a question I don't know. I shiver, and it has nothing to do with the crispness of the air and everything to do with the heat of his gaze.

After what feels like entirely too long and not nearly long enough, he sighs. "Did you really think I was going to serve you a drink?"

My shoulders sink. "I don't know. Maybe."

"You don't really drink, do you? I mean, you haven't been gone that long."

"I've not actually lived here for a year and a half."

He runs a hand down his scruff-lined jaw. "It doesn't feel that long. Then again," he reconsiders, his eyes softening, "it feels like a lifetime."

Our gazes crash together, propelled by enough memories to sink us both. I know exactly what he means. On one hand, it seems as if we haven't missed a beat. But, on the other, it feels as though there's a drift between us that's deeper than ever.

"It's been long enough for a lot things to change," I say. "I'm sure they've changed for you too."

"I ..."

A car pulls up beside us and slows to a stop. I glance over to see Lance, the oldest of the three Gibson boys.

"Well, what do we have here?" he asks.

"Hey, Lance," I say.

"Hey, Had. I didn't know you were coming home." He glances at Machlan. "Did you forget to mention it?"

"No one knew," I interject. "Cross doesn't even know I'm home yet."

"But you're here. With Mach." Lance's brows pull together. "I need some help here, guys. Have you had the fight yet? Or are we still gearing up to it? I can go inside and wait with Peck, if that's better."

"Fuck you," Machlan says.

Lance laughs and pops his car into drive. "Good to see ya, Had." The car starts down the road, but he looks out the window at his brother. "I'll grab some tequila for later!"

I take advantage of Machlan's diverted attention and climb into the driver's seat. I don't get the door shut before he's in the way. Again.

When he grips the doorframe and leans inside the car, there's no ignoring his presence. Even if I wanted to, the way my body hums would be enough to remind me every half a second he's here. It's always been that way with him. I bet it always will be.

"What?" I ask.

"You said you got a new job?"

"Yeah." I give him a small, genuine smile. "I start on the first."

"In Vigo?"

I nod.

He nods too. "I guess that makes sense since you live there and all."

"I'm excited. It's a lot faster paced than where I worked before."

"Did you not like it there?"

"No, I did. I just ..." I look at the sky. I don't want him to feel bad about my choice of words, but I'm not sure how to phrase them. "I really need something fresh. To go a new direction. These past few years have been rough and ..."

My voice trails off as I watch Machlan absorb the weight of the words. I can see it in the way he shifts his weight and in the way his shoulders fall. It's probably because he's the only one who's privy to all the things those words mean.

"I, um, I think that's great." He clears his throat. He leans away, looking over my head in a blank stare. "Anybody would be lucky to have you around."

"Thanks." The word is a whisper. Anything more would be impossible around the lump in my throat. "I appreciate that, Mach."

We exchange a soft smile before he releases the doorframe.

"You going to Cross's?" he asks.

"Later," I say, starting the engine.

I don't want to leave on a sweet note that I'll think about all night. I'll have a hard enough time sleeping the way it is.

"Later?" he asks, furrowing his brow. "Where are you going now?"

"Who knows?" He glares as I reach for the door. "Probably to get a drink first."

"Don't fuck with me, Hadley."

I yank on the door but stop it before it shuts all the way. "Don't fuck with *me*, Machlan."

He steps away as the engine roars to life. There's no doubt he's annoyed, but he's amused too.

As I pull away, I'm annoyed at his incessant need to take over when I'm around. But I'm a little amused too.

All his behavior stems from a really good place. It's not that hard to remember that. Despite our problems and miscommunications and all of that, he's always been one thing: loyal.

Whether I wanted to or not, I could call him for anything. Maybe it wouldn't be the best idea, but he would do anything for me.

Everything but one thing.

The one thing that matters more than them all.

Chapter 4

Hadley

"Kallie, let me help you." I start to push back my chair before my brother's girlfriend waves me off.

"Don't you even think about it. Sit. Relax." The dishwasher swings shut with a bang. "I'm going to jump in the shower and leave you two alone for a bit."

She walks by the table where Cross and I are sitting and stops briefly to press a kiss to the top of his head. He gazes up at her with a soft smile and watches until she rounds the corner.

Settling back in my chair, my stomach full of Kallie's meatloaf and mashed potatoes, I watch my older brother. I never thought I'd see him like this—content and happy in a way that seems to come from the purest, sweetest spot. I study him, wondering what a look like that feels like on the inside.

He lifts a glass of ice water but doesn't bring it to his lips. "What?"

"Nothing."

"That look is not nothing."

I sigh and pick at the hemline of my shirt, hoping Kallie comes back in and needs Cross for some random task. Anything to get me out of this topic.

It's funny in a not-so-funny way that Cross settled down before me. On one hand, he was the wild one between the two of us. When I came to live with him and Dad after our mother died, I couldn't believe how much he got away with. Late nights. Less-than-stellar grades. A best friend who oozed trouble. On the other, I was the good girl. The book nerd. The one who beat curfew by five minutes. All indications pointed to me having my life in order way before my brother. Yet here we are in Cross and Kallie's house while my life is a disaster.

I've spent way too many years pushing in the wrong directions. It wasn't until my ex-boyfriend, Samuel, brought up marriage a couple of times that I realized how much trouble I was in.

I hated my job. I loathed my apartment. And I didn't love the man I'd spent almost a year with.

What kind of life is that?

When I saw a website on his computer about wedding proposals, all I could see was the next sixty years of my life that I didn't want. And when I tried to envision the life I did, it kept coming back to one thing. One man. Machlan.

"I was thinking about how happy you are," I say. "I haven't seen you this way in a long time, Cross. Maybe ever."

He sets the glass down. The ice cubes clink together as the water swishes around. "You know, that's true. When I was with Kallie before, I wasn't ready. I wasn't in a place to appreciate being in this place. If that makes any sense."

"Kind of."

"I'm kind of glad things didn't work out with us until now. It wouldn't have been as good then."

"You were kids."

"We were kids." He parts his lips as though he's about to say something else but doesn't. His head cocks to the side.

I have the distinct feeling this conversation is segueing to a topic I'm not ready to talk about yet.

I glance at the ceiling and study the little swirls that take the place of the popcorn that was there the last time I was here.

"New ceilings?" I ask.

"How did you notice that?"

"Well, if you remember, the last time I was here, Machlan stopped by and a piece of the popcorn fell into his drink ..."

Cross nods. "And you told him you hoped he got asbestos."

"Not one of my finer moments," I mumble. "Anyway, the ceiling looks nice. I love the swirls."

As Cross gets up and refills his water glass, probably giving me a minute to bring up seeing Machlan, I wonder if it would be possible to get up and leave. To not answer his questions. To avoid the full reason I came home—to get advice from my brother and deal with Machlan once and for all—and go.

Before I can get to my feet, Cross is sitting in front of me.

"Okay," he says. "Let's do this."

"Um, let's do what?"

"Someone said you went to Crave tonight."

My forehead rests on the edge of the table. The wood is smooth from years of wear, and I wish I could somehow melt into it and become invisible.

"That someone is named Peck, huh?" I ask.

"Yeah, maybe."

"Fucker."

He laughs, leaning back in his chair and stretching his jeans-clad legs along the side of the table. "Do we want to jump right into why you went to see Mach?" When I don't raise my head, he continues. "Or do you want to tell me why you did it at Crave? I don't have a preference, if that's what you're waiting on. I can't wait to hear the answer to all of it."

"You know what they say—curiosity killed the cat."

"Did your curiosity get the better of you tonight?"

"Uh, no." I lift my head. "I know all about Machlan Freaking Gibson and the hellhole that is Crave. There's no curiosity there, bud."

I think of all the things I wish I didn't know. Like the smell of Machlan's skin first thing in the morning and the way he donates money anonymously every year to the local school to buy winter coats for kids. I wish I didn't know how his voice sounds when he's whispering things in my ear as I drift to sleep and how he pretends not to hear when someone says his parents would've been proud of him.

Mostly, though, I wish I didn't know the way his arms feel like the safest place in the world when I'm scared and how the pad of his thumb catches my tears with such gentleness when I'm falling apart. I wish more than anything that I didn't know how graceful he is under duress. How I can't imagine going through some of the things I have with anyone but him.

I wish I didn't know any of that.

"How are things in Vigo?" Cross asks, changing tactics.

"Fine."

He runs a hand through dark hair the same color as our mother's. Seeing Cross reminds me so much of her that it's hard to even be around him sometimes.

"Should I be worried about you?" He fiddles with his glass. "You're acting weird. Even for you."

"Gee, thanks." I toss him my best smile despite the hollowness in my chest. "I'm fine. Really. Vigo is great. I'm stoked about my new job. The staff seems awesome, and I can't wait to get started. Everything is good."

Cross's grin is smug. "What about Samuel?"

"What about him?" I yawn.

"The last time I saw you, I was pretty sure you guys were serious."

"Yeah, we were. I guess." I shrug. "That's how apathetic I am about him. The only words I have for Samuel is a shrug. How bad is that?"

"Bad is a subjective term. And were is past tense."

"You're so smart, big brother."

He shakes his head. "Are you deliberately trying not to give me any information? Or is this one of those times I'm supposed to push? I'm not sure."

The chair creaks as I settle back. As if he knows we're talking about him, Samuel's name glows from my phone a few inches in front of me. I stare at his name and imagine the sound of his voice.

He's a pretty nice guy. A *good* guy, for all intents and purposes. He's smart, works hard, and balances his checkbook to the penny.

Once the glow fades and the voicemail alert chimes, I look back at my brother.

"We're on a break," I say simply.

"And how do you feel about that?"

I ponder that for a moment. "Relieved." Tucking my foot under my bottom, I ease into this conversation. "Samuel is a great guy."

"Great might be a little strong of an adjective, but I've seen worse."

"He's *nice*, Cross," I say.

"He's kind of a pudfuck."

"He is not!" I shake my head, trying not to laugh. "And don't use that word ever again."

"It fits."

"It does not. Samuel is not a pudfuck, whatever that even is."

"Then why are you *relieved* you're not together?"

I wait for my belly to flutter, for that pang of guilt to swell in my stomach for not answering his call, but neither happen. I feel like someone hit a mute button on my emotions and *that* gives me guilt.

"Maybe relieved isn't the right word," I groan. "Not dealing with him feels kind of nice for a change."

"Is he high-maintenance?"

"Not really. He's ... particular. And that's a great quality," I add quickly, "but sometimes, if the vacuum lines don't look perfect, I can live with that."

"Apparently, you can live without him too."

My smile fades as I see the truth in my brother's words. "Yeah. I can. But I wish I couldn't."

Cross sits up and folds his hands on the table. He dips his head, looking at me with no levity at all. "I'll be totally honest with you. When I met him a few weeks ago, I couldn't figure out what in the hell you were doing with him, Had. You were *blah*. You didn't laugh. You didn't joke around or reminisce about stuff."

It's true. I know it's true. I knew it was true then. That day, when Cross met Samuel, the shift started in my soul.

"I liked him," I say.

"Did you, though?" Cross sits back again. "Or did you like him because he wasn't Machlan?"

"Oh, he's not Machlan." The two of them side-by-side in my head is enough to make me snort. "I just ... Is it wrong to wish I was in love with Samuel? Like I wish I wanted to get married and have his children. I just *don't*."

My brother studies me. His big, green eyes soften, filling with a concern that shine like my mother's used to when she was alive. It rips at me and makes this harder and easier all at once.

A lump lodges itself at the base of my throat, swelling a little more with each breath I take. My chest stings like a fire is smoldering in the bottom of my lungs. If I was sitting across from anyone else, I'd be able to pretend there wasn't the start of a wildfire burning inside me.

"I wish it wasn't this way," I say softly. My guard has fallen and broken into pieces at my feet. There's a relief in being able to drop it for a while.

"What way?"

"Maybe Samuel isn't for me. Maybe that was a decision I made when I was super lonely one night and we reached for the same ice cream, okay? But there is a guy out there for me, and I'll miss him when he walks by because I'm stuck on Mach." I blink back tears. "I'm so stupid."

"You are not stupid, Had."

"I am. I really, really am." My hair swishes against my shoulders as I shake my head, blowing out a breath that takes way too long to expel. "I have the dumbest crush on him, which I know is weird for you to hear, being that you're his best friend and all ..."

"Not new information."

I grin sheepishly. "Something is wrong with me because I can't turn it off. It's like a part of me thinks he and I have a future together, and it's really messing with my life."

Cross presses his lips together. The light in his eyes has dimmed.

"I think I'm emotionally unavailable to men because I feel like I'm in a relationship with Machlan, which is so ridiculous because he's made it abundantly clear he doesn't *want* a relationship with me." I suck in a breath. "I've heard him say this, Cross. This is not some unspoken guess on my part. Yet my heart refuses to get the message."

"You can't help who you love. But you can help how much you let them hurt you." Cross's face tenses. He's clearly torn over what to do. He's been stuck in the middle of this non-relationship between his little sister and best friend for far too long. "I'm gonna talk to him."

"No, you aren't," I say. "Machlan doesn't hurt me. Not intentionally. It's my own damn fault."

"Then we need to get you away from here. Finn Miller has a cabin up on the lake. I bet you could use it if they aren't there."

"No, Cross."

"Kallie would go with you. Or take Nora. She put in her two weeks' notice tonight at Crave."

"She did?" I ask. "That surprises me."

"She's taking classes or something. I don't know. Peck mentioned it. I'm sure this will add rainbows to Machlan's attitude," he groans. "Anyway, I could call Finn and see if he minds."

Just when I think he doesn't get it, I realize he does. There's a hesitation in his tone and a cloudiness across his eyes that clues me in. It's not that he doesn't get it—he doesn't like it. He knows this will probably get uglier before it gets easier ... *if* it gets easier. But he's trying to protect me from it.

"Thank you for offering," I tell him, putting a hand over his. "But I didn't decide to come here on a whim."

"He's my best friend. I see the good sides of him, and there are a ton of them. Hell, I'd congratulate a woman if she were able to wrangle that motherfucker into forever, but Had, you're not just another woman. You're my sister. That changes everything."

"I'm aware of that. And I'm sorry it makes it weird for you."

"I'll be fine. It's not me I'm worried about." He shoves away from the table. "If you two were on the same page, I'd give you my blessing. I love you both. But this isn't easy to watch. It never has been. You've always kind of handled it, but ..." He stops and turns around. "You seem different about it today."

"I'm resolved to the fact that I have to take responsibility for my life. For my happiness."

"That's true."

"I know it is. I've always lied to myself and thought things would change between me and Machlan, but they're not going to. I have to accept that and figure out how to live with it."

"And you think being here is the way to do that?"

"Yeah." I sigh. "I can't avoid Linton forever. I can't avoid Mach either. I want to be able to come home and see you and Kallie and Emily. I want to run into Machlan at the gym or throw Kallie an engagement party and not hem and haw about it because I know he'll show up. He's going to have to be a part of my life, and I have to make that work."

"And?"

"And I'd like to be free to fall in love someday. Get married. Have a family ..." When my voice breaks on the last word, Cross reaches for me, but I wave him off.

He gives me the space to get myself together. I shove all those thoughts out of my head, something I've practiced long enough to be decent at, and get to my feet.

"You good?" he asks.

"I'm good." To help the effect, I give him a thumbs-up. "Any advice?"

I watch with amazement as his cup is rinsed and put into the dishwasher. "I have something, but it'll probably complicate things."

"Not sure it could get more complicated." I stand and make my way across the kitchen, shoving my glass in the dishwasher before he can shut it.

"You didn't rinse it."

"It only had water in it."

He scowls, pulling the cup out and rinsing it before putting it back in the dishwasher. "Kallie wants everything rinsed first."

"Oh, please." I laugh. "Has Kallie whipped you into a baby?"

"Happy wife, happy life. Isn't that what they say?"

"Yeah, but she's not your wife."

"Yet." He almost sounds offended. "Anyway, back to you. If you are really in love with Machlan like I am Kallie, then I don't think you'll ever stop loving him. Even when she left me, I still couldn't move on, and I had women throwing themselves at me."

"Ew."

He chuckles. "Can't help I'm a good-looking motherfucker."

"So. Gross."

We laugh as he closes the dishwasher.

"What I'm trying to say, I guess, is I don't think you can convince yourself you don't love him. Not if it's real love. Not if it's like I love Kallie."

"Yeah, well, maybe it's not like that," I lie, my heart squeezing. "Maybe it's a high school crush that's unrequited, and it's time I make peace with that." I head to the light switch by the refrigerator and look at my brother. "People do this all the time. The percentage of people who marry their first love is actually very low. They survive. I can too."

He walks by, looking unconvinced. "Get a Plan B together, Had. Just in case."

"I have one. I'll hate him." I flip off the light. "I got this. Don't worry."

"I have doubts."

Following him down the hallway, I feel my spirits dip. Cross flips me a final grin before closing his bedroom door behind him.

Standing in the hallway alone, my thoughts an errant mess, I sigh before heading toward the guest room. "Yeah, well, I have doubts too."

Chapter 5

Machlan

My phone rests next to the napkin holder in the center of my kitchen table. Fashionable from the eighties, each plastic side of it has faint etches of apples in the center. It's hideous and probably not worth the effort it would take to throw it in the trash where it belongs, but I can't do that. It was Mom's.

I stare at my phone like it might hop off the table and gnaw off my leg. My fingers itch to pick it up and call a number ingrained in my brain deeper than any other—one of the very few numbers I actually know. With each passing second, my stomach twists harder until it pulls into a knot so tight I wince.

"Fuck it," I say and swipe up the device. I ignore the number I really want to call and press her brother's instead. It's at the top of the list anyway from when I almost called it an hour ago but hung up before it rang.

As I gaze out the window over the sink, the phone rings once. Twice. Three times. My blood soars through my veins as a hundred thoughts speed through my mind. I snatch my keys off the counter when I hear Cross's voice come through the line. The keys clatter to the table.

"Hey," he says. His voice is the equivalent of a blank stare—neutral. Lukewarm. Beige.

"Hey."

He doesn't respond, forcing the onus back on me. Fucker. I don't know what to say. I have nothing *to* say. I just want him to tell me what I want to know and let me get back on with my night.

As I look around kitchen, finding the half-eaten peanut butter and jelly sandwich and untouched glass of milk, I search for words.

"How's the gym?" I ask finally.

Cross chuckles. "Shut the fuck up, Mach."

"Fine. What do you want me to say?" I bark. "Hadley just waltzes into Crave like she owns the damn place and orders a drink like it's her Friday night routine. Am I wrong for wanting to make sure she hasn't lost her mind and that she actually made it to your house?"

The line grows quiet as my words die off. With each passing second, I find it harder to breathe. It gets that much more difficult to keep my hands out of my hair and my voice from shouting demands at my friend.

"She's there, right?" I growl.

"What if she's not?"

"Then where the hell is she?"

"What if it's none of your business? I mean, it's *not* your business, is it?"

I must've misheard him because those are fighting words. Through clenched teeth, my knuckles turning white, I scowl. "It's always my business. You know that."

"Maybe I don't," he says, energized all of a sudden. "Maybe I agree with Hadley that you need to mind your own business."

"Maybe you need to mind your mouth, Cross." I regret the words before they're even said, but I don't take them back. "Is she there or not?"

A long pause settles awkwardly between us as I plot ways to kill him after I find Hadley. I hear Kallie whispering, what must be sheets rippling, and the sound of something creaking, then Cross sighs.

"Yes. She's here," he says.

"Good." My entire body sags against the wooden cabinets. "You could've just said that five minutes ago."

"Anything else you want to ask?"

"Not at the moment. I'll call if I think of something."

"No doubt." The sheets rustle again. "If we're done here, I'm gonna go."

"Wait," I say quickly. "Does she seem all right to you?"

"Yeah. Why?"

I think back to the night she called me late, too late, and told me she thought she was dying. How I sped to Bluebird to find her and a couple of people she never should've been with toasted on rhubarb moonshine. How I scooped her up and took her home with me and watched her sleep all night. I wiped her mouth after she puked and made her sip water even when she didn't want to. I was scared shitless. I made her promise that night she'd never drink again.

I'm sure she has. She's a grown woman. But to come in Crave and order a drink *from me* prickles at my skin. Why would she do that?

"I don't know. She never comes into Crave, never drinks. Not after your mom's accident and the one night she got hammered on moonshine ..."

"Yeah, well, how well do you know her these days?" Cross asks, oblivious to the thoughts I just had. "I mean, how much time have you really spent with her lately? People change. People grow up. People make new choices."

I can barely shuffle a swallow down my throat. She can't change. I know her. I know what makes her smile and laugh and get so incensed she can't see straight. I know she prefers strawberry jelly over grape and has never turned down an elephant ear in her life. I know who she is better than anyone, even her, and fuck him for acting like she's someone different.

"Look, Mach, she's fine. We just had dinner and a long talk about her plans and what she's doing with her life."

"Oh." I wait for him to tell me the details. He doesn't.

"She's in a good place. You don't need to worry about her."

"Oh. Okay."

I work my bottom lip between my teeth as I listen to him and Kallie whisper. Finally, he comes back to the line.

"Sorry," he says. "I gotta go. Kallie's getting antsy." She must smack him because he laughs. "When it comes to Hadley, I got her. She's my sister. You don't owe her anything."

"I ..."

"Good night, Mach."

"Yeah. Bye."

The line goes dead, the screen lit up like a Christmas tree. I hold the device and stare at the screen. On the other side of that last call is Cross and Kallie ... and Hadley.

The phone clatters against the countertop.

My hands go in my hair as I yank on the strands.

As much as I don't want to admit it, Cross is right. I need to step back. There are reasons, big ones, why things didn't work out between Hadley and me. Lines were drawn. Choices made. Things decided that would forever change the two of us individually and together, and I can't forget that.

"Hey. You home?" Peck's voice calls through the house.

My hands go from my scalp to my cheeks as I listen to his footsteps grow louder across the hardwood floors. "Yeah."

He enters the kitchen but stops quickly. Scanning the room, he settles his gaze on the sandwich. A snicker pierces the air as he takes a couple of steps toward the table and deposits the black bank bag with a thud.

"It was a good night." He wraps his hands along the back of a chair. "The register was off ten dollars, but I think it was my fault. Nora got busy, and I had to serve a couple of yuppies from Chicago. They got me talking, and I fucked up the math. I think." He scratches his head. "Anyway, I put the money in outta my pocket so it wouldn't look like it was Nora."

"You didn't have to do that."

"Yeah, well, I didn't want to add to your problems tonight." The chair is whirled around, and Peck sits his ass down. "Nora told me she put in her notice."

"Yeah."

"You replacing her?"

"Already did." My feet are heavy as they trudge across the kitchen. Ignoring Peck's curious gaze, I take my time in pulling out a chair and getting situated across from him. "Do you know Navie Barnes?"

"That would be a negative."

"She starts tomorrow."

Peck wipes his hands down the front of his pants. "Are we feelin' good about this?"

"I'm not feeling good about jack shit." I hang my head. "I knew Nora would quit. She kept saying she wasn't going back to school, but I knew she would and then would feel terrible about having to quit at the last minute. So I hired Navie a couple of weeks ago to start tomorrow."

When I lift my head, Peck is grinning.

"What?" I ask.

"Just glad you have it figured out. That's all."

"One thing out of a million."

His grin pulls wider. "What else you got goin' on?"

I stand and turn to face the window over the sink. It's so dark out I can't see a damn thing except for the security light at the cemetery a ways down. Just as I'm about to find a comfortable mental distance between myself and this mess with Hadley, Peck moves. It reminds me there is no ignoring it. At least, not for now.

"Well," I say, referring to his question. "I have Spencer Eubanks coming by this week."

"Over that building on Ash Street?"

"Yeah." I turn to look at him. "He's not really hyped on letting me do a land contract on the place. Probably for the same reason the bank wasn't either."

"You know what? That's bullshit. You're trying to do something good for this town."

"I guess this is why small towns fall apart. A guy like me—not on the town board, not a commissioner, no one fancy—can't be trusted."

Peck laughs. "I'd trust you over any of those guys all day, every day." He laces his fingers together and rests his forearms on his knees. "Ready to talk about Hadley?"

"What?" I ask, my head spinning. "That's some whiplash."

"I feel like I warmed you up some. Did a little foreplay. Too soon?"

"If that whole thing was your idea of foreplay, this explains why Molly doesn't want anything to do with you."

He raises up, his hands pressed on his heart. "That wounds me."

"Shut up." I laugh.

Peck drops his hand and laughs too. "Hadley looks good, Mach. Funny as hell. You should've seen your face when she said that line about the panties—"

"Thin ice, Peck." I have to turn away. It doesn't seem right to face him when memories of Hadley in her panties are streaming through my mind. The way her narrow hips round around to her ass and the way—

"Dude, I don't even want you to turn around. I get it." He cackles. "I gotta go. I'll leave you here to wonder what she's doing tonight."

"Oh, I know what she's doing tonight."

"What?"

"She's at Cross's house."

"For now." Peck heads for the door. "Who knows what she might do later?"

"You know something, Peck?" I shout after him. He's screwing with me. I'm ninety-percent sure. But that leaves ten percent, and that's ten too many. "Peck!"

"No, I don't know anything."

"I mean it."

"So do I."

I scurry to the doorway just in time to see him at the front door. He looks over his shoulder with his hand on the knob.

It's a struggle not to grab him by the back of the neck and shake him a little until I'm sure he's being honest. "If you know something, I want to know."

"You'll just go apeshit," he says.

"You want to see apeshit? Watch what happens when I find you tomorrow after I hear about it, and make no mistake, I *will* hear about it."

Peck slides his hat around, his blue eyes twinkling. "I don't know a damn thing other than you're too easy to wind up."

I lunge forward, but he's out the door before I get too far.

His truck starts, the engine rumbling from all the tinkering he's done to it at Crank. The sound gets louder before I hear his tires squeal, and the roar drifts off into the night. The only sound breaking the silence now is the whirl of the ceiling fan in the living room.

My back hits the cool drywall, and I rest my head against it too. My brain feels like a bunch of liquor bottles have been delivered and set around everywhere, nothing in their place. I bet I could stay up all night and not organize this mess.

Hadley's golden eyes flicker as soon as I close mine. Her pretty face smiles back at me. I fight to keep this vision of her and not let it denigrate to something more ... realistic.

I bet I could stay up all night and imagine her sweet face. I bet I will too.

Chapter 6

Hadley

"*Oh, Cross ...*"

I pull my pillow over my face, cupping the fabric against my ears, but it doesn't block out Kallie's moans. A quick peek from under the lavender lace trim shows me they've been at this for a good thirty-six minutes. The volume goes up and down, as does the thrashing of the headboard against the wall, while I hide my face again.

"*Cross!*" Kallie calls out from the other side of the wall.

I launch the pillow onto the floor. "I'm done."

Ignoring the sounds of Cross trying to shush his girlfriend and Kallie's incessant giggling, I slide on a pair of yoga pants and a T-shirt. The headboard orchestra begins again as I reach for my bag and purse. I'm out the door as Cross takes over, repeating Kallie's name.

The late-night air rustles against my skin. Fishing my keys out of my purse, I unlock the car door and toss my things in the back.

The neighborhood is dark and quiet as I climb in the driver's seat. Only the streets are partially lit from the lights dotting the sidewalks every few hundred feet. I glance at the clock and wonder where the heck I'm going to go.

Grabbing my phone out of my bra, I find my friend Emily's number.

> Me: Hey. You up?

> Her: Yup. What's happening?

> Me: You home?

> Her: No. Be home tomorrow. Can't wait to see your face!

> Me: Shit. I'm in town early and was going to come by.

> Her: Sorry! I'll be home by noon, and we can have lunch.

> Me: Sounds good.

"Guess I'll be sleeping in the car," I mutter, dropping my phone into the cup holder.

I back down the driveway. Like a sane person, I wait until I'm aimed down the road before turning on the headlights so I don't shine them in anyone's bedroom window.

With nowhere to go, I pitter through the neighborhood. Little houses are tucked in perfect little rows. Minivans are parked in more than a handful of driveways as I make my way into town.

I haven't been out and about alone at this time of night in Linton in a long time. It's calmer than I remember. No one is out driving the loop around town or tapping their brake lights as they pass each other as a small-town "hello" like we used to do. All the businesses are closed. I can't even stop at Goodman's for a tea because their lights are off too.

I drive along in silence, pondering how long Cross and Kallie might be able to maintain that kind of pace and if it's safe to go back, when I make a turn onto Beecher Street. I ease up on the accelerator.

Like everywhere else in Linton, Crave is quiet. There isn't a car on the street. No lights are on. There's not even a person loitering by the back like they do sometimes after closing.

"Keep going," I whisper. And I do ... right to Doc Burns's parking lot. My car pulls beneath a large pine tree at an angle perfect for checking out the back side of Crave.

My heartbeat quickens as I take in the stainless-steel door and large pot for plants that I suspect is filled with cigarette butts. Just to the right of that is an old wooden staircase with chipped white paint. A security light hangs haphazardly atop a tall pole and gives the area a muted yellow glow.

I pick up my phone and open the door.

"You're an idiot," I tell myself. Still, I keep moving forward.

My flip-flops smack against the pavement as I cross Beecher. A truck rumbles somewhere in the distance, but other than that, everything is perfectly still. Everything but the thrumming in my ears from my heart going wild.

I follow the train track that runs through town, over a side street, until I'm at the back of the bar. My breath billows in front of me in the cool night air.

Wishing I had a hoodie over the T-shirt, I gaze in the planter as I walk by. Sure enough, a million pounds of cigarette ash and ends float in dirty rainwater.

I make my way to the steps leading to the one-room apartment above Crave. The railing wobbles under my grip, and I wonder if it's some veiled warning by the heavens not to keep going. Like the brainiac I am, I continue up the rickety steps.

A little window is positioned next to the door. The plaid curtains are split in the middle and I peer through. It's pitch black inside.

My heart twists in my chest as I remember many nights here with Mach. In high school, when his uncle still owned Crave, we'd come up here and have poker nights with our friends. I made my first batch of cupcakes in the oven in there for Machlan's birthday and spent so many afternoons curled up against him while he watched football.

As I turn to go back to my car, I imagine Kallie's breathy moans. The sound is overshadowed by a set of tailpipes coming up the side street. I stand still, not moving a muscle, as I see a truck roll up to the curb and stop.

Peck jumps out. "What the hell are you doing, Had?"

"Hey! What are you doing out so late?"

"Going home. What are you up to?"

I glance over my shoulder and get an idea. "Come up here and give me some help."

"Um, what exactly do you need help with?" He rocks back on his heels. "Why don't you come on down from there?"

"I'm not going to jump."

"Yeah, well, one of us might die even if you don't, and that person probably isn't you."

I flip him a look. "Come on. I need some help."

Peck looks at the sky, working his neck back and forth.

"Come on, Peck," I say again. "I haven't even told you what I'm thinking."

"Why are you not at Cross's again? I know you have a bed over there, and Kallie will probably even make breakfast."

I lean on the rail. My arms almost slide off because of the dew dotting the surface. "Imagine listening to your brother go at it with his girl all night."

Peck flinches. "Got ya."

"See? I can't listen to that. It's disgusting, for one, and two ... well, it's disgusting."

He glances over my shoulder, and then, with more trepidation than I've seen him have, he looks back at me.

I grin super wide in hopes it warms him up to my idea. "You don't think Mach would mind if I slept up here, do you?"

He runs both hands down his face and mutters a few unintelligible things.

"Fine," I say. "I'll just go home with you."

His eyes pop open. "The fuck you will."

I got him. "So you propose, what? I sleep in my car? That sure sounds safe. Machlan's gonna love you for suggesting that."

"Now, I didn't say that."

"What did you say then, Peck? You won't help me sleep here," I say, motioning behind me. "And you won't let me bunk with you."

"Hadley. I. Don't. Want. To. Die. Okay? I haven't made it to the *Wheel of Fortune* yet. I haven't made love to Molly. I haven't even gotten my own dog yet, man," he whines. "Don't make me do this."

"Stop being a baby."

"But I *am* a baby." He looks at me with the biggest set of puppy dog eyes I've ever seen. "Let me go home and forget this all ever happened."

"Why?" I laugh. "Why are you acting like I'm asking you to rob a bank?"

"I'd rather rob a bank than help you break in to this apartment." He gulps.

"You're thinking of this in the wrong way. We aren't breaking in. He'd totally let me if I asked—"

"So why don't you ask?"

"Because then he'd come over here and just, bad things, Peck. Bad, bad things."

I see the start of a grin, so I keep going.

"Let's operate as if I did ask, knowing he'd approve, and he doesn't even have to know. It'll be our secret."

"I promised Mach I was oblivious to your plans tonight, and that if I did find out anything, I'd tell him."

"You don't *have* to tell him anything," I say.

"But bad, bad things will happen if I don't." He laughs. "Damn you."

Propping both hands on my hips, I stare at him from my perch. I can see him break a little more with each second that passes. But after almost a minute, he still hasn't given in, so I start toward the stairs.

"Fine. It's your house then," I say. "I like to sleep on my right side, and if I start to cuddle—"

"Fuck." He storms toward the stairs, shaking his head the entire way. "This is going to hurt. You know that?"

"I don't think so. The window looks fairly easy to pry open. I just need someone to boost me up there—"

"I meant for me. Machlan's gonna milk my pain for all it's worth."

I swat him on the shoulder and lead him to the window. "Oh, he is not, you big baby. Just pretend this never happened."

"I'm a terrible liar."

Ignoring him, I direct my attention to the little window. On the other side is a sink that won't have dishes in it because Machlan can't stand dirty dishes. There will be a bottle of soap on the left side of the faucet and a strainer in the right sink basin.

"Did you hear me?" Peck asks.

"Nope. What?"

He dangles a set of keys in the air.

"Are those to the door?" I ask.

"Unfortunately."

Snatching them out of his grip, I pop them in the lock, and the door swings open. "Peck," I say, handing him the key ring. "You're my favorite person tonight."

"Yeah, yeah, yeah."

We step inside and flip on the light. It's exactly as I expect it.

A sink sits to our right, soap and strainer in place. A little table sits a few feet away with an aloe vera plant in the center that was a start from Machlan's grandmother. A hideous orange and brown sofa is backed up against terrible brown paneling, and a television sits across from it. The long back wall has a futon, a dresser, and a little desk with a lamp.

"Smells a little musty in here," Peck notes. "Maybe we should open the window a bit."

"Yeah."

I venture into the room as Peck wrestles with the window. My heart sits at the base of my throat, pulsing with every beat. I've sat on that sofa many nights, listening to the chaos of the bar below as I waited for Machlan to come up after Crave closed. I've woken up on the futon with my face on his chest with our legs wrapped around each other so crazily that I didn't know where his started and mine ended. I've tasted his lips, felt his skin, loved his heart on those sheets, and my own heart tugs a little as I think about it.

"You okay?" he asks.

I jump at Peck's voice and turn around. "Yeah. Just thinking."

"Just in case you were thinking about it—or not," he adds. "Maybe you weren't thinking of this at all, and now I'm bringing it up and—"

"What, Peck?"

He sighs. "Machlan doesn't bring women up here. He comes in early and does some paperwork before the bar opens. He'll nap up here if the bar is dead and he doesn't need to be down there. He does all kinds of things, but never ... that."

My swallow is hard to pass. My tears are hard to blink back. I manage to do both.

"Thanks for telling me," I say. The words scald my throat as I think of Machlan holding another woman or letting her hear his heartbeat in the dead of night.

My arms fold around my middle. Peck notices.

"If you want me to stay, I can stay," he offers. "Or, despite my aversion to coffins, you can sleep at my place."

"I'll be fine. Thanks, buddy." I give him a weak smile. "I won't tell Mach you helped me."

His brow furrows. "Nah, fuck it. Tell him."

"That's a quick change of heart."

"Maybe it'll be good to fire him up some. It'll keep him off my ass for my tab." He grins and closes the distance between us, pulling me into a hug. "I'm not asking for details because it's safer not to know." He chuckles as he lets me go. "But I feel like you have something going on, and I hope it works out for you."

"Me too," I whisper.

He heads for the door. "If you care, Mach is usually here by ten. Unless you want to deal with him, you might wanna be out of here by then."

"Noted. And Peck?"

"Yeah?"

"Thanks. I appreciate you."

He winks. "Lock this behind me." He waits on the other side until I slide the lock in place. It's only then I hear his footsteps descend the stairs and his truck start and pull away.

The room seems to shrink with only me in it. I stand next to the table, a piece of furniture I know Machlan made in a high school woodworking class, and wait for a chill. An unsettled feeling. A gnawing sensation at the back of my mind.

Meandering through the small area, my lips part in a smile. It grows as I remember making peanut butter and jelly sandwiches on the tiny counter space next to the microwave and gets wider when I remember the night Machlan broke up a fight in the bar. I spent a couple of hours up here tending to his bloodied knuckles and black eye.

My eyes grow heavy as they land on the futon. Yawning, I pull back the navy blue comforter and inspect the sheets. They're crisp and clean. Slipping off my flip-flops, I flop on the mattress. The frame groans under the movement. I nestle in the pillows, yanking the blankets over my body. The entire bed smells like a mix of Machlan's laundry soap and cologne, and I sigh as I float into a dream that I never want to wake from.

Chapter 7

Machlan

You'd think I have a hangover.

My head hurts the way it does after the couple of times a year I kick back with my brothers and get a little heavy-handed with the Jim Beam. A sharp pain rips along the side of my head and shoots across my forehead, threatening to take my sanity right along with it.

What little there is left of it, anyway.

The bright, early morning light doesn't help my cause. As I turn onto Beecher Street and wave at Ruby as she heads to the library, I think my head might explode. The light almost blinds me as I grimace under my breath and pull onto the side street and then into the lot behind Crave.

I rub my temples in a futile attempt to lessen the ache between my eyes. Curiously, Beam headaches are generally less agonizing than this one. This is one I haven't felt in a long time. This is a Hadley headache.

I have all the usual symptoms of this particular affliction. Piercing pain in my skull, extraordinarily high blood pressure, shortness of breath, a quickened pulse. Rock hard cock. Intense chest pains. Feeling of hopelessness and erratic behavior.

That's what she does to me. She makes me a fucking lunatic.

Taking a deep breath, I try to focus on something other than her. The binder for my meeting with Spencer this afternoon lies on the passenger's seat. I have no idea what I'm going to say to the guy to convince him to loan me the rest of the money for the building, and I should know that by now. I sat up with those damn papers all night, trying to come up with a plan. Instead, I just planned all the ways to interrogate Cross later about what Hadley might've said or done.

"Stop it." I look at my reflection in the rearview mirror. "You're a grown ass man who has business to take care of. Stop acting like a juvenile with a hard-on."

My cheeks heat, partly from annoyance that this reminder needed to be said and partly because I'm embarrassed for the same reason. I tuck a phone number Lance gave me into the binder and look up.

My hand stills. I drop the binder.

The window to the apartment I use as a makeshift office slash crash pad is opened a sliver. I rack my brain, searching for the last time I opened it, and come up empty-handed. Peck helped me install a lock on the inside of the window, and it's a bitch to undo.

My teeth grinding together, I step out of the car. Grabbing the bamboo rod I keep hidden against the dumpster, I make my way up the steps.

The clouds clear above me. The sun's rays pelt my back, only adding to the sweat trickling down my spine as I anticipate what I'm about to find.

Nothing up there is worth a damn, but it's the idea of being defiled, the inherent disrespect, that has me itching to teach someone a lesson. I almost feel sorry for the motherfucker who did this. He'll be on the receiving end of a lot of pent-up aggression.

With my back against the wall, I make an effort not to give myself away with my heavy breathing as I lean to the side. Peering into the open slot at the bottom, I can only see a part of the kitchen area.

It looks like it always does.

Nothing's out of place. No mess to indicate a break-in. Nothing but an open window.

My palm rests on the knob, and I attempt to rotate it, but it doesn't budge. Locked tight.

"What the hell?" I whisper. Digging into my pockets, bamboo rod still in my right hand, I find the keys. They slip into the lock, and the door breaks free.

Sunlight trickles through the doorway, illuminating most of the apartment. Confusion replaces anger as I realize nothing's been bothered.

I set the rod on the kitchen counter and walk slowly inside, leaving the door open. I walk around the table and next to the sofa. My eyes adjust to the differences in light as I peer toward the futon and desk. As they settle on the bump on the middle of the mattress, I stop.

Sucking in a breath, my chest burning, I think I must be seeing things. I can't see the person's face. All I can see is a little foot with a scar across the ankle and a wrist with a tiny tattoo of a wing on the inside. Although I haven't seen the tattoo before and that bothers me, I know who is in my bed.

Every cell in my body lunges her way. The draw to her, the fight to not jump in bed and pull her up against me, knocks me off balance. I catch myself on the arm of the couch.

I glance around the room, back to the propped open window, and try to make sense of this. Before I can make heads or tails of this situation, she rustles against the sheets. I freeze. Don't move a damn muscle. Just stand in place and stare at her like some kind of demented asshole.

The blankets are batted away. Her eyes struggle to open as I watch her.

"Oh, shit," she whispers. Her voice is throaty and full of a sleepy grittiness. "What are you doing here?"

"Me?"

She sits up, grimacing. "You need a better mattress on this thing."

I slow blink. Twice. "Am I missing something here?"

Her shoulders rise and fall as she fiddles with the hair knotted on the top of her head. It's falling every which way from the thing she had it up in. Pieces are hanging all around her face and when she blows a lock dangling across her nose, I almost laugh.

"You apparently broke in my apartment, made yourself at home, and now you're bitching about my mattress?"

"Accurate. You still didn't tell me why you're here."

I throw my hands up and turn away from her. This attitude of hers is infuriating and not because I want to scream at her, but because I want to hold her down and kiss her until she stops talking.

"Peck said you didn't ... whoops," she says. "Um ..."

I whirl around. "Peck?" My brows lift to the ceiling. "Peck had something to do with this?"

"*Yeahhh* ... Kind of?"

"That motherfucker said—"

"Just stop." She tosses the blankets off her legs but doesn't get off the bed. "You would've let me stay here if I needed a place to stay."

"So?"

"So what's it matter if Peck *may or may not* have helped me get in here last night?"

I take a step toward her but stop myself before I lose the fight with my body and end up on top of her before I realize it. "It matters because I explicitly told him to tell me if he knew ..."

The look she gives me stops me from saying anything more.

"Well, I *explicitly* told him not to tell you," she says.

It's not the way her breasts fill out the tight little T-shirt she's wearing or how the pants fit the curves of her hips that has me all worked up. It's not even the way her lips form a little bud, still swollen from sleeping on her stomach like she always does.

It's the fire in her eyes. The challenge she's tossing my way. The fierce way she doesn't give two shits about what I say or do. She's going to do what she wants either way, and that pricks at something deep inside my soul that I've never been able to pinpoint. Or stop.

Damn her.

"You know what?" I say, narrowing my eyes. "It's time we get something straight."

"I agree."

Much to my surprise, a reaction I try desperately to hide, she leaps off the bed. Tugging her shirt down over the top of her pants, she props a hand on her hip. Her eyes narrow, still puffy from sleep.

"You got something you want to say?" I ask.

"Oh. Are we going to pretend like you're suddenly going to start listening to me?"

"I was going to, but you're running out of time. Better talk quick."

"You're such an asshole, Machlan."

I scratch my chin. "I know. That's why I find it so interesting that you keep coming around."

She rolls her eyes and goes back to trying to tame her gorgeous, wild hair again. "It's a coincidence."

I yank a chair away from the table and twirl it around. Sitting in it backward with arms draped over the back, I look at her. "There are no coincidences, *sweetheart*."

The last word gets her. Her eyes light up. If I were closer, I'd guarantee you can see the jade flecks.

"Especially if you consider you walked into Crave knowing there was an excellent chance I'd be there since it's *my bar*, then broke into *my apartment*."

"You own the only bar in town, and I've stayed in this apartment more times than I can count—"

"What's that have to do with anything?" I fire back.

Her chest rises and falls with the force of her breathing. "The fact of the matter is that you weren't supposed to be here." Her arms cross over her chest, her nose tipped up in some hoity-toity gesture.

Fuck that.

I go out of my way to stay out of her life. I kill myself every morning and night when I walk by her robe that hangs on the hook on the back of my bathroom door. It's the worst kind of torture to know I could drive to Vigo and see her and probably hold her if I tried hard enough.

But I don't do that. I don't do any of it. Even though I think about it every day, I let her live her life without me. That's how it's supposed to be. That's the result of the choices we made, and I have to step aside. I might be an asshole, but I'm not evil.

My eyes narrow. "I don't give a damn if I was supposed to be here or not. It's my fucking apartment."

"Fine. Get out of here and I'll get my stuff together and go."

"Oh no," I say, standing. Grabbing the chair, I fling it behind me. "You always do this."

"Do what?"

"You start running your mouth and distract me and make me forget what I was going to say. I have a point, and I haven't made it yet."

"Then you better make it."

She grins a cocky, I-got-you kind of smile. If she only knew.

"I can't with you," I say, shaking my head.

Her grin fades. Her eyes drop too. "I think we've already established that."

Our eyes lock together over the thirty-year-old carpet. The exchange says more than her lips ever could and, quite frankly, more than I could ever hear her say out loud.

The wind is knocked out of my lungs at the emotion in her eyes. "That's not what I meant to say."

"No. But I'm glad you did." She shakes her head as if the motion will rid her of thoughts of me. "Anyway, back to the point at hand. Don't even think about bringing this up to Peck."

"I'll do whatever the hell I want." I grab a can of chew out of my back pocket and flip it between my fingers. The rhythm sets a mood I think we both find some comfort in.

"Peck was helping me last night," she says over the sound of my thumb hitting the can. "Cross and Kallie were all kinds of loud, and I didn't have anywhere else to go. I figured I'd be in and out before you even knew it."

"He still should've called me. What would've happened if I'd come in here guns blazing? Then whose fault is it?"

"Mine. It would've started with *my* bad choice." She gulps. "I've had to endure consequences of bad decisions before."

As we stand across from each other, close enough to touch if we tried but far enough away to remember all the reasons why we can't, I just want to hit something. Hard. Destroy something worse than I've destroyed her. Feel the pain on my knuckles, the shots of fire that radiate up my arms when I nail something as hard as I can. Anything to distract me from the hurt bubbling up inside me.

I hate that I can't reach for her. I despise that it will always be this way between us. Our wounds are like the black eye that never quite heals, leaving traces of purple in the corner that you can see if you look at it in just the right light.

She coughs, bringing me back to the little room above the bar. "I'll be out of here in a few minutes."

"Is there anything else I need to know?" I ask, not quite ready to part from her.

"Like what?"

"I don't know. You're a drinker now. You perform breaking-and-enterings. Did you join a biker gang or something?"

She laughs, shaking her head. "No." Light streams in farther into the room, washing Hadley and me in the bright morning rays. She squints as she looks at me. The wheels are turning, and that makes me a little more nervous than it should. "Cross was telling me Nora put in her notice."

"Yeah. Sucks because everyone loves her. But she has to do what she has to do."

"I know you trust her a lot."

"She's better off finishing her degree. We'll make do." I stretch my arms overhead, the adrenaline from thinking I was going to war earlier making them ache. "I'll be a little short-staffed for a while because no one can do all the things and work all the shifts Nora did."

"Hey! I could help you." Her eyes light up like a Christmas tree. "I mean, I don't know how to be a bartender, but I have some time to kill."

"You must be out of your mind."

Even as I say the words, the idea of having her beside me every night appeals to me. I could keep an eye on her, make her smile. Feel her brush against me and hear her laugh.

"I could do it," she says. "I'm just trying to be helpful."

"It's like I don't even know you anymore." I chuckle. "You hate the bar. You hate me, for fuck's sake. What in the world is going on here?"

The fight in her eyes soften. Instead of answering me, she turns slowly toward the futon and starts making the bed.

"Uh, that wasn't rhetorical," I say.

"Maybe," she says, jerking the blankets in place, "I'm trying to evolve."

"Into what? Bonnie and Clyde?"

She glares at me, and it's the cutest fucking thing I've ever seen. "Maybe that was the wrong choice of words." She goes back to making the bed. "Maybe I'm trying to *move on*."

That causes a chill to rip up my spine. It cascades down my legs, rolling down my arms, covering my half-sleeve of tattoos with goose bumps.

"Trying to move on from what?" I ask.

"What do people move on from? The past. Old habits." She sits on the edge of the bed and looks at the wall. "Life goes by so fast. It's easy to hold onto things and ideas that aren't the best things to cling to."

Like me. My heart drops as I watch this girl almost wince as the words fall from her mouth.

Her sigh spills into the room. She tilts her head to the side until her golden eyes find mine. "I didn't drink until last year because my mother was killed by a drunk driver when I was fourteen. What's the sense in that, really?" Her lips form a small smile. "Except that night with the rhubarb moonshine."

Words are on the tip of my tongue—explanations and promises and apologies. Probably a few profanities too. But they're stolen by her soft laugh.

"It's time for me to go on with my life. Stop living in the past." She grabs her phone off the nightstand, gives it a quick look, and stands. "It's time for a lot of things, one being breakfast."

She walks in my direction, stopping a few inches in front of me. The smell of her body floods my senses. There's no distracting myself from her, here, engulfed in the sunshine.

"Thanks for letting me stay," she says, "even if you didn't let me per se. I honestly just didn't know where else to go. This place just feels like ... Well, you know."

I bite my lip, knowing I'm going to say something I'll regret later, but such is life. "You know you can stay here anytime you want. Just tell me first."

She grins. "Oh, I should've felt comfortable asking because you were so personable yesterday?"

"No. You should've asked because it's mine."

She presses her lips together and lets her gaze drift down my body. A path is seared by her eyes, scorching my skin beneath the clothes that now feel way too tight.

Her gaze lingers on my cock for a long second. It's hard as a rock, and there's no way she doesn't notice. There's also no way for me to try to hide it at this point.

When she finally looks back at my face, she doesn't even try to hide her grin either.

"We still taking about the apartment?" she teases.

I'm only a man. I step toward her, my blood running hot, but she steps back with a laugh.

"You better get out of here," I warn. My headache slides back into place as the pent-up aggression I live with on a daily basis reminds me it is, in fact, still present.

With an easy shrug, she steps around me and heads for the door. "What time should I be at work?"

"Not happening, Had."

Her laughter, and a soft one of my own, is all she leaves me with as I watch her go.

Chapter 8

Hadley

"I have to say," Emily says, picking up a breadstick, "it is so much easier seeing you when I don't have to drive all the way to Vigo to do it."

"Like the old days, right?"

I lean back in my chair as the server from Peaches checks on us. Emily tells him we're good and to please bring the check, so away he goes.

"Sorry I wasn't home last night," Emily says. "Josh wanted to go to the Mud Boggs over in Greene County, and we were there until almost three in the morning. I ended up staying the night at his house and coming home today." She looks at me over her breadstick. "What did you end up doing last night?"

Flipping my gaze to my water glass, I shrug. "Oh, not much. Just drove around a while. Ran into Peck and—"

"Ooh. What's he doing these days?"

"What's it matter to you?" I laugh.

"I'll have you know I drive by Crank sometimes just hoping he's working on a tractor or something in the parking lot without a shirt."

"He's like my brother."

"A BILF."

"Oh my God!" I laugh. "That's so gross, Em. Peck's cute, but that entire BILF thought process is wrong."

"He's *not* cute." She shakes her head, her long, black hair shining under the restaurant lights. "He's seriously one of the best-looking guys I've ever seen."

I make a face, trying to imagine Peck in the way she's describing him. "Well, it doesn't matter anyway because he's all up Molly McCarter's ass."

"I hate that bitch."

"Tell me what you really think."

She shrugs. "I will. I think she's a terrible human being that has no class or couth. She'll suck anything that gets put in her mouth."

I lift a breadstick and inspect it as though it's the most fascinating thing in the world. "Seen her around much?"

Emily's gaze is heavy on my face, but I don't look up. If I do, she'll call me out and ask me why I didn't just ask if she's been in Crave ... or with Machlan. I didn't ask because I don't want to know in the same way I do want to know.

I toss the breadstick back in the basket.

The waiter reappears with our checks and tops off our water glasses. Emily swipes up both tickets, pointing a French-tipped fingernail my way in warning not to argue with her, then hands her credit card with the checks to the waiter. They get into a conversation about credit card companies, and my thoughts drift to Machlan.

If I hadn't put my guard up immediately this morning, the day would've ended up going a whole different way. I would've been sitting here crying, having been shut down by him again or fired up from one of our infamous arguments. Lucky for me, lucky for us both, I saw him before he realized it, and that bought me a few seconds to get myself together.

Well, as much as I can when he's around.

It's hard with him because it's not. Not really. Not about anything besides being together.

"Earth to Had." Emily rests back in her seat, the waiter long gone. "What are you thinking about?"

"Nothing."

"That's fine. You can lie," she says. "I actually already know you're thinking about Machlan."

"And what would lead you to believe that?"

"Because I've been your friend forever, and I know the look you get on your face when you're thinking about him. What did he do now?"

"*He* didn't do anything," I protest. "I actually, um, I stayed in his apartment last night."

She sits upright, forcing a swallow. "With him or without him?"

"Without him. Obviously."

"Yeah, of course. Otherwise, you'd still be there." She sighs. "Why did you do that, Had?"

Although I know she's not judging me, it feels like it on some level. I wad up my napkin and set it on my plate before looking at her again.

"I didn't have anywhere else to go," I point out. "Cross and Kallie were ... occupied. You weren't home. What was I supposed to do? Stay with Peck?"

"That's what I would've done," she jokes.

"And Mach would've killed him."

"And why would he have done that?" She waits for an answer I don't give. Then she grins. "Of course, we both know the answer to that."

"Because he's an overbearing asshole?"

She rolls her eyes. "Not where I was going with that."

"But it's the truth," I push. "He doesn't want me. He—"

"He loves you. He just doesn't know what to do about it."

It's not true. I know it. But just hearing it postulated into the universe does something to the pulse of my body. Everything hums. Everything electrifies. Everything seems brighter and happier for a split second—until I remind myself she's wrong.

"Well, that's too bad because I'm here to convince myself to fall out of love with him."

I really don't have to explain it to her because I know she's reading between the lines. She knows about Samuel and how he wanted to talk marriage before we called everything off. How that conversation, the one about me being emotionally unavailable and in need of figuring out what I want out of life, was the saddest and angriest I've ever seen the otherwise sweet, sober man. Emily knows my storied history—most of it, anyway—with Machlan and how he's the one I can't get out of my mind.

She was there the night, years ago, when I cried so hard I almost passed out. It was her shoulder I leaned on when I decided to move to Vigo eighteen months ago. Emily has heard me fight with myself over every little decision in my life because ... *what if?*

The what-if is not happening.

"Has Samuel called?" she asks.

"He texted me last night to see if the dog sitter is scheduled for the rest of the month. I just texted back yes, and he left it at that."

"So responsible."

I groan. "I know. We had our life in such sync. I did these things, he did those. We didn't even live together, and it was like we were on the same calendar."

"His calendar," she points out.

"But it was a joint calendar. One where my presence was wanted." My shoulders sag as my spirits sink. "But, yeah, his calendar. Which is why, I guess, it's a good thing we split up."

"Do you miss him?"

I think back over the past couple of days and what's been on my mind. Coming home, seeing Machlan, starting my job, seeing Emily —that's what I've been thinking about. Not Samuel.

"You don't even have to answer that," Emily says.

I look at my water glass and wish it was vodka. "I need a therapist."

"You need to get laid."

"Em …"

"Orgasms paint the world rosy. You're in need of a good painting."

"That's what got me in this mess," I point out. "It was in a tent on Bluebird Hill, and the stars were almost magical. The orgasm *was* magical."

Emily snorts. "Thinking about Machlan delivering orgasms isn't going to help you."

As she says it, I can almost feel his palms on my skin. Taste the sweetness of his breath. Feel the heat between my thighs.

"You're right," I say, shivering. "It's definitely not going to help." I grab my purse and find a few bucks for a tip, then put them under the salt shaker.

"If I loved someone like you love Machlan and he didn't love me back, I think I'd hate them."

"Let's not embarrass me, okay?"

She sighs, grabbing her purse. "You have nothing to be embarrassed about. You're brave. Much braver than I would ever be." She takes out a tube of red lipstick and strategically paints it on her lips. "I see your predicament. He can be a complete jerk, and then he's the first to jump to your aid or fuck you real good."

"Emily!"

"Just going by what you've told me." She smacks her lips together and puts the lipstick away.

"*Anyway,*" I continue, "I think I need to change my plan. I need to figure out how to be around him without loving him or hating him. Just look at him like another guy I'm friends with. Like Peck," I add, proud of myself for the comparison.

"Peck is boy-next-door hot. Machlan is front-cover-of-women's-porn-magazines hot. Good luck with that." She laughs as she climbs out of her seat, taking her credit card from the waiter.

I follow her out the door. Once we're in the parking lot, Emily stops and turns to me. Her arm goes around my shoulder as we head to our cars. "Can I tell you a secret?"

"Sure."

"I'm glad you're not with Samuel anymore. He's *so* lame."

She continues her opinions as I climb into the car. Despite all the confusion in my life and all the questions I don't have answered, I can't deny it's awfully nice being home again.

Chapter 9

Machlan

"Just the man I was looking for," I say.

Peck stops in his tracks, and the door swings shut behind him. The thud sounds ominous as it echoes through the bar, sealing the sunshine out and him ... inside with me.

"I'm gonna need to know how pissed you are before I come any closer," he says.

"What an interesting thing to say." I shove my tongue in my cheek. "Why would I be pissed off?"

"Oh, *I* don't think there's anything to be pissed off about. *You*, on the other hand ..."

Tossing the rag down on the bar, I slap both palms flat against the wood. "Cut the shit, Peck."

"Oh, yeah. That's right," he says, tapping his temple. "Letting her stay at my house was a better idea. Or would you have rather I let her sleep in her car?"

"I would rather you had called me like I fucking told you to do."

"And then she would've been pissed, which I know really doesn't bother you, but I don't like the look in her eye when she's mad, okay?"

He sighs. "Besides, I left the window open so you'd know something was up. I did you a solid, bro."

"*You* did *me* a solid?"

He shoots me his stupid, goofy grin that makes it hard to be pissed. "I did. You just might not see it yet."

"You're right. I don't."

"You will." He starts to move forward but stops. "Before I come any closer and grab a beer, how pissed are ya?"

"What's the scale?"

"One to ten."

"Oh, about a seven point three."

Peck's laugh is quick and loud. "Hell, I've made you madder than that without trying. Now grab me a beer, will ya?"

I shake my head, grabbing the rag I had a few moments ago to finish cleaning the area where I cut the limes. Peck takes a seat across from me. When I don't get him a beer, he hops over the bar.

He rummages around the liquor bottles and helps himself to the contents of the candy dish by the cash register. I'd bust his balls on a normal day. Lucky for him, today is as abnormal as they come.

I love this bar. Coming in here every day isn't work to me. It's not just entertainment as Lance assumes it is or just a paycheck like Walker thinks. It's not even some attempt to stay young and half-assed irresponsible like my sister, Blaire, points out every other time we talk.

I've seen people come in here ready to drive off a cliff and leave with a smile on their face. Why? Because I poured them a shot and listened to whatever bullshit they had to say, or they ran into a friend they haven't seen in a couple of weeks and got distracted. People let their guard down here, admitting their feelings. Others cut loose and enjoy Friday night because it's fucking Friday night. This place brings people together in a way most don't understand, and being a part of it makes me feel as if I'm doing something worthwhile.

Today, I can't remember any of that. I can't find the good this place usually brings. There's only a wobbliness that started when I walked into the apartment earlier.

It's as if I've forgotten how calming Crave is to me and the only way to get that peace is to skip back in time to this morning. To her lying upstairs on my futon. To the sleepy look in her eyes.

"Who's that?" Peck asks as he walks behind me.

"Who?" I glance up, annoyed to have my attention drawn away from Hadley. Following his gaze as it settles near the storeroom, I see a head of blond hair with purple streaks framing a heart-shaped face. "Oh, that?"

"Yeah. *That.*"

"That's Navie."

Peck climbs on the stool across from me again. This time, he's not looking at me. He's looking at her.

I expected as much when I hired her. Hell, I hoped as much when I hired her—not so much from Peck, but from patrons.

Navie is pretty. Tanned, muscled body, full lips, and cheekbones that nearly touch her blue eyes. She's smart and cool and can talk to anyone about anything. But it's her moxie that makes her perfect for this job.

"Hey," she singsongs as she approaches. "I hope you don't mind, but I just swept the storeroom."

"Why would I mind?"

"Because it doesn't look like you've done it in maybe forever. I thought it might be some barkeeping superstition or something. Like if you don't sweep the floors, you get good luck."

"Nah," Peck says, leaning forward. "Mach's just a mess."

Navie turns her attention to my cousin. Her body follows suit. "And he's apparently also rude. I'm Navie."

"Nice to meet ya. I'm Peck."

They exchange a smile that has me rolling my eyes.

"You're on the clock," I tell her.

"This is a part of my job. I'm just getting to know the customers," Navie says.

"He's not a customer."

"I am too!" Peck bristles. "I'm in here almost every day."

"Customers pay," I point out.

Navie laughs. "Is he the one you were telling me would rack up charges?"

"That's him."

"I always pay, though," Peck protests. "Don't let him fool ya, Navie."

She laughs again. The melody does something to my cousin. As she walks back toward the storeroom, Peck floats behind her. I almost yell at him to leave her alone, but before I do, my gaze lands on my binder at the end of the bar.

A sinking sensation washes over me as my head muddles. I *should* be training Navie. I *want* to reminisce about Hadley. I *need* to be preparing for the meeting I have with Spencer Eubanks in less than an hour.

Sliding the book around, I open it. My entire business plan is sprawled open—including my proposal to Eubanks. Bank statements and credit letters and all the other bullshit he wanted are organized in little clear inserts for his viewing pleasure.

I wish it didn't come to this. But even if I used all of what's left of my inheritance from my parents to buy the building on Ash Street outright, I wouldn't have enough left to do the renovations necessary to make it what I want it to be. I need him to let me give him half and pay the rest in installments.

Sweet-talking people has never been my strength. Lance got all of that in the gene pool. I sure as hell don't kiss ass either. Lance got that too. What I did get is a stubborn streak that might just come in handy for the first time in my life.

"What are you doing?" Peck asks before a fresh bottle of beer cracks open.

"Looking at this shit for Eubanks." I flip a page in the binder. "This is probably my last shot at convincing him. If it doesn't happen today, it's not gonna happen."

"You know if I had the money, I'd loan it to you."

I look up at Peck as he takes a long swig of his drink and am reminded why I like him. As much crap as he gives me, and I give him, he's good people. The best people, really.

"I know," I say, looking back down. "I appreciate that."

"I mean, if I loaned you money, you'd have to be lenient on my tab, right?"

A glare is what I aim to fire at him, but a laugh comes out instead. "You're a jackass."

The door opens, and Spencer walks in. A crisp white button-down with khakis looks as out of place in Crave as a nun would. He takes in the space as if he's grading it, measuring my worthiness to pay back a loan by the looks of my bar.

My teeth grind together as I remind myself to be nice. Play nice. Let this judgmental asshole do his thing while I do mine. Peck turns his back to Spencer and makes a face before tipping back his beer and disappearing from my peripheral vision.

I take a deep breath and unlock my jaw. "Thanks for coming by," I say. Clearing my throat, I extend my hand. Spencer takes it and shakes it like a wet noodle. "Good to see you."

"Nice to see you too, Machlan," he says. Propping his briefcase on a stool, he makes no attempt to hide the fact he's surveying the bar again. "How's business?"

"Closed, right now. But it's good otherwise. I wish you'd come in last night. You could've seen for yourself."

He adjusts his collar. "Not really my scene."

My fingers clench at my side as I remind myself, once again, this is a business deal. I can't tell him off and escort him out. I can't lose my temper.

Yet.

Business deal or not, if he steps over a line—he steps over a line. The line of respect is there for everyone whether they wear an ironed shirt or not.

"I gathered all the data you asked for," I say, scooting the binder his way. "Financial statements. A business plan. Letters from my suppliers showing I pay on time every month."

His gaze falls to the blue plastic container and then back at me. "You know, Machlan, I appreciate you jumping through these hoops. I do. And it means a lot. But ..."

"What?"

"You're asking me to extend a line of credit that's pretty substantial."

He looks down his long, angular nose at me as though I'm the gum on the bottom of his designer shoe. My instincts buck against the insinuation, my body falling into a specific role I always do when dealing with situations like these—situations where someone thinks their shit don't stink and mine does.

Looking him directly in the eye, appreciating the way he's smart enough to squirm, I square my shoulders with his. "I'm not asking you to loan me thirty grand. I'm asking you to let me give you thirty thousand dollars and then take me at my word that I'll give you the next thirty thousand in installments over the next six years."

"I—"

"With interest," I add. "You'll make more money off me than off someone who can cough up sixty grand right now. You know that. And, if I don't pay up, you still have thirty thousand in your pocket and get the property back too."

He takes off his glasses and tucks them at his side. "I understand the way this works. Clearly. It's what I do for a living."

"Then why is this a hard decision?"

His shoulders fall as a breath streams in the air. "I'll be honest with you. I'm not sure you'll turn a profit over there. Not with the demographic you plan on going after."

"Kids?" I laugh. "Kids spend more money than their parents these days."

"But not at your price points. Look, Machlan, you're not going to make a living off a juvenile version *of a bar*."

I'm not sure if it's the eye-roll I think he adds in as the glasses slide over his face or the way he nearly spits the words like my idea is the most ridiculous thing he's ever heard. Either way, I heard a chuckle roll past my lips that most people are smart enough to realize isn't a reaction to something entertaining.

Spencer isn't that smart. He laughs.

"Look, Spencer. I'm not trying to make a living off your building, man. I make a living here." I lift a brow, hoping he chooses this as a fight to pick, but he doesn't, so I continue. "The building is something I want to do because I want to do it."

"Let me get this straight. You don't want to make money off this venture?"

"I didn't say that. I said I don't expect to make a living off it. I want to make enough to cover my costs. If I pocket anything after, that's great."

His glasses come off again. "I don't understand why you'd go out of your way for this. That building needs a lot of work. It's not easy starting a business. Getting permits. Getting tax papers in order. Why bother if you're not turning a profit?"

I look at the ceiling. A barrage of memories trickle through my mind as I try to come up with words that would explain to someone like Spencer, someone who probably had the world handed to him on a silver tray, why this would matter to me.

When I look at him, he's not as irritated with my lack of a response as I thought he would be. Instead, a curious look paints his face.

"When I was a teenager," I tell him, my throat all of a sudden going dry, "my parents died in a boating accident. I was supposed to be there, spending quality family time. I promised them." A swallow barely passes down my throat. "Instead, I was off with my buddies doing dumb shit, and they didn't know where to even look for me."

"So you were an irresponsible youth?"

"You have no idea." I jerk my brain off that slippery slope and back to reality, ignoring the sadness that seems to fill every cavern in my body.

"Kids do dumb things," he says.

"They do. But they do less dumb things when they have smart things to do instead. And that's why I want this building, Spencer." I flip open my binder and whirl it around to face him. My finger jabs a page with a mock-up of the interior I plan on installing. "If anyone in the world understands young, dumb kids, it's me. I wrote the book on it."

He looks at me over the rim of his glasses. "You aren't really helping yourself here."

"This place is a bar. People think of bars as places lushes go to get tanked. That's true to some extent, I guess, but not completely. This place keeps a lot of people from drinking down country roads. From staying home when they're lonely and drinking themselves to death. Instead, they come here, catch a conversation, maybe a game, and then they go home. Alive. Maybe even feeling a little better than they were when they arrived. I want to recreate this with pool tables and game systems and—"

"And not turn a profit." He closes the binder and sighs. "The truth of the matter is a business relationship like this demands a lot of trust, and that's something I don't give easily."

I can't argue with that.

My gaze lands on the binder. Sandwiched inside that plastic cover is weeks and months of planning. Of a harebrained, half-assed idea that consolidated into something I want to do. I need to do, really, in some weird way.

His hand goes to his briefcase, and I look up. He's ready to walk out of here, money still in his proverbial pocket, and I don't know how to keep him here. I don't know what to say. I know what he needs to hear, but nothing I can say will work.

There's nothing I can do that I haven't already done.

What I need is a miracle, and it's been proven I'm not the miracle-getting kind of guy.

Chapter 10

Hadley

Having no plan is better than having a bad plan.

I think.

Looking up at the unlit letters of Crave, I wonder if Machlan plans to fix the 'a'. It seems to drop a little more every time I see it. Knowing him, he probably thinks it makes the place seem less yuppie and fully expects to just let it hang until it eventually breaks free and falls to the sidewalk.

Kind of like me.

Rolling my eyes at my dramatics—although not completely untrue—I take my keys and stick them in my pocket. But I don't move. I just sit in my car and look at the bar.

I don't know why he loves this place so much—more than he might've ever loved me.

There are nights when I'm lying in bed thinking about my past, and I wonder, if Machlan hadn't bought Crave, would we have had a chance? Was the bar the nail in our coffin or the stamp on an ending that was predestined from the start?

Samuel's name flashes on my phone. I silence it while wishing I could silence myself.

Climbing out of the car, I take my time walking down the sidewalk. There's no hurry because I don't know what I'm going to say.

I tug open the door. Cool air rushes against my skin as my stomach tumbles at Machlan's energy pummeling me from somewhere close. My eyes adjust to the light.

Machlan is standing at the end of the bar, wearing a pair of jeans and a black collared shirt stretched over his body. The sleeves are short enough to display the end of the colorful art decorating the top of his right arm. It's only when the person beside him turns to face me do I even realize he's not alone.

"Hadley?" Spencer Eubanks's face breaks into a smile. "Is that you?"

"Mr. Eubanks," I say, hoping I'm covering my confusion. "What are you doing here?"

Machlan stands behind Spencer. His hand motions between me and Spencer and ends with a shrug. I give him a subtle shake of the head.

"I was talking with Machlan about a business proposal," he says. "What are you doing here?"

I ignore his second question and, instead, focus on the first. "A business proposal? This sounds interesting."

"It's not." Machlan flashes me a look. "What do you need, Had?"

Climbing on a barstool a couple of seats down from the end to leave plenty of space between me and the men, I smile. "I wanted to talk to you about a proposal of my own."

There's a glimmer in Machlan's eyes that tells me he took that the wrong way. My thighs pull together in an ill-fated attempt at dulling the combustion at the seat of my core.

The fucker somehow reads this, or at least predicts it, because the corner of his lip flickers toward the ceiling. I glare at him for good measure.

"Do you know each other well?" Spencer asks. His question feels like someone just walked in on me dressing, and I actually jump.

I laugh. "I'm sorry. What did you say?"

"I asked if you know each other well."

"I've known Mach since I was fourteen," I tell him. "We've been friends for a long time."

Machlan shakes his head, walking around the bar and positioning himself between Spencer and me. My focus starts to waver as the intoxicating mixture of his cologne and energy wallops me from head to toe.

"Friends," Machlan repeats. His lips twist in amusement. "That's us. *Friends.*"

"Maybe that's too strong of a word." I flip my gaze back to Spencer. "We've been acquaintances for a long time. My brother and Machlan are best friends. We're just in the same circle, I guess."

Machlan completely ignores Spencer's presence. He pierces me with his gaze. I shift in my seat and try to block out the questions Machlan is burning into my brain.

I take a deep breath and try to redirect this mess. "How is your mother?" I ask Spencer.

"Oh, she's good. She and Dad are leaving for their end-of-summer vacation next week. It's all I hear about."

"Did they pick Oregon or Maine?" I ask.

Spencer starts to answer, but Machlan cuts him off.

"How do you two know each other again?" he asks, obviously perturbed.

"Hadley has worked in my mother's dental office for quite a while now," Spencer says. "Mom thinks a lot of her."

My cheeks heat. "Well, your mom is pretty amazing."

Spencer releases the handle to his briefcase. His arms cross over his chest as he looks at me, then at Machlan, and finally back at me.

The feeling in the room changes, shifting from an easy banter to something more serious. Machlan feels it too because he takes a step toward me.

"Hadley ..." Spencer takes a deep breath, looks briefly at Machlan, and then rests his attention back on me. "Do you come here a lot?"

I have no idea what's going on. The way he asks this question makes me immediately uncomfortable, and Machlan's reaction to it worries me. He stretches his neck like he does when he's frustrated, and that's never, ever a good thing.

Suddenly, I'm curious. Probably too curious for my own good.

"I do," I lie. "Why do you ask?"

Machlan mumbles something under his breath, but I can't make it out.

"How much do you know about this business?" Spencer asks.

"Let's leave her out of this," Machlan says.

"Um, let's not." I lean against the bar and settle in.

Spencer sighs. "I know Hadley. I trust her judgment."

"That'd be your first mistake," Machlan says.

I rise up. "Excuse me?" Not that I particularly care what this is all about, but I'm not about to be excluded from it now. Not after that little comment. "I know a *ton* about this business."

"You do, do you?" Machlan asks.

Spencer smiles. "Have you ever worked here?"

My heartbeat quickens as I see my opening. Machlan sees it too. His lips part to interject before I can say something stupid, which I'm about to do. But, lucky for me, I can talk faster than him.

"Funnily enough, I'm starting here this week." The words come out in a rush—almost as quick as the glare from Machlan. "I have a couple of weeks before I start my new job, so I told Mach I'd come by and help out."

"Oh my God," Machlan groans.

Spencer picks up his briefcase. With a distinct nod of his head, he turns to Machlan. "I'll have a contract sent to you tonight."

"What?" Machlan's eyes grow wide.

"I don't know." Spencer laughs. "Not that your presentation wasn't compelling, but I feel better about this knowing Hadley knows you. You know how it is in this day and age. Who do you trust?"

"You can trust him," I say, softer than I intend. "You can trust Machlan."

The rise and fall of Machlan's chest matches mine—in and out in such rapid succession that it makes it hard to actually even breathe. Spencer says something about faxing the contract again, and Machlan nods. I wave without looking as Spencer says goodbye.

Before I know it, it's just me and Machlan. And Machlan doesn't look happy.

Machlan

"What the fuck was that?"

My words are ringing through the air as the door slams shut behind Spencer. There's a bite to my tone, a jagged edge to each syllable that's delivered with precision. I wait for Hadley to react. All I get is a slight roll of her eyes.

"What's what?" she asks.

My head spins, the events of the last few minutes tumbling through my mind and clamoring against each other. I can't make sense of any of it.

"You don't trust me," I say. "So what was that all about? Why did you lie for me?"

"I didn't say *I* trusted you."

"You just told Spencer he could."

She jumps off the stool and places her hands on her narrow hips. "That's Spencer."

She's inches away, close enough for me to actually hear every breath she takes. Each soft intake of air feels like an invisible arm pulling me toward her.

Everything inside me is screaming—from the elation, and relief, of getting the building. From the irritation of Hadley intervening. From the proximity of her body to mine and from the smug look she's flipping my way.

"Did you want this or not, Mach?"

"Clarify *this*."

"Fuck you."

I grin. "Is that an offer?"

Her arms cross over her chest, but the posture is muted by the way her lips part. "Clearly not." She flushes. "But thanks for going there."

"It was *your* mind that went straight to the gutter."

She drops her arms at the same time she pulls her lip between her teeth. She's definitely not doing it for my benefit because she has no way to know how hard it is for me not to reach forward and run my thumb along her jaw and free it. There's no way she knows this is the exact look, complete with the lust in her eyes I'm scared of never seeing again, that I replay as I lie in bed alone and get off to memories of being entangled in my sheets with her.

"You could've just said thank you," she points out.

"I could've."

"You should've."

"I would've if you hadn't sidetracked me."

She tilts her head to the side. "Whatever. You've never thanked me for anything in your life."

I step toward her until her back is pressed against the bar. Her eyes are wide, her breathing as heavy as mine, but she makes no indication this isn't where she wants to be.

"I can think of a few times I've thanked you," I say. My voice is as thick as the air around us, gritty with the pent-up frustration I've had since she walked her tight little ass into Crave. "Are you going to pretend you forgot?"

"I never pretend."

"So you remember when I thanked you for making those cupcakes up here for my eighteenth birthday?" The memory of what we did with that icing hits me in the groin.

Her pupils widen. "Yes."

"And you remember when I *thoroughly* thanked you for picking me up the night Peck and I got caught throwing corn at the sheriff's cars out by Bluebird?"

Whether it's intentional or not, I don't know, but she angles her body subtly toward me. Her breath is hot against my skin with every little gush of air that escapes her lips. Every move she makes floods me with the scent of her floral perfume and the sweet smell of her skin.

She swallows. "Yes. I remember that. Very well, actually."

I don't move. I'm rooted in place by her stare. It's for the best because I'm not sure what I want to do first—shove my face into the crook of her neck or twist her around and bend her over the bar. Neither of which is probably a good idea if I really think about it. Good thing that not thinking things through is one of my best qualities.

My arm raises until my hand cups the side of her face. She gasps before a full-body shiver slides across her delicate skin. Her eyes are wide, glued to my lips, as I lower them to her.

She lifts her chin to me, her eyelashes fluttering closed. She lays a hand on the center of my chest. Her fingers flex against the cotton material. If she feels how hard my heart's ricocheting off my ribs, she ignores it.

My lips hover over hers. She inhales sharply right before we touch—

"Hey, Machlan! I told Navie ... *Oh, shit.*"

Still holding Hadley's face, I twist my gaze to Peck. He looks like he's seen a ghost. Or his executioner.

"Are you fucking kidding me right now?" I growl. My eyes almost pop out of my head from the force of my teeth grinding together.

Peck stands there, mouth agape, but he's shrouded in the red of my fury.

"Trust me when I say I had no idea we were about to walk in on that." Peck gulps. "You're gonna kill me now, aren't you?"

"Brutally."

Hadley slips from beneath my grasp and slides to the side. Immediately, I miss the softness of her skin, the warmth of her proximity. I want to jerk her back, swallow the excuse on the tip of her tongue, and kiss her like she needs to be kissed. Like I need to be kissed.

"Stop it," Hadley says. She smooths out an imaginary wrinkle in her shirt and makes a point to stand a good few feet away. It's not so much that point that boils my blood, but more of the wall I sense between us again.

She doesn't look my way. Doesn't acknowledge me at all, really. Just fixes her gaze on Peck and Navie and that's what bothers me the most. That she doesn't see me. That she can pretend she wasn't just pressed against me and willing to let me touch her.

Damn it.

"I'm Hadley," she says to Navie, clearing her throat.

Navie looks between Hadley, Peck, me, and back at Hadley with a curious bend of her brow. "I'm Navie. It's nice to meet you."

"I'm sorry. Things aren't usually this awkward," Hadley says.

Peck laughs. "She's lying. They're always this awkward between the two of them."

I glare at him again. Everything inside me is lamenting the missed opportunity, and as I look at her, I'm not sure I'll get it again.

"This should be fun." Navie laughs, running a hand through her hair. "So on a different note, I just want to remind you that I have to be out of here early tonight, Machlan. I mentioned that a few weeks ago. Just wanted to make sure you remembered."

"I can help out," Hadley offers.

I don't even look at her. "The fuck you can."

"I work here now, remember?"

"The fuck you do."

"I told Spencer—"

"I don't give a rat's ass what you told Spencer," I say, turning to face her. "You don't know the first thing about bartending, for one. For two, I'm not about to let you in here at night alone."

"I can stay with her ..." Peck gulps as I flash a look his way. "Forget I said anything."

My chuckle is low and angry. But as I take in my cousin, I realize I'm not actually mad at him. Or at Hadley. I'm mad at *me.*

Something in my genetic makeup makes it impossible for me to ignore Hadley Jacobs. It's like God created me with a chink in my armor, then He created her to fit that weakness, and I can't get around it to save my fucking life.

As I look at her across the room, I can't figure out what it is that lures me so hard. She's beautiful, but I've seen women who are technically prettier. She's smart, but I've met smarter. She's funny but not quite as funny as she thinks she is. She's good and honest, but even she holds secrets and most of them are with me.

That's why I can't just write her off. I'm bound to this woman by scars etched on both our hearts; scars we share with only each other.

I tune back into the conversation as Navie picks up the remote for the television above the bar. "I love poker," she says.

"A lot of us meet up at Machlan's a couple of times a month and play. You could come sometime, if you want," Peck offers.

"Really?" Navie looks at me.

I just shrug.

"He cheats," Hadley says.

"I do not."

"You totally do," she says. "You change the rules halfway through the game—"

"No, I don't. You don't know the rules and think I'm changing them when they don't go your way."

She puts a hand on her hips. "Then how do I beat you every time?"

"Because I let you."

Navie's laugh fills the bar. "You two sound like an old married couple."

Hadley's hand falls to the side as she flips me one final gaze. She starts off toward the back of the bar. "I asked him to marry me once. He rejected me, so that won't be happening again."

I hear Navie's gasp and see Peck's jaw drop out of the corner of my eye. I wait for Hadley to look over her shoulder, to give me some clue as to why she just said that in front of an audience, but she doesn't. She just opens the door and lets it pop closed behind her.

My eyes close as I count to ten. I don't get to four before my legs start toward the back door too.

Chapter 11

Hadley

My sneakers squeak on the asphalt as I pivot to make my way up the splintered staircase. Bursting up the rickety steps, the handrail wobbling in my palm, I make my way as quickly as I can to the apartment.

I have no idea what led me to admit that out loud—in front of Peck and Navie, no less—but my cheeks are hot to the touch as I step into the kitchen.

This is not how this was supposed to go. I'm not here to let him kiss me.

But oh, God, I wish he would've.

My phone lights up on the table, and Samuel's name is on the screen with a text message. I walk right on by, leaving it untouched.

My hand touches the spot on my cheek where Machlan's hand rested.

I'm an idiot.

The entire point of being here is to figure out how to forget the touches and smiles and kisses, not to create memories of more.

I reach for my sweatpants on the bed when the sound of someone barreling up the steps stops me in my tracks. My back to the door, I wait for Machlan. I don't have to wait long.

The door opens, rocking against the wall and rattling a picture of an old man praying before dinner on the wall. His presence takes up the entire room.

I clutch the nightgown to my chest and wait for him to speak. When a few seconds pass and he doesn't utter a word, I look at him over my shoulder.

His hair is all mussed up as though he ran his hands through it on the way up here. There aren't lines bunching his forehead like I imagined. Instead, a softness tints his features that has me blowing out a thankful breath.

"That took about three seconds longer than I anticipated," I say.

"What are you doing?" he asks, not humored by my observation.

"Getting my stuff together."

"That's not what I asked."

"Um, actually, it is."

We're face to face, my sweatpants and sunshine from the open door the only things between us. My gaze drops to his right hand. My cheek tingles at the thought of him touching me. And when I look back up at him again, I know he knows what I was thinking.

He smiles carefully. "I told you to stay here."

"It's a bad idea, Mach."

"Why?"

"Because of you. And me," I add before he can object. "Look at us. One of us can't even do something nice for the other without a fight."

He considers this. "Yeah, you're right."

"I am? I mean, I am, but you agree with me?"

His gaze settles off into the distance. "Thank you for what you did with Spencer. I guess I should've led with that."

"You think?"

"Oh, so you are blaming it on me?" He grins.

"I'm not blaming *this*," I say, motioning between us, "on you. I'm just as much at fault."

"*This* is your fault," he says, motioning between us too.

"What? No. You touched me," I say, tossing my sweatpants on my bag. "You broke the barrier."

"And you came home, love."

My knees go weak, and I grab the wall for support. I think it just slipped—him calling me love—but the glimmer in his eyes makes me consider otherwise.

I press my lips together, trying to get my head on straight. He shakes his head, a cheeky smile splitting his cheeks.

"Unless you want to be almost-kissed again, stop it," he says.

I take a step back, but I can't fight the smile on my face either. "I hate you."

"Yeah. Sure looks like it."

My phone rings from its spot on the table. It sounds louder than it's ever sounded before and more urgent than it's ever buzzed. Machlan side-eyes me as he leans forward and looks at the screen.

"Who's Samuel?" he asks.

"A super nice guy who I've been dating."

"You're dating him?" He moves to pick up the phone.

"Don't you dare."

His hand stalls midair. "You're dating him?" This time, there's a gruff tone to his voice, a caution that pokes at my heart. He runs his tongue along the roof of his mouth as if going over a blueprint for war.

"No," I admit. "I'm not currently dating him. We're on a break."

"Why?"

"Do you care?" I ask.

"Depends on the answer."

He turns up the thermostat in my body with one pointed crook of his brow. I think I might melt to the floor as he leans against the wall and runs a hand up and down his bicep.

The colors of his tattoo draw me in, making it hard to look elsewhere. There are new designs etched in his skin, and I want to look closer. I want to drag my fingers down the designs and ask him why he chose each image.

"Hey," he says.

When I skirt my gaze back to his, he nods, as if prodding me to answer his question.

Sucking in a deep lungful of air, I steady myself. "We're on a break because I apparently have commitment issues."

"Good." He laughs. The jerk laughs.

"It's not funny." I head across the room again and find my flip-flops under the bed. When I stand again, he's on the other side of the bed watching me with an amused smirk. "Don't look at me like that."

"He thinks you have commitment issues? Does he even know you?"

"He knows me well enough to know I'm unable to commit."

"Since when?"

"He's known me since—"

"Since when do you have commitment issues?" He gives me a disapproving look. "And on that note, what the fuck is with you saying shit to Peck and Navie?"

"I didn't say anything that wasn't true."

I toss my flip-flops on top of my bag. He moves behind me. I just carry on into the kitchen and grab my toothbrush and toothpaste off the sink.

"Are we telling everyone everything about us now?" he asks.

My head whips to the side, and my eyes find his. "No."

He nods like he doesn't care, but I see the relief on his face.

My shoulders sag. I go about putting my things on top of my bag. They form a pile, teetering back and forth, as I add a notebook to the mix.

"Had ..."

"If this is about ... *that*," I say, my throat thick with emotion, "then don't."

His hand reaches for me and rests on my arm. I stop in my tracks and stare at the point where his skin touches mine. My chest refuses to allow enough air inside to keep me even-keeled. A flurry of memories, of hopes and dreams all gather in the corners of my eyes.

I refuse to look at him, even when he says my name again. I look away, focusing on a pile of papers on the makeshift desk next to the microwave.

My tears are hot. My nose burns. My brain wrestles for control of my overstimulated nerves. Gently, I shake my arm free from him and turn completely away.

"I've never talked to anyone about *that* but you," he says in an almost-whisper.

I sniffle, wiping my nose on the sleeve of my shirt. "I haven't either."

"I'd hug you if I didn't think you'd hit me."

I can't suppress the soft laugh. "How can you be such a jerk and then almost sweet in the same minute?"

"It's what happens when you're the fourth sibling. You get whatever genes are left. My bag of DNA didn't include enough of either, I guess. I kind of hop back and forth between them."

"You really stay on the jerk side most times."

He shrugs. "Probably." He finds my car keys on the nightstand and holds them in his palm. He looks them over as if they might tell him something, before sitting on the bed. "Let's get back to this Samuel guy."

Plopping down on the sofa, I tuck my legs under me. Machlan watches but doesn't press, and that concerns me. He's a presser. The kind of guy who doesn't give you a chance to get yourself together. But here he is, giving me space to articulate a response.

It's enough to make me want to answer him.

"He's nice, Mach. He ..." I look around the room, trying to figure out the words to use. "He's kind and smart and responsible."

Much to my amazement, Machlan doesn't laugh. He doesn't grin or smirk or give me some one-liner that makes me want to throat punch him. Instead, he leans forward and rests his elbows on his knees.

"I've been seeing him a while," I add.

"Does Cross know this?"

"Yeah."

He mumbles something I can't hear. His knuckles turn a bright white before fading back to his usual skin tone. "I'm gonna have to disagree."

"On ...?"

"All of it."

"All of what? There's nothing to disagree with," I say. "I told you my opinions."

"And I told you mine. Look, Had. If this guy was so fucking great, first of all, he'd be here trying to get you back."

"No. Part of what makes him great is that he gives me room when I ask for it."

"You don't want room," he scoffs. "When you say that shit, you really just want someone to chase after you."

My legs drop to the floor. A tinge of sadness sits over my heart because it shows why he didn't come after me when I left town. "Well, I'm glad to know you know that."

We exchange a long look. He shrugs but looks at the floor. "I'm glad to know you want someone kind and smart."

"What did you think I want?"

"I don't know."

He might say that, but he doesn't mean it. There's an idea of what he thinks I want that he won't say, and I wonder why. Before I can ask, he jams his hands in his pockets.

"You won't commit to the kind, great guy. That's what's going on?" he asks.

"Basically." I stand, too. "I'll be honest with you."

"I wish you would."

"I want to be in love with Samuel."

Machlan stills. He narrows his eyes just a touch, as if trying to comprehend what I said, before his hand slides in his back pocket.

Out comes his can of tobacco, and the thumping of his thumb against the lid strums through the room in an easy rhythm.

"You can't just 'be in love' with someone," he says finally.

"Tell me about it." I sigh. "No matter how hard I try, I can't be in love with him."

The thumping stops. "That's not a bad thing."

"It kind of is."

"No, it's not. Do you really want to wake up one morning next to someone you made yourself love?"

I look at the floor. "Sometimes I think it would be better than not having anyone to love at all." Shrugging, I flip my gaze to him for a moment because I can't linger on the sadness I see in his eyes. "I'm being dramatic."

"You still being honest?" he asks. "'Cause I'd like to know why you're here. For real. No bullshit."

When I turn away, he touches my arm lightly. I let him spin me to face him.

I wish I hadn't.

His eyes search mine with a tenderness that makes me want to curl up in a ball and cry. It's my favorite Machlan look, the one that I've only seen a handful of times. Usually, he's too guarded and ornery to let himself be exposed like this, but when he does, it's a sight to behold.

I stare at him for a long time, letting my heart find a steady pulse.

"Why are you here?" he asks again.

Without breaking eye contact, I tell him. "I need to put you in a box I can manage."

"What's that mean?"

Tears slip quietly down my cheeks. I don't think Machlan notices. His eyes don't leave mine.

"Hadley ..."

"This is so embarrassing," I admit.

He swipes a few napkins off the table and hands them to me. Our fingers touch as I take them, but he jerks his away before I can relish the micro-second of contact.

My heart pounding in my chest, my body warmed by his proximity, I do what he asked. I tell him the truth. "I'm here to figure out how to make peace with you. I fell in love with you when I was a little girl, and I can't seem to find a place in my heart to love anyone else."

"You don't love me, Had."

My jaw drops to the floor. I look at him, expecting him to laugh. Maybe grin. Chuckle, even. He doesn't.

"How could you?" he continues, sober as a judge. "I'm not fishing for gratuitous compliments because fuck that. But look at me. Look at what I've done to you, what we've been through. How could you love *me?*"

"It was pretty damn easy." I sniffle.

"This is my fault. All your memories go back to me. You moved here after your mom died, and I was the one inserting myself in your life when you should've been making friends and grieving."

"I did make friends. And I did grieve."

"And I was right there, nosing myself in."

I force a tear-filled swallow. "I'm pretty sure I let you."

He shakes his head, running a hand through his hair. "What's dickhead's job?"

"Who?"

"Fucking ... what's his name?" he asks, motioning toward my phone.

"Samuel?"

"Yeah. Samuel," he almost spits. "What's his job?"

"He's an auditor."

"That's what you need, Had. Someone like that. Not *him*," he adds, "but someone like him who makes you smile and laugh. Not someone like me. Someone like me just fucks shit up."

I hold my hand out for my keys. He's confused for a split second, then digs them out of his pocket and places them in my hand. This time, he lets his hand rest against mine.

The warmth of his palm, the way his fingers drag over mine, kicks my tears back into high gear. My stomach knots. My chest aches.

"What can I do to help you?" he asks.

"Stop trying to kiss me."

He almost cracks a grin as he draws his hand away. He shoves his chew can back in his pocket and trudges to the door. He pulls it open, light filling the room in a happy flood of sunshine. Neither of us smiles.

My phone rings again. We both look at it. Machlan grimaces, biting his bottom lip, before stepping outside.

"Lock up behind me," he orders.

"I told you I was leaving."

He leans against the doorframe, his bicep flexing as he grabs the top of the door. "And I said you were staying."

"Mach—"

"Let me win this one, Hadley." He drops his arm. "Just give me this. Please."

The sweetness in his eyes, the way he looks at me with such genuine care makes me give in.

"Okay," I say.

I ignore the flutter in my heart and shut the door. I flip the lock. It's only then do I hear him descend the stairs. It's only then, too, do I turn my phone off and climb into bed in the middle of the afternoon.

Chapter 12

Machlan

"What smells so good in here?"

I step through the screen door and scare the shit out of my poor nana. She jumps and clutches her chest. "Machlan Daniel. Don't you do that to me." Wielding a wooden spoon in her hand, she waggles it my way.

My hands go up in self-defense. A spatula doesn't feel great when your nana whips it through the air and wallops you on the back. I made the mistake of mentioning she decorated it with cocks one time. Just once. I've avoided the spatula since.

She sticks her cheek out as I approach. I place a kiss on the side of her face as I walk by. "Sorry, Nana."

"You boys are gonna be the death of me."

"Let's not talk about your death."

"It was an expression, Machlan," she says. She turns back to the stove and stirs something in a copper pot.

"It was an expression I don't appreciate." I hop on top of the island, knowing damn good and well she'll swat me down when she turns around. "You didn't answer me."

"About what?"

90

"What are ya making? Smells good."

"I have a ham in the oven and have some—get your hiney off my counter!" She swats my leg. "Goodness gracious, boy. Were you raised in a barn?"

I shrug. "Maybe."

"You were not. Now get off there."

Her orders, delivered with the firmness of a sergeant but with the smile of a grandmother, make me laugh. I sit at a stool and watch her cook.

She meanders around the space, lifting lids and getting things out of the refrigerator. She rattles on about some television show she watched that said a kitchen is dirtier than a bathroom, and I tune her out when she switches topics to her soap operas.

I don't have time to listen to that crap. I'm living a soap opera of my own.

The corner of my lips turn up as I think of Hadley. I don't know what I'm going to do with that girl. It was easier when she was in Vigo and Cross withheld information. I could rationalize that, tell myself she was happy and to just let her be. But now, with her right under my nose, I can't pretend she's not there. I can't pretend I don't want to be near her. I don't want to.

My breath comes out in a long, slow drawl. It's enough to have Nana turning around with a concerned look.

"A ham on a weeknight?" I ask before she can dictate the direction of this conversation. "Seems weird. You got a boyfriend or something?"

"Not that it would be any of your business, but no. I don't." She furrows her brow as she turns back to the stove and shuts off a timer. "Lance called. He and Mariah are coming for dinner."

"And I wasn't invited? I'm hurt."

She glances at me over her shoulder. "You're always invited, honey."

"I kinda don't remember the phone call saying, 'Hey, Machlan. We're having dinner tonight.'"

She sets her spoon on a little tray on the counter. "I think Lance is up to something."

"Lance is *always* up to something."

"No, I mean a serious something. Do you know anything about this?"

I balk. "Nana, are you asking me to gossip about my brother?"

"Gossip? No."

"Yeah. You are." I shake my head as if I'm utterly amazed at this revelation. "Wasn't the pastor just preaching about gossiping last week?"

Her mouth hangs open.

"And about my brother, no less," I add. "I'm disappointed in you."

She recovers, grabbing a dish towel and throwing it at me. "You're so full of it."

"Full of what?" I goad, ducking as the yellow-and-white checkered rag goes over my head.

"Nothing good." She swats my shoulder as she walks by to pick up the errant towel. "At least you were listening in church, though. That's a good sign."

"I always listen. Sometimes to the pastor too."

I watch as she moseys back to the oven. She opens it, and the entire room is filled with the sweet, smoky scents of baked ham and pineapple.

"You really don't know what Lance wants?" she asks, resting the baking dish on a towel. "I have no idea what to expect from that boy."

"I really don't know. You know I'd tell you. I mean, you feed me."

She laughs, shaking her head. She gets out a plate and busies herself at the stove. I slide my finger along the edge of a cake on the island and plop the icing in my mouth while she isn't looking.

"You staying for dinner?" Nana asks.

"I wasn't invited."

"I won't ask again."

"Oh, you will too."

"I just hate the thought of you going home alone and eating by yourself."

"Which is why you totally called me tonight, right?"

She fires a warning look over her shoulder. "Keep it up and no cheeseball for you on Sunday."

I make a face. "Wow. Going right for the jugular, huh?"

Nana busies herself again, going off on a tangent about how nice her yard looks. Walker apparently mowed it yesterday, and you'd think he shit gold.

Through the window above the sink, I see the evening sky. It's almost like a painting. I can't see a sky like that and not think of Hadley.

Evenings are her favorite time of day. I remember when she wanted to be a painter her sophomore year of high school. I bought her all these fancy paints and an easel for Christmas. She spent hours of her life outside, watching the sun go down and trying to capture it on a canvas.

"If you won't stay for dinner," Nana says, setting a plate down in front of me, "you can at least eat before you go."

"Lance is gonna be pissed I got a plate before him." I smile as broadly as I can. "That really makes me happy, Nana."

"You and that mouth."

"Just think," I say, picking up the fork beside the plate. "I kissed you with this mouth."

She makes a face but laughs the entire time. As I take a bite of ham, she meanders around the island and hoists herself on a stool beside me. She groans as she gets situated, and a stab of fear races down my spine.

"You okay?" I ask, my fork suspended in midair.

"Oh, I'm fine. My back is just a little sore."

"Want me to take you to see Doc Burns tomorrow?"

She places a hand on my arm. It's not a swat and isn't accompanied with a laugh or a joke about getting old. Instead, it feels a lot like a plea not to talk about it.

My throat squeezes shut as I look at her wrinkled skin. Her wedding ring still sparkles on her finger even though my grandfather has been dead for ten years.

Nana is my consistent, the woman who looked after me after my parents died. The one who makes me chicken noodle soup when I get a slight cough—even when she's knows I'm faking just to get the soup. She's not to blame for the bad parts of me, but the credit goes to her for most of the good parts.

The idea of something happening to her makes me want to be sick.

"Ready to talk?" she asks.

I shove a spoonful of scalloped potatoes in my mouth. "About what?"

"About whatever brought you here."

"Don't I come here to check on you all the time without wanting to talk?" I ask, still trying to shake off something being wrong with Nana.

"Yes. You're a good boy and check on me all the time. But you do it differently most days."

"You're nuts."

She tilts her head to the side. "No. I think I'm observant."

I load my mouth with potatoes again so I don't have to respond.

She starts a story about my parents. Just the mention of my mother and the taste of the home cooked dinner has me lifting the fork a little slower.

I miss this. A lot. More than I'd ever admit to her or my brothers or Blaire. It's why I don't miss Sunday dinners at Nana's and why my ass is in a pew nearly every Sunday. As much of a heathen as I am, a part of me really likes the slower pace of family dinners. The way you can relax and catch up from the week. How someone cared about you enough to fix you dinner. How someone would miss you if you didn't show up. How maybe, despite all the bullshit you do and have done, it can be okay somehow.

Nana's face is animated, her hands waving through the air as she finishes her story. I wonder what will happen when she does pass away some day. My stomach roils. I drop my fork.

"Is it okay?" she asks, looking at my plate.

"It was really good."

"But you didn't clean your plate."

"I, uh, I grabbed a sandwich a little while ago."

She doesn't believe me but doesn't push it. "I talked to Blaire today. She seems to be doing good."

"I think she got laid on her trip to Savannah."

She shakes her head. "Don't talk that way around me."

I lean forward, resting my elbows on the counter. "Oh, come on, Nana. It's not like you don't know what happens."

"Of course, I know," she says, patting her silver hair wrapped in a bun high on her head. "It's not like I was always this old."

"I bet you were a maniac," I tease.

"Well, I wasn't a wallflower, if that's what you mean."

"Nana!"

Her cheeks flush as she rinses my plate and sticks it in the dishwasher. "Your poor grandpa didn't stand a chance."

"So you're where we get it."

"Get what?"

I look at her and try not to laugh as reality settles over her cute little face.

"Well, I guess it could be true ..." She smiles sheepishly.

My laughter comes quick and loud as I hop off the stool. "Lord, I love you." I pull her into a one-armed hug and kiss the top of her head. "Thanks for dinner."

She wraps her arms around my waist and doesn't let go. "I love you, Machlan. Even if you're ornery."

"I love you especially when you are."

She smacks my stomach. Despite her playfulness, I sense something else on the cusp of spilling over. I do quick math and wonder if I can get out of here before she brings whatever it is up.

The answer is no.

"I'm worried about you, sweetheart," she says.

"Why?"

"When was the last time you brought a young lady over here?"

I bite my lip. "Two thousand fifteen? Fourteen, maybe?"

She smacks me again. "I'm being serious."

"Me too." I dodge the next slap and step away. "I'm fine."

"I know you are. But I want you to be great."

"Fine. I'm great, Nana."

She rolls her eyes. "Your brothers both have a woman in their lives, and Blaire might even have a man."

"What makes you think I don't have someone?"

"Because you're at your grandmother's way too often to be a man with a lady waiting."

This is true, and I have a hard time disagreeing with her logic. I am here more than most mid-twenties men who are in good shape and make decent money. I also never bring women around. This is mostly because I don't fuck around too much, but I heard she thought Lance was gay once and really don't want to have to spend time making her believe I'm not.

"Maybe I like you better than her," I offer with a shrug.

"Or maybe she doesn't exist."

"Are you saying I can't get a woman, Nana? Wow. What's with you and the hurtful comments tonight?"

"I'm not being hurtful. And I wasn't saying that either." She goes to the cabinets and takes out a container. "I'm just saying I want you to have someone to look out for you. And I definitely want to see some grandbabies from you."

My heart drops to my knees. I grab the side of the counter and force a swallow. "Maybe someday."

She thrusts a container at me. "This is for later."

"Thanks."

"Are you ignoring that grandbaby comment?"

"I said maybe someday. What did you put in here?" I ask, shaking the lidded box.

"You didn't eat enough tonight."

"Did you give me cake?"

"No, but if you come see me tomorrow, I'll make a lemon pie just for you."

"You know," I say, draping an arm over her shoulder, "if I get a girlfriend one of these days, she probably won't want me coming over this much."

"I'll still cook for you and drop it off at your house. And if she doesn't like that, then she's not the right one for you."

"I'll add that to the checklist." I wink. "Good luck with Lance."

She frowns. "A part of me hopes Mariah is pregnant. The other part of me just hopes it's not bad news."

"There's some optimism for you," I joke. "Why don't you just hope for something good?"

"That's what I said."

"No. You said you hope it's not bad. That's not saying you hope it's good."

She shoos me toward the door. "Get out of here. You're giving me a headache."

"Night, Nana."

"Love you, sweet boy. And get a haircut before Sunday, will you?"

"I'll think about it."

I trudge down the back steps. The sun is almost completely over the horizon, the night sky a deep blue with stormy looking skies. Silver stars begin to sparkle despite the clouds, and I wonder if Hadley is looking at them.

I imagine holding her in my arms as we sit on the swing on my back porch and having her point out all the little shapes she can find in the sky. Stopping in my tracks, I look up at the bright flecks and smile.

"Hey!" Lance calls out as he and Mariah turn the corner of the house. "What are you doing here?"

"Eating your dinner," I tease. "Hey, Mariah."

"Hey, Machlan." A bouquet is in her hand. "How are you tonight?"

"You warming Nana up for something?" I ask, nodding at the bouquet.

"Yeah. No. Maybe?" She looks at Lance. "Maybe this is a bad idea."

He whirls his girlfriend around and plants a loud, wet kiss on her lips. "It's not," he tells her. "Go work your magic with her, and I'll be inside in a second."

Mariah grins as she gives me a little wave and heads up the steps to the back door. Lance, though, stops beside me.

"You got Nana all fucked up," I tell him. "She tried to get me to rat you out."

"You don't even know why I'm here."

I shrug. "True, but I almost made something up just to look like the hero."

"Well, I should've told you so you could get a feel for her reaction before I go in." He rubs his forehead. "She's not gonna like this."

"What's happening?"

"Mariah and I want to elope." He cringes as I burst out laughing. "Stop it, asshole."

"She's never gonna go for that. As a matter of fact," I say, cutting off Lance's attempt at interjection, "she was just trying to get me to settle down."

He jabs a finger my way. "Now *that's* funny."

"Right?"

He sticks his tongue in the side of his cheek, his eyes sparkling with some dickhead comment that I try to brace myself for.

"How are things with Hadley, anyway?" he asks.

I roll my eyes, my heart clamoring at the sound of her name, and head to my truck.

"Oh, come on," Lance calls from behind me. "I was just kidding."

"It's really not funny."

"No, it's not."

I stop walking and turn to face him. "Can I ask you a question?"

"You just did."

I sigh. "What made you stop fucking everyone you met and want to just be with Mariah? And elope now, apparent-fucking-ly?"

"Why do you care?"

"Don't you wonder if you're rushing this?" I ask. "I mean, why do you need to get married right now? It seems like only yesterday we were looking at some sex app and now you're getting fucking married?"

Lance just laughs and heads up the porch. "First of all, it was a dating app."

I lift a brow. "I believe you used it for sex, not dinner parties."

He looks at the house guiltily before turning back to me. "Will you please lower your voice?"

"Fine. *Dating app*. But how do we go from *that* to *this*?"

"Because if I don't marry her, someone else will." He stops and flashes me a smug smirk. "Better think about that, Machie boy."

I watch him disappear inside the house, his laughter at my expense trailing behind him. As I climb in my truck and buckle in, I pause. Looking up into the night sky once again, I wonder if he might be onto something.

Or not.

The gravel flies behind my truck as I pull on the road.

Chapter 13

Hadley

A shot of lightning catapults through the air. It illuminates the sky before a crack of thunder roars through Emily's backyard.

"Looks like rain," I note.

"Feels like it too. I think the temperature just dropped ten degrees." Emily refills her wine glass with a light pink Moscato. "We'll be switching this out for hot chocolate soon."

"I'd take hot chocolate over that stuff now."

"I can't believe you don't like wine. How are we even friends?"

I squish my nose. "Wine is so bitter. Or flat. Or ... something. There's nothing to it."

"Ever had Moscato?" she asks.

"No. And I'm quite okay with that."

"Your loss." She takes a long sip before resting her head against the deck chair. "I told Josh to go fuck himself tonight."

Twisting in my chair, I feel my eyes bug out. Her eyes close. I'm not sure if she's in complete thought or blocking out thoughts altogether, but she seems *peaceful.*

"What happened?" I ask her with a heavy dose of caution. "I thought things were going great?"

100

"They were."

"And then ...?"

She lifts her head and looks at me. I scan her eyes for tears or a sign that she's unsure about her decision, but there's none of that. We could be talking about anything factual—Pilates is overrated, buttercream icing is better than whipped, or how no one really looks good in orange.

Or, apparently, how she and Josh weren't mean to be.

"I'm so confused," I say after a long silence.

She pulls her knees to her chest. "He never wants to do anything I want to do. It's always about him and, to be honest, I'm sick of it." She looks at me and makes a face. "Everything is what he wants—what we do on the weekend, where we go for dinner, how we have sex. I mean, sometimes I really want to be bent over a damn chair! Is that too much to ask?"

I know she's being serious, but I can't not laugh. I also can't formulate a good response. Luckily, my reaction seems to settle her in some way because, before my chuckles end, she's shrugging.

"Well, it's true," she says.

"Hey, what about that guy from the lumber yard? What was his name?" I snap my fingers. "Jeremy! What about him?"

"He's cute, and based on the errant thing he whispered in my ear that night at Crave a couple of weeks ago, I'm one-hundred percent positive he'd bend me over a chair. But I don't even want to think about dating again." She sighs. "Finding a good man is like ... buying an avocado."

"Ridiculously expensive?"

"No, but that's true too." She laughs, pointing at me. "I was thinking more like a terrifying gamble. You can't just go for looks because that perfect skin and amazing tan that leads you to think it's spent the entire season getting perfectly ripe just for you may be a lie. The inside might be rotten. So you give it a little squeeze—firm, gentle pressure to kind of test the waters." Her brows waggle. "Is it hard enough for a good time but soft enough to watch a romcom? Maybe. Or maybe it took a little blue pill and has mommy issues."

"Dude. Stop drinking," I tell her.

She picks up her glass and downs whatever is left in it. A burp belts through the air. "Okay."

I don't dignify her belch with a response. Instead, I settle back in my chair and gaze into the night sky.

If there was a way I could blink and be as flippant about relationships as Emily, I would do it in half a heartbeat. She dates men, falls in love, practically moves in with them, and then casts them away when things don't pan out like it's the crust on a peanut butter and jelly sandwich.

Why can't I do that?

Why do I have to be cursed with feelings for one boy?

"What?" Emily asks.

I turn to look at her. "What what?"

"You just groaned."

"I did?"

"You did. And if I were your best friend who knew all your groans and snarls, I'd label this one as being rooted in Machlan."

My head hits the back of the chair with a loud thud. "Ouch!" I rub the spot, trying to distract both myself and Emily more than massage out a knot.

"I was right. Surprise, surprise."

My emotions well up against the dam I built inside to keep them all back. I can feel them roaring against my lips like a hurricane lashing against the shores.

Since Machlan left the apartment, my brain hasn't left me alone. My mind doesn't even feel like mine anymore, and that's a tough thing to reconcile. One minute, I'm reminiscing about sweet moments with him, and the next, I'm almost in tears over others. Then everything flips again and I'm ready to kill him, and then reality hits and I feel helpless.

Helpless is something I loathe. I call bullshit on it most times.

You're never helpless; you can always do something. I just wish I could figure out the *something* about this.

Wine sloshes against Emily's glass as she fills it again. "Just thinking I might need this to get through this convo." She takes in my reaction. "Or you might need it. Either way, I'm prepared."

"A regular survivalist," I joke.

She leans back in her chair again. "Okay. Let's hear it."

"I don't know." It's almost a whine, but I'm too overwhelmed to care.

"No, you do know. And I know, and he knows, and the whole damn world knows."

I groan again, louder this time. So loud, in fact, that my voice fills Emily's entire backyard, and her neighbor's dog starts to howl right along with me.

"Stop." Emily laughs, shoving me in the arm. "I think you've officially lost it."

Lost it. Her words send a shiver across my skin. The thought of losing Machlan knocks the wind out of me. How I thought I could do that—just distance myself from him forever—seems idiotic now.

It's always this way once I've spent time with him. Five weeks, five days, five hours—it's always the same. Maybe it ends badly or we drive each other crazy, but I always walk away knowing two things: one, I love him and, two, he'll never commit to me.

"What if I lose him completely, Em?"

My friend doesn't need a further explanation; the look on her face shows she gets it.

My chest shakes as I take a breath. It's the kind of shake that happens when your body is full of adrenaline, prepping to keep you going through some perceived danger. There may not be a lion in the area, but I'm on the cusp of getting eaten alive anyway.

She lays her hand on my arm, giving it a gentle squeeze before removing it. "Isn't that what you came here for?"

My entire body sags, pressing down in the wooden deck chair so hard I think I hear it crack.

"Yes. No. I don't know anymore. When I'm away from him, he's what I want, and I tell myself I have to make it stop. Then I'm with him, and it's really apparent I *can't* make it stop." I cover my face with my hands. "I just want to be one of those women who is all confident and independent. One who calls a number and meets up at a hotel when she needs a man."

Emily snorts.

"I mean it." I look at her with every intention of being serious but end up laughing as soon as our eyes meet. "Stop making me laugh!"

"It's my job."

"Well, make it your job to help me figure out how to live my life. Just make all my decisions for me, will ya?"

"You need to relax," she says. "Seriously."

"I know."

The temperature seems to drop. I run my hands up and down my arms as the crickets in the lowlands get louder. It makes me think of camping with Machlan—campfires and s'mores and the taste of bug spray. I close my eyes and imagine his red tent with the hole in the top from the summer night when Peck forgot to watch the fire and the top of the tent went up in flames.

What a fun time of my life that was—being with my favorite people, doing the simplest things. Making memories that are still some of my most precious possessions.

"How do people survive this?" I ask. "How do they love someone who doesn't love them back and go on and have a happy life with someone else?"

"Maybe they don't."

"Oh, gee. Thanks."

She laughs. "Maybe those people never get married because they refuse to see the big sea and all those other hunky fishes swimming around them. Or maybe they do get married and are never truly happy because they keep thinking about the fish from the reef back there."

I struggle to keep a straight face. "You're so super helpful."

"Hear me out," she says, waving a hand to shush me. "You know how you can go three days and not eat cake and as soon as you say you're on a diet, all you can think about is cake?"

"Wait a minute. What happened to the reef?"

"They're connected. I promise. Stick with me."

"*Okayyy ...*"

She shimmies in her seat. "Okay. So, all you can think about is cake, right? Well, it's the same thing here. It's the same thing as Fish Girl."

I pretend to think. "Nope," I say, shaking my head fervently. "I'm not following you."

"Gah!"

"Cake and fish should never go together."

"They go together in this way: you want cake on minute one of a diet because it's what you can't have. As soon as that luscious piece of heaven slathered with buttercream goodness is off-limits, you need it like you need air. Am I right?"

"Yeah."

"Okay," she says, her eyes lit up with excitement. "And it's the same for Fish Girl. She's swimming in this vast ocean that comprises like three-quarters of the world and can't see all these ah-mazing fish she encounters every day because she's still all obsessed with Reef Boy."

"Look, Em ..."

She shakes her head. "You want what you can't have. It's basic human nature."

My gaze drops to the glass of wine, and I contemplate guzzling it. It certainly couldn't make me more confused or sick to my stomach.

Not everything she's saying is resonating. I don't want Mach just because I can't have him. I want him because he's so threaded in my life—in who I am and how I got to be this person—that I can't imagine not having him. Or not wanting him.

"Maybe I have to accept I won't have him like I want him," I say, testing the idea out loud. "Maybe I need to ..."

"Maybe you need to take the pressure off it. Stop 'being on a diet'," she says, using air quotes. "You stress constantly about your relationship with Machlan—how it's defined. What it is. What it isn't. Maybe you just need to let it be."

"Let it be, huh?"

"Yes," she says, grinning. "Let it be. Let it be whatever it is. Give it the organic room to just develop into a great friendship or an intense hatred or a friends with benefits or maybe just mutual acquaintances. You'll never know what it can be if you don't stop trying to shove it into one of the two boxes you've already decided it has to go in."

I gulp, my mind processing this too quickly. Everything kind of jumbles together as if I did drink the wine, but at the same time, it seems clear. And possibly logical.

"I almost kissed him today," I say. I toss it out there as though it'll change her mind. She only laughs.

"I'm sure you did. The two of you together is like watching two people have sex without the sex."

"That's gross." I stand, stretching my arms overhead. "I need to get going."

"You got somewhere to be?"

"Yeah. Bed."

She yawns, getting to her feet too. "I'm tired myself and that bottle of wine didn't help."

I pull her into a quick hug before heading toward the gate at the side of the house. I wave. I might even respond to something she says offhandedly as I walk away. I'm not sure. All I do know is that I have to figure out if I can just be friends with Machlan Gibson or if that's a recipe for disaster.

Chapter 14

Hadley

I slide my toothbrush over my teeth.

The sky is a hazy mass of grays. Buckets of rain aren't pouring from the sky, and the wind doesn't sound like it's two seconds from ripping the stairs off the front of the apartment either. Both were constants all night as I lay on the bed and listened to the weather be as contrary as my feelings.

By the time the rain switched to a drizzle and I finally drifted to sleep, I had worried myself into an emotional coma. Now that it's morning, or early afternoon if the clock isn't lying, a sort of peace blankets me. I have no solution to my predicament. There isn't some grand plan to wrench my heart out of Machlan's hands. But there does seem to be a confidence that I'll figure it out and that feels good.

That feels like me.

I spit, rinse, and spit again.

Plucking the toothbrush back in the coffee cup next to the window, I think through a highlight reel of my relationship with Mach. The only consistency throughout the years is that there was always pressure.

Pressure not to be together from Cross.

Pressure to be together as a result of our choices.

Pressure not to be together because things were too hard, and then pressure to be together because it really felt like our final shot.

"Maybe Emily's right," I say. "Maybe I just need to let it work itself out."

The words barely get past my lips before my palm hits my forehead. It sounds so simple to say those words. It seems so easy in concept. But giving up control when it comes to this particular situation is so crazy hard for me.

It's too important. I'm too vulnerable. There's too much on the line.

"Ugh." My stomach rumbles, reminding me I haven't eaten since the three bites I had of Emily's frozen lasagna last night. I head to the couch to grab my purse when my phone rings from the table.

I ignored two texts from Samuel last night and one call that could be classified as early morning. Grabbing the device, I sit on the edge of the bed and answer it.

"Hello?"

"Hey, Hadley."

I wait for a flutter of butterflies or at least a semblance of familiarity at hearing his voice, but nothing changes inside me. I might as well be talking to Cross or Peck.

"How are things going down there?" he asks.

"Oh, they're good. How about you?"

"Work is killer today. We balanced a couple of accounts this morning and ..."

My attention wanes, drifting to a certain tattooed bar owner instead of Samuel's tales of the accounting tape. I wonder what Mach is doing and what he had for breakfast and if he still sleeps on his right side with a pillow between his legs.

"Am I boring you?" Samuel asks.

"Sorry," I say, faking a yawn. "It was a long night."

The line quiets. "I wondered why you didn't answer. Anyway, I'm glad to hear you're having fun with your friends."

"Yeah. Me too." I scrub a hand down my face. "Are you having fun with yours?"

He laughs, and it pains me a little. The idea of Samuel having friends—the real kind, the kind like he knows I have—shouldn't be funny.

"We worked until three this morning. I guess the slight conversation we had outside of numbers and figures over cold pizza could be construed as a good time," he says.

"You need to have more fun. What about that one guy? Ryan? Brian? Whatever his name is. You guys should go out and have some drinks tonight."

"We're all too busy. Hey, how's your brother? I thought of him today. A guy tried to write off his gym membership, and it made me think of Cross's gyms."

I flop back on the mattress and think about the awkward meeting between Samuel and Cross a few weeks ago. How Cross kept looking at me like I was crazy, and Samuel couldn't understand why Cross didn't want to man-hug when he left.

"He's good," I say. "He and Kallie are living together now. They're pretty happy."

"That's good. I bet it's nice for you to stay there and spend so much time with them while you can."

"Yeah." I get to my feet and begin to pace the small room.

A long, awkward silence fills the line. I walk back and forth, passing the table each time, wondering what in the world we're supposed to talk about.

When did it get this hard to talk to him? Has it always been?

Papers rustle. "Well, that's good. Do you think you'll be home when I get back from Salem?"

"Samuel ..." I close my eyes and kick myself for answering the phone in the first place.

"I know, I know. You can't commit right now. But I'm hoping if we get some time away from each other, maybe you'll change your mind."

"We're on a break. We mutually agreed to that."

He sighs like this conversation is a distraction. "We did, but agreements change. Right? That's why we took a break and didn't break up. We can salvage this."

I stop pacing and look at the wall. *Salvage.* "What kind of word is that?"

"What kind of word is what?"

"Salvage," I say, wrinkling my nose. "It's like garbage. Like a salvage yard where they take parts off old cars or something."

"It's a proper term. It means to rescue."

"I know what it means, Samuel." I sigh, feeling a weight on my shoulders. "My point is, is that what you want? To salvage our relationship?"

"Frankly, yes. I do. I want to rescue it from its current situation. With a few tweaks, Hadley, I think we can bring it in the black."

Bring it in the black? I groan, and I know he hears it, but I just can't make myself care.

I consider the possibility of going back to Vigo and seeing Samuel again. It would be *nice*. Orderly. Predictable. We'd have date nights on Fridays and intelligent conversations about business. We'd read separately before bed and fall asleep on crisp white sheets. But as my mind drifts to other possibilities, to ornery bar owners and spirited discussions and jokes, the idea of going back seems like turning off my favorite rock song and putting on elevator music.

"I don't think it's going to happen, Samuel."

"Why?"

"Do I make you happy? Really? Do you come home with butterflies in your stomach to see me?"

"That's the most overused analogy in the history of analogies."

"You know what I mean."

"Yes, I look forward to coming home every day and seeing you. I get excited to spend the weekend with you. And I can't wait to get home from this trip and convince you to ... maybe move in with me."

My eyes almost pop out of my head.

"It'll make things a lot easier," he says. "I won't have to rush home so our schedules meet because you'll be there. And you won't have to rush into that new job of yours either. I can more than cover our rent and necessities."

"That's not what I asked."

"Is it not?"

"No. You don't ask someone to move in because of ease," I say with a sad smile on my face. "It should be about more."

"I don't know how much *more* you can get than synchronizing our lives."

I want to tell him about all the *more*—the staying up late and breaking down the best songs of the nineties. Taking a truck to Bluebird to see if we can get it stuck in the mud. Sitting around a campfire with your friends and telling stories. I would tell him, but I don't think he'll understand.

My head hangs. "You know what? I need to go," I say. "I hope you have a great day."

"I hope this vegetable juice kicks in soon, or I'll be dragging all evening."

"Goodbye."

"Goodbye, Hadley."

I think he's going to say more, like say I love you, so I end the call before he can. And before I can look at the phone and replay that entire conversation, I grab my purse and head to Carlson's Bakery for lunch.

I wave to Dave, a little old man who's driven the same black Ford Ranger since I moved to town. He waves back as he putts down Beecher Street.

Puddles are everywhere. The gutters are full as water streams into the storm drains under the street. Tugging my jacket around my body, I jog across the street to the opposing sidewalk.

The closer I get to Carlson's, the more the air is scented with cinnamon and freshly baked bread. My stomach rumbles in response.

Just as the bakery comes into view, a clap of thunder cracks above and a downpour of rain comes out of nowhere.

"Ah!" I yell, the cold droplets hitting the pavement and splashing me a second time. I bow my head as if it'll do any good and speed walk in the direction of Carlson's. Pausing at the next intersection, I can barely see through all the rain. Just as I start to cross the road, a truck pulls up to the stop sign.

I don't look over. Before my foot can hit the asphalt, the truck's engine revs.

"What are you doing?" Machlan's voice works its way through the rain.

Squinting, I shrug, the water sticking my hair to my face. "Getting lunch."

"Get in here." He grins, reaching over the console and opening the passenger's side door.

I waste no time rushing to the truck. Getting inside requires a little hop, which amuses Machlan to no end. The door closes with a thud barely heard against the weather.

Smoothing my hair away from my face, I watch water drip off every inch of me. "I'm going to soak your truck."

"I think you already did." He hits the gas. The truck rips through the intersection before he eases up on the pedal. "Where were you going?"

"Carlson's."

"Why didn't you drive?"

"Fresh air, I guess."

"That worked out well for ya."

He watches me out of the corner of his eye before reaching forward and adjusting the temperature. The air warms immediately, and I relax back in the soft leather as we roll through town.

The wipers streak against the glass. With each swipe, the quickness of the last few moments dissipate, and my present situation becomes clearer.

And hotter.

And squirmier.

I reach up and turn the heat down.

"I figured you were cold."

"I was. Now I'm not." I point at the bakery. "If you could drop me off there, I'd appreciate it."

"You can't have lunch there."

"And why not?"

He grins. "Megan McCarter works there. She'll poison you or something."

"Molly's sister?" I laugh. "She will not. What would she have against me?"

He bites his lip, and I know whatever is about to come out of his mouth is going to get a reaction out of me—one in addition to the way my thighs clench together as I look at his lips.

"The first thing she'll have against you is you have a vagina," he says. "That's enough for her to want to maim you for life."

"That's terrible!"

"That's true, and you know it."

I think back on the McCarter sister's escapades. Like how Megan was accused of sleeping with the gym teacher in high school and he lost his job. Or how Molly slept with half of the football team her senior year so she'd be crowned Homecoming Queen. Not because she wanted it, but because she didn't want Jessica Grimes to get it.

"You might be right," I admit.

"And the second thing," he says with a tease in his tone, "is she wants my cock so bad she could taste it."

"Well, I'm good to know she hasn't tasted it," I say.

I turn toward the door so he doesn't see the flash of jealousy in my eyes or the way my jaw tenses at the thought of that little hoochie being with Machlan.

He laughs, his hand gripping my thigh and shaking it a little as though it's the most natural thing in the world. A bolt of flames extends from the center of his palm down my leg, up my side and radiating out until it settles at the base of my belly.

"Ooh, did that spark a little jealousy, Had?" he teases.

"Nope. I just don't like thinking about all the women who have tasted you."

He roars with laughter. I bite my lip so hard I think it might bleed.

"I'll tell you a secret," he says. "I haven't actually slept with everyone you probably think I have. I mean, I'm a good-looking motherfucker. I get it. But Lance slept with all of them, and I don't really like sloppy seconds."

My lip pops free with a laugh. "I'm so glad your confidence isn't waning."

He grins, amused I'm playing along. It's infectious. I find myself grinning back, my cheeks aching.

"How's your confidence these days?" he asks.

"My confidence is fine, thank you."

"I just thought since I shared some insight into my sex life, maybe you'd want to share some into yours."

"Um, no," I say. I consider riling him up but enjoy the playfulness too much to risk it. "You would actually be bored to death if I talked to you about my sex life."

He takes his eyes off the road for a lingering moment. They're filled with a mischievousness that really is a Machlan trademark; a glimmer of naughtiness that could go a plethora of ways. "Your sex life is my favorite sex life."

My jaw drops to my lap. I think I misheard him, but my heart is screaming that I didn't. I try to keep my gaze pinned to his eyes and not on the way his lips purse together. Or the way his neck has the perfect amount of scruff dotting it. Or the way his white T-shirt, covered with an unbuttoned flannel, is cut in a way that gives me a peek of his broad chest.

He flashes me a smirk before looking back at the road. "That's the danger of Megan. She knows."

"Why would she think that?" I fumble for words. It's hard to say a set of words when your brain is repeating another.

"Why would she think there was anything between you and me? Oh, I don't know," he grins.

A heat rises to my cheeks. I'm unsure if he's just messing with me or insinuating there *is* something between us.

A mixed response catches in my throat. Clearing it with a frazzled cough, I point as we fly by Carlson's. "You just passed the bakery."

"Yeah."

We stop at the stop sign by the library. As we wait our turn, Machlan's fingers tap against the steering wheel.

The rain has slowed to a drizzle. Everything is quiet and peaceful. His truck smells like his bedroom. His breathing slows my heartbeat to match his tempo. Looking at his profile as he chews on his bottom lip makes me so comfortable I could curl my legs up and drift away into an easy slumber.

On a normal day, I'd start to panic, to feel pressure of the unknown and start prodding. A bubble of alarm wants to burst and spread through my veins as Machlan turns his head. I think of Emily's advice and *pause*.

"They're having taco salads at Peaches today. You like them, right?" he asks.

I nod.

He motions for the car on our right to pass through the intersection. "No onions, no beans. Extra olives. Right?"

I nod again, this time with the biggest smile.

He nods too and settles back in his seat. I'd normally comment on how smug he looks, but this time, I let it pass. I'm probably a little smug too.

Chapter 15

Machlan

The brown paper bag holding the Peaches take-out crinkles under Hadley's fingers. She sits quietly beside me, the taco salad on her lap, and gazes across the soybean fields at the rainbow stretching across the sky.

Nana told me a story once that a rainbow is God's promise not to flood the world again. I remember sitting on her lap on the porch and having her read me this story from a little green-bound book she had. I don't know why that stuck with me all these years, but it did. Every time I see one, I think of her. I don't think of her long today because I can't think of anything besides Hadley sitting in my truck.

I hate that I like it so much. The way I feel calmer with her around is something I crave. I don't feel this way around another person or in another spot. Just with her.

I tell myself it's because I know she won't hold anything I do or say against me. Not really. If she would, she would've stopped speaking to me years ago.

She should've.

She could've.

I would've had the roles been reversed.

"Where are we going?" she asks as I steer the truck in the opposite direction of Crave and the apartment.

"You got somewhere to be?"

"No."

"Okay then."

She looks at me, expecting clarification or a reason, but I don't give her one. She'll assume it's because I'm being a dick, because I usually am, but this time, she is wrong.

I don't answer because I don't know where we're going.

All I know for sure is I saw her leave the apartment and didn't think too much about it. Then it started raining, so I went after her on the small chance I'd find her stranded … and I did. And here we sit in the cab of my truck filled with her perfume, the heater on low, the music switched from my usual rock station to some country channel she loves.

Heaven and hell don't work together, but it damn sure feels like they do.

"Thanks for picking me up," she says. The bag crinkles again. "And for buying my lunch."

"No problem."

Easing up on the accelerator, I run my hand down the front of my jeans. We've been in this situation so many times—her in the front seat of my truck while I drive around town with nowhere to go. It's how we killed many Friday nights back in the day.

Back in the good old days.

The silence fills every nook and cranny. The two of us are the sole occupants of the truck, but it feels like there's no room left. It's almost too crowded to even breathe. I need to say something, anything, but come up empty. So, like a dumbass, I keep driving and leave George Strait to do the talking.

"You need a haircut," she says. "Getting a little long back here."

Her fingers brush against the back of my neck, ruffling the too-long strands that do need a trim. My neck flexes against her fingers, trying to deepen the touch. The warmth from her touch trickles through my body. I can't remember when someone touched me like this—without an end game or to get something. Just because she actually cares.

It fucks with me.

"I can't believe Nana hasn't said anything," she says.

I fiddle with the cruise control button to keep my hands busy so I don't reach for her. "Oh, she has."

"I bet. Do you remember when Peck let his almost turn into a mullet?" She throws her head back and laughs. "I thought Nana was going to have a coronary."

"Oh, yeah. How do you forget that? The harder she rode him about it, the harder he fought against cutting it."

"The best was when he would wear a bandana and push it all back like they did in the eighties." She looks at me with the sweetest, simplest smile. "You boys put her through a lot, you know that?"

I regrip the steering wheel. "Yeah, well, I think we put everyone through a lot. Don't ya think?"

The truck turns toward Bluebird Hill. The tires hit the gravel, the sound ripping through the air as we slow. Hadley rolls down her window and takes a deep breath.

"Like the smell of wet gravel?" I laugh.

"It's the smell of my youth." Even she laughs at that. "I have Peaches take-out, gravel, the grass still wet from the rain ... and you." Her smile fades. "That was a really weird thing to say."

Weird? Yes.

True? Also, yes.

Awkward? Hell, yes.

My stomach sinks with that heavy, uncomfortable sensation that won't budge. It just sits inside you and makes you miserable. I shift my weight in the seat and loosen the white-knuckle grip I have on the steering wheel in hopes of releasing some of the stress.

It doesn't.

I take a quick right, causing the sunglasses on the dash to drift to the passenger side and rattle against the glass. Hadley grips the door as the truck climbs to the top of the hill. We're nearly vertical, the engine groaning because I didn't flip it in four-wheel drive. Hadley's grip stays tense until we're safely settled at the peak.

I cut the engine, and George's voice melts away. It's just Hadley and me—two people trying to figure out what to do with the other.

She looks at me warily as she sets the paper bag on the floorboard. The little clover pendant rises and falls about the same hectic speed as my breath. She gives me a half-smile, one loaded with a hundred questions, before she opens the door and climbs out.

Her arms stretch to the side, her face tilted to the sky. The rust-colored shirt brings out the redness in her hair, and I wonder if Samuel knows it gets less red as the seasons change. Then in the summer, the sun will kiss her again and the coppery strands will pop like they do now.

I wonder if he knows anything about her I don't. The idea pummels me yet sparks an entire line of thought I don't want to go down.

It's not even about her making memories with someone else. It's that they aren't with me. That feels completely selfish, but I can't help it. Just as I can't help how wrong it feels to have sections of our lives that don't intersect.

Lance's stupid one-liner floats through my head like a digital banner, blinking its message over and over. *If I don't marry her, someone else will.* The only problem is, when it comes to me and Hadley, I can't marry her. I can't do that to her or even ask that of her, no matter how much she thinks she wants it. But *that* means I'm going in some arbitrary box in her head, and I don't even know what that means.

Would she call me if something happened and she couldn't get a hold of Cross? Because she does that now. Like nine months or so ago when she popped a tire on her way back to Vigo. She called me. Or the time before that when she thought someone had broken in her house—she called me. Would that stop too?

Nah, fuck that.

I shove open the door so hard it bounces the springs.

Hadley looks over the hood of the truck at me. "You okay?"

"I'm just gonna fucking say this," I say, planting both hands on the damp truck. "And I want you to listen."

"Oh, this should be good."

"Don't start. Please."

"Uh, I believe it's you who almost broke the door off its hinges and proclaimed you had something to say." Both hands go to her hips as she squares up with me. It's a defense mechanism loud and clear, and the fact she goes there automatically makes me feel like shit.

"I don't wanna fight, Had."

"You always wanna fight."

I press off the hood and walk around the front of the truck. "I do always want to fight with you."

Her shoulders drop. "Well, there ya go."

"And on that note, I've been thinking ..."

She blows out slowly, pressing her lips together in resignation. Her eyes flutter closed for no more than a second before she stands tall and opens them again. "I've been thinking too, Mach."

A pain shoots across the back of my neck. "You first."

As I watch her wrestle with what to say, as I feel the air between us swirl with the unknown, I almost wish I hadn't seen her walking today. That I hadn't picked her up. That I hadn't bought her lunch or brought her to this place—*our place.*

"I always make this weird between us," she starts. "I—"

"You don't make anything weird. You're honest." I bite the inside of my cheek out of pure frustration. "That's more than I can say for me."

"What's that supposed to mean?"

"It means ..." I sigh. "It means you're not to blame for us not getting along."

The can of tobacco in my back pocket is suddenly very present. Needing the relief a quick dip would provide, I start to grab it.

"You make it very clear what you want and don't want," she says, enunciating the words carefully. "It's me who puts the pressure on us and makes everything awful."

I forget all about the tobacco. "Everything isn't awful."

"Not right now. But a lot of the time."

"Hadley, look ..." I move until I'm standing just a few feet away from her. There's a resolution in her eyes that gives me hope that we can work it out. I can't not have her in my life, but I can't be in it so deep I fuck her up either. "We have to figure this out."

"Figure what out?"

"This. Whatever it is."

There's a pull from somewhere deep inside me that draws me to her. That makes me want to take her in my arms, bury my face in the messy, rain-mussed hair on the top of her head, and hold her tight. It's so strong it takes all my strength not to reach out, pull her to me, and never let go.

She clears her throat. "Emily and I were talking last night."

"Was she drinking? Because I've seen that girl drink more than anyone her size should be able to get away with."

"She was." She grins. "But her advice was spot-on, I think."

"Which was?"

"Yeah." She takes a deep breath. "She says I need to relax."

A laugh flows from me before I even know it's happening. "I've said that for years."

"Well, it sounds more logical coming from her."

"Of course, it does."

"And that surprises me because Emily isn't logical about much of anything." She laughs. "Guess you never know where good advice might pop up."

"Trust me. I know. Believe it or not, I found a little wisdom in something Lance said last night." I cringe as I bring it up. His words echo in my brain again, and I feel them in my soul.

"Oh, this I have to hear."

"If I go quoting Lance, the world might go up in flames."

She laughs freely. "Taking advice from Lance might ensure the same ending." She makes a face. "Did it have anything to do with dating apps?"

"No. I think Mariah would kill him if he even mentioned that."

"I think I like Mariah."

"You would." I nod. The tension in my neck eases, bringing a relief I didn't know I needed. "She's pretty and smart and feisty like another woman I know."

Hadley's cheeks pink.

"Hadley—"

"No. Let me go first," she says, cutting me off. "For the first time in your life, let me go first."

"Oh, yeah, like you don't always end up dominating a conversation."

"What? I don't. You're crazy."

"And"—I smirk—"can I point out I *always* let you go first?"

If her cheeks pinked before, they're full-on red now. It's adorable and sexy and even brought this conversation here, I need to redirect it. Immediately.

I laugh. "If you don't hurry up and say whatever it is, I'm gonna eat your taco salad."

"Don't touch that or I'll cut your fingers off." She gathers herself. "Okay. So a lot of our problem is me being too focused on putting how I feel about you in a box with a neat little label. I've never been able to just see you like another guy. I don't have to brand my relationship with other men. I shouldn't brand you. Or ... *us*."

"You should be able to do that pretty fucking easy with other men. 'Friend' isn't hard."

"I'm not just friends with every guy I know, Machlan."

"Oh, really?" I say. Crossing my arms over my chest, I try to ignore the irritation gaining traction in my stomach. "How many guys are you not 'just friends' with?"

"Enough." She draws out the word before busting out in a fit of giggles. "It's you who needs to relax."

"This is as relaxed as I get."

"And that's sad. But true," she says. "Anyway, Em says I need to treat you like any other guy. Like I would a guy I met at the dry cleaners, for example, or an old friend."

"You want to treat me like Peck?"

"Well, maybe." She shrugs. "I guess."

"This should be fun," I grumble.

She swats my shoulder as she walks by. When I turn around, she's facing where the sun would be if it were visible.

"You want to be my friend?" I ask the question slowly, getting a feel for it as I say it. "Is that what you're saying?"

She considers this. "I think a friend label will work because we've always been friends, right? I mean, more or less. At least until I figure it out, I guess."

"I'm tired of your guesses. You want to hammer this out? Then let's hammer it out."

She turns to look at me. She's a warm fixture on a backdrop of pine trees and the slate sky, a bright spot in an otherwise bleak day. The slant of her lips is down, not up, and I can't see the gold in her eyes either. It's a stark reminder of the reality of this situation.

"Fine. Do you want to be my friend, Machlan?"

"Is this a George Strait thing? Is there a box to check yes or no?"

Her chest shakes, but she doesn't allow me the laugh. "This is not a George Strait thing. But I might make you cross your heart when you answer."

"I can't with you and country song references."

Despite the ache in my chest that says otherwise, I don't want to be in her life on that kind of level. I don't want to be her friend at all.

What I want is to hear about her day at the dental office before I leave the house for the bar. I want to come home to find her snuggled up in my blankets with a book beside her. I want to hear her jab me about haircuts and take her to Nana's for Sunday dinners and plan my whole weekend around a bunch of chores she wants done—chores I'll bitch about just to see her get worked up.

That's what I want. I want her on every fucking level. I want her so much I can't do it to her.

Lance's voice filters through my mind again. *If I don't marry her, someone else will.*

What the fuck do I do now?

Chapter 16

Hadley

The view from atop Bluebird this time of year is my favorite. The leaves are starting to change, giving hints of the show they'll put on a few weeks from now. It's still subtle now with just touches of golds and crimsons. It's pretty, but my favorite view anytime, anywhere is standing just a few feet behind me.

I wonder if he's pacing, and if he is, why. I don't want to turn around and look, but I feel his presence. He gets closer, then farther away, then closer again. My lungs hold the air that's filled them. My heart rattles in my chest, and I can feel my pulse pounding in the side of my neck.

Something has been different between us today. Initially, I thought it was my attempt at a new mindset courtesy of Emily. But the longer we're together, the more I think it's not just me.

"The truth is," he says, making me jump, "I don't want to be friends with you."

I shake my head, hoping it loosens the fog in my skull as I try to process Machlan's words.

Silence settles on Bluebird Hill. The only sound is the rush of oxygen my lungs finally let go.

My bottom lip starts to quiver. *I don't want to be friends with you.* He can't mean that.

Fighting tears, I clutch a hand to my chest and try to steady myself. This is exactly what I wanted when I came to Linton, and now that I'm getting it, it feels like I'm being sliced and there are no bandages big enough to stop the damage.

His palm cups the edge of my shoulder. His long, muscled fingers wrap around my arm.

Closing my eyes, I remind myself this is exactly why I'm here, and that maybe, just maybe, the universe is helping me for once. My eyes open as his hand slips from my shoulder and I turn to look at him.

"I knew that," I say, the lump in my throat obvious. "That was sort of a rhetorical question."

His forehead mars, the lines forming above his eyes deep and many. "I didn't mean it like that."

"There's kind of only one way you can take it when someone says they don't want to be your friend," I say, forcing a laugh. Turning to the truck, I continue. "Besides, this makes that whole box thing easier—"

"Stop." His hand touches my shoulder again but pulls away immediately this time.

I stop. I stop and listen for his voice, wait for the explanation that I think is going to come. What kind of an explanation it is, I don't know. I don't even want to guess at it. But something is coming. I can feel it.

"The truth is," he says, giving my words back to me, "you aren't just any girl to me, and you never will be."

There isn't even a warning. My eyes fill with tears—red-hot, guppy-sized dollops of water cloud my vision of the truck.

"Fuck, Hadley." He steps in front of me. On his face is a scowl he wears so well. It's usually aimed at me, but this time, I get the feeling it's not. That maybe it's aimed at himself.

"What are you doing?" I ask. I fight so hard to keep the tears from streaming down my face. If the dam breaks and one passes, it'll be a cascade of emotions I can't control. I have it under wraps until I look him in the eye.

My knees wobble as I see something in those orbs I've only seen a couple of times in my life. On the other occasions, I thought it was love. I believed this look to mean he felt something for me in line with what I felt so deeply for him.

Now, I'm not sure what to think.

Or maybe, I'm afraid of what to think.

"I'm really out of my wheelhouse here," he says.

I give him a half-smile. "So this has nothing to do with alcohol, cars, poker, or sex?"

He grins sheepishly. "It has a little to do with sex."

Blowing out a breath, the tears absorbing into my body, I find a kernel of steadiness inside myself and hold onto it for dear life.

"You kind of fucked me up a little with that whole 'I want to love Samuel' bullshit," he says.

"It's not bullshit."

"No, I know it's not. I know you want to fall in love with some respectable guy and have the whole house and kids and dogs thing you didn't have growing up. I get it."

It takes everything I have to force the weight in my chest away. "I do want that. I'm ready for it now. And ..." The weight comes back with full force, barreling its way through my defenses and filling my abdomen. I can't blink the tears back this time. I can't fight the lump in my throat either. My nose burns as my gaze settles on Machlan.

He stiffens, his eyes going wide before filling with a mix of fear and confusion. A half-step is taken back as he runs a hand along his stubbled jaw. The breeze whips around us, rustling a clump of wet leaves stuck to our shoes.

His mouth opens as if he's about to speak, but nothing comes out. As if he's afraid to bring up the topic he's pretty certain I was about to broach—one we've only discussed a handful of times.

A sadness creeps across his handsome face and settles deep in my heart.

Energy drains from my body. If I could drop to the cold, wet ground and curl in a ball, I would. The edges of the rocks and the sticky mud would be preferred over the hell of looking into Machlan's face and seeing my own feelings reflected.

My gaze hits the gravel because I can't look at him. I consider heading to the truck and ending this conversation when he speaks.

"And what, Hadley?" His voice is low, careful. Almost like he was forced to ask it and definitely like he already knows the answer.

My heart races, my palms sweat despite the cool temperatures. Maybe it's my imagination, but the air around us picks up too, and the world around us seems to go faster.

I close my eyes and see her sweet little face all bundled up in a pink blanket Machlan bought at a discount store the day before I went into labor.

"And I hope someday I'll make her proud."

The last few words come out in a hiccup. I'm not sure they even make it into the air before Machlan pulls me to his chest. His arms envelop me in the warmth of his body as my own torso shakes with a force it only does when I cry about *this*.

About *her*.

About *our daughter*.

I don't cry a lot. Sometimes on her birthday when I'm alone and wondering what she would be doing if she were with me and not with the wonderful couple who adopted her that April afternoon. There's just something about having this conversation with Machlan that feels overwhelming today.

The longer I cry, the tighter he holds me.

I think about waddling into that little store and watching Machlan choose a blanket as though it was the most important purchase he'd ever make. How he woke up that morning in the dingy little motel and this was the only thing he wanted to do—buy the baby a blanket.

His cheek lays on the top of my head, and I'm not sure if he's holding me or I'm holding him. My own trembling makes it hard to tell if it's all me or if some of it is coming from him too. Either way, as deeply as it hurts, it feels better to know I'm not hurting alone.

It's only when I've thoroughly soaked his shirt and my chest stops vibrating and my tears turn into whimpers does he loosen his grip. He plants a kiss to the top of my head that I think I'm not supposed to feel before he lets me go.

"Sorry," I mumble, stepping back. I dab my eyes with the corner of my damp shirt. "I didn't mean to break down on you like that."

He brushes a lock of hair that's matted to my cheek off my face. His thumb glides over my skin, his palm cupping my cheek before he withdraws it. "Do you think about her a lot?"

"I think about her every day," I whisper. "I wonder if she still has your dark hair and my eyes."

"I wonder if she still has my mom's widow's peak." He runs a hand over his face, his Adam's apple bobbing. "She had two crowns at the top of her little head. Remember that? And the lines on her left hand ran together instead of splitting into two."

I purse my lips so I don't cry. "Yeah."

"Damn it, Had. I'm sorry." He looks away, gulping. "I'm so damn sorry."

"It's not your fault." My heart breaks in two. The pain of watching him replay that day hurts as much as replaying it myself.

He walks in a circle, shaking his head. His hands go to his hair, and he yanks on the tresses, pulling the locks in a display of utter frustration.

"Machlan. Stop it," I beg.

Much to my surprise, he does. He stops.

"You know what I do first thing every morning?" he asks. "Before I get out of bed or take a leak or make coffee? I think about her. Every fucking morning. Then I think about you. And I think about how everything could've been different if I'd had my shit together."

"Machlan—"

"Then I say a prayer," he says, ignoring me. "I ask God to watch over her and keep her safe and to let her always feel how much we love her, you know?" He turns to me completely, and the look in his eye—completely and utterly raw—almost breaks me. "Then I pray for you. That you have a life you deserve and that, somehow, by the grace of God, everyone can forgive me for being such a massive fuckup."

"Machlan—"

"Don't even," he warns, shaking his head.

"Don't even what?" I cry. My eyes are wet with tears as I watch the man who did the best he could in that situation blame himself. Doesn't he understand how I would've fallen apart without him? How him never leaving my side from the moment I told him I was pregnant until we laid our precious girl in another set of arms meant everything to me? How he held me when I broke down and gave me the courage to go on? Doesn't he understand any of that?

"Don't even try to act like you can forgive me," he warns.

"*We* made that decision together," I remind him. "I was eighteen. You were almost twenty. Neither of us had parents. Neither of us had a plan on what to do. We didn't have any money. Your inheritance didn't get released for a couple of more years. Don't you remember that?"

"I'll tell you what I remember. I remember loading up my truck and lying to everyone, telling them I got a job in Ohio and we'd be gone a few months. And then getting there and trying to find a place to stay and trying to see how we felt about everything and me getting two jobs in the first six, seven weeks and getting fired because I couldn't manage my fucking temper."

"You were a kid," I say. "I was too. Which is why we weren't ready to have one of our own."

He bites his lip, unable to stay still. He paces around the hilltop, jamming his hands in his pockets and then pulling them back out. His eyes darting at everything but me.

I wish I could help him understand this from my point of view. But I know if I get too close right now, he'll push me away.

Finally, he stops moving. "I'm sorry for doing that to you. I'll never forgive myself for putting you in a position to have to give up the baby."

"I didn't *have* to do anything. But it was the right choice at the time, and I don't regret it," I say. Guilt rears its ugly head because, despite knowing it was absolutely the right choice, a part of me will always feel like I failed her. "It's not easy to say that, but I don't. I'll never forgot the look in those people's eyes when they came into that room to get her ..."

My head bows as the tears come again. They don't roll down and hit my shirt. They roll down and hit Machlan's.

I'm pressed to him again, my cheek against his chest. My arms around his waist and his around mine. I don't sob this time. It's a quiet cry that comes from a different place inside my heart.

"Do you think she'll find us one day?" I ask.

"Do you hope she does?" He rests his chin on the top of my head as I burrow into him deeper. "Sometimes I do. I want to see her face and hear her voice and see if she laughs like you or me."

"Sometimes you don't?" My brow pulls together.

"That's a trick question."

"How do you figure?"

He adjusts his arms around me. "That was the hardest day of my life." His voice cracks, but he forces on. "As a man, as a *father*," he says, tripping over the word, "I failed. I had this little version of the two of us in my arms and the best way I could protect her was to put her in another man's ..."

The tremble doesn't come from me this time. He sniffles, clutching me for dear life.

Making it a point not to look at him, to give him space, I just hold him. "That's how she'll know we loved her," I tell him quietly. "We loved her so much we made the hardest choice anyone can ever make."

Tears run down my face. Machlan lets go with one hand to wipe his eyes.

"You didn't walk away from me when I told you I was having a baby," I say softly. "You didn't pressure me to do one thing or the other." I pull him tighter to me. "You held me when I needed held and pushed me when I needed pushed. You did the best you could, and that's all anyone can do, Mach."

"Sometimes I think about saying fuck it," he says, sniffling again. "I think about saying to hell with it all and just selling everything and being done."

"Why?" Leaning back, my fists still wrapped in his flannel, I take in his puffy eyes. "Why would you do that?"

He smiles sadly. "Because my chance is over."

"It's not. How can you say that?"

"What am I supposed to do, Had? Live some great life and have our daughter come back someday and be like, 'Oh, glad you missed me'?"

"You think she expects us to have shitty lives because we couldn't take care of her? She might be half you and as hardheaded as an ox, but she's half me too, so she's logical."

The flicker at the sides of his lips raises my spirits some.

"I write her letters sometimes," I tell him. "I tell her about how much we love her and how we've tried to build our lives, and we think about her all the time."

"You tell her about me?"

"Of course." I grin against his chest as he pulls me back into him again. "I pretend she's an adult, and I'm giving her a peek into our life as the years go by. Maybe it'll help her understand if she ever does come find us."

"How do you explain *us*?"

"Well," I say, clearing my throat of the emotion rising again. "I tell her the truth, without adding in how much of an asshole you can be."

He laughs. "Thanks."

"You're welcome." I want to pull away, to see his face, but there's no way I can remove myself from his arms. "I tell her what I know—

that you're running a business. That you're the silent force behind your family."

"I'm the what?" He chuckles. "Silent force?"

"You are. You check on Nana. You keep Walker and Lance straight. You send Blaire flowers on every holiday because you know your father would've and you don't want her to miss out." My voice breaks. "As much as you hate to admit it, you're there for Peck. You always have my brother's back."

I look up. All I can see is his profile as he gazes into the tree line. A soft smile he doesn't know I can see plays on his lips.

"It's true," I say softly. "I know you think you're a mess, and you *are* a lot of times, but there's a lot of good in you, Machlan."

He looks down and catches me watching. Rolling his eyes, he playfully shrugs me off him.

I laugh with a shrug of my own. "Anyway, that's what I tell her in the letters."

"Thank you for that," he says, the easiness of the moment lost to a somberness only he and I could understand. "That's really nice of you."

"Well, you never know what could go in a future note," I say, turning toward the truck.

I don't get far. He spins me around. When I stop, I'm facing a Machlan I've never seen before.

There's a levity in his features, a lightness in his eyes that seems to expand from somewhere inside him. The lines around his eyes that sort of disappear in the hazy afternoon. A dimple settles in his cheek as he narrows his eyes.

"I still don't want to be your friend," he says. "But I want to be something."

"Like what?" I ask even though I'm almost too afraid to. My hopes go higher than they should, high enough that I can't bring them back down.

He shrugs. "I don't know. I just don't want you to write me off or force yourself to pretend you're in love with some joke of a guy just so you can cram me in some category and move on."

I like this. I like it a lot.

A thousand pounds lighter, I smile the purest, realest smile his way. "Let's just take the pressure off and figure out how to co-exist in whatever way that organically means. Deal?"

"Deal," he says.

I extend a hand to shake. Instead of taking it, he slaps me on the ass, making me yelp, as he walks around me toward the truck.

"Hey, now," I say, shaking a finger his way. "There won't be any of that."

"Just testing the waters, seeing what feels right."

I climb in the truck and the engine roars to life. "That did not feel right."

He pops it into drive but keeps his foot on the brake. "I beg to differ." He revs the engine again. "Everything about that felt absolutely right."

Before I can respond, before I can stop my heart from leaping out of my chest, he slams on the gas and throws me back in my seat.

Chapter 17

Machlan

"Here you go," I say, sliding the truck up against the sidewalk.

Hadley lifts the bag from Peaches onto her lap. She grabs the door handle but doesn't pull the lever. Instead, she looks at me over her shoulder.

There's usually a spark of fire there, either from being extremely annoyed or from an anger that's burned hot for years. I'll take what I see now over that.

A level of apprehension is evident. She doesn't quite trust that I'm not going to say something ridiculous and piss her off. She's right not to. But over top of that unease is a comfort that I would give my life to keep there.

The first time I saw this girl, sitting on the floor in Cross's living room folding laundry, I knew I had just encountered someone my life would be twisted with forever. I was fifteen and couldn't explain it. She was so pretty, so sweet, and her laughter was the last thing I heard going to sleep almost every night after that. But it was her strength, her refusal to put up with her brother's shit or my smartass remarks, that really got me.

She never lost those things—she's as beautiful, witty, and kind as ever. But she was missing that air about her that I love, *that I stole*. Seeing it now, even vaguely, I feel like I can breathe again.

The bag ruffles in her fingers. "I just wanna say one more thing."

"What?"

"Thank you."

The look in her eyes tells me it's not for picking her up or buying her lunch.

"You're welcome."

She nods, biting her lip, and pulls on the handle.

"Hey, Had?"

"Yeah?" she asks. One leg dangles from the truck as she stills.

"Thank you too."

She doesn't turn around, doesn't look my way, but she doesn't have to. I get everything I need from how she rebounds when her feet hit the ground.

I watch her walk to the stairs and make it to the top. She sticks a key in the lock but stops short of going inside. Instead, she pivots slowly and looks at the truck. After a little wave, she disappears into the apartment.

It takes a lot of energy to put the truck in drive and pull away.

I take the corner around Crave and coast down Beecher Street, my thoughts still on Bluebird Hill. Normally when I let my brain wander and it unsurprisingly lands on Hadley, I end up breaking something or wanting to. Today, not so much. I almost feel ... at peace.

The only thing I've ever really wanted out of life was Hadley. No matter how much I tell myself I'm wrong for her even though she's perfect for me, or that I could fill her spot in with another face, I can't. It was laughable when I tried.

Living in my skin has been a complicated adventure. The only thing I've learned so far in my life is this: my best usually isn't good enough. I don't know what all that says about me, but it's true. I'm a guy without a real career, without a real care to have one. I've botched every important moment in my life, and I can't ask for any favors, and I shouldn't be trusted with any either.

My wipers switch on as it begins to sprinkle again. Crank is on my right. Walker and Peck are in the side lot, inspecting a piece of farm equipment. I throw the transmission in neutral and rev the engine. My brother flips me off.

With a chuckle, I hit the button on my steering wheel to pick up an incoming call.

"Hey, Blaire," I say.

"Am I on speaker?"

"Why? You have something juicy to tell me?"

"No, asshole. I just like to understand the audience before I speak."

I roll to a stop sign and wave a truck hauling logs through. "You're such a lawyer, you know that?"

"Are you avoiding my question for a reason?"

Hitting the gas, I laugh. "I'm alone. Just heading home for a few before I go to work."

"Where have you been?"

"Why?"

I get situated in my seat, resting my elbow on the door. Swiping at my bottom lip with my thumb, I find myself doing something I don't do a lot—grin for no reason.

"I was just curious," she says. "Don't answer if you don't want, especially if you were doing something with Cross that's going to result in a call later asking how to deal with a situation."

"Oh, come on. When's the last time that actually happened?"

She laughs. "Let's think. I believe it was when Peck 'borrowed' the tractor from an unsuspecting farmer."

"But that had nothing to do with me." I laugh, shaking my head, as I pull into my driveway. "That's all Peck."

"Um, if I remember correctly—"

"You're a lawyer. You remember whatever version of events best fits your argument." I flip the engine off. "What are you doing today?"

"Working. Although I'm considering leaving for lunch today."

"Wow. Living on the wild side."

"Shut it," she says. "It's hard to get out once you're here."

"And to think you spent all that money on a degree to do that."

"Hang on a sec."

She sticks me on hold. I grab my phone and get out of the truck. The mist is thick. You can see the water droplets falling lazily to the ground.

These are my favorite days. They remind me of when I was young and Mom would open all the windows and cook something amazing. Dad would come get me and make me go to the garage to work on something. I'd bitch and moan at first, but by the time Mom called us in for dinner, I wouldn't mind the day so much.

I kick a rock off the driveway as Blaire comes back to the line.

"Sorry," she says. "Promise me something."

"What's that?"

"Never be the guy who gets married and becomes useless." She sighs. "A partner in the firm got married a few months ago, and it's starting to ruin my life."

"Bruce? Isn't he like sixty?"

"Fifty-two, but that's not the point. The point is he's had this amazing career, he's one of the smartest men I know, and he gets married, and then all of a sudden, he's worthless. I just had to remind him that he doesn't pay my bills or sleep in my bed. He needs to direct his inquiries elsewhere."

Bursting out laughing, I lean against the truck. "It's amazing you have any friends at all."

"Who said I have friends?" She laughs. "I am calling my baby brother, after all."

"I'm the last resort, huh?"

"I wouldn't say that. You're just the only one I call for reasons other than to make sure they're alive."

"Reasons like ...?" I prod.

The line goes quiet. Then she sighs. Then she clicks on her keyboard.

"Hey, Blaire."

"Yeah?"

"I actually have shit to do today."

"Sorry," she groans. "I just ... You know the guy I was telling you about?"

I start to answer her seriously. I *should* answer her seriously. Blaire doesn't talk about men—not to me, not to my brothers, not to anyone. If she dates at all, it's news to me. But hearing her all tripped up over this guy she met while on a vacation my brothers and I made her take in Savannah a few weeks ago has been nothing short of hysterical.

"I'm having a hard time remembering which guy you'd be talking about," I joke.

"Holt. The guy from Savannah."

I chuckle. "Of course, I remember. He's the only guy I think you've ever mentioned. I was starting to think you were batting for the other team."

"You know what? You're a jerk."

"Anyway ..."

"Anyway," she goes on. "He wants me to come down for a long weekend again."

"And ...?"

She groans. "Do I go?"

"How the fuck should I know?"

"I mean, if I go, does that mean something?"

"Yeah," I deadpan. "It means you want to be fucked."

"Machlan!"

"What? You asked."

She groans again, but there's a little chuckle laced in there that makes me smile. Blaire doesn't lighten up much. Everything is cut and dry with her. Right or wrong. Clean or dirty. She doesn't have fun like Walker. She doesn't do relationships like Lance. And she doesn't blow smoke up people's asses like I do. So to hear her all fucked up over a guy is pretty fantastic.

"Well," she says, "I kind of do."

"Blaire!"

"What?" If Blaire was capable of giggling like a normal girl, this would be a giggle. "It's been a while."

I shove off the truck. "I don't want to hear about your sex life."

"Good because it would be a boring story. I'm not like you guys."

"I love how you think I'm some kind of whore."

"Aren't you?"

"No. That was Lance before Mariah came around. I've always been more of a discriminate fuck."

"Speaking of, I heard Hadley was around."

"Yeah ..." I sigh, reaching for my back pocket.

The chew can nestles in my palm. My thumb beats a rhythmic tap on the lid that takes the edge off my exposed nerves.

"How's that going?" Blaire's tone is softer now, knowing this is dangerous territory. "I know it's hard for you when she's around."

I slide the can in my pocket again. "It's okay this time, I think."

"Really?"

"I don't know. Maybe? We talked a little today, and there was no bloodshed. That's a step in the right direction, right?"

"What do you think changed?"

Good question.

Walking to the planters that line both sides of the porch, I look at Mom's rose bushes. She used to keep them pruned perfectly, but I don't. I leave them there because I can't rip them out, but I don't take care of them. They take care of themselves. They stretch opposite ways for sunlight and dig deeper when they need more nutrients, I guess.

"Maybe," I say, wondering how insane this is going to sound, "we realized we're gonna have to figure out how to breathe the same air. I mean, our roots are so tangled that we can only dig deeper, you know?"

"No." She laughs. "I don't. Are you on drugs?"

"No, just looking at Mom's rose bushes and making analogies." Swiping my finger over the wet petals, I head to the front door. "I think you should go to Savannah."

"Yeah," she says with a pointed sigh. "I think I should too."

"Long-distance relationships usually don't work, but knowing you and your anti-social ways, it might be perfect."

"I totally hate people."

"I know." I unlock the door and step inside. "I need to get ready for work. Hired a new bartender and she's there alone right now."

"Go. I need to get back to work anyway."

"Be good. And let me know if you go to Savannah just so I know you make it home." The hardwood floors creak under my weight as I amble toward my room. "I mean, I'm sure this guy is a real winner, but you never know."

She gasps. "I'm being irrational, aren't I?"

Laughing, I flip on the light in my room. "No. Don't overthink it. Just use that brain of yours and you'll be fine."

"Mach, maybe not. Maybe I should—"

"Go, Blaire. Both back to work and to Savannah. Love ya. Goodbye."

"Love you. Bye," she says.

My phone goes flying through the air and lands in the middle of my bed. I want to flop down beside it and rest for a few minutes—get my head together before I throw myself into a weekend night at Crave.

Instead, I turn toward my closet but stop.

My heart pounds in my chest as I step to my dresser. My hand goes around the corner of the television and finds the edge of the four-by-six frame. I pull it out.

Holding it with both hands, I bring the picture closer. Hadley wasn't looking at the camera while I snapped the only photo I have of her and our baby. She's looking at the chubby faced little girl with a shock of dark hair and the prettiest complexion I've ever seen.

"Daddy loves you, baby girl," I say, my thumb stroking the image.

A lump springs to my throat as a wetness coats my eyes, and I put the picture back and get ready for work.

Chapter 18

Hadley

"That was so good," I say, rubbing my stomach.

Cross hands the waitress his credit card. "That was, quite possibly, the best taco salad I've ever eaten."

"I'd have to agree, considering it was the second one I've eaten today."

"You came here for lunch?"

"Kind of."

I roll my straw around my glass, fighting a huge smile from swamping my face. It's been plastered on my lips ever since Machlan dropped me off this afternoon.

My brother pulls his brows together. Setting his wallet on the table, he crosses his arms over his chest and watches me skeptically. "What are you not telling me?"

"Well," I say, letting go of the straw. "I kind of came here today with Mach."

"You're shitting me."

"No, I'm not, and that choice of words is horrific," I say, wrinkling my nose. "What does that even mean? Does anyone actually shit you? How would you do that? Like, I don't get it."

"It's a form of expression. Don't change the subject."

"I'm not."

"Then did I hear you just say you came to lunch here with Machlan?"

"Yes, nosy. I had lunch with your best friend today."

I hate how smug I feel and how I know Cross is picking up on it. How could he not? A total stranger could see how satisfied I am right now. I can't help it, though.

I've replayed every second we spent together today. What surprises me the most is my favorite moments aren't the ones when he held me or touched me or gave me hope that things might find some normalcy between us. My favorite parts of today are the ones where I looked in his eyes and saw *him*. Not the man who owns the bar or the one who has commitment issues. Not my brother's best friend or the guy who broke my heart.

Today, he was Machlan.

The guy who whispered "I love you" one Saturday night while we watched a movie on his nana's couch.

The man who gave me the opportunity to feel a child growing in my stomach and be a mother even if for only a few hours.

Today, when I looked in his eyes, he was the boy I fell in love with.

If I thought about it too much, I'd flip into terrified mode. I'd start overthinking this whole thing and realize how awful I'll feel when things don't work out or how lonely it'll be when I leave and he lets me. Again. But the beauty of today is this: I don't overthink it. I embrace Emily's advice and Machlan's words and just *let it be*.

"I can honestly say I'm surprised," Cross says. He takes his credit card from the waitress and thanks her before turning back to me.

"Why?"

"I thought you were going a different direction."

"Yeah." I sigh. "I tried. And I still don't know what direction we're going, per se, but I like this ... whatever it is. Being able to spend time with him. It's nice."

"I've always told you whatever you two figure out is fine as long as you don't get hurt in the process." He takes some cash out of his wallet and places it in the center of the table. Then, just as our dad used to do, and I do, he takes the saltshaker and places it on top. "You ready?"

"Yeah."

We stand, scooting in our chairs, and meander through the tables at Peaches. Cross holds the door open for me and a couple of ladies coming in, before following me outside.

The air is crisp and the wind gusty as we make our way to his truck. We get situated inside and don't speak until the heat is on.

"Can I ask what led to you and Mach having lunch?" he asks. "I mean, it's none of my business, and I'm totally okay with that, but I have a feeling I'll end up hearing about it from one of you on the back end. If I have some background, it'll help."

I watch clouds tumble across the sky, deep gray billows across the light gray backdrop. "I was walking to Carlson's for lunch, and it started pouring. He happened to drive by and pick me up."

"Sure, he did." Cross laughs, putting the truck in reverse.

"What?"

"He didn't happen to see you do shit. Fucker was probably stalking you."

My heart skips a beat. "No. I don't think so. I think it was random."

"Sure, it was."

We lurch forward as he shoves the transmission in drive. Cross laughs again, this time more to himself than me. I watch the amusement dance across his features and wonder what he's thinking. I'm too afraid to ask.

Biting my lip, I look out the window but don't really see anything. All of my attention is on my brother's assessment of the situation. I turn to him, curiosity winning.

"What did you mean by that?" I ask.

"By what?"

"By saying he didn't happen to see me."

He rolls his eyes. "When it comes to you, nothing Machlan does or says or sees is random." He quiets as he pilots the truck onto the exit ramp back to Linton. "If you're in a ten-mile radius, Mach can't focus on anything else."

"Really?" I grin.

"Seeing you grin like that makes me happy. I get it. Trust me," he says, a look sweeping across his face that I know means he's thinking about Kallie. "But just be careful, okay?"

"Be careful? That doesn't sound good." My grin falters as I look out the window again. "I know what you mean. Things could flip around in a heartbeat."

He turns the heater down and the radio off. "That's true, but let's focus on the good part of the day. What did the two of you do?"

"He picked me up, took me to Peaches, and we drove around a while. Ended up on Bluebird."

Cross makes a show of leaning away from me. "What happens on Bluebird stays on Bluebird, and it's definitely nothing that should be heard by your brother."

"We just talked." My emotions level out, and a calmness settles over me. "It was nice. We kind of came to an arrangement or something."

"I'm afraid to even ask."

"Then don't."

He swishes his head side to side. "Is it sexual in nature?"

I punch his shoulder.

We both laugh as he takes the exit to Linton, and we pass the turnoff to Bluebird. There's a relief on his face that I know well; it's one I feel in my bones.

"Whatever deal you struck," he says, "I hope you can keep it up. I kind of like being able to bring up his name and not have you rant."

"I kind of like it too."

He flashes me a knowing smile and takes a right at Goodman's.

We trudge through town, the roads still wet from the rain. The streetlights come on, and a hazy glow shines over town. It reminds me of fall days after school the year I moved to Illinois from San Diego. I couldn't get over the way the leaves changed and how quickly the temperature dropped.

It was an eventful fall that year. So much time spent learning how to be a country girl—camping, fishing, and going to football games in the back of trucks. The smell of Carlson's pumpkin bread and Machlan's body after a football game trickle through my mind.

I miss those things. All of them. Not necessarily in that order.

"You still planning on going back to Vigo?" Cross asks, bringing me out of my reverie.

"Of course." I look at him over my shoulder. "Why wouldn't I?"

"I just thought maybe if you and Machlan could make peace, you'd come home." He takes his eyes off the road and winces. "Does that make you feel bad for leaving? Because if it does, I'm not sorry."

Giving him a sad smile, I sigh. "It does make me feel bad. Thanks."

"I worry about you, Had."

"I'm fine," I say. "Really."

I jabber on a host of run-on sentences that are clearly more for my own edification than to convince him of anything. The whole time I'm telling him how excited I am to get to work at the new office, to hang out with Emily more now that Samuel is out of the picture, and how I can come back to visit whenever, I fight the rumble in my belly that reminds me how much I wish I felt the enthusiasm I'm trying to extend to Cross.

Being in Linton is comfortable. It's like walking in a warm house on a cold day and taking off your boots and getting handed a cup of hot chocolate. It's having people wave as you go down the road and seeing familiar faces in the gas station who ask how you're doing and really mean it. It's being with Cross, the only family I have, and it's being with my friends. And it's being with Machlan.

I gulp. "I'll be fine," I say again. "Besides, when you and Kallie have babies, I'm sure I'll reconsider. Get to work on that." I make a face. "Who am I kidding? I heard you. You're totally working on that."

Cross chuckles, shaking his head as he pulls next to my car behind Crave.

Cars and trucks are parked everywhere, and people loiter on the sidewalks. Every time the back door opens and people come out to smoke, music from the inside filters out.

I wonder if Machlan is in there, and if he is, what he's doing. I wonder if he's thought of me since this afternoon and how he thinks of me, if he has.

Biting my lip, I gaze at the back door, but I'm interrupted as Cross bumps my shoulder.

"Huh?" I ask, tearing my gaze to my brother.

"You want to go in? Kallie is at her mom's for a while tonight, so I have some time to kill."

I shouldn't. I should leave well enough alone and just go to the apartment and read like I had planned. But the longer I don't answer and the wider Cross's smile gets and the more times the back door opens, the bigger the little bubble of excitement in my stomach grows.

"You know what?" I say, opening my door. "Let's do that."

Chapter 19

Hadley

"People get here this early?" I pause outside the door of Crave and take in the cars lining the street. "I guess I thought this was a late-night thing."

"Machlan has a good thing going here."

"Lots of drinkers in town, huh?"

"Believe it or not, people come in and don't drink alcohol."

"Really?" I flip my attention to my brother. "Why?"

Cross shrugs. "I guess they just like the atmosphere. Everyone in town filters through here at some point during the weekend. Hell, Machlan makes more here than I do at both my gyms."

"Are you serious?"

"He'd never admit it, but yeah. I'd bet that's true."

This sparks a moment of pride in me. It's not about the money because I know Machlan doesn't care about that. But that he took something he enjoys, something I'm just realizing means something entirely more to him than I would've ever guessed and made it a success.

That makes me happy for him.

A roar of laughter ekes through the closed door. The windows are blacked out, so I can't see in, but if I weren't already curious, I would be now.

"There's a bar in Vigo," I say. "It's a great place to go until it gets dark out. Then all hell breaks loose, and it becomes a shit show."

"Yeah, well, that doesn't happen here. Machlan doesn't hesitate to toss people out on their ass."

Stepping to the side to let a couple pass, I look at my brother. "Think he'll toss me out?"

"He'll have to get through me."

"So think he'll toss me out?" I repeat with a laugh.

Cross shakes his head and reaches for the door. "You act like it's a given he'd win."

"Because he would."

"Have you even considered that I'm an actual fighter? Like I've been in sanctioned boxing matches. I own two gyms. I train people how to fight."

"And Machlan would kick your ass." I laugh. "But I still love you, and I'll always lie in front of Kallie about that."

"I ..." He holds a hand on his heart and yanks open the door. "I'm hurt."

"Yeah, yeah, yeah."

It takes a couple of seconds for my eyes to adjust to the dim lighting. The salty scent of the bar mixed with the perspiration from the throngs of people already dancing hit me quick and hard.

Blowing out a breath, I give myself a moment to adjust. The place is hopping in a very controlled manner. It's not what I was expecting even though I don't really know what I was expecting.

Cross touches my shoulder and nudges me to move as a crowd of people come in behind us. I take a few steps before my feet falter.

Machlan is behind the bar. Dressed in jeans and a black T-shirt that hugs his body like it was made just to show off his muscles, he's hard to look away from. The colorful tattoos on his right arm peek out from under the sleeve of the shirt while his hair does the same from beneath a plain black baseball hat that's turned around backward.

I'm nudged forward again. My heartbeat picks up as I get closer, knowing he hasn't seen me yet. A part of me wants to fade into the background and just watch him from a distance. Another side of me wants to climb him like a damn tree. Thank God for the rational side that tells me to breathe, smile, and *let things be.*

"Well, lookie there," Peck says. He scoots over one stool and pats the one he just vacated. His eyes light up like a bright summer sky. "What's happening?"

"Not much. What about you?" I ask.

"Oh, just having a beer. Watching the game," he says, nodding his head toward the television above the beer cooler. "Also, kinda trying to flirt with the new bartender." His face scrunches together as though he's embarrassed.

I sit down beside him. "Yes! She's super pretty and seems really nice. I love her for you."

"Settle down," Cross says. "He didn't say he was marrying her."

I press my elbow backward, and it lands in my brother's stomach. "You stay out of this." Taking a quick check down the bar to see Machlan's gone, I look instead at Peck. "Navie, huh? Much, much better than Molly. I approve."

"Now, let's not go hating on my girl. I'm still marrying Molly someday," he says. "I'm just testing out my flirting skills on Navie. I don't think she minds."

He gives me the cutest smile, the one I think of when I think of Peck. It's adorable with a hint of disobedience that makes you want to hug him and hit him at the same time. It's pretty charming, actually.

"No, I bet she doesn't," I say. "I ..."

My cheeks flush as my gaze finds Machlan's. He seems oblivious to the guy he's handing a beer to. His chin is dipped ever so slightly as he narrows his eyes as though he's unsure if he's seeing things— meaning *me*—correctly.

My heart skips a beat. Then two. He nods absentmindedly to the patron who just took the beer and ignores the money being flashed his way. As he stalks his way toward me instead, it skips a third.

The unknown buzzes through my veins. The glow of the pink flamingo lights hanging above the antique mirror that frames the liquor bottles gives him a warm, roguish glow. The hottest thing, besides my cheeks, is the way he looks *at me*.

One hand cups his chin, his fingers working back and forth over his mouth as if he's trying to hide a smile. His eyes are trained on me so intently I squirm in my seat. Desire pools in my lower belly. My stomach topples over itself, unable to steady against the fire coming from his gorgeous eyes. My palms dampen.

Breathe, Hadley.

"You ready for this?" Peck cracks beside me.

"Ready for what?" Cross asks, looking up from his phone. "Oh, shit."

"Incoming in five ... four ... three ... two ... one ... liftoff," Peck whispers, bringing a bottle of beer to his lips.

"Hey, Mach," I say, hoping to take some of the wind out of his sails by speaking first.

He plants both palms on the bar. *Hard.* His gaze lingers on me for a few long seconds before he rips them away and plops them on my brother. "Really, Cross?"

"We were just coming in to say hi," he says.

"Hi," Machlan deadpans. His fingertips strum against the counter, a sound I only barely hear over the roar of the crowd.

He extends a finger toward my hand, and I hold my breath, thinking he's going to touch me. The longer we sit, the more the edge of frustration wavers off his face.

"I can't take this," Peck says. "Somebody say something." He looks back and forth between us. "Fine. I'll go. What a great game. I have no idea who is playing, but I'm for the green team."

I snort. "I thought you were for the Navie team." My shoulder bumps his. "Get it? Navie. Navy."

Peck laughs. "So witty tonight, Ms. Jacobs."

"Yeah, I try."

I also try super hard not to whip my gaze right back to Machlan, but I fail. It's like he can order my body to do what he wants from the other side of the bar. Like I'm Pavlov's dog—he dangles the treat and I start salivating. It's unfair, really.

"I need to get out of here," Cross says. "Kallie just sent me a text that she's home, and you know ..."

"We know," Peck groans. "Kallie is home, and you're pussy whipped. Congratulations."

"Fuck off, Peck," Cross says atop my laughter.

Peck just shrugs.

"So you guys are going?" Machlan asks. He looks at my brother, then at me, then drags his eyes back to Cross. "Is that what I heard?"

"I don't know about Hadley ..."

Machlan stands tall. His posture is on point as he looks at Cross. "Oh, I do. Trust me, Cross. A case of blue balls is gonna hurt a whole lot less than the knot I put on your head if you leave her here."

"Asking me to take her home would go a lot smoother if you do it nicely," Cross counters.

"Excuse me?" I start to get off the stool but stop when Peck rests a hand gently on my forearm. Shaking him off, I sit back down. "I am right here and perfectly capable of making a decision on where I want to be tonight. Thank you. *Both*," I add, looking over my shoulder at my brother.

"Excuse *me*, but I have a business to run tonight. If I don't pay attention to what's happening in here, it'll all fall apart. Thank you. *Both*," Machlan says, unwavering.

He's dropped the bite in his tone a few decibels. There's a certain level of sternness in his words, but something that might be the beginning of a plea too. I start to respond when a shriek breaks out from the back.

We all jump as the sound breaks from near the pool tables. Voices rise over the music and the other customers' chatter. Instinctively, I grab Peck's arm.

I can't see what's happening over the crowd of people, but my heart pounds out of control. Machlan wastes no time jumping on top of the bar in front of me.

Any vulnerability I might've seen in him today is long gone. He stands like a soldier, looking menacingly down at an unidentified person in the back.

He looks tall and dark and sexy as fuck. And even though I'm latched on to Peck for protection, my body is wound around Machlan.

"Darren!" His voice booms through the room. Everything stills. If it weren't for the music playing through the speakers, you could hear a pin drop. "That's your one! One more time and you're gone. Got it?"

Machlan watches something, or someone, intently before hopping back to the ground. Slowly, the noise level picks back up. I might start breathing again too.

Peck and Cross both say something. I'm not sure to whom. I'm too busy melting into a puddle of goo under Machlan's gaze.

His face is flushed from the situation, but it only makes me want him more. It gives him a little unruliness to his otherwise contained appearance.

"Look, Had. If you're here, I'm gonna be watching you." A ghost of a smile flirts with his cheeks. "If I'm watching *you*, I'm not watching *them*."

I bite on my bottom lip to keep from breaking into an ear-to-ear smile.

"I have an idea," Peck chimes in. "I'll watch her."

Machlan rolls his eyes. "I wouldn't trust you to watch my dog."

He tips his empty bottle Machlan's way. "You let me help close the bar the other night."

"So?"

"So that establishes a certain level of trust."

"He has a point," Cross says. When Machlan shoots him a look, he points a finger his way. "What are you gonna do, Mach? Tell her she can't stay? Good luck with that." He pats me on the shoulder.

"I'm going home to my girl. You guys can do whatever you want. Peck, you'll make sure she gets to the apartment, right?"

"As long as Machlan doesn't kill me."

I lay my head on Peck's shoulder. "You protect me from the boogeymen in here, and I'll protect you from Machlan."

"Who's gonna protect you from me?" Machlan's eyes twinkle as he says the words.

My jaw hangs open in a very unladylike fashion. I can't pick it up. I can't speak, but I am grateful when Cross does.

"Can we not?" my brother asks.

Machlan turns to address someone shouting his name from the other side of the bar. He holds up a finger and turns back to Peck. "Don't let me down, Peck."

"Have I ever let you down?"

"Don't ask that," Cross and I say in unison, making everyone laugh.

Machlan shakes his head and starts toward the guy yelling for him.

"Can I get another beer?" Peck shouts his way.

"And I need a drink, please," I say before Machlan is out of earshot. He just shakes his head harder.

Cross leans in and tells me he'll call me tomorrow. He and Peck have a hushed conversation before Peck turns back to the television and Cross turns toward the door.

My attention naturally turns to Machlan.

He has a bottle of a clear-colored liquid in one hand and a glass with ice in the other. His biceps flex as he moves behind the bar, pouring and mixing and shaking things together. The longer he stands in one place, the more people gather. It appears as though he's telling a story because the patrons seem to hang on his words. It's a very different Machlan than I'm used to seeing.

I've seen him control a room. He keeps a solid grip on every situation he's in. It's no surprise that he's the go-to guy when someone in his family needs a favor. Those are the situations he's most comfortable in. That's the role he likes to play. But seeing him like *this*—not only in control and comfortable, but relaxed, maybe even enjoying it, on a whole other level, is fascinating.

"Hey, Hadley!" Navie's voice draws me out of my spy-fest. "Can I get you something?"

"Please, for the love of God, order water," Peck groans.

"Did I miss something?" Navie laughs. Her giant gold hoop earrings catch the light and twinkle. "Why do you have to order water? Oh, my God! Are you pregnant?"

"No, no, no. Nothing like that." I let out a single laugh as I look up. My gaze is snatched out of the air by Machlan's. He lets it settle over me, lets my body temperature spike to the point of explosion, before pulling it away and back to the bottle in his hand. "I ..." I stammer, clearing my throat. "Just ... can I get a water?"

"Sure." She digs in the cooler under the bar and pulls out a bottle. "Here you go."

Forgetting all about the game on the television, Peck leans toward Navie. Her red lips part into a wide smile as Peck slides his beer bottle from hand to hand.

"What can I get you?" she asks in a much softer, sexier tone than she used with me.

"I could really use another beer."

She leans closer to him. "Is that so?"

He nods, grinning wildly. "Unless you'd like to dazzle me with some drink making skills."

"Oh, I have lots of dazzling skills. The problem is figuring out which to show you first."

Whether he folds under the pressure or loses his cool, I don't know, but he starts chuckling. His cheeks are as pink as Navie's shirt.

It's her turn to smile like an idiot, and I can't help but feel like I'm intruding. Just when I start to get up, I see Molly and sit right back down.

"Hey, Peck," Molly says, coming up to the other side of Peck. She pointedly ignores Navie as though she's not even there. "How are you, *baby*?"

I flinch, pulling away from the two of them and look at Navie. She looks surprised at the intrusion and at the term of endearment. I hold out a hand to motion for her to wait. That there's more to this story than lets on.

"I'm good." Peck sits back in his chair and focuses on Molly. "How are you doin' tonight?"

"Good." The sweetness drips off her words like poison, like the fake sugar known to cause cancer. You can feel the tumors grow with each breath she takes. "Just saw you up here and thought I'd say hi."

Rolling my eyes, I look at Navie. Molly glances quickly at Navie, too, and then bends toward Peck. Her boobs nearly drop to Peck's lap as her buzzed eyes set on me like I'm the enemy. "Well, hello, there, Hadley Jacobs."

"Well, hello, there, Molly." There's no love in my tone.

There's no love in the look she shoots me either. She turns back to Peck, who is putty in her hands. "I wondered if you'd look at my car. I'm afraid to try to leave here in it without someone taking a look at it."

"Oh my God ..." I groan.

"What's it doin'?" Peck asks, oblivious to anything but the girl in front of him.

Molly angles her cleavage toward Peck. "It's *moaning* and the ground was all *wet* underneath it when I got here."

"Sounds like a piece of shit," Navie mutters.

I can't help but laugh, but she's not talking about the car. And she's not wrong either. Molly glares at the two of us before going back to work. "Think you could take a look, Peck?"

"Yeah, of course." He stands and takes the last pull of his beer. "Sit right here, okay? Don't get up."

"Are you seriously going outside to look at her car now?" I balk. "It's dark, dude. All you're gonna see is the game she's playing."

"Be nice," he whispers. "I'll be right back." With a pat on my shoulder and a quick glance at Navie, he follows a smug Molly out the door.

Navie's jaw drops as Peck walks away. "I have a feeling I don't even want to know who that girl is."

"Molly McCarter. Resident town slut and I don't use that term lightly. I actually selected that word from my expansive vocabulary. It was the only one that fit."

Navie giggles. "Please. Tell me more."

I take a sip of water, ignoring Machlan's stare. "A whore just sleeps around. I have no problems with that. But a slut acts inappropriate, unconcerned with little details like marriage or prior commitments. She's in it for the drama and attention, not the sex."

"Love the description." She looks at the door. "Hate that Peck is out there with her. He seems like a good guy."

"He's a great guy. And he's in here flirting with you, and she can't take it. She usually ignores him, which is sad, but he's better off for it, actually."

She grabs two beers from the cooler and hands them to a couple of guys at the end of the bar. "Does he like her?"

The question is poised as if it was an afterthought. Being that I've tried to pry information out of people almost my entire life about Machlan and hoped they didn't catch on, I catch on.

"He has this crush on her. It's more like a kid with a puppy than an adult relationship. It won't last." Shaking my bottle at her, I throw out an idea. "He just needs someone else to rewire his brain. He can do so much better."

"I'd do him better."

"You know what? I like you." I laugh.

"And I like you." She glances over her shoulder. "And so does my boss."

Following her line of sight to Machlan, I catch him watching me out of the corner of his eye. He looks away. I don't.

Despite the handful of people clearly waiting on his attention, he pauses in front of an old man. The man seems to be fumbling over his words. His finger is crooked with age, and he jabs it toward Machlan with a smile on his face.

Machlan keeps his body square to the old man. He nods his head, smiles at various points, and even laughs a couple of times.

My heart warms just watching him. How he gives so much of himself to these various people is beyond me. I'd be pulling my hair out by now.

"He's a good guy," Navie offers.

"Yeah. He is."

"How long have you known him?"

I settle back in my chair. "Since I was fourteen. I moved here with my father and brother, Cross, when my mom died."

She nods and then looks over my shoulder. "Okay, then. Since you grew up here—who the hell is *that*?"

Chapter 20

Hadley

Woah.

There's no confusion as to who she's talking about. If the word stunning was ever supposed to be used to describe men, it was for these two.

They're tall, fit, and definitely not from Linton. One has on a button-down with the top two buttons undone, the other dons a polo shirt that shows off his physique. Their hair is perfectly imperfect with a nice, straight trim along the back of their necks and their fancy watches catch what little light there is overhead.

They laugh the kind of laugh that makes you sad you didn't hear what was said. Their smiles make you jealous of the women in their lives. Their confidence reminds me of Machlan, but in a more polished kind of way.

"Know them?" Navie asks.

"Nope."

"It's my job to see if they want a drink, right?" Navie giggles.

"Yeah, if you can do it without giggling like a little girl," I tease.

"What are we giggling about?" Peck slides into the stool in front of Navie. "What did I miss?"

"I'm not telling you anything since you let Molly order you around," I say.

"I did not."

"You did too." I cross my arms over my chest. "Navie? Did he or not?"

She grabs an order pad and shoves it in the front of her apron. "I'm not getting into it. Instead, I'm going to get back to work."

She walks away without looking back. Peck watches her in confusion.

I grab my water bottle and twist off the lid, but before I can raise it to my lips, a hard body is pressed behind me. I start to jump but stop when I smell the heavenly scent of Machlan.

My arms go weak as all the blood in my body rushes to my head. The bottle slips from my fingers, but Machlan catches it before it falls.

His breath heats the shell of my ear. "How do you feel?"

I nod, knowing I'm bending my neck for his use but unable to help it. A live wire running through my body both electrifies and freezes me at the same time. "Feels organic."

Waiting for him to touch me is hard. Anticipating the zing of energy across my skin is frustrating. Not having it happen is infuriating. All I get is a little snicker as a response.

I turn to face him, but he steps away. With a wink that I feel between my legs, he rounds the bar.

"Machlan," I call after him.

He stops. "Yeah?"

I let my eyes drift down his body before bringing it back up to his face. "You okay?"

His tongue rolls around the inside of his cheek. Nodding and fighting a grin, he proceeds to the end of the bar.

I love this feeling. Seeing how I affect him feels powerful but allowing myself to feel him affect me is even more so.

I've second-guessed every decision I've made for years—probably my entire life. I can't think of a time I let my guard down and didn't feel like I was swaying on my feet from the first moment after.

Machlan looks at something Navie shows him on a notepad. He's so kind to her, patient as he goes through the protocol or whatever he's explaining. I love this side of him. I love even more when he pauses midsentence and looks my way.

He nods toward the water bottle in front of me and grins. I roll my eyes, lifting the bottle and taking a drink. This makes him laugh. That makes my heart soar.

"Anyone wanna tell me why—" Peck is cut off by Walker's hands resting on his shoulders. "Hey, Walk."

"Hey." Walker looks at me. "What's up, Hadley?"

"Not much." I grin at Machlan's older brother. He's a darker, slightly heavier version of Machlan with just as much piss and vinegar.

Sienna, his girlfriend that I've met once before, comes up to his side. She gives Peck and me a little wave.

"Hey, Slugger," Peck says. "Any chance you could make some blueberry muffins for breakfast on Monday—ouch!" He rubs the back of his head where Walker smacked him. "What's that for?"

"She's not your maid. Or your girlfriend. Fucker." Walker scowls.

Sienna laughs. "I'll make you something and sneak it in."

"That's why I love, er, appreciate you so much," Peck says, ducking another smack.

"We're gonna sit in the back," Walker cuts in. "Sienna's family is in town to check me out, make sure I'm not a serial killer."

"They are not," she insists. "My sister and her husband are watching Deacon Love fight in Chicago tonight, so a couple of my brothers hitched a ride and are staying with us."

"As I was saying, if you two want to sit with us, you're welcome to. Actually, I'd appreciate it if you did."

Sienna splays a hand on Walker's stomach. "I'm going to go find my brothers before Lincoln meets Machlan on his own. I feel like a buffer needs to be there when that happens. Linc's already had a couple of shots."

"Yeah, go." Walker sighs. "I'll be back there in a minute."

Once she's gone, Walker stretches his neck. "Pretty cool guys but they fuckin' talk all the damn time."

Peck laughs. "I bet that's fun to watch, Mr. Social Butterfly."

Walker groans. "At least they're cool. Graham is actually really smart about a lot of shit. We've had some good conversations about business."

"What about the other one?" Peck asks.

"Lincoln is all right. Kind of a goof but cool." Walker grins. "As a matter of fact, I bet you two would get along great."

A host of laughter comes from the back corner of the bar. We all look back, but there's nothing to see but a table in the corner with Sienna's family having a good time.

"I better get back there," Walker says. "Where's Mach?"

"She's here." Peck jams a thumb my direction. "So, my guess is somewhere within a twenty-yard vicinity."

Walker chuckles. "Sounds about right. Now come back here with me and entertain the crowd. Keep them from wanting me to talk all night."

Peck stands. "Let's go, Had."

"Oh, no, you guys go on," I say, waving them off.

They stand in front of me and don't move. I fidget with the wrapper on my bottle. I don't know what to say to them, that this is a family thing and I'm not family. I don't want to intrude, and I don't want to feel like a burden they have to lug around.

"Come on," Peck says again.

"You know what? I need to go to the apartment. I'll be fine."

Walker takes my hand and guides me to my feet. "You will be fine because your ass is gonna be at the back table with us."

"Walker, thank you. Honestly. But—"

"But fucking nothing. Just because my dumbass brother hasn't figured out how to get his tail from between his legs doesn't mean you aren't family."

My heart turns to mush. I can't answer him with words because I can't find any to say. To see this burly, broody man imply I'm family to him would make me cry if we weren't in a bar full of people.

Peck guides us through the crowd toward the sitting area nestled next to the billiards tables. Navie is there and taking everyone's drink orders when we get there. I sit between Peck and Walker.

Sienna does a quick introduction of her brothers. Graham, wearing the button-down, nods. Lincoln, the one in the polo shirt, waves.

"Do not bring Lincoln a bottle of Patrón," Graham says to Navie. "Whatever he offers you under the table to do it, I'll double."

"I'm a married man, thank you." Lincoln gasps. "And so are you. Kind of."

Graham turns to Navie with a raised brow as though Lincoln just proved his point.

"No tequila for this guy." Navie laughs. "Got it."

"I've only had two shots," Lincoln says. "And we're on vacation."

"You've had three, and your wife said that's your limit," Sienna tells him. "I'll have a glass of red wine, please. And bring Walker some tequila. I think he's gonna need it."

Lincoln shakes his head and looks at his sister. "He gets another shot, and I don't? What the fuck?"

"Because I can handle my liquor," Walker says.

Lincoln flinches. "And I can't?"

"No," they all say at the same time.

They continue ribbing Lincoln, but I'm distracted by Walker. I follow the direction of his gaze to see Machlan heading our way. Everything else drowns out.

His swagger is present, his confidence intact. But the closer he gets and the more I see of him, the more questions I have.

There's a question sitting on the tip of his tongue. I just don't know who it's for.

I hold my breath as he reaches our table and doesn't stop until he's behind my chair. I feel his hands brush against the edges of my hair. His fingers skim the back of my neck so lightly that I wonder if it was an accident.

A shiver rolls down my body, and I hope no one notices.

"Guys, this is Machlan," Sienna says, starting off a new round of introductions. She names each person at the table, and Machlan exchanges a hello with each of them.

"This is your place?" Graham asks. "Looks like a good revenue stream."

"It doesn't do bad," Machlan replies.

"Doesn't do bad, my ass," Walker says. "He works half as hard as me and makes double the money."

"Sounds like Lincoln," Graham says.

"I can't help I made playing professional baseball look easy." Lincoln looks at Machlan. "You can't help you're smarter than Walker and picked a job that got you a lot of money and pussy. Am I right? I mean, that's how I feel about baseball—not that I'm getting a lot of pussy now. I'm happily married. Let's make sure to clarify that so I don't get beat with my own bat when I get home."

Machlan's fingertips drift across the back of my neck. It's not an accident this time. They sweep from side to side, the contact growing a little more each time.

"Ah, I don't use this place to get laid," Machlan says. "It was never about that for me."

He says the words to Lincoln, presumably, but I feel like they were said to me. He rests his hand over my shoulder, his thumb pressing on the back of my neck. It's like he's telling me he's there. To pay attention. To be in the moment. I don't know how much more in the moment I could be because a flame of hope lights in my chest that I know I'll have a hard time putting out at three in the morning when I'm lying in bed alone.

"I need to help Navie out for a second. I'll come by and check on you guys in a while. It was nice to meet you all," Machlan says.

He squeezes my shoulder again before heading back into the crowd.

My body buzzes as though I've had a drink. I hear the sounds of everyone laughing, talking, enjoying themselves, but I can't pay attention to any of that until Machlan is out of sight.

"Okay," Lincoln says. "There's Walker and Machlan and Blaire. We met her when she came down to get the corporation papers. Isn't there another one of you?"

"Yeah, Lance," Peck chimes.

"What's he do for a living?" Graham asks.

"He's a history teacher," Peck says. "Total nerd."

"Graham will love him then," Lincoln says, earning an eye roll from his brother.

Graham takes two shot glasses from Navie and then turns to Peck. "Who are you in the grand scheme of things?"

"We're first cousins. Well, me and them. Not Hadley. She's not related or that'd be weird. And illegal, maybe."

"You're with Machlan?" Graham asks, taking a shot.

"Oh, no. I ..."

"Yes, she is." Peck sighs.

"I am not."

"You are too." Sienna smiles at me. "If you think you're not, go talk to a guy in here and see what happens."

"But that doesn't mean we're together," I contend. "That means he doesn't want me with anyone else."

Lincoln grabs a shot glass in front of Graham and hammers it. Graham smacks him on the back of the head, but he swallows it with a laugh. "I'm going to give you some advice," Lincoln says.

"First thing you should know about Linc," Graham says, "is that you never take his advice. If he's had any tequila, that warning triples."

I can't help but laugh.

"Okay," Lincoln starts. "Here's what you do. You—"

"Don't listen to him. Really," Sienna says. "He just convinced our oldest brother to buy a winery. Our family knows nothing about grapes."

Lincoln snorts. "That's not what I heard."

"I think I'd like that story," Peck says.

"I'll fill you in, man. Your girl will love you forever."

"He does not mean Molly," I say. I turn as Peck starts to speak but don't see Navie between us. The entire tray of drinks goes in the air. It's slow motion as the liquids separate from the glass and splashes into the air.

"Oh, no!" Navie gasps as Peck and I try to get out of the way.

We don't.

Liquid crashes down on both of us like an angry wave. My shirt is soaked, my hair sticky from the sweet alcohol.

"I'm so sorry," Navie gushes.

"Don't worry about it," I say, standing up. Taking a step behind the chairs, I fling off what liquid I can. "I'll just go change. Really. It's no big deal." I look at Peck. "You look like a drenched puppy."

He laughs, running a hand through his hair. "I feel like one. I have an extra shirt in my truck."

"I'll just go out the back door and up the stairs. If I'm not back in ten," I say, seeing the hesitation in his eyes, "you can come get me."

"Had ..."

"I'll be fine. Go change."

Not waiting for an argument or answer, I head around the table. "I'm going to clean up. It was nice to meet you all," I say and hurry out the back door before anyone can stop me.

Chapter 21

Hadley

The cool air wallops me as I push through the back door. A couple of men standing next to the makeshift ashtray give me sideways glances.

My shirt sticks to my skin, my hair clumped to my forehead, my arms and face sticky from the drinks.

The farther I get from Crave, the harder it is to breathe.

Everything feels too tight. Too fast. Too *pressurized.*

The events of the day spiral around me in a turbulent blast. The music from the bar adds to the cacophony inside my body every time the door opens and the patrons' laughter slips out to add to the mix.

It's sensory overload.

My mind tries to find one thing to grab on to, one thing to process, but there's just too much. The images of Machlan emotional over our child. The feel of him in my arms. The heat of his touches and the warmth of his grins.

Walker's declaration that I'm family.

My flip-flops pound the stairs as I wonder how this day got away from me. How I made a decision to go out for lunch in a break from the storm and ended up ... here. A situation I don't even know how to describe or, much less, what to make of it.

I just need a few minutes alone. Just a few minutes to regain control.

Let it be, I remind myself. I pop the door open and step inside. With an exhale, I swing it shut, but it just swings back with full force.

"Ah!" I startle. Only now considering someone followed me from Crave, I spin around.

Machlan stands in the halo of light from the security lamp outside. His chest rises and falls, the easygoing look in his eye from earlier gone. There's no grin, no winking, no question to explain why he's here. Nothing but a fire in his eye that reduces me to a puddle.

"I bumped Navie ..." I force a swallow. "Peck is changing. Not here," I add quickly before he takes that the wrong way. "In his truck."

He closes the door.

Taking a deep breath, I feel my chest vibrate. The clover on my necklace is cool against my skin as I blow the air from my lungs in hopes it settles me.

"You can be mad," I say, "but I legit walked out the back door and up the stairs. And be mad at me because Peck wasn't given a choice, nor should he have been saddled with watching me like a child."

"That's not what he was doing."

"Oh, it wasn't?"

Machlan walks across the room like a man on a mission. He doesn't blink, doesn't flinch, doesn't break stride until he's standing mere inches from me. "He was watching you like you're a woman who's special to someone." He takes a deep breath. "To me."

My head explodes. Every synapse misfires. Every beat of my blood echoes his words.

My plan to prove Machlan is bad news is backfiring. Like a snowball in the desert, my scheme is melting faster with each passing second.

I take a step back. He takes one toward me. I take another, but my back hits a wall. He closes the gap with no apology.

"You can't say that to me," I say.

"I can't say what?"

"That I'm special to you."

"Why not?"

"Because I don't want to hear it." My back is against the warm wood paneling, and it creaks as I lean my head on it too. I need all the support I can get as the man in front of me looks at me like I'm the crazy one. "It's unfair, Machlan."

He reaches up and drags a clump of rum-infused hair off my face and tucks it behind my ear. "You wanna know what's not fair?"

"What?"

"That I have to watch every guy in my goddamn bar look at you and not smash them in the face."

"I *am* a single woman," I say.

The vein in his temple pulses.

"Machlan, look, I—"

The words are shushed with his thumb pressing over the bud of my lips. He leans closer, the room between us barely enough for his hand. "Every time you start a conversation like that, it ends badly."

"Don't most of our conversations end up like that?" I ask from beneath the pad of his thumb.

He drops his arm but doesn't move away. It takes everything I have not to grab his waist and pull him against me, to wrap my arms around his neck and kiss him like he's everything to me.

"The last one we had didn't," he says.

Each breath I take sounds like a little gasp. Each time that happens, Machlan's eyes narrow. Every time he does that, my knees wobble a little more.

Emily's advice rolls through my brain as if she knows the position I'm in and wants to torture me. As if she's encouraging me to let things happen. To do what I want and not what I think I should.

I know what I want to happen. Right now, in this time and place,

I want to be with him. It feels entirely organic to touch him, to kiss him, to get around this stupid wall we've put between us. And as I look into his eyes, I think he feels the same way.

My stomach clenches, pulling my body tight, as I get the courage to move. My palms dampen as I reach up with one hand and touch the side of his face. There's two, maybe three, days' stubble dotting his cheeks, and the hair is rough against my palm.

Machlan doesn't move. Not a twitch. The only thing that reacts is the light in his eyes.

"I'm warning you," he says. "you keep this up, and my restraint will be gone."

"You don't have restraint anyway."

"I've managed to breathe the same air as you for two minutes now and not touch you. Trust me when I tell you it takes more restraint than I ever knew I had."

"That's too bad ..." I drop my hand and smile. "I was really hoping you'd—gah!"

My back hits the wall with a ceremonious thud. Machlan's body is pressed against mine, pinning me between him and the wall. His mouth covers mine roughly. It's not a sweet or sensual motion. It's purely primal. Animalistic. *Exactly* what I need.

He thrusts his tongue in my mouth and moans as if I'm the best thing he's tasted in his his entire life. The feeling of his voice vibrating against me with need sets me ablaze.

I dig at the button of his jeans as he brings his lips to mine again. Somehow, I get them unfastened in my haste.

His mouth is hot, his breath sweet, as he sweeps his tongue inside my mouth again. I shove his pants over his hips and grip his cock in my hand. It's thick and stretches from the tips of my fingers up the bottom of my forearm. It's heavy in my hand and the head sticky from a drip of pre-cum. Wetness coats the inside of my thighs as I hold him with both hands.

"You've done it now," he says, ending the sentence with one final kiss.

"If only you'd do it now."

He pierces me with a look that's feral. "Oh, love. I'm gonna do it."

Shorts drop. Flip-flops off. I've never undressed faster in my whole damn life. The faster I move, the harder my heart beats, and the more I want him to touch me.

He hooks an arm around my left leg, hoisting it up to his hip.

"Oh, shit," I gasp. My insides melt at the way he grips me as though I'm his, the way his fingers sear into the sensitive flesh on the insides of my thighs.

My urgency is reflected in his eyes. I drag in a jagged breath as he positions himself at my opening.

"Do I need a condom?" he asks.

"No. I have an IUD—*holy shit!*" I cry.

He fills me so quickly I'm forced into the wall. The picture of Linton from the 1800s rattles on the little nail where it's hung for decades.

My eyes roll closed as I stretch around him. His hands cup my ass, and he lifts me. My other leg curls around his hip. When I open my eyes and look into his, I think he's going to come undone.

His teeth are gritted together, a bead of sweat dotting his forehead. "Damn it," he groans, his tone full of grit and gravel.

He slips out and pushes right back inside me, hitting every nerve ending in my body from this angle. My hips push against him, craving the contact. He squeezes my behind, digging his fingers into my flesh before he strokes inside my body long and hard.

"Oh, God," I mutter. The two syllables take more than two syllables to get out as my body begins to convulse. My teeth almost chatter at the intensity of the moment.

My shoulders dig into the paneling as my lower half wraps around this delicious man. The sound of our bodies sliding against one another producing an erotic layer over the rock music from the bar below. I can't take it. I've needed this for far too long. I've needed *him* for far too long.

"Harder!" I shout, the words coming out through my clenched teeth. "Please. Harder."

"Like this?" He hammers into me with no caution or concern, no tenderness like I've experienced with him before. There's nothing personal about this—this is fucking.

"*Ahhh ...*" My voice gets louder as the beat of the song below increases and as the drum hits, so does my orgasm. "Fuck!"

As I grip his shoulders, my body explodes around him. The walls of my vagina pulse with each ripple of sensation he delivers. He brings me higher and higher until I think I'm going to rip in two.

"Machlan!" I scream.

The wall bites into my skin and my nails dig into his as he grips my hips and presses me down hard. Through the aftershocks of my own orgasm, I can feel him releasing into my body, filling me with his own pleasure.

His head falls back, a low hum emanating from his throat. Sweat trickles down the side of his face, glistening over his skin.

Panting, finding it impossible to get enough air in my lungs to steady myself, I watch him come back to Earth. His eyes are almost bloodshot. His hat gone. His shoulders red from the marks of my fingernails.

"How organic was that?" he asks.

He's trying to play it cool, referring to our earlier conversations, but something's amiss in the way he says it. It's not cocky or even neutral. It's ... careful. And that makes my stomach drop.

I shrug in an attempt to seem as nonchalant as I can. "That's one way to put it."

He sets me back on my feet. My legs shake, threatening to give out, so I lean against the wall.

"This is gonna make me an asshole," he says, "but I gotta get back down there."

He keeps his head down, his voice as gruff as I've ever heard it. He busies himself with getting put back together. It doesn't go without notice that he keeps his distance.

My nakedness suddenly feels wrong. I scoop up my clothes, avoiding eye contact. "No. No, go ahead. I get it. Completely."

His zipper breaks the silence before he rummages around, finding his hat behind the chair. "You're okay, right?"

My throat tightens. I search his face for some hint as to what he's feeling but find nothing. Just a guard in place that I've seen too many times to count.

I've never been stung in the chest by a wasp, but this is what I think that would feel like. A quick stab. A slow roll of poison. A burn you can't shake for a while.

"Of course, I'm fine," I say, plastering on a smile. "That was letting things be organic. I don't expect anything from you." *And now the natural thing is for you to leave.*

If I'm not mistaken, something washes over his eyes. It's another bee sting in the center of my chest. Lucky for me, the first one stings too bad to really feel this one.

"Just make sure you lock this," he says. He takes his hat off, watching me as he runs his hands through his hair, and then puts it back on again. Only now does he start toward the door.

And just like that, he's gone.

Chapter 22

Machlan

"I think that does it," Navie says. She zips up the money bag and tosses it on the counter. "Everything is squared away."

"You did good tonight."

"Thanks." She looks quite pleased with herself as she leans against the bar. "How good did *you* do tonight?"

That's all it takes for my mind to be pulled right back to Hadley. One stupid little sentence that might not even be about her—that probably isn't—and I'm lost to everything else.

I looked over my shoulder all night. I don't know what I wanted more—have her in walk in the bar and spar with me or walk my ass back upstairs and finish what I started. Or re-start what I finished. Either way, it ends with me getting fucked. She's probably directly above me, just feet away, yet it feels like she's on the other side of the world.

I'd ask myself what I was thinking, but I already know. I wasn't. Not with the head I should've been.

"It was that good, huh?" Navie asks.

Putting the last clean glass back on the shelf, I look at Navie through the mirror. "I have no idea what you're talking about."

"Oh, okay." She's laughing when I turn around. "Look, I know I just started here, and we're not friends or anything. And you totally don't have to tell me anything ..."

"But?"

"But I want to know." She pouts. "I see the way she looks at you like you're the best thing since yoga pants. And you look at her like you want to eat her."

I pretend to consider this. "Fair enough."

She laughs again. "See? You don't even dispute it!"

"Anybody ever tell you that you're a busybody?"

"Lots of dumb, stupid people." She raises her brows. "I saw you chase her out of here."

It's like she wants me to deny it. I can't. I don't have the fucks to give to lie.

I chased her.

By all accounts, I fucked her.

But if it was only fucking, then why do I want to run back up there?

God help me.

I rough a hand down my face. "I pay you to keep the customers' tabs, not keep tabs on me."

"Well played, boss. Well played." Pulling a gray sweatshirt over her head, she then hops on a stool and gets comfortable.

"Why are you looking at me like that?"

"Like what?" A few moments go by before she gets it. "Oh, like I'm expecting you to talk to me?"

"Yeah."

"Because I'm expecting you to talk to me."

"I'm not the talking type, Navie."

Liquor bottles are right behind me. I back up to them. A quick shot might dull some of the insanity in my brain, but it's against my own rules. I never drink at work.

A shot glass magically appears in my hand. Whiskey jumps from the shelf and splashes into it, and I down it without a second thought.

Navie watches with an unbridled curiosity. "That's probably why you aren't actively screwing Hadley. You won't talk."

"What the fuck are you talking about?"

"Explain it to me another way then," she challenges. "Or don't because communication issues seem to be your thing."

"I don't have to explain anything to you."

"And I don't really want answers unless you feel compelled to give them. In that case, I'll totally listen. But," she says, wagging a finger through the air, "I do want you to think about it."

The shot slams down my throat. It burns as it rolls, splashing into the acid already pooled in my stomach. One measly shot isn't going to do shit; I'd need the whole damn bottle to make a dent in this night.

The whiskey mutes just enough to pull my defenses down and bring her reaction front and center—the one I've fought since I walked out of there. It's a look I'll never love. It's a look that, every time I put it there, I swear I won't do it again.

This is why, at the end of the day, we will never work. I can't be trusted with making her happy. Even if I try to, *even though I want to*, I'll mess it all up.

There's a rotten feeling in my gut, a disappointment that's directed internally. It sprung as soon as I pulled my pants up. And when she didn't ask me to come back, it gnawed at me.

"Does this lull mean you're thinking?" Navie asks.

"What are you? Some kind of pseudo-therapist?" I ask as I pour another shot. "I don't want to think about anything."

"Clearly."

This shot goes down much easier.

"Keep it up and you won't be standing much longer either," she observes.

"Two shots? I'm gonna be all right."

"But are you?"

"For fuck's sake, Navie. Yes. I'm gonna be fine. I've fucked shit up a hundred times, and I've come out okay. Trust me." I reach for the whiskey again but reconsider. "Have some faith."

My reflection stares back at me in the mirror above the bottles. Stress lines form around my mouth, the vein in my temple pulsing every time my heart beats.

A part of me wants Navie to hurry the hell up and get out of here so I can find Hadley. Make sure she's okay. Apologize for being a dick. Another part of me points out that encouraging this shit with her makes me a dick, and I should really just stay away.

"Okay, want to know what I heard in all that?" Navie asks, resting her chin on her folded hands.

"No."

"Too bad. What I heard is a whole lot of fear."

My head falls back, the alcohol making it heavier than normal. It feels good to give in. To let the relief, what little of it there is, course through me.

"What are you afraid of, Machlan?"

"Being employee-less when I fire you," I say, still facing the ceiling. "It's gonna suck ass, but it'll be better than dealing with this."

She sighs with all the drama of a soap opera. "Okay. I'm gonna just talk frank."

I lift my head. "You mean you weren't?"

"Ha." She drops her hands. "Look, you're a nice guy and good looking, but don't let that go to your head. You have a helluva business here. Everyone, and I mean everyone, loves you. You have a super-hot cousin who you could totally hook me up with as a signing bonus type of thing." She grins, waggling her eyebrows. "And you also have a girl who's so in love with you it makes me in love with your love."

I scoff, turning away.

Hadley can't love me. She might think she does, but she can't. How could someone like her love someone like me, a shitshow of a guy? A guy who knocked her up when I couldn't take care of her. A man who could never offer her the things in life that she needs.

What she wants out of life isn't a mystery. I've known that since I met her: she wants the life she never had. A husband who comes home after a nine-to-five. Kids she can dote on. A stable, predictable life she can relax in for the first time ever.

I own a bar. I know what the inside of a jail cell looks like. I'm never going to be the guy the Chamber of Commerce adores or be the responsible one in any lineup you can put together.

I've ruined her life once. I'll do it again. I have no faith in me.

"Have you talked to her about your feelings?" Navie presses.

"For the love of God." I slam the shot glass down, but it's accompanied with a chuckle. "I don't have feelings. Okay? Let's get that straight."

"Oh, so you're a liar too. Good to know."

I want to be pissed she's calling me out. It's way out of line and probably setting a bad precedent. But I hired her because she has that indistinguishable charm that makes people want to talk to her—me included. Even if I don't actually want to talk.

"Will you stop it?"

"No," she says as though she's insulted. "I won't stop it."

I slide my hands down my face again.

"Fine, fine." Navie slides off the stool. "I'll forget about it."

"Thanks."

"I'll forget all about how she watched you mix drinks and how you went straight for the table when you saw her sitting with those hotties in the dress shirts."

My hands fall to my sides, but my fists clench. A surge of jealousy strikes again even though I now know Camilla's brothers weren't here for Hadley.

But I'm the one who left her upstairs.

Guilt slips in place, shoving the jealousy out of the way. The whiskey sloshes. My brain tortures me with screenshots of Hadley's face when I told her I had to leave. I hear the sound of her voice, pretending to be strong, telling me she doesn't expect anything from me.

But she should.

I want her to. When she does, I feel like I'm ten-fucking-feet tall even if her expectations are impossible.

Damn it.

I drag the keys out of my pocket. "You ready to go?"

"Yup."

We head toward the door. Navie takes her time, fishing her keys out of her purse. I try to walk faster in hopes it speeds her up, but it doesn't.

"You have big plans for the rest of the night?" she asks.

"It's two in the morning. I'm pretty sure tonight is over."

"True enough."

We step into the darkness and find the air a good ten degrees cooler than it was earlier in the day. Navie shivers in her sweatshirt as I lock the door. Once it's secure, I walk her to the little blue car next to the train tracks.

As soon as I can see the back door, my attention is there. The light is off. Hadley's car is parked by the dumpster. Everything looks normal, only I know it's not.

She's up there. And I'm not.

Climbing in the driver's side, Navie starts the engine and flips on the heater. "Hadley's in the apartment, huh?"

"Yeah."

"You should check on her," she says softly. "I get it—the stuff between you two isn't easy. But it never is."

Still looking at the apartment, I sigh. "I think it's a little harder for us than most."

"Then you should work extra hard to make it a thing."

"Huh?" I ask, turning around.

"If it's that hard and you're still in it, then it might be worth the extra fight." She closes the door but rolls down the window. The fog on the windshield clears slowly, the sound of the air blowing on it comforting. "If a guy ever looks at me the way you do her, I hope someone is smart enough to tell him to find me."

This I can work with.

Gripping the door frame, I choose my words carefully. "But what if he was a clusterfuck of a guy? Wouldn't he be better off staying the hell away from you?"

"No." Her laugh is simple, as if this should be obvious. "I'm a giant clusterfuck myself. Sure, it looks like I have it all together, right? I mean, I'm working two jobs. I'm well-adjusted, have great parents, and take my birth control regularly. I don't smoke, have perfectly straight teeth, and I can balance a spoon on my nose."

"What?"

"*Anyway*," she says, "the point is those are my statistics. The 'good column', if you will. People don't see my 'bad column' as easy, but we all have one."

"I'm still stuck on the spoon thing."

She looks at the ceiling and sighs. "Look, Machlan, Hadley is a smart girl. She really likes you. And I don't know what happened between you when you—wait, yes I do." She shakes her head. "You have a stain on your shirt that I've seen before after a quickie ..."

I look down at the tail of my black T-shirt as Navie makes a face. Sure enough, she's right.

"I don't think anyone else noticed. I just notice things. *Anyway*, after *that*," she says, pointing at my shirt, "she's probably lying up there right now wondering what's up. Like, did you just one-and-done her? Are you going to call? Do you care? What did that mean?"

What did *that mean?*

My throat squeezes, and I fight the urge to look at the apartment again. Every cell in my body draws backward to Hadley, and I grip the doorframe harder so I don't turn around and run to her like a pussy.

My fingertips strum the roof of the car. "I should stay away. Let her think."

"Yeah, if you wanna be a dick."

"Navie ..."

"Sorry. The truth hurts." She shrugs. "If you wanna tell yourself you're letting her think, fine by me. It doesn't affect me. But if you *do* give a shit about her, and I know you do, then do the right thing, Machlan. Treat her with the same decency you treat everyone else."

The whiskey must wear off because my entire body cools. I shiver as a rash of goose bumps break out across my skin.

"Now, I gotta go," she says. "I'm tired and emotionally spent from this love affair you have going on. Plus, I have to rationalize Peck's love of Molly before I can go to sleep, and I'm not sure how long that's going to take."

"None of us have figured that out, so good luck."

"He's so cute. And she's so ... mean," she groans. Shoving the car in gear, she waves. "Have a good night, Mach."

"You too."

She drives off, her taillights disappearing around the corner before I even pivot. When I do, I almost wish I hadn't.

A light is on in the apartment. It's faint, barely visible, and looks to come from the back of the room. My feet start walking that way before my head even tells them to.

At least I don't run like a pussy.

———

Hadley

Knock, knock.

I sit straight up in bed with my eyes glued to the door. The clock shows it's possible—it could be Machlan. I stifle a nervous chuckle because if it's not, it's probably a serial killer, and I'm dead, and I don't even care.

My back aches from the springs of the mattress. If I could've forced myself up more than once to pee since Machlan left, it probably would've helped. But I couldn't.

I shouldn't be surprised by any of this, and I'm not, really. Rationalizing it took some time, but in the end, this one is on me. I knew what I was getting in to. I pushed. I accepted his pushbacks, and I don't regret it. I only need to temper any expectations that this will go anywhere. It won't.

The knock raps again, a little louder this time. The covers are tossed to the side. Grabbing my phone in case it's not Machlan and I need to call 911, I shove it in the pocket of my shorts like a girl who doesn't care about her life.

"Who is it?" I ask, hand already on the knob. A bubble of excitement is on the verge of bursting as I wait for a response.

"Who else are you expecting at two thirty in the fucking morning?"

He came back.

Running a hand over my still-damp hair from the sponge bath I gave myself in the kitchen sink, I say a prayer and swing the door open.

"Never know," I say, trying not to show how happy his arrival makes me. "Could've been the guy from the other day."

"That would be your best bet. Pretty sure you could take him."

He's standing, both hands shoved in his pockets, the start of a grin on his face. The wear of the night shows in the puffiness of his eyes.

Despite the late hour and the trickiness of how we ended things earlier, he came back. I don't know what that means, but it's a good sign. I think.

I turn away to get myself together. The door shuts softly. I turn back around to see him standing in the middle of the room. He doesn't touch anything. He doesn't look anywhere but at me.

This is a look I can't decipher. He doesn't look angry or apathetic, just like a guy in the middle of a room.

"How was your night?" I ask to break the silence.

"It was good. I kept having to refigure tabs, and Navie had to balance the drawer at the end of the night, but it was a clean, bullshit-free night for the most part."

"For the most part?"

"Yeah." He rocks back on his heels. "I had a girl run me up a little. She had a mishap in the bar. Went to check on her and she ended up sticking her tongue down my throat." He can't contain his grin.

I can't contain mine as I buckle with relief. "Not exactly how I heard it went down, but whatever works for you."

"Oh, it definitely worked for me."

Staring at the wall above the bed, pointedly not looking at Machlan, I will my face to return to its normal shade of peach. I tell myself to stay calm and not put too much hope into this. He's walked away enough times after giving me something to hold on to.

"About earlier ..." Machlan says. His voice resonates deep in my core. I'm drawn to the timbre of his voice, to the way it wraps around me in the gentlest of ways.

"I've overanalyzed it enough for both of us."

"I don't want it to be that way, Had." He sighs.

"I don't either. And I'm trying really hard to go with the flow but ..." I look at him over my shoulder as my voice falls away.

"But it's me and you, huh?"

"Yeah. It's me and you."

He reaches for me. I hold my breath until the tip of his finger touches the bottom of my chin. He lifts it so I'm looking at him.

Each breath I take is much louder than it should be. My blood runs hot while my body shivers at the tiny bit of contact; the contrast enough to make it feel like I'm losing my mind. I close my eyes to regain my composure, but he nudges my chin again, and I open them.

"I thought you'd come down tonight," he says, peering at me. "Why didn't you?"

My insides trip over themselves as I scurry to make sense of the mayhem I've been dealing with all night. It's hard to pinpoint why I stayed up here and didn't go to Crave. I wanted to. I wanted to so badly. But something changed when he walked out.

As I laid in bed and looked at it from every angle, the only difference in this time and most is that I had some control. I chose to spend time with him, knowing damn good and well it wasn't going to end with some fantastical proposal. I came to town and went straight to the bar. I got in his truck. I let him hold me on Bluebird, and I sat down there tonight and received his advances while giving some of my own.

I'm never surprised when he walks away. I always just go into it hoping he doesn't push me away. Even though it stung tonight, I had the Band-Aid ready.

"You left," I say. "I figured you knew where I was if you wanted to see me."

His eyes burn hot as he continues to cup my face. He peers so deeply, I swear he's searching my soul. I have nothing to hide. He won't find anything buried in there he doesn't already know if he's honest with himself.

"I want you to promise me something," he says, a grit to his tone that makes me shiver.

"What?"

"Don't ever change who you are for anyone. Not for me. Not for some dickhead auditor. Not for *anyone*." His hand falls away from my face.

"What's that supposed to mean?" I gulp.

"It means ..." He twists his hat around. "You've always done exactly what you wanted. You have an uncanny ability to follow your gut, you know?"

I don't answer. My stomach churns, unsure where this is going. Unsure I even want to know.

He fiddles with his hat. "Whether anyone likes it or not, me particularly, you do what you want. And that's something I've always admired about you," he says, talking in a rush. "When you've had enough, you leave. When you want more, you come back. And I just hope that's something you never lose, you know?"

"Where is all this coming from?"

He licks his bottom lip. "The truth?"

"I don't know. Would I rather you lie to me?"

He holds my gaze until we both laugh softly. He shakes his head as my stomach settles.

"I went back to the bar," he says, "and was fairly sure you'd reappear. And then you didn't—which is fine. But as the night wore on and the place emptied out and you didn't show up, I hoped you stayed away because you were stubborn ... and not because you were scared."

My throat tightens as he looks at me with an uncertain glimmer in his eye. "It was probably a little of both."

His face falls.

"The weird thing," I say carefully, "is I'm never scared of the big things. Like when I told you I was pregnant." Tears dot my eyes. "That's huge, and I wasn't scared to tell you that. It was the biggest thing I think I could ever say, and I knew you'd be there. I wasn't scared to tell you I love you. I wasn't even that scared to ask you to marry me." I blink back the tears. "But to tell you I wanted you not to leave tonight? Terrified. Because that's something you can brush off, and those are the things that really hurt at the end of the day."

"Had ..."

"No," I say, looking up again. "I knew you had to go. But I won't say I wondered if you would've left had the bar not been open."

He slips his can of chew out of his pocket. He doesn't open it. Doesn't flip it between his fingers. Just slides it around his palm while he watches me.

I try to look away but feel him pulling my eyes back to his. "It occurred to me while I laid here and listened to the music blaring under me that we've always kind of pussyfooted around each other. We've never had a real adult relationship."

His grin turns mischievous. "Oh, I think we adult amazingly well together."

"Not that." I swipe his shoulder as I walk by, needing the space. "What I mean is, we've always interacted with all this baggage."

He glances at the messy bed and at my bag on the couch. "You ever wonder what would happen if we met each other now? Like you moved to town or came in Crave and we met for the first time?"

"All the time."

"What do you think would happen?"

"Probably what happened up here a few hours ago," I say.

The chew can slips back in his pocket. "I don't think so."

"You don't?"

He laughs to himself. "I'd want to. But I think I'd be a little intimidated by you."

"Ha. I knew it." I laugh. "I scare you, don't I?"

The levity in his features melts away. Before I know it, the playfulness is gone.

I try to figure out how to rewind the last few seconds and bring back what we had before. It's nearly a panic inside, a 'no, no, no' chant in my head not to let him start backpedaling. Bracing myself for the inevitable, for Machlan to leave, I take a deep breath.

"It's been a long night," he says. "I need to get home."

"Okay."

"Why don't you come with me?"

I grab the back of a chair as naturally as I can. There isn't a breath deep enough to steady myself from that.

There's no response from me. I wait for him to rethink his offer, for him to walk to the door on a phone call and leave me standing. But the longer I wait, the more certain he seems.

It's a tedious ledge, and I feel myself falling over the side. This is what I want. But if I reach out and take it, attempt to walk the ledge that's so slippery it shines, I'm risking everything. What if I can't recoup? What if I'm not the adult I think I am? What if sleeping with Machlan and having a fun few days isn't something from which I can recover?

When I fail to respond, he moseys toward the couch and lifts a shirt off the floor. "You have a lot of laundry here. And—"

"You know, this probably isn't a good idea." My eyes squeeze shut. "I'm good here."

"I know you are. But ... I'd like you to come home with me."

My eyes open. He's watching me with a wariness I know intimately. He wants this now. But what happens tomorrow? Letting it be was easier when it didn't involve sleepovers. I'm already in deeper than I can afford to be.

"This can just be sex," I say.

He tosses my shirt on my bag and walks toward me. "You and I both know it's never just sex between us."

"But it can be," I offer, my hand trembling at my side.

He stops a couple of inches in front of me. I can feel his breath on my face, smell the hints of mint from the tobacco he must've chewed tonight.

The room is perfectly still. There's not a sound to be heard. The only break in the silence is my ragged breaths and the energy pulsing off Machlan, something I'm sure I hear.

"I'm a little fucked up about this," he says. "I don't know the right answer."

I lean away as he tries to touch me. "I don't know the right answer either, but I do know I have to be careful with you."

"Didn't you come here to figure things out?" He drops his hand. "Because I feel like we're doing that somehow."

"Yeah, that's why I came here. But honestly, I thought it was going to go a different way."

"You wanted me to be a dick so you could feel good about leaving?"

"I didn't want that," I say, "but I expected to be able to justify moving on when I left. You're making that super hard right now."

He moves too quickly to stop him from touching my arm. Like a jolt of electricity, my body sings at the contact.

"I don't want to make your life hard," he says, his fingertips pressing into my arm. "But I don't want you leaving and not wanting to talk to me again either."

I focus on the softness of his words and not the way I begin to sway. "Mach ..."

"Look, it's late. You're up. I'm up. Just come home with me."

I want to. I might never have wanted something so bad in my entire life. And *he's asking*—not assuming or manipulating and I'm not winding up there by chance.

"Machlan, I—"

He touches his finger to my lips. "Before you say no, hear me out." He waits for me to nod before dropping his hand. "I don't know what in the hell I'm doing, okay? I'm walking this line of trying to leave you alone so you can go on about your life, but it's so fucking hard when all I want to do is be around you."

I force a swallow, tears flirting with the corners of my eyes.

Seeing this side of him isn't something I've seen before many times. I can count them on one hand. I know how hard it is for him to let himself be vulnerable, to put himself out there like this, and all I want to do is hug him.

This is the man I fell in love with. Not the guy I slept with first or the one who saved the day when I drank too much. This is the guy who clasped a necklace around my neck after a night at the Water Festival and told me I was the prettiest girl he'd ever seen.

To think this man, the one who can be so considerate sometimes, can think he should let me go on about my life is ridiculous. But I don't have the energy to point that out.

"It's not as if you have anything else to do," he points out. A hint of a grin is back.

"Are you sure?"

"You're the one who said we need to just see where things settle between us. I'm just trying to do what you asked, and right now, this feels like where it should settle."

He doesn't blink. Doesn't flinch. Just stands in front of me waiting on me to break. And even though it might not be the best answer if I think it out completely, I don't. I give in.

"But you're sure?" I ask with a grin of my own.

He laughs, grabbing my bag. "No, I've stood here for the past ten minutes not sure. Yes, Hadley, *I'm sure.*"

"Fine." I suck my cheeks in to keep them from breaking in half and head to the door. "If you're sure."

He swats my ass, making me yelp. "Keep it up."

"That's what she said."

I don't look back as he starts laughing. I make my way toward his truck with the lightest steps I've ever taken and the best music in my ears.

Chapter 23

Hadley

The hardwoods creak as I make my way down the hall. The house is dark, pitch black in most areas. A night light glows from the living room, and I know without looking that it's a little plug-in shaped like a tea rose. It's been there since the first time I came to this house. It belonged to his mother.

I venture through the house in a pair of shorts and an oversized T-shirt with a slogan from an athletics company on the front. My hair is wet from the quick shower I took while Machlan took a call from Walker.

The air is crisp as I mosey around, like a window is open somewhere. Scents of pine from the trees surrounding the house and a hint of cleaning product and tobacco flood my senses. It's a weird combination, but one that's definitely Machlan.

I've walked this hallway a hundred times before. I know each plank that will give a little when I step on it, and that the section by the front door will echo a little louder than the part in the back. The closet to my left is filled with coats and shoes, and the door to my right used to be Machlan's dad's home office.

Out of all the houses I've ever stayed in, this one feels the most like home. My mother and I had to move too often to afford rent in California. Living with Dad and Cross, and then just Cross when Dad took off for Reno and never came back, wasn't very heartwarming. This place, though, always felt cozy and smelled vaguely of fresh flowers and home cooked food. It still does.

My movements slow as I near the kitchen. The light is bright ahead of me. Soft rustlings and the snap of a refrigerator door roll from the room. The soft material of the burgundy rug lining the last few feet to the kitchen caress the soles of my feet.

Hand over my mouth, I stifle a yawn as I reach the threshold.

Then I stop in my tracks.

Machlan is doing something at the counter with his back—his bare back—to me. He's naked except for a pair of gray sweatpants hanging from his narrow hips. Each movement causes the muscles in his back to ripple. The pushing and pulling of his perfectly sized muscles make me gulp.

Knowing he was in the shower earlier and not peeking was super hard. The door was cracked, so it wouldn't have been hard. But going in there and not making things even more complicated would've been impossible, so I didn't. I busied myself by texting Emily instead.

"You gonna stare all night or what?" he asks.

"Maybe I'm not here."

His body vibrates with a chuckle. "I see you in the window, genius."

"Oh." I yawn again, forcing it a little this time, as if to say I'm tired and not completely turned on. He grins smugly, seeing through it, but I ignore his delicious smirk. "It's after three."

"Nice you can tell time." He turns and hands me a plate. There's a perfectly browned grilled cheese sandwich cut into four little squares. "Thought you might be hungry."

"You come home from work and make grilled cheese sandwiches?" I ask, taking the plate.

He takes a square off my plate and pops the whole thing in his mouth. "Fuck, that's hot!" His mouth pops open, and he waves his hand in front of it. A dollop of cheese is stuck to his bottom lip, and I want to wipe it off, but I don't. If I touch him with his six-pack abs looking all glorious, it would be the end of me. I'd have an orgasm holding a grilled cheese.

"That's why you shouldn't steal." I sit at the table and pick up a piece. I hold the sandwich so it looks like I'm giving it serious attention when, in reality, I can see across the golden crust and watch Machlan pour two glasses of water. "When did you learn how to cook?"

He pads across the floor and hands me a glass. Our fingers touch as I take it. I pretend not to notice.

"I hardly think grilled cheese is considered cooking." He grabs another plate off the counter and then sits across from me. "But I can reheat food like it's nobody's business."

I take a bite. The cheese oozes out the sides and melts in my mouth. It's buttery and gooey, and the crunch on the outside is so satisfying. He grins as he takes a careful bite of his.

"This is good," I say, licking my lips.

"You should see what I can do with Nana's fried chicken."

"Oh, really?" I eat another piece in two bites. "What do you do with that?"

"You take the chicken and put it in a brown paper bag. Turn on the oven and put the chicken in there. Grab a shower and when you're out, the chicken is warm and crispy."

"I don't think you're supposed to put a paper bag in the oven, Mach."

"I've done it a hundred times, and nothing bad has happened yet."

I laugh. "I think that's just part of your charm."

He shoves another section in his mouth. "What's that mean?"

"You do a lot of things a hundred times and nothing bad happens. You better hope it doesn't start catching up with you."

His eyes go wide before he grabs a napkin and cleans his hands. "You gonna eat that last piece?"

"No. I hate eating this late. I'll wake up with an upset stomach."

"Then why did you eat any of it?" he asks, sliding my plate in front of him.

"I can say no to a lot of things but not grilled cheese. Even I have limits."

"Good to know." He slides the last bit into his mouth and washes it down with a long drink of water. "You ready for bed?"

A bit of panic creeps through my body. Raising my glass, I take a drink. A long one. One that nearly drains the entire glass into my stomach. Getting waterlogged is a better alternative than answering that question the wrong way.

I have no idea how this is going to work. Every time I've been here before, I've slept with him. Every time I've been here before, I've left without him. This is no different, and I know it. Not even if he's being nice or thoughtful or considerate—it changes nothing in the long game.

Machlan watches me. The longer it takes, the wider his grin gets. Only when it's stretched ear-to-ear does he cross his arms over his toned chest and laugh. "I didn't realize you were so dehydrated."

"Yeah," I say, setting the glass down. Sucking in oxygen in a wild gasp, I shrug. "Really thirsty."

"Or really avoiding my question."

"No, no, no." I get up and gather our glasses and put them in the dishwasher. There's a dishrag in the sink. I use it to wipe a few crumbs off the counter but stop when Machlan's hand rests on my shoulder.

"I didn't bring you here to clean up after me."

The rag goes into the sink with a plop. I look at him in the reflection in the window.

"You clean when you're nervous," he says, holding my gaze. "Why?"

"I feel like maybe I should go back to the apartment."

His abs ripple as he chuckles. I try to ignore them and the way my stomach clenches.

"You want to go back now?" he asks. "Why?"

I spin around, letting the panic hit. "I've talked a good game. Better than I thought I could, really. But I don't know if I can do this," I jabber. "Coming home with you doesn't feel like just sex, which we've talked about, and now that I'm here, I think it's a terrible idea. I think I'm gonna wake up in the morning and—"

"Breathe," he says. He takes in a lungful of air and blows it out, encouraging me to do the same. "See that? That's how you don't sound like a lunatic. You breathe between words. Try it."

I make a face. "I don't sound that crazy, do I?"

"Yes." He bends forward until he's inches from my face. "You do."

He steps back and really takes me in. When he usually does this, it feels like he sees all the way through me. Right now, though, it feels like he's wrapping me in a warm blanket.

Under the haze of the yellow-hued light bulb in the kitchen, I relax. And as I do that, I realize how easy it would be to *totally* relax, to fall into his bed or into some fantasy like I usually do.

No matter how good this feels, how right, it's still me and Machlan. Nothing has changed there. I have to remember that.

"I'll sleep on the couch," I say.

"You will not." He turns toward the hallway.

"I'm not sleeping with you." I follow him out of the kitchen, flipping the light off as I go. The hallway is dark, and I can only make out his silhouette as I go. He takes a left, and the light comes on in his bedroom.

It's decorated as I remember. A slate gray bedspread stretches over his king-size mattress. Four pillows lay at the top with black and white pillowcases. There's a television facing the bed and a dresser beneath it. A chair sits in the corner with a pair of jeans thrown over the back.

He disappears into his closet and comes back out with a hand-made quilt. "I'll sleep on the couch." His irritation is palpable.

"What do you want?"

"I'm just taking your cues."

"That's not what I asked."

"Yeah, well, that question sounds a whole lot bigger than where I want to sleep." He looks at me before shaking his head and disappearing back in the closet.

A yawn comes out of nowhere. I stretch overhead, too tired to spar with him anymore. My bottom sinks into the soft mattress. Blinking back the tears that spring with another good, deep yawn, I lie back on the soft blankets.

Everything smells like him. It's like being in a cloud of Machlan, and it's the most comfortable I've been in forever.

Rolling on my side, my knees to my chest, I let my eyes fall closed.

The sound of a blanket being dropped whispers through the room. My head is so tired, so calm, I can't open my eyes to see what Machlan's doing.

Every second that goes by, the farther I fall into the abyss.

The bed dips. I feel a warmth settle over me like a blanket is tugged over my body.

I barely hear it when Machlan's voice whispers, "You look really pretty tonight."

"You make really good grilled cheese ..."

I wonder if I'm dreaming, or if he's really there.

If it's a dream, maybe I won't wake up.

Chapter 24

Machlan

Bacon.

My eyes open one at a time.

The house smells like bacon and eggs.

The light is too bright for eleven on a Sunday morning.

I'm on the wrong side of the bed.

My head twists on the pillow I only use when I pull it against me in the middle of the night, and I remember why—Hadley.

Glancing at the clock, I realize I've missed church. I only fell asleep a couple of hours before services would've started. After picking Hadley up and laying her under the covers, I stretched out and watched her sleep because I sure couldn't.

This is a blessing and a curse. It's like the time Blaire sent me a bottle of a particular Kentucky bourbon you can't ever find. It's top-shelf stuff that masks the alcohol content with big splashes of vanilla and caramel. Drinking it is like a gift, but the hangover the next day is akin to hell.

Sleeping in the same bed as Hadley is a present. Having her leave today will feel like I've been robbed of everything I actually give a damn about. Because fuck if I don't.

It's really, really hard to keep my distance. It's so easy with her. She knows everything about me, knows how to talk to me and when to joke around and when to let it be. If God asked me to design a woman for myself, I'd just point at Hadley and say, "Yeah, you already did."

It never gets easier to realize you can't take care of someone like they need. That you'll inevitably embarrass them or fail them in ways you haven't imagined yet. That fear sits in my core, positioned in a place it gets rubbed every time I start to get comfortable with Had. It reminds me how sick it feels to look in her eyes and see disappointment.

My phone rings, and I have to dig under my pillow to find it. When I see who it is, I hit the green button and say a quick prayer for help.

"Hello?" I ask.

"I'll have you know, young man, that you were the only grandchild of mine with your behind not in a pew this morning," Nana says.

"I'll have you know, young lady, that I'm not sorry."

"Machlan Daniel—"

"Nana. I'm kidding," I say, smoothing my hair back off my face. "I have a good reason."

"There are very few reasons good enough to miss Jesus."

A long bang comes from the kitchen. Hadley issues an expletive loud enough for me to hear.

Throwing the blankets back, I sit up on the edge of the bed. The floor is cool under my feet, the air chilly on my naked torso.

"I had company last night," I tell my grandmother.

"Company, huh?" She pauses. "Is that company fit enough to come to my house for dinner?"

The feel of Hadley's thighs in my hands last night and her arms wrapped around my neck has me getting hard. "Oh, she's fit all right."

Nana scoffs. "That's not what I mean, sir."

"Are you implying my house guest might be a one-night stand?" I gasp. "I'm insulted."

"Now, that's a lie if I've ever heard one."

"What's that supposed to mean?"

"You're Lance's brother. The concept of a one-night stand is not new or insulting."

I chuckle. "When did you get so savage?"

"I don't know what that means, but I want you over for dinner."

Reaching my free hand over my head, I feel my muscles stretch. A rumble flows from my stomach as I move, and the scent of bacon gets stronger. It rumbles harder when I think about taking Hadley with me to Nana's.

I'm not sure I could handle it.

My brothers take their girlfriends to dinner every week while Peck and I sit together like two losers with no dates. It used to not bother me—Hell, it felt easier being alone. But lately, it feels like something is missing, and no matter who I think about inviting over just to fill a spot, it doesn't feel right.

It does today. It feels perfect.

"What are you fixing?" I ask.

"I'm frying chicken just for you because you guilted me for having Lance over the other night. And I'm making a cheeseball, and I'd hate for Peck to have all of it."

"Are you bribing me with food?"

"Of course. I'm a grandmother. It's what we do."

"You do it well."

I know she's smiling on the other end. I can hear it in the way she smacks her lips together in satisfaction. "We'll eat around three o'clock. If I know you're coming, I'll make you a butterscotch pie."

"I'll be there if I can bring home leftovers," I tease.

"You'll have to fight Walker for the chicken."

"That I look forward to," I say, getting to my feet. "I always love a Nana-approved duel with Walker."

"I meant that figuratively. Don't go getting him in one of those head-lock things in my dining room, or I'll kick your behind."

My phone buzzes, indicating the battery is dying. I pull it away from my face to see I have less than ten percent left. "I gotta go because my phone is dying, and you know, I need to entertain my company."

"Oh, dear. Goodbye."

Laughing, I head to the other side of the bed. "Bye, Nana."

I fish my charger out from behind the bedside table and plug it in. Setting it beside the lamp, I spin around but stop when I see Hadley's bag on the chair in the corner.

Her shorts are sitting on top of the closed bag as though she tossed them there as a side note. If someone walked into this room right now, they'd think that gym bag was supposed to be there. I kind of feel that way too.

Scratching my head, I walk into the hallway and hear music playing softly. Sunshine pours in from the windows.

Walking as lightly as I can, I pause in the doorway. She's buttering toast over the sink. Crumbs falls into the basin as she rakes the knife along the bread. The movement slow as she looks through the window with a thoughtful gaze.

Her hair is a wild mess piled on top of her head, and she's changed into a pair of my sweatpants. They're two sizes two big and nearly fall off her waist, but I've never seen a more beautiful sight in my life.

Hadley in my clothes in my kitchen. Happy.

"Hey," I say before I can get in my head too deep. I ignore the way my chest feels like it's going to burst and open the refrigerator. I don't need anything, but maybe it'll cool me down.

The corners of her lips turn up before she looks over her shoulder. There's a hint of trepidation there. "I made breakfast."

Overriding my natural reaction to walk across the room and plant a kiss on her lips, I shut the refrigerator door. "What can I do to help?"

"Don't die when you eat the bacon." She makes a face. "The expiration date was last week, but it smelled fine."

"Shit. I don't even know when I bought that."

"Or half the things in the refrigerator," she mumbles. "Seriously. I threw away a bunch of crap this morning."

"What did you throw away?" I say, letting my jaw fall open just to rile her up.

"Nothing you'll ever need or it wouldn't have been expired."

"You don't know what I need."

She walks toward me, an arch to her lips. She reaches right in front of me, almost brushing against me but not quite, and pulls out two plates. "Oh, I think I do know what you need."

My breathing stops as I adjust to her proximity. I'm suddenly very, *very* awake.

The sweetness of her skin drifts around me, luring me to touch her. The pout of her lips begs for a kiss, the sliver of skin between the hem of her shirt and the top of my sweatpants taunting to be gripped.

My eyes narrow as I squelch the reaction I want to make. "Humor me. What do you think I need?"

She falls back on her feet slowly. It's clear she didn't anticipate this question and is unprepared to give me an answer. I'm not sure what kind of an answer to expect, either, and I'm not sure why in the hell I asked that this early.

Turning away, she begins to fill one of the plates. "This morning, you need four strips of bacon, two eggs over medium, and two slices of toast."

"Over medium, huh?"

"I know you like over easy, but I overcooked them because I dropped a jar of mayonnaise that expired last year." She shoots me a look. "Last. Year."

"Good thing I like them over medium these days, huh?"

She nods. "Good thing."

"I also like coffee," I say, walking away before I get too comfortable watching her move around my kitchen. "You want some?"

"Yes, please."

We work silently, me making coffee and her getting the food to the table. Every now and then, we catch each other's eye and smile or sort of softly laugh at nothing in particular. It's weird sharing the space with her but so damn amazing at the same time. It has all the hallmarks I love about Nana's Sunday dinners but at home. With Hadley.

This could get me in trouble, yet I have no intention of ending it. Not right now. This may never happen again, and I want to suck it up for all it's worth while I can get it. It gives me a quietness that comes from the inside that I haven't felt since we lived together.

When she stayed with me before she got pregnant, and then when we lived together while in Ohio, my favorite part of the day was waking up next to her. The morning routine of getting ready—preparing for the day, having her there and knowing she'd be there when I came home—was the best part of my life so far.

We sit down. She curls one leg under her.

"Did you sleep okay?" she asks.

"Yeah."

"I think I kind of passed out. I remember sitting on the edge of your bed and hearing you talk and then nothing until I woke up this morning." She reaches for a piece of toast. "Which brings me to this question. How did I get in your bed?"

She lifts a brow as she takes a bite of toast.

"You seemed to enjoy my mattress, so I tucked you in."

Her lips part, the furrow in her brow warning me she's about to argue. Then strangely, the wrinkles vanish. "Thank you."

"Wow." I laugh, slicing into my eggs. "That was unexpected."

"What? I'm being polite."

"I know. Unexpected." She taps my leg with her foot under the table. "I'm not sure if I should thank you for holding me so tight I couldn't move this morning."

My fork almost drops out of my hand. The tines clink against the china before I regain control. "I did?"

"You did. And it was kind of nice." Her shoulder comes to her chin in the sweetest gesture. Batting her eyelashes, she grins. "Now, enough of this being nice stuff. What can we fight about?"

I pick up my coffee cup and sit back in my chair. She rattles on about a story Kallie told her about Cross, and I tune out. Watching her talk—her hands flying through the air, her eyes bright and happy as she jabbers away—is enough.

Sipping the caffeine instead of guzzling it like I usually do, I enjoy the peace of a Sunday morning instead of avoiding it, which is a new thing. A thing I could get used to. A thing I'd love to replicate with her.

But as I begin to process that idea, her words from last night come back to mind. *"You do a lot of things a hundred times and nothing bad happens. You better hope it doesn't start catching up with you."*

It will catch up with me. It always does.

"Are you listening to me?" she asks.

"Yeah." I sit my cup down and grab a piece of bacon. "Nana called and ripped my ass about church."

She snorts. "I'm not sure you should say ripped my ass and church in the same sentence. While not quite sacrilegious, it doesn't feel right."

"Okay. She busted my balls. Better?"

"I'm with Nana. You needed Jesus today."

"I'll pray extra hard at bedtime to make up for it," I say, crunching down on the meat. "Anyway, she's making dinner and demanded I come."

Hadley's fork rests on her plate. The light in her eyes dims as she reaches for a napkin. "You should." She swallows hard. "I need to see Emily today, so I can have her pick me up here, or you can run me by on the way."

That's the best solution. The easiest. The safest. And it absolutely won't work.

"Nah, see, neither of those will work," I say with a casual shrug.

"Cross can come and get me."

I watch her until she lifts her eyes to mine. She's adorable when she's unsure, when she lets her guard down long enough to let me see it. I should be as unsure as fuck about this, but I'm not. I've not been so certain about anything in a long time.

"Nana said you have to come," I say. Even though that's not totally the truth.

"Oh, I don't know ..."

"Tell it to Nana. I'm not." I take my cup back to the Keurig. As I pop in another pod, I look at her out of the corner of my eye. She's grinning with her hands folded together in front of her face. "She said we're eating at three, which means we have to be there *by two*. She gets really pissed if you show up when it's time to eat."

"I can understand that."

The coffee stops. I take my mug and walk back to the table. Instead of sitting, I lean against the chair. She looks up at me with big, wide honey-colored eyes.

Sunday dinner has never looked so appetizing.

"It's eleven," I say. "That gives us a few hours."

She gulps. "To do what?"

I take a long, intentional drink and watch her squirm. Once she's sufficiently worked up, I swallow. "Do you know how to prune rose bushes?"

She punches me in the stomach and laughs, getting to her feet. "I hate you." She laughs in what I think is relief. "I hate you so much."

"Is that a yes?"

"Yes. You know I know how to prune rose bushes." Her hair wobbles as she reaches for her plate.

I don't know what it is about this moment that does it, but I can't help myself. I wrap an arm around her waist and pull her into my chest. She gasps but doesn't fight it. Every place her body touches mine lights up. Her eyes do the same as they meet mine with a hopeful anticipation.

I could say something funny here and let her go, and nothing would be worse for wear. But we're going for what feels right, and nothing feels more right than her in my arms.

If it bites me in the ass later, then it does.

I touch my lips to hers. We melt together in perfect sync, retracing the steps of a dance we perfected years ago. Her lips are soft, her breath sweet, and her hands perfect as they rest on my chest.

I break it way before I want to. The smacking sound sings through the room just like in the movies. She watches me back away, the smile on her face matching mine.

"I'm gonna get a shower," I say, adjusting my cock as discreetly as I can. "I'll clean this up if you leave it."

She doesn't stop grinning. "I'll get it. I need to call Emily and cancel our plans for today, so I'll do it while I talk to her."

"Fine," I say.

"Fine," she says.

As I walk by her, we both laugh.

Chapter 25

Machlan

"There you are. It's about time you showed up." Nana waves a spoon in my direction. "I was just saying if you didn't get here in a few minutes, I was sending Lance after you."

"Lance? Come on, Nana. At least send Walker. Make it worth my while."

"Hey, fuc—dge you," Lance says as he scoops up part of my favorite cheeseball on a cracker. "I caught myself, Nana. I don't want to hear it."

"You boys." Turning to me again, she starts to speak but stops when she sees Hadley beside me. She looks at Hadley, then at me, before stalking toward her like a madwoman. "Oh, Hadley. It's so good to see you, sweetheart. Come give me a hug."

Hadley envelops my little grandmother in her arms. She holds her tight, much the same way I do. Much the same way I hug both of them.

I'm pretty sure Hadley stops and sees Nana when she visits town, making sure to avoid me most of the time. They've been close since I brought Hadley here for one of Nana's famous tonics when she was sick in high school. Nana can do no wrong in Had's eyes. Hadley is

Nana's favorite, besides Walker. Me? I'm just happy to see the two of them in the same room as me.

My cheeks ache as I grin, watching them chat about Nana's fried chicken. I don't dare look at Lance. He'll laugh at me, for sure, but there's nothing I can do. Seeing these two together makes me a pussy.

"Don't start," I say to my eldest brother. "And give me the cheeseball."

"I'll share, but you can't have it."

"There's another in the fridge, you two," Nana says, releasing Hadley. "But don't get it out until Peck gets here."

"Forget Peck." Lance points at himself proudly. "Did you hear that? I didn't even almost say fuck. I'm learning. All those years of riding my ass worked."

"Until you just said ass," I point out before a load of cheeseball goes in my mouth. "Where's the golden boy?"

"Who?" Nana asks.

"You know. Walker. The favorite," I say.

"I don't have favorites, Machlan."

"Yes, you do," Lance says. "You've always liked Walker most. But that's okay. Parents always like the dumbest child most. It's why everyone likes Peck."

Hadley comes up to my side. Her fingers drag across the small of my back. She doesn't look at me or acknowledge that she did it, nor does it feel like a sexual invitation. It's more intimate, like she's acknowledging I'm here, and she's here, and we're here together. And I'm not sure what to do with that.

"Actually," Hadley says, "everyone likes Peck because he's nice. Hi, Lance."

"Everyone likes Peck because they feel sorry for him. Hi, Had."

They exchange a smile.

"Where is he?" I ask.

Lance rolls his eyes. "That's why she was going to send me to get you. Walker is with Sienna, taking her family back to the airport."

"Aren't they loaded?" I ask. "Why wouldn't they just rent a car?"

"They did, but Sienna, Camilla, and Mariah went shopping yesterday, and I guess it was a tight fit with the bags or something." Lance looks up at Hadley. "Mariah's home sick today. I know she's been looking forward to meeting you."

Hadley looks at me through her thick lashes. "I didn't know she'd know who I was." When she realizes she's not talking to Lance, she blushes and turns to him. "I hope to meet the woman who tamed the beast someday."

"Don't get it twisted," Lance says. "I'm not tame."

"You're a pussy cat." I laugh.

"I heard pussy." Peck's voice rings through the room as he steps through the open sliding door. "That means Lance is here."

"Fuck off," Lance says.

Nana swats him with a spoon as she moves behind him. He yelps, caressing his butt cheeks, and grimaces.

"You boys get to the table. We're ahead of schedule today," Nana says. "Peck, grab the tea."

"Can I help you with anything?" Hadley asks right before I give in and pull her to me.

My grandmother pulls my girl into a quick hug again. "It's so nice having you here, sweet girl." She looks at me over Hadley's head. "I'm guessing you're why he missed church—"

"Don't blame her," I say. "I overslept."

Nana releases Hadley and grabs my chin as she walks by. "I'm not blaming anyone. It's nice to see you have a girlfriend."

Hadley's gaze finds mine as Nana floats that word out there as though it's a given. She smiles nervously before turning and sorting through the silverware drawer.

I want to say something, but I don't know what. All I can think is how I don't hate the idea, and I don't hate that she'll be sitting next to me at the table today.

"And yet, no one thinks Machlan might be gay." Lance stands in the doorway, his arms stretched in front of him. "Anyone want to explain that?"

I grab a last bite of cheeseball before heading to the dining room. "Well, I've never had a pocket protector, geek."

"I had one in sixth grade. You can't possibly even remember that."

"There are pictures," Peck says. "We've all seen them."

"I didn't think you were gay either," Nana says, handing Hadley a handful of large spoons. "I just said if you were, I'd still love you."

Lance continues his whining as we make our way to the table. I pull out Nana's chair after she sticks a spoon in every dish. Once she's settled, I take a seat next to Hadley. Peck says grace, and we dig in.

Usually, I fight for the chicken legs. They're the crispiest pieces and my favorite, but I look at Hadley for a second too long, and Peck and Lance take them to spite me. So when Peck reaches for the gravy, I take one off his place.

"You can't do that," Hadley whispers with a laugh.

"I just did. Here. Want some green beans?"

"Yes. Thanks." She shakes her head. "This all looks great, Nana."

"Thank you."

Something about Nana's voice makes me look up. Her face is beet red, a line of sweat dotting her forehead. She's as pale as a ghost.

"Hey." My chair scoots against the floor. "Nana? You okay?" The sound of silverware clattering to the table pierces the room. I kneel next to Nana's chair. "You feeling all right?"

"I'm just tired," she says softly. She takes my hands in her clammy palms and pats them. "You're a good boy."

"Do you want to lie down?" Peck asks. "We'll help you to bed."

"No. I'm fine. I just needed a second to rest."

Her eyes struggle to open. Under the cake-y makeup she wears every Sunday, I can see the tiredness etched in her features. I know she's old; I've purposely thought of that in case something happens to her, so I won't be shocked. But I think I'll be shocked anyway.

Hadley's hand finds my shoulder as I squeeze Nana's in mine. "Did you take your medicine today?" she asks Nana.

"Yes. I took them all before church. I'll be fine, kids. Just give me a minute to get my bearings."

My heart sinks. "I'm calling Doc Burns."

"Don't you call him on a Sunday," she protests. "I'll call in the morning and get an appointment."

"I'll be doing that," I say.

She squeezes my hands this time. "I will do it, Machlan." She looks up at Hadley with a sweet look in her eye. "You have things to do. You don't need to be babying me."

"Apparently, I do because you were supposed to make an appointment the other day, and I'm guessing you didn't."

"I got busy."

"That packed schedule of yours must be impossible to rearrange," I say, getting to my feet. "So I'll be calling him this time. *And* I'll come and get you and take you."

She tries to glare at me but fails. "You just want to hear what he says."

"You're damn right I do."

Hadley's hand falls from my shoulder, slipping down my back. Her presence doesn't do anything to fix Nana, but it does soothe something deep inside me.

I'm afraid to feel that for long. So, I focus on my grandmother instead.

The room grows quiet. The color slowly comes back to her face, and her palms return to normal. Kissing the top of her head, I return to my chair.

Hadley sits too, watching me with a worried expression. When her hand hits my thigh, I don't think about it. My hand goes to hers and laces our fingers together. She stills next to me before working her fingers deeper into mine.

My heartbeat settles, and I get comfortable in my seat. Hadley gives me a gentle squeeze, bumping her shoulder with mine.

"This might not be the right time for this," Peck says, "but Machlan stole my chicken leg."

The table erupts in laughter—everyone but me.

"You know they're my favorite," I point out.

"Yeah, well, if you weren't making goo-goo eyes at Hadley, then you could've gotten it yourself."

"I did get it myself." I lift the leg and take a big bite of it. "Damn, that's good."

"Don't taunt him, Machlan," Nana says. She fans her face with her hand. "I think I'm getting too old to fry chicken. I'm pooped."

"Then who will cook for us?" Lance whines.

"Um, you have a girlfriend," I point out.

"Yeah because Nana won't let us elope." Lance takes a bite of mashed potatoes. "I really wish you'd reconsider."

"I really wish you'd stop talking nonsense," Nana tells him.

"You know what you need?" Lance asks.

"I'm afraid to ask."

"You need a day to teach our girls how to cook like you. You know, just in case you get too old to fry chicken." Lance makes a face. "I can't believe I just said that out loud. You can't forget how to fry chicken, right? Like, that's not a thing."

"Can we not talk about this?" I ask.

Hadley tries to pull her hand away, but I tighten my hold.

"You need a day with Mariah and Sienna and Hadley and I'd say Blaire, but that's a joke," Lance says. "She'd read you a legal brief while you fixed food."

"I'd actually like that," Nana says. "Not a bad idea."

"I like this idea too," Peck says. "It's like having backup Nanas. I have a fear of starving, you know."

"Would you be interested in that, Hadley?" Nana asks.

Hadley fidgets in her seat. "Um, yeah. Of course. I just, you know, don't want to intrude."

"I love how we pretend Machlan and Hadley aren't together," Lance says.

"Shut up, Lance," I say.

"What?" He takes another bite of potatoes. "When's the last time you had a girl over here? Never. You two need to get over yourselves and—"

"You wanna do this?" I ask. "You wanna put her on the spot like this?"

"Machlan ..." Hadley touches my bicep.

"Looks like I put you on the spot, if you ask me," Lance says, wiping his hands on a napkin as if I'm not threatening to kill him. "I'm sorry, Had, if I made you uncomfortable."

"That's okay," Hadley says. "You didn't."

Rattling my teeth as I bite them together, I give my brother a final warning glare. Hadley pats my arm again.

"It's fine," she whispers.

Nana laughs out of nowhere. "Do you remember when I had you help me make macaroni and cheese on that Christmas Eve, Hadley?" Nana smiles fondly. "You forgot to add the macaroni and boiled all the water right out of that pot."

"Not a good sign for the future," Lance says, winking at me.

"Fuck off."

Nana smacks my hand. "Don't do anything to him in my house."

"Oh, but he can kill me as long as it's not in here?" Lance asks.

"Oh my God. Nana just authorized Lance's death." Peck gasps.

"I did no such thing." She laughs. "Lance is a smart boy. If he wants to push Machlan, he knows there will be a pushback." She turns to Hadley. "You let me know when you're free, and we'll have an afternoon together," Nana says.

"Okay," Hadley says.

"It'll be fun. Mariah is a pretty good cook now, and Sienna is catching on. She usually gets frustrated and wants to cater everything. But between the three of you, maybe I'll turn over Thanksgiving and see how you girls do."

Hadley stares at her chicken as though it's the most interesting thing in the world. She pulls her hand away again, and this time, I let her.

I think about Thanksgiving and how we all pile in here for the day. We watch football, eat all fucking day, and then, before we go home, we get out Nana's Christmas decorations. It's my favorite holiday, and I look forward to it all year. But as I look at Hadley and realize she won't be here, Thanksgiving doesn't seem that exciting.

"You know," Nana says, "I always wanted a daughter. And I got one, but she didn't want anything to deal with my things. I would love someone to teach all my tips and tricks. Someone to give the little love notes that your granddad sent me when we were young."

"You have Blaire," Peck offers.

"And Blaire is too busy for all that. Such a smart, industrious girl, she is." She sets her glass down, the sweat along the outside creating a ring on the tablecloth. "But now I have your girls. And you've all picked very good girls."

"As long as Peck doesn't wind up with Molly," Lance says.

Peck throws a napkin at my brother. "I'll get her even if it takes a hundred years."

"Your dick won't work in a hundred years. Sorry, Nana," Lance says.

"Stop it," Nana says. "Let me tell you something. Things work out when they're supposed to. I hear all the time these newfangled ideas about making things happen and forcing your way through stuff, and let me tell you, you can't do that."

"I might disagree," Lance chimes in. "If you don't press for what you want in life, it'll never happen."

"True. But you can press and press all day long, and if the time is not right, it won't matter." She settles back in her chair, wincing as she moves. "When you get to be my age, you can look back on life and see it. Things happen when they're supposed to. You get a little distance between yourself and a situation, and you can see how if you got everything you wanted when you wanted, how wrong it all would've been."

Hadley swallows. "What do you mean, Nana?"

"I wanted a baby as soon as we got married. All I'd ever wanted to be was a mother, and I couldn't figure out why on earth God would deny me that. Now, I look back and see all the things I would've missed if I'd been caring for a baby then." She smiles at some memory we can't see. "Staying up late with my husband, talking all night. I got to know him in those years before we had the boys. Being available to travel with him when he worked for the oil company. We made so many memories going from state to state in our beat-up truck. The one we had to stop every couple of hours and add coolant to." She chuckles. "Or when my husband, back before we were married, asked and asked me to go out on a date with him, and I refused. I was so smitten with Johnny Lindsfeld." She laughs. "Oh, dear. I forgot about him."

"Did you date him?" I ask.

"In a roundabout way."

"So, you slept with him," Lance deadpans.

Her eyes light up like a little girl. "No. Well, maybe, but that's not the point."

As everyone laughs and Nana gets flustered, I peek at Hadley. She's watching Nana tell her story with rapt attention. I wonder what it's like to be her with no family but Cross. No stories to listen to, no holidays to share traditions with.

"The point is, I learned a few things from Johnny that served me well later in life, and I would've missed out if I'd have dated your granddaddy right away."

"So, he taught you how to—"

"Don't you dare," Nana cuts Lance off, her face flushing again. "Oh, Lance. What am I going to do with you?"

My family breaks out into a conversation about Molly again. I take Hadley's hand and hold it on my lap, wondering if what Nana said is true. And if it is, does that mean there is hope for me?

Chapter 26

Hadley

The truck kisses the curb and rolls to a stop. The leftovers Nana sent home with Machlan perfume the air, and I could sit here for the rest of the day and be content. Belly full. Heart fuller. If only things could stay this way forever.

Machlan's fingers tap against the steering wheel to a tune I can't hear. His gaze is settled off into the distance, an almost forlorn look written into his skin.

He's been quieter since Nana got sick at dinner. Even his smiles don't quite seem as genuine or as wide as they were before.

"Hey," I say, resting my hand on his arm. "You okay?"

"Me? Yeah." He pulls his gaze to me. "You?"

"Yeah."

He gives me a half-smile, one his heart isn't fully into. "Do you wanna take some of this food? She gave me enough to feed an army."

"I think you asked for that much."

"Only so Peck didn't get it." His smile slips wider. "I'll share with you, though."

"I couldn't eat any more. I'll pop."

He turns the heat down, then fiddles with the radio. Taking his chew can out of his pocket, he turns it over and over in his hand.

I hate seeing him like this. Nana is so special to him. Even as a teenager, he'd check on her. Make everyone promise not to tell her about his shenanigans. Mow her lawn. Help her with her garden. I don't know how he'll cope if something happens to her.

"She's going to be fine," I say softly.

"Yeah." He clears his throat. "She'll be fine. I'm not worried about it."

"It's okay to worry about it, you know."

"I know. But I'm not. There's no sense in it."

The can lays in the palm of his hand. He moves it so the light reflects against the metal lid and shines a light in the air.

My heart sinks for him, and I just want to ease his burdens, if only for a minute.

"Thanks for a fun day." The slices along my forearms from the rose bushes are bright red from the irritation of the dishwater at Nana's. I hold them up for Machlan's viewing pleasure. "It's been a blast."

Machlan tosses the can in the cupholder. "You look like you've been in a fight."

"The question is: do I look like I won?"

He laughs. "You look like you took a hell of a beating, but there's hope the other guy looks worse."

"He does. I chopped that rose bush to pieces." I laugh too. "Seriously, though. Thanks for a fun day. I really did enjoy it."

"Me too." He looks out the windshield again. "It's kind of weird, huh?"

"What's kind of weird?"

"Spending a day together."

His head turns to me first, and then he angles his torso to me. He stares at me for a long while, biting his bottom lip. This typically has me squirming in my seat because I don't know what he's going to say. But, today, I don't squirm at all. Not a bit.

"I think," I say, "it's more that we spent a day together being normal that feels so different."

"I didn't think we had it in us."

"There's a joke to be made there, but I'm gonna let it go."

He grins as I pop open the door.

The evening sun streams in the truck. Machlan looks so handsome sitting in the driver's seat, the button-up he put on before we went to Nana's rolled up to his elbows. He looks as calm and relaxed as the day has been, and if I don't climb out of the truck now, I won't.

"I better get going," I say.

His brows pull together. "You have plans?"

"Emily might come by." The heat in my throat causes it to tighten as I toy with my next sentence. I might as well bring it up—sort of test the waters—because it's going to happen whether I want it to or not. "Because, you know, I head back to Vigo soon."

Machlan shifts. I feel his energy move, but I can't look at him. I just look out the window at my car sitting at the base of the steps.

I'm going to have to get in my car soon and leave again. This time, the idea is to have some peace about where I stand with Machlan. And now, I struggle with getting out of his truck, knowing I'll see him tomorrow.

This plan of mine isn't working. My stomach roils.

As if he can read my mind, he sighs. "When do you leave?"

"I need to be out of here this coming week. I have to get things ready to start my new job, get the things I left at Samuel's house ..." Those words weren't planned, but I don't take them back because they're true. "Just stuff to do, you know?"

My breath holds, a ball of stress sitting smack dab in the middle of my stomach, as I will myself to stop, hoping he'll ask me to stay. I can't stay even if he does. A few good days between the two of us doesn't fix the years of problems we've had. I can't change everything I've worked for because of a hopeful heart.

He reaches across the console and touches my leg with the tips of his fingers. A chill ripples down my spine as I watch his strong, tanned hands contact my bare skin.

If I don't leave now, I won't.

"I gotta go," I say. I give him a quick kiss on his cheek before sliding out of the truck. Reaching to the floorboard, I grab my bag. "Have a good night, Mach."

"Yeah. You too."

I hoist my bag over my shoulder and make my way to the apartment. I give him a little wave before going inside. It's only after I lock the doors do I hear the engine fire and tires squeal as Machlan pulls away.

Flipping on a light, I look around the little room. It's the same as I left it early this morning, but it feels totally different. Bigger. Vacant. Lonely.

Before I even put my bag down, I fish my phone out of my pocket and dial my brother.

"Hey," Cross says. "What's up?"

"Hey. I was wondering what you're doing tonight?"

"Well, Kallie and I are in Merom having dinner. There's a kid who takes boxing lessons from me in a play over here. We're gonna see that in a few. Why?"

My bag hits the floor. "No reason. I was just gonna come by."

"You can come with us. The play doesn't start for an hour. You can make it if you leave Linton now."

"No," I say, feeling my spirits sink. "You guys have fun. I'll find something to do."

"Where's Emily?"

"She might come by later. I'm just bored, I guess." I sigh. "Go have fun. I'll come by tomorrow. You working at the gym?"

"Yup. Come by and I'll let you kick my ass for a while."

"Deal. Bye, Cross."

"Bye, Had."

I set the phone on the table, and it goes off immediately. Samuel's face flashes on the screen, and I silence it without a second thought because I have no thoughts to give. They're all with a dark-haired bartender that I hope I can figure out how to live with. And without.

———

Machlan

"I can't live with her," I say to myself. "And I can't live without her."

A wrench flies from my hand into one of the red toolboxes lining the garage. It gives a satisfying ping as it clamors against the metal.

My hands are a greasy mess, and my shirt is soaked with oil. Working on my dad's old truck usually takes my mind off everything, but it failed me today.

Rinsing the grime off my skin in the basin by the door, I wish it were as easy to do the same to my brain. A little water, a pump of soap, and boom—Hadley is gone.

"I didn't know you still knew how to do that." Walker's voice makes me jump.

I knock my elbow into the side of the sink. "Ouch." Flicking the water off my hands, I cradle my arm and turn to face him. "What are you doing here?"

"We just got back from the airport, and Sienna passed out. She went nonstop the whole time her family was here." He shrugs. "Guess I just thought I'd come by and see what you were up to."

"Should've called and I would've waited on you to help me with this thing." I knock my knuckle against the side of the truck. "Every time I fuck with it, I tell myself it's a pain in the ass and I should just get rid of it. But, you know ..."

Walker comes into the garage. "Yeah. How do you get rid of Dad's pride and joy? I mean, it's not worth shit and just takes up space, but what are ya gonna do? Sell it?"

"Exactly."

I take in the hunk of metal my dad loved more than anything

except Mom and us kids. He and our grandfather rebuilt it from the ground up, and although Dad never drove it anywhere, he changed the oil in it every few months. So, I do too.

Even though I bitch every time I come out here with the new filter in my hand, I do it. And the whole time I'm working on it, griping under my breath, I think about my dad.

I hate I didn't really get to know him as a man. There are a lot of things I'd like to chat with him about, things I'd like to get his advice on.

I'll never forgive myself for not going with them that Fourth of July.

"I heard Hadley was at dinner at Nana's," Walker says, testing the waters.

I nod, biting the inside of my cheek as I test the waters right beside him.

"That's good," he says. "She's a good girl, you know."

"I'm aware."

"Then what the fuck are you waiting on?"

My cheek pops free of my teeth, and I turn my back to Walker. I busy myself with sorting wrenches until I hear my brother laugh at me from the other side of the garage.

"You know what? Fuck you," I say.

"I'm getting plenty of pussy. It's you that I'm worried about. You're not getting any, and it's turning you into one."

As much as I want to argue with him, I can't. I *am* turning into a pussy. My silence only proves his point.

"I get this shit is hard," Walker says. "Do you even know how much of my work Sienna just gives away like I'm running some charity operation? I've had to ban her from Crank most days just so I'm not in the red." He leans against the truck. "It's not easy. But if it was, would you want it?"

"I'd want Hadley either way."

Walker raises a brow. I look the other way.

"Seems to me," Lance says, strolling into the garage, "that

someone once told me to grow a pair of balls. To stop overcomplicating things."

"Yeah, well, that's when it was you." I face my oldest brother. "Why the fuck are *you* here?"

"Just driving by and saw Walker's truck and thought, 'Eh, why the hell not invite myself over?' Is this a private conversation? Not that I care if it is."

"This wasn't even a conversation until you assholes showed up." I head into the house and leave the door open behind me because I'm certain they'll follow.

They do. Jabbering back and forth, they trot after me like puppies until we're standing in the kitchen.

Walker tugs open the refrigerator door. "Didn't I leave this beer here like a year ago?" He jerks one out and pops the top.

"Probably." I watch him take a long drink. "Guess it's a good thing it didn't get thrown out."

That's all it takes for Hadley's face to float through my mind. I hear her laugh. Smell her perfume. Feel my spirits sink.

Lance pulls out a chair and sits. "So, Mariah and I aren't eloping."

"Am I supposed to be surprised by that?" I ask as Walker and I sit too. "There was no way Nana was letting that shit slide."

"You actually asked her?" Walker takes another drink. "That's ballsy."

"I think it was more ballsy not to," Lance says. "Besides, I'm kind of glad she said no."

I raise a brow.

Lance's eyes dodge mine. "I can't say I'm all that upset at having to see her in a dress and have the honeymoon and all that. I'm kind of looking forward to it."

"You're both turning into pussies. You know that?" Walker deadpans.

"Come on, Walk," Lance says. "You've never thought about watching Sienna walk down an aisle? Never? Not once?"

Walker lifts the beer again. We sit quietly as if Lance proposed some profound idea that requires loads of thought. He didn't. But I still find myself envisioning Hadley wearing white with Cross by her side, walking her down a church aisle.

For a moment, everything feels right. I like it. Too much. So much that I get to my feet and scour the refrigerator for another beer.

"Don't worry about Sienna and me," Walker says as I sit again with a cold one of my own. "Let's worry about dipshit over there." He tips his bottle my way. "What's going on with you?"

"Nothing." I down half the bottle.

"You letting her leave?" Lance asks. "I heard her tell Nana she was leaving soon."

I down the rest before standing. Flexing my fingers to relieve some of the pressure in my joints, I look at Lance. "I can't stop her from doing what she wants."

"No," he says. "But you could let her do what she wants by asking her to stay."

"I can't," I almost hiss.

"You fucking can too," Lance fires back.

My blood pressure spikes because this motherfucker just doesn't get it. No one gets it. They would if I told them the truth. Hell, if they knew the truth, they'd probably be disappointed in me too.

I can only imagine their faces, the two men who are my two role models in life, two good as fuck guys who have some internal compass I lack, if I told them what they don't know.

That her dad left the week before she turned eighteen for Reno with a note written on the back of a grocery receipt as a goodbye. I was nowhere to be found when she broke down because I thought it was a good idea to get hammered the night before and pass out in a hayloft on the other side of Merom after running from the police for speeding about thirty miles over the limit.

That she discovered she was pregnant the next week—the same day I was fired for missing too many days of work.

That I couldn't pull myself together fast enough to make her think having a baby with me would be better than living with giving our child up for adoption.

I'm a joke of a man. All I've managed to do with my life is fail the only girl I'll ever love in the worst of ways over and over again.

"Maybe I could make her stay," I say, my voice eerily calm. "But I won't."

"And why the fuck not?" Walker asks.

I glare at him. "Sometimes life isn't about what makes you feel good. Sometimes it's about what makes you able to live with yourself."

"Explain to me how, if you really love her, you can live without her," Lance says. "Because I don't get it."

"Maybe it's really hard to look in her eyes and see my failures, all right? Maybe I'm a pussy, like Walker says, and I can't stand to think what a bitch I am every time I fucking see her. How I'm responsible for the worst part of her life. How she'll never be whole because of fucking me!" My breath comes out so hard, so hot, my nostrils flare. "How her life will be a constant state of fucked up because I can't be a fucking adult, all right? I mean, I own a goddamn bar. I'm begging an asshole in a suit to trust me enough to loan me a basic fucking loan so I can start another business I have no business running."

I throw my hands in the air. "I mean, for fuck's sake, guys. I'll never be able to take care of her—not like I should. Not like she deserves."

I barely catch my breath when Lance laughs.

"Well, that was impassioned," he says. "Have you considered open mic night at the bar? I think you could really do something with that."

"Fuck you."

Walker holds a hand to Lance, stopping him from a retort.

"Look, Mach," Walker says, letting his gaze linger on Lance until he's sure he's shut up. "I don't know what happened, but I'm sorry it did because it's obviously fucked you all the way up."

"You have no idea," I mutter. "The bar was the nail in our coffin."

"Why is the bar such a problem for her?" Walker asks.

My head hangs. "Her mom was killed by a drunk driver. So, she had this immediate reaction like it was the worst idea ever, which, in retrospect, it might've been. I don't know. She didn't get why I wanted to buy it off Uncle Vince, and honestly, I don't know if I understood it then."

Squeezing my eyes closed, I think back to the day I asked Uncle Vince if I could buy it from him. He laughed and said my mother would've killed him had she known her only brother was selling her son a tavern. He tried to talk me out of it, but he was dying of cirrhosis, and I was dying of the heartbreak of losing my daughter and Hadley. Even though she was still around, she was only there out of habit. I knew she'd leave eventually.

It wasn't too long after I bought it for less than a used car that Hadley asked me to marry her.

I said no.

She left.

And I've lived my life sort of floating around with no anchor since.

"Do you understand it now?" Walker asks.

"Understand what?"

"Why you wanted to buy it."

I walk across the kitchen and blow out a breath. My entire body is tight. My shoulders slump like the whole damn world is sitting on them.

"I like it," I say simply. "I like hearing everyone's stories and watching their lives play out. I like giving my two cents. And I like having something that was in our family, which might sound weird." Flicking the bottle cap Walker left on the counter, I watch it hit the edge of the sink and bounce in. "I don't have a lot of options. You have Crank. Lance has his teaching bullshit. What do I have? I'm not good at anything."

"I got this one," Lance says, pointing a finger at Walker. "I get why you're a little rough on yourself for owning a bar."

"Not helping, Lance," Walker grumbles.

Lance waves him off. "But that's all superficial. Let's break this down."

"Make it quick. I gotta piss," I lie.

He rolls his eyes. "Historically, what are you good at? What are your strengths? I'd say partying. Causing mayhem. And ..." He looks at me. "Observing people and taking care of people you care about."

"I—"

"Shut the fuck up. I'm not done," Lance says. "Walker, you got my back if he lunges, right?"

Walker chuckles. I try not to laugh.

"*Anyway*," Lance continues, "the bar is the perfect place for you. When I help my students narrow down their career choices, I tell them to look at their strengths and pick something that falls within those boundaries that interests them. You did that. Maybe you didn't do it with that thought process, but you did it anyway."

It makes sense, but I don't care. It doesn't solve my real problem.

Walker stands and heads to the trash can. After polishing off the rest of his beer, he tosses the bottle in the garbage. "I'm out of here. Do what you want. Just don't fuck your whole life up because you made some bad choices. We've all done it." He swings the door open. "Call me if you need anything," he says over his shoulder as the door shuts.

"I gotta go too," Lance says. "Mariah wants chicken noodle soup, and I have to drive all the way to Peaches to get it because Megan McCarter is working at Carlson's. Did you know that?"

"Yeah."

Grinning at the memory of picking Hadley up in the rain, I sigh. I can still feel her in my arms. I can taste her lips, feel her body against mine.

I look at my brother. "Are you ever worried you'll fall back into your old ways?"

"No." He doesn't laugh or smile or even pretend to be amused by my question.

"Seriously? Like you never think you'll ever want to sleep with some random girl you see on the street?"

"Is that what this is about?" he asks. "Do you want to fuck around?"

"Not at all."

"Then why ask that?" He studies me closely. "Are you worried you'll turn back into a punk?"

"Gee, thanks." I snort.

He laughs. "Mach, you were an asshole for a long time. I was there for all of it. Or most of it," he reconsiders. "But I have faith that you won't get arrested, punch anyone who doesn't deserve it, wreck a car, or lose your money in a high-stakes poker tournament again." He heads for the door. "Now I'm going to get some soup and then go home to the one girl who makes all the pussy I miss out on worth it."

"Later," I say as he leaves.

Once I'm alone, I survey the room. I wonder if Hadley would be happy here. I try to imagine her watching the sun go down out the window over the sink or hearing her sing while she takes a shower.

Lance's words come back to mind. I haven't gotten in a fight in a long time. My arrest record as of late is pretty clean, and even when it was active, it wasn't for anything really serious, I guess. The car wreck wasn't my fault, and I've only lost money a couple of times in poker in the past year. Both times to Walker. Fucking asshole.

Maybe there's potential for me. A small amount, but possibly enough to work with. Enough to be in Hadley's life in some way.

I peel my T-shirt off and study the ink on my arm. A new cluster of tattoos sits on the underside of my arm just on the side of the ridge of my bicep. They're positioned so if look down, they're what I see.

A rose for my mother lays longways. Just beneath it is a four-leaf clover with a little pink bow wrapped around the stem.

"Let it be," I say to myself. "Just let it be."

Rolling my eyes, knowing damn good and well I can't do that, I head to the shower.

Chapter 27

Hadley

"He's home," I say to myself.

I've thought this idea to death. My stomach twists in excitement but tosses the opposite way toward anxiety as I pull my car in behind Machlan's truck.

I haven't seen him since he dropped me off last night after dinner at Nana's. His truck was at Doc Burns' this morning, presumably with Nana, and I warred with myself whether to call Machlan to check on her. I finally broke down during lunch with Emily and sent him a text.

Turning the car off, the grocery bags rattling in the back seat, I pick up my phone. His last text is still pulled up.

> Machlan: Nana was ordered to take it easy for a few days. She'll be okay. I'll probably stay home for a while this evening if you get bored.

My thumb hovers over the keys as I rethink my plan. I read his text again. Nowhere does it say to go buy groceries and bring them over. It doesn't ask me to make him dinner. It doesn't even technically ask me to come by, although I think it does. I hope it does.

I nearly came by a dozen times last night. It was really hard to think about being with him and knowing he was in the same town and all I really had to do was drive a few miles to see him again. But was it the right choice? I didn't know. It felt like it. It still does. But will I regret it tomorrow?

My attention going back to the phone, I decide how to tell him I'm here without looking overconfident. Before I can type something out, it dings in my hand.

> Machlan: Are you going to sit in my driveway all night or what?

I look up and see him standing on the front porch. He's leaning against a column barefooted in jeans and a plain white shirt. I almost whimper at the sight.

Instead of getting out, I text him back.

> Me: That depends. Have you had dinner?

> Machlan: No. Will you get up here, please?

> Me: Maybe

I laugh, my thumbs flying over the keypad. I got presumptuous and thought we could have dinner. I watch the chat bubble bounce as he types his reply.

"Ah!" I jump as my car door opens, and I nearly fall out. He catches me with a chuckle.

"Scare you?"

"Yes." I laugh as I get out of the car. He helps me to my feet. "I'm not intruding on anything, am I?"

"Kind of." He glances in the back seat. "What's this?"

I swallow hard. "Groceries. I thought we could make dinner. Together."

It takes longer than I want for his face to break into a smile. It's the soft one, the shy one, the one I love the most, and it's totally worth the wait. It wraps me in the fuzziest feeling, embracing me with everything right in the world.

He grabs the bags out of the car without saying anything. I lock it and follow him to the house. As we're going up the stairs, I remember what he said when I got here.

"Hey," I say. "You said I was intruding on something."

He holds the door open for me. "You were. But I'll set it aside for now."

"Oh, by all means. I can leave," I say as I enter the foyer. Before I can turn around and follow that with another comment, I feel his breath against my ear.

"Don't even think about it."

A flurry of goose bumps covers my skin. I feel myself come to life as though a button has been pushed, and I grin like an idiot.

"Fine," I say, my words tinged with laughter. "If you're sure."

He steps around me and heads down the hall toward the kitchen. The grocery bags swing in his hands. "I was thinking about getting a dog."

"A dog?" I try to focus on Machlan getting a puppy, but it's hard not to watch his back muscles ripple with each step he takes. "Why do you want a dog?"

"Why not?" He disappears around the corner.

Realizing I'm still standing just inside the door, I scurry down the hallway. "I don't know. I guess there's nothing wrong with getting a dog. But are you sure you want to potty train a puppy?"

I turn the corner and stop in my tracks. He's leaned against the stove, his hands gripping the ledge behind him. With his bare feet and slightly damp hair, he looks like a picture straight out of a magazine.

My breath stolen, I try to recover. "Um, you know, they pee a lot."

"Yeah." He grins. "I guessed that. All animals pee, don't they?" He lets his gaze linger on my face, driving home the fact he's a witness to my flustered state, before turning to the bags. "What did ya get?"

"Steaks. Potatoes. Salad," I say. I help empty the bags onto the counter. "I thought if you had a grill, we could do that. And, if not, we can use the oven."

A package of dinner rolls hits the counter. "Do I have a grill? I'm a man. Of course, I have a grill."

"How was I supposed to know?"

"Well, I'd hope it was a given," he says, side-eyeing me.

"Right. It should've been. Because you're such a *normal* guy."

He wads the bags up and looks at me. "Are you implying I'm not a normal guy?"

"Let's see ..." I say, tossing a tomato in the air and catching it. "Where do I start?"

"You know what? Don't answer that." He fishes out a lighter from what appears to be a junk drawer. "I'll start the grill. You start the salad. Deal?"

"Deal."

He brushes against me as he walks by. He smells heavenly, like freshly washed laundry mixed with a deep, heated aroma. My body tingles as he walks out the back door.

Instead of cutting the salad, I watch him out the window over the sink. He pauses next to the grill and gazes down the hill toward the cemetery below. A soft grin plays on his lips before he shakes his head and gets to work.

One plays on mine too.

I move around his kitchen, pulling open drawers and cabinets until I find what I need. It's fairly organized, and I'm surprised he actually even has a cutting board. I'm also surprised how easy it feels being in this space.

As I rinse the vegetables, I think back on my relationship with Mach. How all the phases we've been through together, the ups and downs and twists and turns, changed how we interact with one another. But at the end of the day, we've never been able to truly walk away.

I'm slicing through a tomato, lost in thought, when he walks in.

"Grill is fired up," he says. "What can I do in here?"

The knife clatters against the cutting board as it presses all the way through a tomato. "Can you grab me a paper towel? This thing is juicier than I thought."

He reaches above my head and pulls a roll out of a cabinet. I turn to see his arm flex but stop when I see the tattoo on the inside of his arm.

I drop the knife onto the counter.

My throat seals shut as my gaze locks on the ink emblazoned on his skin.

"Here you go ..." He takes a step back. His arm falls slowly to his side as our gazes lock.

His lips part, his chest rising and falling as he waits for my reaction.

I take a deep, shaky breath. Tears gather at the corner of my eyes as I reach for his hand. He gives it to me without a fight.

His palm is heavy in mine. His skin is warm from the grill. With a dose of uncertainty, I turn it over so his arm rotates and I can see the underside of his bicep.

And there it is.

I press my finger against the four-leaf clover with a pink bow laced around the stem. My brain races, sorting the odds that I'm way overthinking this and it doesn't mean what I think it means—it isn't for who I think it's for.

Still touching the design, I bring my eyes to his. "What's this?"

His Adam's apple bobs. "It's what you think it is." He reaches carefully for the charm on my necklace, the one I've barely taken off since I was seventeen years old. The little clover lays on the pad of his finger. "This is probably the nicest thing I've ever bought you, huh?"

I wrap a hand around his wrist. "Because that day is one of my favorite days of my life."

A faint grin touches his lips. "We played in that co-ed softball tournament that weekend."

"And we ate all the elephant ears and corn dogs and drank all the lemon shake-ups we could stand." My heart fills with the memories that I've clung to as my life has fallen apart at various times.

"We rode the Ferris wheel," he remembers.

"And it started raining, and I fell in the mud."

"And then I won this to make you feel better," he says, dropping the charm back to my chest. "I didn't think you'd be wearing it this many years later."

As I let go of his hand, the sweetness of that weekend is replaced with the bitterness that came after. I step away as if it will distance me from what happened next.

"I'm glad you are, though," he says. "As dumb as it might be, every time I see it around your neck, it ... would it be wrong that it makes me proud?"

"It should. You gave me the last carefree, fun weekend of my life."

He takes my hand this time and squeezes it. "You've had fun since then."

"Not like that weekend. That weekend I had you. I had a little naivety that life might work out all right. I had a parent who gave a fuck."

His eyes are a warm raft to cling to as I sort back through my dad leaving. And how Cross went crazy when he found out, and I thought for sure he was going to do something stupid and get arrested, leaving me too.

"I sat on the floor in the living room and cried and begged Cross to get his shit straight. But he was a kid too, really, and here he was forced to take care of me or let me fend for myself."

"Cross wouldn't do that to you. Even then."

My stomach churns, kicking up the pain of those few weeks like it was yesterday. I can't look at Machlan, so I look at the floor.

"I got pregnant at the absolute worst time in my life," I say quietly.

He doesn't say anything, but he doesn't have to. His body releases a frustration, an anger I know is directed at himself, as he stands in front of me.

"I didn't know what was going to happen to me," I say. "Mom was dead. Dad was gone. I didn't know if he'd come back. And I was having a baby."

His arm flinches, but I still don't look at him.

Talking about this wasn't on the docket, but it feels right. There's a relief, almost, in talking about this because I never do. Machlan is the only one who knows about this part of my life. It's like it's this secret that I have to keep but one that claws at me from the inside to get out.

He tugs gently on my hand, bringing me a step closer to him.

He doesn't say how it's his fault or go into a rant or start apologizing like a man with a burden he can't shake like he usually does. He *listens*.

"I've never been more scared in my life," I say, a nervous laugh lacing through the words. "I remember thinking I had a human growing inside me, but I felt the most alone I'd ever felt. It was the oddest sensation."

"You had your life turned upside down in the matter of a few days." He frowns. "And God knows I wasn't much help."

I shake my head. "You did all you could at that moment. It wasn't easy for you either."

He grits his teeth. The struggle warring inside him is written on his face. "It wasn't about me. It shouldn't have been about me."

"But it was about you," I insist. "You look back on it and think you should've looked at things differently then, but you didn't have the tools to do that. Think about it, Mach. Your parents were dead. Your siblings were off living their lives, and you were kind of stuck here in a way."

"It's no excuse."

"No," I say, touching his arm. "But it's a good reason. That's a different thing."

"I could've stepped up," he says, his voice rough. "I could've held a job. I could've ..." He hangs his head. "I could've stopped breaking up with you the years before you got pregnant and given you some hope that I could be rational. I don't blame you for not trusting me to raise a kid."

"Not trust you? You think that's what it was?"

My heart breaks, the split inside my body so intense I feel like I'm ripping in two. "I didn't trust *me* to raise a baby, Machlan."

He looks at me as though he's considering this for the first time.

"I remember my mom working two, three jobs when I was growing up," I say. "She'd go from the bank to a grocery store and sometimes a pizza shop at night. And you know what? We still barely got by." I close my eyes as thoughts of my mother wash over me.

He exhales harshly. I know he hates when I bring this up, but I can't help it. I need to prove this to him once and for all.

"It seemed so irresponsible to bring a baby into the world when I wasn't sure if I was going to be able to feed myself."

I blink back tears as fast as they gather.

Machlan's face falls. "You had no faith in me."

"I had no faith in me either," I say as a tear slips down my cheek. Machlan brushes it off with the tip of his finger with a gentleness that makes me want to just fall into his arms and release all the emotions I have brimming inside my soul. "I had no parents. No job. No schooling. Nothing. *And I only had you sometimes.*"

I take a piece of the paper towel he retrieved and dab my eyes. My heart is exposed, lying between us as he searches my face.

Love was never our problem. It's still present, still rumbling between us even now, even after all the shit we've been through. We may not have been able to get on the same page or work out our problems, but there's a relief that the love, in whatever form, is there.

"Do you think we would've been able to deal with it?" he asks. "Do you think if we would've kept her, we would've made it?"

"Do you?"

He chews his bottom lip while he looks around the room. Finally, he exhales. "No. I hate to say that, but I don't."

Tears flood my eyes again. "I don't either. I mean, we didn't make it as it is. Can you imagine us trying to make it with a baby?"

"No." He forces a swallow. "Nana would've tried to raise it, and she was old then. But, by God, she would've tried. I couldn't saddle her with that, you know?"

"Yeah. I know."

A silence blankets us with stillness we both need. Machlan fiddles with our hands. He laces his fingers lightly through mine, rubbing my ring finger with his thumb.

"It eats at me every day that I didn't tell Nana," he says quietly.

A lump settles in my throat. "We did what we had to do. If you would've told her, like you said, she would've talked us into a decision we know wasn't the right one for us or our baby girl."

"I just can't see the disappointment in her eyes," he says over a lump of his own.

"That's why we went to Ohio, right? To avoid all the outside pressure and judgment and see if we could be parents."

There's a flurry of sadness that settles deeply in the lines of his face. And while I understand it, while I feel it to the bottom of my soul just the same, I don't want him to be sad.

I take his hand again and pull up his arm. The tattoos stare back at me. "So that clover is for me?"

He nods. "The week before I got it, the preacher was saying in church that there's a Christian legend that says Eve took a four-leaf clover with her out of Eden so she'd have a piece of paradise with her." He twists his lips in embarrassment. "It's like having a piece of you with me."

I rest a hand on his chest and don't dare speak. My lips tremble at the sweet genuineness of his words, and if I even try to comment, I'll cry big, fat, ugly tears.

"And the pink ribbon is for her," he says.

I look at the sweet little mark tied to the clover. Our daughter and I are wrapped together on Machlan's arm for the rest of his life. All the years since her birth, the years we've struggled and fought and couldn't get on the same page, he was thinking of us.

Blinking back tears, I smile. "I think it's perfect."

"That's the hardest thing we'll ever have to go through, huh?"

"I can't imagine anything being harder than giving your baby up for adoption."

"But we did that," he says. "You know why? Because we loved each other, but we loved her more."

Tears spill down my cheeks in a soft, quiet stream. I wonder when he came up with that—when this big, burly man who has an incredible heart buried under his tough exterior came up with words that sweet and perfect.

We loved her more.

"We did. We loved her more. I like that," I say.

He presses a kiss to my forehead before turning away. "I also like steak. You ready to get this thing started?"

There's no pause for an answer, no follow-up question. He walks by, clearing his throat, and busies himself with the rest of the meal prep.

I dry my face and turn back to the tomato.

Chapter 28

Machlan

"Here you go." The chains holding the porch swing jingle as I sit beside Hadley. She smiles as I tuck a quilt around her shoulders. "Is that better?"

"Totally."

She curls up under the fabric and nestles against my side. The air might have a bite to it, but I don't notice because she's right. This is totally better.

Back and forth we go, our stomachs full of a dinner we almost burned because we couldn't stop telling stories and laughing long enough to remember the grill. I could close my eyes and live in this moment. It's felt good with Hadley many times in my life, but it's never once felt like this.

It's never just us. It's me and her and all the baggage we carry. It all piles together until there's a giant wall that feels impossible to scale.

How do you scale all that? How do you look at someone you care about and think, *Okay, I'll risk your happiness for my own?*

I don't know. What I do know is that sitting on the porch with her on this cool, quiet night makes things feel not quite so impossible.

Not totally uncomplicated, but not quite complicated either. It's what I've always thought spending time with a woman you care about would feel like, and that's scary as fuck.

"Look at the stars," Hadley says. Her arm stretches across my middle against my stomach. When contact is made, she starts to pull back, but I stop her.

"They're beautiful," I say, my hand resting on her forearm.

Her profile is the same one I've studied countless times. Her nose curls up just a bit at the tip. Her lips form a little bud at the center as if she's just been kissed. It takes everything I have not to do that. Not yet. As good as that would feel, it wouldn't be better than just holding her like this ... and it might ruin everything.

She looks up at me through her thick lashes. "You aren't even looking at the stars."

"Oh."

She shakes her head, her kissable lips forming a smile against my side. "My favorite nighttime skies are the ones after it rains. I don't know if it's because we get so used to the storms and the clear skies are such a relief, or if the rain just washes away all the yuck. But I love nights like this."

"Me too." My arm rests over her back as we swing. "Do you have plans for tomorrow?"

"I'm supposed to do something with Emily," she says. "She wants to go to Crave."

My initial reaction is to flat-out tell her no. Every worst-case scenario dashes through my head, and all I can envision is some guy grabbing her, or her getting shoved, or some unsuspecting asshole hitting on her in front of me.

But as she gazes up at me with her honey-colored eyes, she looks different somehow. Stronger. Wiser, even.

My gut reaction is to protect her from everything I can—to keep her out of harm's way. That's why I can't have her in Crave. Why I threaten every asshole I see talking to her. Why I stay away myself.

As we rock and I hold her close and think about the things

we've talked about tonight, how she's survived so much loss and turmoil and came out on top, maybe she's okay. Maybe I can ease up a little.

I summon all my strength and gaze into the darkness. The swinging slows until it stops. "Be careful, okay? I've seen your girl Emily on the verge of fistfights, dancing on tables, and I have a suspicion she swindled some bikers out of a hundred bucks at the billiards tables. She's reckless."

Hadley sits up. "That's it?"

"That's what?"

"Be careful." She cocks her head to the side. "No warning not to come? No threat to only order water or to sit at the bar next to Peck?"

I pull her back down against me again. "No."

"Well, okay, then."

Rifling my hands through the fabric until my hand is on her back, I start swinging again. "I figure you know what you're doing. Right?"

"Right," she says, squeezing me tighter. "Besides, you want to know something funny?"

"What's that?"

"Crave isn't so bad."

I snort. "Well, I agree, but it's funny to hear you say that."

Her fingers strum against my side, sending waves of warmth through my body. "It's important to you in a way I didn't understand. I don't think I completely get it now but watching you in there isn't like I thought it would be."

"So, no strippers?" I laugh.

She makes a fist and jabs me in the side. "Anyway, Emily wants to come in and see Peck."

"I don't get the Peck thing," I say, confused. "I think Navie has a thing for him too."

"Navie totally has a thing for him." She laughs. "Peck's cute, Mach. He's funny and kind, and he has a good job. He's a great catch."

"He's a goof."

"A lovable goof." She sits up and looks at me. Her eyes rival the stars with their sparkle. "Does it make you jealous?"

"What?"

"That everyone is loving Peck?"

I grip the blanket on either side of her like the lapels of a jacket. Her eyes go wide, and I tug her toward me.

My heartbeat kicks in high gear as the heat of her breath gets closer. The playfulness in her eyes hits me somewhere in my gut, and I set my defenses to the side, all the way, and just enjoy this moment in time.

"Does that 'everyone' include you?" I ask.

She wrinkles her nose. "I like Peck, yes."

"I know you like him. Are you loving him?" I tease.

"Loving him? Well ... no."

I scoop her legs and lift her, pulling her onto my lap. She laughs, her eyes going wide, as she's situated across me.

Her weight on me sends a fire ripping through me. The feel of her body on top of my groin is enough to make everything around me, except for her, completely invisible.

Fuck it. Fuck every reservation I have and every reason I can come up with not to take this any further.

I brush a strand of hair out of her face. "What are you loving these days, Had?"

"Let's see," she says, playing along. "I love pistachio ice cream. And this show about an office that's on re-runs, but I missed it originally, so it's new to me." She taps her chin as though she's in thought. "I also love deep purple nail polish for fall, but I haven't had time to get a manicure in forever."

"Great info." I roll my eyes.

"It is, huh?"

"I was hoping for something more in-depth."

She laughs. "There's nothing shallow about nail polish, bud."

"Noted."

"Give me something in-depth, then. What are you loving these days, Mach?" she asks with a mega-watt smile.

"Burnt steak," I say, earning a giggle. "Brothers who call before they show up. And I'm really into the Illinois Legends but haven't had time to catch many games so far."

"Sha-llow."

As I watch, her eyes become flecked with green. Her lips part in an almost pout that sends a shock straight to my cock. Her ass presses down on my lap in a slow, controlled gesture that's coupled with a hooded gaze.

I grip her hips. A swallow barely slips down my throat. "What are you feeling right now, Had?"

She stills. Her pupils dilate as her breathing gets heavy. "It's a weird thing, actually. I feel ... *wanted*. And I trust you enough to tell you that."

That's it. Her vulnerability, her willingness to trust me at this moment, is my undoing.

My hands run up the length of her sides, brushing against the mounds of her breasts on their journey to her face. She gasps at the contact of my palms against her beaded nipples. The quilt falls off her shoulders onto the porch floor.

The breeze rattles around us as if it is cheering us on. I cup her face in my hands and start to kiss her but pull back.

The clover bounces on her chest, her breath coming out in hurried wisps. She pulls her brows together, wondering why I didn't kiss her, but too afraid to ask.

I'm probably going to hate myself tomorrow for this. I'm going to wake up and realize I've fought my whole life to avoid giving her too much hope when it comes to me. Yet there's nothing I want more right now, need more right now, than to make her understand one fundamental thing.

The words claw at my throat, scraping away my defenses until they're on the tip of my tongue.

"You are wanted," I whisper, looking into her soul as deeply as I can. "You're all I've ever wanted, love."

Her lips find mine in a kiss I feel in every cell of my damn body. For once, I trust her enough to let her take control.

I don't try to protect her from me, keeping her at arm's length to make it easier to break apart later. I succumb to her demands. When she presses, I open my mouth. When she swipes her tongue past my lips, I let her control the pace. When she wraps her legs around my waist and rests her forehead on mine, I relish the contact.

She's so small, wrapped around me. But even so, I can feel the force that is Hadley Jacobs. I wonder if she's always been like this, or if I'm just now seeing it.

A shiver ripples through her body, and I reach for the quilt and can't quite get it. I pull her against me instead.

This will end too soon if I don't stop it. And despite my surprise, I don't want it to end.

"Hey," I say, my breathing ragged.

"Hey, what?" she whispers against my neck.

"Can I interest you in a hot bath with a fancy fizzling thing Blaire left here at Easter?"

"Will you get in with me?"

An arm goes under her ass as I stand. "That was the plan."

She leans back and looks at me. There's something on the tip of her tongue, something just under the sweet little smile she gives, that has my heart skipping a few beats.

Instead of sharing whatever it was, she rests her head against my shoulder again. "Can you hurry? It's cold."

I smile into her hair and carry her inside.

Chapter 29

Hadley

I'm too warm.

One foot slides out from under the blankets, but the air is too cold, so back in it goes.

There's a light coming from an odd direction. My eyes flutter open.

The ceiling fan above Machlan's bed whirls quietly, ruffling the edges of a wall tapestry in blues, grays, and black. The blinds have been pulled on the window that looks across the backyard, but the room is still bright from the sun.

My hand juts out to find an empty spot beside me.

Sitting up, I stretch. My limbs ache from the activities of last night as I look around the room. There's no smell of coffee, no sound of anyone moving around. It's only when I start to climb out of bed do I notice a piece of yellow paper on the bedside table.

Had,

I have to meet some people at the property on Ash Street. I didn't want to wake you. I should be back by eleven.

Take that bath we didn't get to last night if you want. I'll bring lunch.
    Machlan

I flop back in bed with a giant smile on my face. I need a cup of coffee, but I don't want to get up—not because I'm tired. I'm not. But because lying here feels so indulgent.

Scooting over to Machlan's side, I twist myself up in his blankets. His scent is all over the linens. The mattress dips only slightly where he usually lays, and I wiggle around until I bury myself there.

My eyes fall closed. If I lie still, I can pretend he's here with his arms around me. And if I'm quiet enough, I can hear the words he whispered as I was drifting to sleep a few hours ago.

I'm glad you're here, he said into the shell of my ear. *Thank you for trusting me tonight.*

This is the only place I've ever wanted to be. And now that I am, in his home, in his bed, it's hard to process. I keep thinking there has to be more to it. There has to be something I'm not panicking about or some dark hole to walk around, but there's not.

Something was different about him last night. He let me in. He even gave me the reins at times. None of that is like Machlan, and while I can't explain it, it gives me so much hope.

I smile into the pillows until my ringing phone snaps me back to reality. I consider letting voicemail pick it up, but by the fourth ring, I reconsider.

Army crawling to the other side of the bed, I swipe the phone off the table. It's a Vigo number I don't recognize.

My throat clears as I sit up. "Hello?"

"Is this Hadley?"

"It is."

"Hello, Hadley. This is Jamie from the Human Resources

Department at Boseman. You're supposed to start here next Monday."

"Oh, yes," I say, tossing the covers off my legs in hopes the chilliness will wake me up. "What can I do for you?"

"A big favor, actually. We're actually hoping you can start on the nineteenth."

I yank back my phone and hit the home key to check the date. "That's in two days."

"I know. And I'm sorry to hit you with this at the last minute, but when Kyle interviewed you for the position, he thought Sandy would be here longer than she is. So, if we want her to train you for a couple of days, we really need you to start on the nineteenth . Do you think that's possible?"

My heart sinks. I squeeze my temples with one hand and try to ignore the dread coming at me in droves. "I actually am out of town." I wince. "Let me see what I can do, and I'll get back to you later today."

"That's fine. And I understand this is our mistake, but if there's any way we can get you in with Sandy, it will make the transition so much smoother. If you can make it happen, we would really appreciate it, Hadley."

"I understand. Thanks for the call. I'll get back with you before the end of the day."

"Take care. Talk soon."

"Goodbye."

My phone drops unceremoniously onto the blankets. The thud is soft, muted by the extra comforter Machlan added before we climbed into bed for actual sleep.

A sharp pain shoots across my forehead. I whine, a fake cry drifting across the room.

The rational part of my head reminds me I was leaving anyway. The illogical half tells me I can't. It's too soon. I haven't had enough time with Machlan.

Crawling across the bed, I dive into his spot. I burrow as deep into his sheets as I can.

"What am I going to do now?" I ask aloud.

The room gives no answers.

The sweet way he looked at me last night, the loving way he caressed me as he didn't fuck me but made love to me more than a couple of times, gives me hope he will ask me to stay.

Surely, he wouldn't make himself that vulnerable if he wasn't in a different place. That has to mean something.

"Ask me to stay," I whisper, my eyes fluttering closed. "Ask me to stay and I will."

My phone rings again, and I pick it up. Holding my breath that the universe heard my request and is coming through, I look at the screen.

Damn it.

"Hey," I say in the line.

"Hi, Hadley," Samuel says. "How are you?"

"I'm good."

Looking around Machlan's bedroom and hearing Samuel's voice triggers something deep inside me. Regardless of what happens with Mach, whether he finally realizes he can commit or not, doesn't matter. My heart is not in it with Samuel. And even though I've prayed it would be, it won't.

"I'm glad you called," I say.

"Really? That's promising."

My heart sinks. "Listen, Samuel. You're a nice guy. You're everything a girl should want."

"There's a but, isn't there?"

"Yeah," I say softly.

He sighs, a heaviness in it that isn't missed by me. "I really hope you find what you want. Even if it isn't me."

"I hope that for you too."

"Promise me something, though."

"What's that?"

He takes a deep breath. "Don't settle, Hadley. Don't let anyone walk all over you or twist yourself up to make people happy. Your spirit is what I love most about you, and I'd hate for anyone to dampen it."

"Thank you."

"There's no reason to make this longer than it has to be," he admits. "You have a few things at my house. I'll gather them when I get back, and you can come get them, or I'll drop them off."

"Okay."

"And Hadley?"

"Yeah?"

"If you change your mind, I'll be here."

I open my mouth to tell him not to be, to meet some girl at his audit conferences and fall madly, deeply in love. To find someone who makes him feel what I feel when I'm around Machlan. To find someone he simply can't live without. That he would fight for.

But before I can do that, the line is dead.

———

Machlan

A flashy sports utility vehicle flies up the road. The tires hit the dirt lot before the driver locks the brakes. The vehicle slides a few feet before it comes to a complete stop.

Spencer is over an hour late. He seems to either be unaware of this or completely without a fuck as his loafers hit the gravel.

He adjusts his tie as he strolls my way. I don't get up from the bench I've been sitting on for the past thirty minutes. Fuck him.

"Well, good morning," he says. "Glad to see you're on time."

"I was. An hour ago."

"Really?" He looks at his watch. "I had a quick meeting this morning that apparently ran over. I apologize."

He doesn't. There's not a hint of respect in his tone to lend any credence to that at all.

It's not only that I left Hadley asleep in my bed and could've been there with her for the better part of the morning that has me annoyed, but also that the key wasn't here like it was supposed to be.

"Wouldn't have been so bad if I could've gotten in," I say, alluding to the key.

"You mean a guy like you couldn't figure out how to break in?" His laugh is loud and grating. It's enough to bring me to my feet.

"What's that supposed to mean?"

"Oh, nothing. Just a little humor to lighten the mood, you know?" He pats me on the back. "Let's go inside. I have a couple of things I want to talk to you about."

As he unlocks the door and makes a meal out of turning on the lights and inspecting the thermostat, I take inventory of the space.

Billiards tables will go along the back wall—two or three, probably. A kid Lance knows, Ollie, is going to make me some furniture out of old pallets for the area to the right. We'll have game systems and a couple of computers. It'll work great.

Spencer tosses a file down on the sole table in the room. "What do you think of the place?"

"It's gonna work out great. The whole plan is in place. I'm just waiting on the signed contracts to pull the trigger."

"Interesting choice of words," he mumbles. "I'm just going to be frank, okay?"

"Yeah. Go."

He walks around the table, effectively putting it between us. "On the advice of my attorney, we had an addendum drawn up."

"Wait. What? What for?"

Everything was covered in the original contract. I had Blaire look at it, and it was fine. She didn't love some of the terms, but she doesn't love much of anything on the first try.

"What's going on, Spencer?"

"You said a few things the other day that, upon second thought, made me a little nervous about loaning you the money."

"Like what?" My hands flex at my sides as I try to stay calm.

"For one, because I'm carrying your loan, I'll need to be insured on the property. That means I have something to lose."

"I get it. Cut to the chase."

He opens the folder and shoves a stapled stack of papers in my direction. "You can obviously have your attorney, if you have one, look at these."

"My sister is an attorney at Litchfield and Sparks in Chicago," I say, not giving a fuck what that means, but knowing it's a big deal to people who care. "I'm sure she'd love to see these before I sign them."

"Oh. Well, okay," he says, straightening his already straight tie. "She can tell you what they say then."

I cross my arms over my chest and ignore the fire smoldering in my stomach. "I'd really like to hear it from you."

"Fine." He picks up the document. "This part says you have to be closed to all underaged people by eight o'clock on school nights and ten on the weekends."

"What? Why would you do that?"

"With all due respect to your business plan, I'd rather not have a bunch of kids here at night tearing the place up."

I hold my hands in front of me. "That's the exact reason I'm doing this. So they don't go tearing shit up."

He takes off his glasses and holds them near his mouth. The way he looks at me, down his nose as though I'm some kind of fucking idiot, makes me see red.

"Kids aren't inherently bad, you know," I say.

"Machlan. You own a bar. You know people, in general, are inherently bad."

"Don't tell me what I fucking know. That's not true. And if you want to know the real ridiculousness of those hours you've written in there, it's this: most juvenile crimes happen in the hours right after school lets out. Not at night."

"I think you're wrong."

I think he's a cocksucker too, but I'm not going to say it.

Pacing a circle, I try to settle myself. I take in all the potential this place has and remind myself of the end result. That if I can deal with this asshole and get this building, I can do something real and valuable with my life. That I can be more than bar owner. That I can give back to a community I've fucked with relentlessly in my life.

"Tell me this," I say. "What did you do after school when you were growing up?"

"I either went to golf practice or went home."

"And who was there?"

"My mother. Why do you care?"

"Because when I was growing up, both of my parents worked. I came home to an empty house. And when my parents, who were good fucking people, mind you, died when I was a teenager, my grandmother had to chase me around. My best friend, Cross, had basically no one. His dad didn't give a fuck."

He looks at me as though I'm telling him the weather forecast.

I blow out an exasperated breath. "When you have nothing to do, no one waiting on you, you get in trouble. From the hours of eight to three on school days, even if you hate school on the surface, you appreciate the routine of it all. People who care where you are. People who shove a lunch in front of your face. Somewhere warm and dry and, for a lot of kids, that's more than they get at home. Once that bell rings, they have nothing. Do you know what that feels like?"

"No."

"That's my point."

"Their parents should do better." He chuckles. "I love your passion for this project, but it's ... Quite frankly, it's a waste of time."

I try to stay calm, but my nerves bounce, ready to explode.

"If Hadley hadn't been in there that day, I probably would've pulled the deal completely," he says.

Hearing her name on his tongue doesn't help, nor does the way he grins after he says it. As though lewd thoughts are spilling through his pussified brain.

"Let's leave Had out of this," I say.

"Had, huh?" He quirks a brow.

"Leave her out of it."

"Let me give you a piece of advice." He tosses a pen on the papers. "I don't know how well you know her, but she's a little rough around the edges. A sweet girl. Great tits. But she's basically the same kind of customer you want in here, and those people don't make you any money unless you own a strip club."

I'm so shocked that I'm certain I misheard him. I expect my brain to filter it all out and make it make sense at any moment. Instead, he laughs, licking his lips, and makes it absolutely clear.

"All right. You sign this addendum and we—"

"We ain't signing shit." I stalk across the room. My breathing is eerily calm; my eyes narrowed on the dick in the suit.

I need to stay calm. I know that. I need to let this arrogant bastard get his rocks off however he does it and not fuck up my plans. But the longer his words echo in my brain, the lesser my grip on logic becomes.

"Don't get testy." He laughs. "And don't let a girl like Hadley get to you like this, Machlan. Women always ruin a good man."

"You think *she* ruins *me*?" I shake my head, the words getting jumbled in my mind. It's almost a plea because something in his eyes, something right under the surface, tells me he's going to press. And if he presses like I think he's going to, it won't end well. "You don't know jack shit."

"I know enough to know I was going to turn your offer down, but the fact that she knew you made me more comfortable. But seeing you now, all hyped up over her, makes me rethink your abilities."

"This isn't me hyped. I'll assure you of that," I say. "And what I do when people like you talk about her has nothing to do with the contract."

He twirls his glasses in the air. "I disagree. If you get wound up so easily by me, how do you think you'll survive a room full of teenagers?"

"Because they aren't assholes."

He drops his glasses; his thin lips pressed together. The wheels are turning in his peon brain. I've seen it a hundred times. I'm usually really good at ignoring it when a pussified motherfucker thinks they've found your weakness and chooses to push. Today might be different.

"Tell you what," he says, his eyes twinkling. "I don't really want to lose this sale. As you said, I'll make more money off you than I would if I sold it outright. So, have your attorney look over the addendum, and if it's manageable, it's a deal. I'll even knock off five thousand if you tell me how tight Hadley is." He snickers, picking up his pen. "She probably has a sweet little cunt, doesn't she?"

"You motherfucker," I growl, my pulse hitting me so hard I can barely hear his cackle. "I'm gonna fucking kill you, you bastard."

He grabs his phone and presses a few keys as I stalk around the corner of the table. I could hit him with one hand and end his fucking day, but I want to enjoy this one. I want him to feel every word he just spit at me. I want him to taste the blood on his lips. To remember it the next time he tries to open his mouth.

The table legs scratch across the floor as he shoves it around, trying to keep it between us.

"Look at you running like you were just running your mouth," I say, my voice eerily calm.

I step right. So does he. I step forward. He steps back.

I laugh. "You do know how bad this is gonna hurt, right?"

"Let's calm down," he says, his voice trembling.

"Nah, you wanted this. Cause and effect, bitch."

It's only going to take one shot to knock him out, and that won't feel nearly as good as seeing the fear in his eyes does.

Spencer looks over my shoulder, then back at me. "I hope Hadley is smart enough to stay away from you. It makes me sad for her that she's gotten caught up with trash like you."

Adrenaline rockets through me as I charge around the table. Spencer runs toward the back of the room.

The door swings open behind me. I glance over my shoulder before pursuing Spencer.

"What's going on here?" Kip asks, taking off his sheriff's hat. "We had a 911 call."

I stop in my tracks; my teeth still pressed together so hard it hurts.

"Machlan?" he asks. My cousin raises his brows. "What's going on?"

"Not a damn thing," I say. "Just teaching this pudfuck some manners."

Kip motions for me to come toward him. "Come here."

"Give me five minutes. Nah, two," I beg. "Just walk out of here for two minutes."

Kip doesn't blink. "You don't want an assault charge. You'll lose your license for the bar. Now come here before you lose everything you have."

Looking over my shoulder at Spencer, I point a finger his way. "You have one coming."

"That's a threat," Spencer says. "Did you hear that, Sheriff?"

Clenching my hands at my sides, my nostrils flaring as I try to rein in my fury, I head toward Kip.

"Did you hear that?" Spencer shouts again. "That's clearly a threat."

"I didn't hear anything. Go get in your truck," he says under his breath. "And go home. Got it?"

"Our contract is void," Spencer shouts from the other side of the room.

I whirl around. "You think?"

The door slams behind me.

Chapter 30

Hadley

The clock on the stove moves past another hour.

My hair is almost dry from the bath I took around eleven in hopes he'd return and join me. The dishes from the leftovers I heated up around noon have been washed, dried, and put away. The bed has been made, a reality episode consumed, and now I sit at the kitchen table unsure what to do. Phone in hand, I unlock it.

His name is at the top of my text messenger. *Running late* is the only thing I've heard from him, and that was around the time I climbed out of the bath.

I wish I hadn't eaten. The steak and potatoes are too heavy on my stomach, and every time I move, my stomach churns. I jump at every sound I hear, thinking it's him.

As comfortable as I was earlier, I'm not now. Whether it's the stark difference in the note and text or that he hasn't come back, I don't know. There's an uneasy knot in my stomach I can't shake.

"He probably just got busy," I tell myself. Brushing a bit of salt off the table, I get to my feet and head to the hallway.

My steps echo through the house. A loneliness burrows in my gut, and I try to kick it out and find the happiness I had when I woke up, but it's hard. I really thought today would be different and he wouldn't leave like he used to do. And as much as I tell myself he might not have, that there's a perfectly logical explanation for this, I worry.

I gather my things. I try not to look around, to overthink anything, to see the spot on the couch where he spread me last night and buried his face between my legs.

The hair on the back of my neck prickles as I slip on my shoes. Leaning against the wall, I pull out my phone again.

> Me: I'm just going to go back to the apartment. I hope everything is okay.

I watch as the chat bubbles start. Then stop. Then start again. Then stop. Finally, as I start to type again, they come back on and remain.

> Machlan: Probably a good idea. I'm sorry.

> Me: No worries. I'll see you tonight. Em is coming around six.

I wait, sure this will get a reaction. There's not even a start of a chat bubble this time.

My mouth dry, my stomach twisting, I exit the house and climb into my car. My phone pairs to the Bluetooth when the engine turns over, and a loud ring blares through the car as soon as I put it in drive.

"Hey," I say.

"How's my little sister doing today?" Cross asks.

"You know what? I'm not sure."

"I don't like the sound of that."

Trees line the streets leading back to town. They're tinged with burgundies and oranges and, if I wasn't so perplexed by Machlan, I'd drive slower and appreciate them.

"Have you talked to Mach today?" I ask.

"No. I think he had to go to the building he's buying at some point."

"Yeah." I bite the inside of my cheek as I take a left. The farther I get from the cocoon of his house, the more turbulent my nerves get. "I stayed all night with him. He left this morning to go do that but didn't come back."

"What?" Cross asks. "What do you mean he didn't come back?"

"I think that's self-explanatory, isn't it? He left, and I haven't seen him since."

My chest tightens, smooshing together my insides until I'm squirming in my seat. Talking about it out loud makes me wish I'd never answered the damn phone.

"Maybe he got busy with something else," Cross offers. "You know how he gets."

"I do. I know how he is better than anyone. But I just feel like something's ... off. I can't explain it. It's like intuition or something."

Beecher Street approaches much faster than I anticipated. I suck in a deep breath as I pull next to the stairs leading to the apartment. I do a quick scan of the area and don't see his truck.

My lungs expel the breath I've been holding as I place the car in park. Navie is outside the back door of Crave. A broom is propped up next to the wall next to a large garbage bag.

"I got a call today from my new job. They want me to start in two days," I say.

"Are you going back tomorrow then?"

Machlan's cologne is still on my shirt. My body's still tense from being wrapped around him all night. My heart is still tender from his sweet whispers.

Maybe that's all it is. I'm too tender. I'm too on edge from everything and just making a mountain out of a molehill.

I swallow hard. "I'm not sure what I'm going to do. If he wanted me to stay, I'd stay. But this morning makes me think maybe I should go."

"Can I ask you something?"

"Sure," I say, watching Navie use the broomstick as a microphone.

"Do you really think it'll be any different between you guys if you stay?" Cross asks. "I mean, I hoped it would. God knows my life would be easier."

"Ha."

"I mean it, Had. You're confident. You make decisions. You're stronger than I've ever seen you. As much as I hate to admit it, Vigo seems to have done you some good."

"Yeah, well ..."

Cross sighs. "Just promise me that you won't let Machlan get to you. You can't fix someone else's problems, no matter how hard you try."

"I'll be fine. Promise."

He sighs again. "Come see me before you leave, okay? And call me if you need me."

"I will. Love you, brother."

"Love you too."

Ending the call, I reach for my purse when my phone buzzes again. This number I don't know.

"Hello?" I ask, blowing out a breath.

"Hadley?"

"Yes. Who is this?"

"Spencer Eubanks."

Sitting up, I wonder how he got my number. My eyes flip to Crave, and I wonder if something has happened to Machlan.

"What can I do for you?" I ask. "Is everything okay?"

"I know we don't really know each other, Hadley. And I'm sorry

for getting your number from my mother, but I thought it was impera-
tive we speak this afternoon."

My mouth is dry. "Okay. What's going on?"

"I had a meeting with Machlan today."

"I know."

"Hadley," he says with a gush of a breath that isn't a chuckle, but
more like an exasperated reaction. "How well do you know him?"

"Very well. Why?"

"He threatened to kill me today. It was ugly. I've never seen
someone snap like he did."

My jaw drops to the floor. I almost drop my phone.

"What?" I open the door, needing the fresh air.

Nothing about this makes any sense. Is this why Machlan didn't
come home? Where is he? Is he okay?

"He literally threatened to kill me," he says again.

"That's not like Machlan, Spencer."

"He went into a rage when I told him my attorney had issues
with his business plan. Had I not called the police when I did ..."

My eyes bug out. "You called the police?"

"It was that or get hurt. Hadley, the man is reckless. Please,
please be careful around him."

"I ... What?" My head hurts, pain streaking over my forehead as I
attempt to reconcile this information. "Spencer, this doesn't make any
sense."

"I agree. It doesn't. But you need to watch yourself around him.
He's ... impetuous."

The way he spits the last word out snaps me back to reality. I
switch the phone between my hands, the sun warming my back just
enough to make me sweat.

Imagining Machlan snapping on someone without just cause
doesn't seem likely. He might have a temper, but it's never unjusti-
fied. And the longer I think about Spencer pushing him or needling
him to get a reaction, knowing he'd get one, the angrier it makes me.
Because that's what had to have happened. It's the only explanation.

"I appreciate the call," I say, a rush of energy pulsing through me. I need to find Machlan. "Take care."

"You don't believe me, do you?"

"If Machlan lost his cool, it was for a good reason."

Spencer chuckles angrily. "Remember that when he's in your face ready to hit you."

My jaw drops. "Excuse me?"

"Don't look the other way, Hadley. Men like him are dangerous."

"You know who is dangerous? *Men like you,*" I snarl. "I don't know what happened between the two of you, but I'd bet my life that Machlan didn't start it. And I'd bet even more that he'd never hurt me. This call you just made? It was to hurt me as a way to hurt him because you obviously feel like he got one over on you today."

"Hadley—"

"Goodbye, Spencer."

I end the call. Stepping out of the car, I head for the stairs and decide how to find Machlan. The railing wiggles as I yank on it and start the ascent. Only then do I hear Navie.

"Hey, Hadley!" she exclaims, popping her earbuds out of her ears. "How are you?"

I don't stop. "Good. How's it going?"

She laughs. "Good. Machlan taught me how to do the ordering today, so I think that means I have some job security."

My foot falters. I turn to her, my hand on the rail. "Mach was here today?"

"He came in about halfway through lunch. I'd keep some distance today. He's in a really bad mood."

"Hey, Navie," Machlan's voice drifts through the air.

I look up. His eyes meet mine somewhere over the ashtray, and he clearly didn't expect to see me.

My heart slams against my ribcage, my breath caught in a gasp and an exhale. Whether it's the way he holds his body or the steeliness of his eyes, I don't know. But I can't smile or walk to him. That much I know.

He holds my gaze for a long second, maybe even two, before he gives me a twitch of a smile and turns to Navie.

"Did we order any brandy?" he asks.

"Yeah. Two bottles, I think," she replies. "Remember? You made a comment about how you never sell it, but if you stop carrying it, everyone orders it."

I watch them banter back and forth, my heart splintering in my chest. He was here. After all that with Spencer. And he couldn't even call me, let alone come to me?

My stomach drops, and I consider just going to the apartment. But just as I do, he drags his eyes back to mine.

"How are you?" he asks carefully.

"Confused."

Navie gathers the trash bag and broom. "I think I'll go inside. If, um, yeah ..."

Machlan steps outside and holds the door open for Navie. It closes softly behind her. He looks at me but doesn't speak. He doesn't have to. I've seen him pull away from me a number of times in my life. This look hasn't changed.

What has changed, though, is I'm not going to just let it happen and go suffer quietly. No. I'm done with that.

"What happened today?" I ask.

He leans against the brick wall of the building and angles his chin to the sky. "Nothing."

"No, Mach. What happened?"

"I don't really want to talk about it."

"Well, I do. You didn't come back. You didn't text me, and clearly, you were right here. So why wouldn't you have told me to just come here with you or at least told me you had work to do? Why leave me to sit there all day not knowing what was going on?"

He squeezes his eyes shut before lowering his chin. He still says nothing.

We're having two different conversations on two different wavelengths. He's not hearing anything I'm really saying. We've been here a million times before, and despite what I'd hoped, he's still on *that* level.

Frustration pours through me as I set my jaw. "What happened with you and Spencer?"

His head whips to mine. "Why would you ask me that?"

"Because he called me and said there was an incident that ended with the police being called."

"He called you? That motherfucker called *you*?"

"He seemed to be more talkative about his day than you are." I glare at him. "I love getting information like this secondhand."

He shoves off the wall. "He ..." His lips press together as he shakes his head. "Yeah. We had words. The deal is off."

"Can I do anything?"

"He called Kip on me, Had. Do you think there's anything you can do? Not that I'd want you to at this point anyway." He refuses to look at me. "Everything's fine."

"He called the sheriff. It doesn't seem like everything is fine. But what do I know? I'm getting my information from the enemy."

"Oh, so it's my fault?" Now he looks at me. "I mean, I get it. I'm the bad boy. Always my fault." He turns to the door, but I won't have it.

"Go ahead. Walk away. That's what you do best."

He spins around. "I walk away, so you don't get drawn into my fuckery. Don't you get that?"

"I'm already drawn into it, Machlan."

"And you shouldn't be, and I hate that you are," he says, his eyes on fire.

"You want to know what I told him?" I say, my teeth gritted the same as his. "I told him I was behind you one-hundred percent even though I didn't even know what happened. Yet you don't have enough faith in me to even fucking tell me."

Something shifts in his eyes, but it doesn't stay. Instead, he pulls the door open.

We stand, staring at each other, a hundred emotions flittering between us. I fight back a set of tears as I feel whatever we had last night dissipate.

If I could reach out and grab it and hold onto it forever, I would. But as I look at him, see the coolness come back to his eyes that I've seen so many times over the past few years, I realize what reality is. And what dreams will never come true.

"I'm supposed to go back to Vigo tomorrow," I say. "They want me to start this week."

My breath stalls in my chest as I hold onto the final strand of hope that this will be the moment I've waited on—the moment when he asks me to stay. That he'll see our fate is in his hands.

He can ask me to stay or tell me to go. As he looks at me with a crooked brow, I say a silent prayer he'll come to his senses.

He slips the chew can out of his pocket. He opens his mouth to say something but closes it just as quickly. He looks at the ground and shakes his head. "Drive careful." And then he's gone.

Chapter 31

Hadley

"I don't know, Em."

My best friend tucks her bra strap under her shirt. "I do. You're going to go out strong."

Rolling my eyes, I gather the last of my things scattered around the apartment and stuff them into my bag. Everything will be a wrinkly mess when I get back to Vigo, and the bottle of lotion tucked between a shirt and a pair of socks may or may not have been completely closed.

Oh, well.

That's the least of my worries.

"How do you feel about everything?" Emily asks. "You're kind of freaking me out a little with how cool you're being."

I'm kind of freaking me out a little with it too.

Tears gather in my eyes again, and I force them back. I catch myself every so often wanting to run down the steps and throw open the door and let him have it. But I won't. I won't be the one to try anymore.

My stomach somersaults without fail, rolling around and around as I see Machlan's face as he says, "Drive careful."

Then the tears come back again.

"What am I supposed to feel?" I ask, yanking the bag closed.

"I don't know. Sad. Hurt. Pissed off. I mean, if your story from last night is true, probably a little sore at a minimum."

I flop down next to the bag. "Do we seriously have to go there?"

"Nope. We can totally focus on the positive in all this."

"Which is?"

"Which is ... now you know where things stand."

"Maybe not," I say, scooting over to make room for her on the couch.

"Had." She towers over me with her five-foot-eight frame. She sits. "I'm not saying he doesn't love you in his own way because I know he does. I've seen the boy. Machlan loves you. But he's never been ready to commit for whatever reason. And it looks like he's still not."

He's not.

If only I understood why he refuses to give in and allow himself to feel the way I know he does. Because for the first time in my life, I know, without a shadow of a doubt, that Machlan Gibson loves me. I also know, with the same certainty, it doesn't change anything for him.

Despite the rock weighing down my emotions so I don't lose complete control before I get home, there's a comfort in this. *This* I feel completely.

Knowing my love wasn't unrequited, only displayed in a way I don't understand, does make accepting this reality a tad bit gentler.

"You're right," I say, my voice garbled. "Nothing is going to change with him."

"And that's fine. I mean, it's not fine," she adds when I shoot her a dirty look. "It hurts you. I know that, and I get it. But he's the one stuck in whatever misery he's in, and you can't pull him out. God knows you've tried."

I have tried. For so long. And accepting I can't try any more strangles my heart.

"I hate he's this way," I say, my heart aching.

"But he is. So cry over him if you want."

"Oh, I will. I'm sure. I just gotta get out of here first." I look at my friend. "I guess this means I got my answer and can go on with my life."

She puts her arm around my shoulders and gives me a gentle shake. Her head rests against mine.

Tears come again, but this time, they aren't for Machlan. They're for me.

"I want you to do something," Emily says.

Wiping the wetness off my face, I laugh. "If this has a punchline, I'm not there yet."

She laughs. "It doesn't." Pulling away, she takes in my mess. "Forgive him for hurting you, okay? And accept him for who he is. Not because he's worth it or deserves it, but because you do."

"Wow. I didn't know you were so poetic."

"I have moments." She gets to her feet. "Now get off the couch. Wash your face. Change your shirt."

"Em ..."

"I didn't come here to see you. I came to see Peck." She takes my hand and pulls me up. "I've sat here and given you therapy; now you can go with me into the bar and see the guy I want to give me babies."

"Oh, my God."

"I wonder how many times he'd make me moan that?"

As I process her request, to follow her to Crave, I have no problems forgetting Peck. "What do I do about Machlan?"

She flaunts across the room and rifles through a drawer in the kitchen. "You're going to have to see him again at some point. You might as well do it now." She removes a dishcloth and dampens it. "This is like getting back on the horse once it bucks you off. We're taking the fear out of it."

It's a crazy proposition. I'm crazier for taking the cloth and cleaning my face. And for putting on mascara. And for changing my shirt. And when I'm walking into the bar just a few seconds later, I legit consider I might be without a damn mind.

Machlan

"Are you going to tell me what's up your ass tonight or not?" Navie leans into the cooler and plucks out a beer.

"Or not."

"You are one frustrating man, Machlan."

Every noise the crowd makes has me ready to blow a gasket. Every laugh, every cheer, every shout of something I'd probably find amusing most nights is like nails on a chalkboard. But even if I went home, there would be no relief.

I don't know where this fucking day went wrong. How do you wake up beside the girl of your dreams and end it with her leaving because you told her to?

Because I'm me. That's how.

Maybe someday she'll get it. Maybe she'll understand I did her a huge favor. Maybe she'll see when she finally falls in love with someone else that life can be good for her. She can look at me then and realize she deserved better than a guy who fails at everything he touches, who risks everything he has at the drop of a hat.

As much as I don't want to admit it, Kip was right. If I would've lost my head today, I would've lost everything.

Planting both hands on the cooler, I hang my head. The music starts up again, and I just wish for it to stop. I wish all these people would go home and someone would lock the door behind them so I could sit here and drown everything out.

Navie's hand rests on the small of my back. "I'm really kind of worried about you, boss."

"I'm fine."

"Okay. Good. Glad to hear it. Hadley just came in, so maybe that will help."

I shove off the cooler and jerk my attention to the door.

There she is.

In a green shirt with sleeves that come down to her elbows and jeans that shows off her ass, she watches me blank-faced. It's a blow that hits in the center of my chest.

She doesn't look away like she usually does when she doesn't want me to see what she's thinking. She doesn't smile or laugh or even glare. I'd take any of those three things right now.

I take a step toward her. This makes her look away. She says something to Emily that makes her friend laugh, and they head to a table on the opposite wall of the bar.

Swallowing takes more energy than it should. Breathing is a little more complicated. Ensuring I don't run over there and tell her I'm fucking sorry as shit takes everything I have.

"Want me to get that?" Navie asks. Her bright blue eyes shine with a look that reads there's a problem, and she's correctly identified me as the cause.

I take an order, dole out two beers, and give the customer change without looking away from Hadley. Her shoulders are tight, her smile practiced, and her attention pointedly not even coming close to me.

Puke bubbles in my stomach, the taste bitter and disgusting. My voice is so loud inside my head, screaming at me to do something, that I can't do anything at all but wince and watch.

Navie comes back and takes a beer and a bottle of water from the cooler. "Hadley ordered water," she says.

A faint smile graces my lips. I wish I could look at her and grin, tease her a little, but that's over with.

"How is she?" I ask.

"I don't know," she says, grabbing a fresh order pad from the stack by the register. "Why don't you ask her yourself."

I glare at her.

"Why do you do this, Mach? The girl loves you."

"You want to know why?" I growl, leaning toward her. "Because I love her."

Navie's eyes go wide. Whatever she was expecting, it wasn't that. I can't blame her because I didn't expect it either. That doesn't make it any less true.

"You said you love her," Navie points out. "Mach."

"What?"

"You said you love her."

"So?"

"Guys don't say that without it being big!"

"What's big?" Peck sits at the bar, smacking his hands off the top. "I mean, I know something that's big …"

Navie laughs. "Oh, do tell me more."

I grab a beer and slide it to Peck. "Here. Be quiet."

"Oh, it's one of those nights," Peck groans. "I'll be over there if you need me, and by *there*, I mean anywhere but near him." He winks at Navie and takes off through the crowd.

"I have these little fantasies," Navie says, "that Peck says he loves me in the throes of passion."

"I … That's … Great," I say.

She laughs. "I wonder if he is big?"

"I don't fucking know. I …" I spin around to face her. "We can overstep this boss slash employee relationship if you want. That's cool. We can be friends, but we aren't gonna be those friends, all right? I'm not the one to talk about cock sizes. I. Am. Not. The. One."

She laughs harder. "Okay. Fine."

Tuning her out, I look to the side. Hadley still isn't looking at me. She's seemingly engrossed in something Emily is saying while Peck stands next to their table.

I wonder how much she's thought about what Spencer said. I wonder if she believes even an inkling of what she heard.

I can't go the rest of my life and have people whispering things to her about me. Eroding that look in her eyes like I hung the moon.

Tearing away the faith she has in me. Destroying the bond we have that keeps us linked despite everything else.

If she's mine, that's what it'll be. People have a lot of feelings about me. My name was in the paper a lot growing up. I'm the kid with no parents who went a little wild for a period of time. I'm the guy who owns the bar downtown. I'm the one people whisper salacious things about because I'm the easy target.

The door opens, and Logan strolls in. He winks at Navie as I pour a bourbon neat for a customer. I watch him wander through the room.

There's a cocky strut to the asshole that I don't like or appreciate. The guy is on a mission to wreak havoc. He's on that mission every time he's been in here this week.

"Here you go," I say, handing the drink to the guy across from me. "That'll be ..."

Logan stops at Hadley's table. He brushes against her arm in a move that's intended to appear innocent. I know it's not. Hadley knows it too. She scoots away from the edge of the booth.

My teeth grind together as I watch this bastard make a play.

"How much is it, Machlan?" the customer asks.

"It's on the house."

I step away from the bar slowly, watching Hadley. She smiles, but her body tells something different. As Logan talks, Hadley moves her water between them in some unconscious defense mechanism.

Logan touches her arm. Hadley pulls away.

I jump across the bar, sliding across the top, and stalk my way toward their table.

"What's happening over here?" I ask, my voice hitting them long before I actually arrive.

"Hey, Machlan." Emily grins. "How are you tonight?"

"This is gonna be fun," Peck grumbles.

"What are you doing, Machlan?" Hadley sighs. Everything about those five words is heavy. Weighted. Burdened.

"Are you with him?" Logan asks, motioning toward me over his shoulder.

For the first time since she walked in, Hadley looks at me. There's a puffiness to her eyes and a pout to her lips that tells me she's been crying. I wish she wouldn't have looked at me at all.

My heart splits open. I know what she must be thinking. Here I come again after pushing her away, but what the fuck am I supposed to do?

"I'm not with him," Hadley says, ripping her gaze from mine.

I shiver as a chill catapults up my spine. My mouth opens to argue with her, but I can't.

Logan looks at me and cackles. "Lucky me." He licks his lips with a wink before turning back to Hadley. "Do you want to get a drink, beautiful?"

The chill is replaced by a fury that's hard to contain. "She doesn't."

"Don't speak for me," Hadley says.

"Just trying to help."

"I don't think she needs your help, *pal*." Logan laughs.

"I'm not your fucking pal."

"No, you're not." He grins. "And apparently you aren't hers either."

My fists clench, my arms primed by a shot of adrenaline. Hadley's eyes go wide as she watches the two of us.

"You're gonna need to walk away," I say to Logan. "Do us both a favor and just get out of here."

"Fuck you," he snarls. He squares up with me, facing me head-on. "What do ya got to say about that, bud?"

Peck grabs my arm. "Easy there, Mach."

I shrug Peck off. Loosening my shoulders, I keep my gaze pinned on Logan. "I'd say you're running out of time."

"You wanna go with me?" He looks at Hadley over his shoulder. "Because I'm not getting great vibes in here."

Hadley doesn't move. She looks at me with a sadness in her face. A resolution, maybe. "I'm not getting great vibes in here either."

"Then let's go." He reaches for her hand.

I turn to the side, a punch loaded.

Peck jumps between Logan and me, making it impossible to unload without hitting him in the process.

"I can only save you for so long," he says to Logan.

Hadley looks my way as she climbs out of the booth. "I'll walk you out, Logan."

"The fuck you will," I say.

"Yes," she bellows, whirling around so fast her hair follows in her wake. "I *will*. I will talk to who I will. And date who I will. *And fuck who I will.*" She glares at me. "But don't worry. I'll drive carefully."

I stand so we're only inches apart. My heart pumps so fast I think it might spin out of control.

"I won't stand here and watch you walk out of here with him," I say, blocking out everyone around us. "He's no good, Had."

"And how do you know that?"

"He was just trying to fuck Navie yesterday. He was with Molly in here two days ago."

"He what?" Peck barks.

I ignore him. "This guy will chew you up and spit you back out, and I'm not gonna stand here and watch it."

She shoves her delicate shoulders back and looks at me with a sadness I'll never un-see. "Then don't."

It's a challenge, a plea to walk out of here with her myself. It's a dare I don't take.

Her face falls. "You ready, Logan?"

He grins at me. "I'll let you know how it goes."

I step toward him but keep my attention on Hadley.

I never see the punch coming.

His fist connects with the side of my face flush, the bones cracking upon contact. I'm knocked to the side and into Peck before I even realize what happened.

"You son of a bitch." I fire a right, then a left, then a right hook into his kidney before he gets his hands up. Each punch lands, punishing his flesh. The sound of cartilage popping rings through the bar.

Logan wobbles on his feet. "What the fuck?"

Peck stands in front of me and waves his hand once through the air. "Point made. Enough."

Slowly, as the haze of the adrenaline begins to lift, do I realize the spectators. And only after that realization hits do I see Hadley.

A single tear slides down her cheek as she watches with her mouth agape. "*You* are a fucking idiot."

"Logan threw the first punch," Emily says. "What was Mach supposed to do?"

I can't even thank her for the defense. My heart is too busy breaking under Hadley's gaze.

"I'll get him out of here." Peck sighs.

"Here." Navie thrusts a towel toward Logan. "Get this on his nose. I don't do blood."

"You can have her. That better be some good pussy," Logan says, his voice muffled from the towel.

Peck shoves him toward the door. "My God, man. Shut the hell up."

The crowd slowly dissipates. It's encouraged by Navie who offers a sale on vodka. I don't even care.

"I'm sorry," I say. So many things roll through my mind that I can't sort them. I can't do anything but look at her and hope to God this makes sense to her. That she gets it.

"You know what? I don't even care anymore." She shakes her head, a lump visible in her throat. "You're only sorry now because you got your way."

"That's not true."

"No, it is true. You don't want me, but you sure as hell don't want anyone else to have me either."

"Had ..." I drag in a lungful of air in hopes it steadies the panic taking over my insides.

"Don't. I'm done. This is not how this works anymore."

My stomach lurches. Bile rises into my mouth, but I swallow it back. "Don't do this."

"Me? Don't do this? Machlan, I would've followed you to the ends of the Earth if you would've just asked. But you're either too chickenshit or don't care enough to even ask."

The break in her voice breaks me. My heart shatters as my worst nightmare plays out right in front of me. She's right, though. I'm too chickenshit to ask her for anything.

"I came here in hopes of figuring things out with you so I could go on with my life. I didn't think you'd make it this easy." Her eyes fill with tears as she turns away. "Don't follow me."

She passes Peck at the door as I watch her leave.

Chapter 32

Hadley

"Good morning," I croak.

Squinting, I take in the mess in my living room. The ride to Vigo took forever with Emily driving last night, and by the time we got to my house, I didn't care about anything but lying down and making the heartache stop.

My bag sits on a chair; the contents spewed across the room from where I dug through them last night. Emily is lying half on and half off the sofa. On the coffee table are an empty pizza box and two bottles that held wine a few hours ago.

"Is this what a hangover feels like?" I ask, squeezing my temples.

"Yup," she says, with a pop on the p. "Who let us drink that much?"

"You. You were in charge."

"That was your first mistake," she groans, struggling to sit up. "What time is it?"

"Nine." I head into the kitchen. "I'm going to find my phone and call Cross and go back to bed. What do you take for a hangover?"

"Hangovers and heartbreak are the same. Both take time."

My feet hit the cold linoleum as I enter the kitchen. I shiver, spying my phone next to the coffeepot. The idea of coffee makes me nauseous. The prospect of looking at potential missed calls makes me sicker.

If Machlan called, I'd fight myself from calling him back.

If he didn't …

I look at the screen.

He didn't.

My eyes close again as another shiver rips through me that has nothing to do with the temperature of the floor.

"Try some crackers," Emily says from the living room. "And bring me some, please."

Fishing a box of saltines out of the cabinet and a couple of bottles of water from the fridge, I make my way back through the living room. I toss her a drink and the crackers. "Here," I say. "I'm going back to bed. And if you ever let me drink again, *ever*, we're not friends."

"Are you a mean drunk? Because I don't remember you being mean last night." The crinkle of cellophane dances through the air. "You were pretty funny, actually."

"I was?"

She shrugs, taking a bite of a cracker. "From what I remember."

"Fabulous," I mumble, heading to my room.

I climb into bed and tug the blankets over me. They aren't as soft as Machlan's, and I don't sink into my mattress like his either. I also don't remember when the bed got this big.

As I lie in my dirty clothes from last night and feel the wine churning in my stomach, I try to sleep. But as soon as my eyes close, my mind starts to drift.

The pain I numbed last night comes barreling back. A hand goes to my chest, the sadness cutting so deep it physically hurts. The worst part of all is pinpointing what hurts worse—the pain of losing him or the pain of never really having him at all.

Just as my nose starts to burn, alerting me of tears to come, my phone rings in my hand. I pull it to my face and see Cross's name emblazoned across the front.

"Hey," I say with no enthusiasm.

"I heard you left town last night."

"You heard right."

"I also heard Machlan punched a guy in Crave over you. Again."

"You heard right," I repeat. "Again."

"What the fuck happened, Had?"

"Why don't you ask him?"

"Oh, I'm going to," he tells me. "But I thought I'd get your side first."

Groaning, I sit up. My head throbs from the movement. My body begs me to quit the day and just burrow down in the blankets and sleep it off.

Cross sighs into the phone as I take my time propping myself up with pillows. By the time I'm ready to talk, he's out of patience.

"Can we get on with it?" he asks.

"Oh, I'm sorry. I'm over here trying to figure out how to sleep off a heartbreak. My bad."

"A heartbreak?" The question is cold. Pointed. Full of promises he doesn't have to verbalize.

It's my turn to sigh. "No. Not a heartbreak. I mean, yeah," I babble. "I don't fucking know."

"Well, Peck called me late last night and just said there was an incident and you were fine but left town."

"How'd he know I left town?"

"He's Peck. You don't think he made damn sure you were okay?"

My heart fills as I think of my sweet friend.

"He had eyes on you until Emily was driving your car and you were on the highway back to Vigo. But he wouldn't really say what happened. And, Had, I wanna know."

He's at his wit's end with this. I can hear it in his voice.

It must be hard for him, being Machlan's best friend and my big brother. He loves us both. And he should. Machlan is a great friend to him.

The idea that Cross and Machlan would have a wedge between them because of me makes my head hurt even more, and the longer I ponder it, the more I realize I can't let that happen. I can't ruin their best friendship because I have this stupid love for a man who refuses to let me do just that.

I could spin this story a couple of different ways if I wanted to be a jerk. But I don't. I don't want to do that to them.

"This guy, Logan," I say, "was hitting on me. Machlan didn't like it too much."

"Oh, I bet he didn't."

"In Machlan's defense, Logan hit him first. I don't think Mach even saw it coming," I say. My stomach drops as I remember Machlan's head jerking to the side as Logan's fist pushed across it. "All Mach did was hit him back."

"Once?"

"Eh, a few times. It was actually kind of impressive."

"What made you leave town then?"

"I just ... He's not going to change, Cross." My words are barely audible as I sniffle. "I told him I was leaving, and he told me to be safe or something stupid like that. Even after the days we spent together, you know, it was just back to the old Machlan."

"Don't cry."

"Well, it's hard not to," I say, wiping a tear. "But I'll be okay. For real this time. This time, this one is on me."

"How do you figure?"

"I came back. I asked for it. And I got my answer. I can't blame him for that."

My head starts to swirl, his laugh filling my mind. His touch is hot on my skin, his breath whispering against my ear, and then it hits me. I'll never have that again. I got a glimpse into a world I can never have.

"Do you want me to come up there?" Cross asks. "Or send Kallie? Or ... something."

"No," I say, drying my face with the blanket. "I just need to cry it out today. I'll be okay. Emily is here, and I'm going to eat all my feelings and probably watch a sappy movie or two and just be done with it. Tomorrow, I start my new job. Tomorrow will be the first day of the rest of my life. Today, I'll mourn the last day of my old one."

"Had, look, I know this sucks, and I know you're hurting right now. I just ... I don't know what to do about it."

I relax against the pillows. "The fact you would do something is enough. You're a good brother."

"I will always be there for you. And I can't kick Mach's ass, but I'll sure give it a shot if you want me to."

Giggling, I snuggle under the blankets. "Not yet. Maybe tomorrow. We'll see how the day goes."

"I'll get limbered up." He laughs. "I'm gonna go check on Kallie. I think she got Mariah's virus. She was up puking all night."

"Gross. Go. I'll be fine. Sorry I didn't call last night."

"I'm just glad you had Emily with you. Now go eat or watch television or whatever it is you do. Call me if you need me. I can be there fast."

"Love you, Cross."

"You too. Bye."

"Bye."

I drop my phone on the blankets and pull a pillow over my head. I still miss him. And that's pathetic.

———

Machlan

"Can you fix it or not?" I ask my brother.

"Can I fix it? Yeah. But it'll cost you more than if you just buy another one." Walker goes back to the tractor parked in Crank's lot. "What the fuck did you even do to it? You completely fucked that tire up."

"Hard to say."

He whacks a screwdriver against a bearing. "That good, huh?"

"Yeah. I'll leave it here until you get it fixed if Peck can give me a ride home."

Peck comes out of one of the shop bays. He sees me and slows his steps. "Hey, Mach."

I lift my chin in acknowledgment of his presence.

My cousin has seen me act like a fool more than both my brothers combined. We were closer in age and both had an interest in things that went fast or were stupid. I never care what he thinks about the things I do. I am curious what he thinks about last night, and that bothers me.

"I grabbed that ratchet off the wall, but it's too small," Peck says to Walker. "Where's the one you had last week for that dozer?"

"Fuck, I don't know," Walker says. He wipes his brow with the back of his hand. "Let's put that on hold for a minute."

"Yeah ..." Peck looks over my shoulder. "Let's do that."

I spin around to see Cross turning into the parking lot. He kills the engine before the truck is even in park. His feet are on the ground before the dome light comes on.

I face him. There's nothing worse than letting a pissed off Cross think you're submissive. It gives him power. I can kick his ass, but it's close. Too close to let him get a head start.

"Hey, Walk," Cross says. "What's up, Peck?" He doesn't wait for their response before setting his sights on me. "Can I talk to you for a minute?"

"Sure."

He lets his fingertips trail the hood of my car as he walks around it. The squeal of the metal cuts through any hope I had that this conversation could be civil.

"Just got off the phone with Hadley," he says.

"How is she?"

The question comes out before I can think about it; my inherent need to check on her taking precedence over logic or etiquette. Of course, I shouldn't ask about her. Not when Cross has that look in his eye.

"Let me tell you something," Cross says. "I've put up with the two of you for years. Practically my entire fucking life. You're on. You're off. You love her. You hate her."

"I've never hated her."

He's not thrilled with my interruption. "I stay out of it all I can because I love her and I like you. But by God, Mach, when I have to hear her cry, it cuts through me."

It's a gamble, a big one, to run my hands over my face. It takes my sight off Cross for more than a half a second. He could fire a punch and, if it hits just right, could knock me on my ass. But it's a gamble I take because I can't stand the look in his eye.

"Why do you do it?" he asks. "Why do you fucking humor every fucking whim she has? If you don't fucking want her, let her fucking be."

"I do fucking want her," I tell him.

"Then what the fuck is this?" He holds his hands to his sides. "Because I'm not following you. And God knows she's not."

My pulse pounds in my temple, my neck screaming with tension.

"I got in two fights yesterday," I tell him. "Did you know that?"

"I heard."

Not what I was expecting. I try again. "I lost the building on Ash."

"I heard."

"So ... why are you here?" I shout.

He looks at me like I'm not making sense. "Are you fucking stupid?" he bellows.

"No, but I'm starting to think you are."

Peck is beside us. His hands are in front of him, his back foot planted in case all hell breaks loose. "Listen, guys. Let's calm down just a second."

"Fuck it, Peck," Walker yells from the tractor. "Let 'em fight it out. Maybe Cross will knock some sense into Mach."

"Why don't you shut the fuck up?" I shout back.

A wrench rattles off the tractor as Walker throws it to the ground. He storms our way, reminding me of the few memories I had of our father when he was pissed.

I haven't seen Walker mad like this more than twice in his life, and neither time was at me. I could take him—that I'm sure. But looking at this bull of a man stalk my way is a lot less appetizing than watching Cross get pissed.

Biting my lip, I watch Walker's face swirl with an anger I'm not comfortable having directed at me.

"Listen, fuckhead. We're all sick of this shit," he says.

"You don't think I am?" I ask. I look at my family, Cross included. "You think this is fun for me?"

"Guess what? Life's not fun," Walker says. "But we all manage."

"And you don't think I manage? Fuck you, Walk." My head is going to explode. I know it. I'm going to blow into a million pieces in the middle of this parking lot. "Aren't you guys hearing me?"

"Loud and clear," Peck says.

"Then what's there not to understand?" I ask. "I lost my shit on Spencer Eubanks yesterday and lost a building because he said some shit about underprivileged kids and some things about Had I won't even touch." My fists clench at my sides. "He's alive because Kip walked in."

"What did he say?" Cross asks.

I laugh angrily. "And then," I say, giving Cross a look not to push, "Logan Jerrell bled all over my fucking bar last night." I look at them all one by one. "I'm a mess, you guys. A fucking disaster. Why aren't you guys telling her to run?" I look at Cross. "Especially you."

"You know why?" He slips his hands in his pockets. "You know why I'm not telling *my* little sister to run away from the biggest asshole I've ever met?"

"I'd love to know," I say, my back flexing with pent-up aggression.

He takes a step toward me. "Because you don't deserve her. She's way out of your league, Mach."

"You don't think I know this?"

"But here's the thing," he says. "She deserves you."

Peck raises a hand. "Excuse me, but I'm not following." We all look at him. His arm lowers. "Okay. It's just me. Got it."

"As I was saying," Cross says, "Hadley deserves someone who will fight for her. Who isn't afraid to step up and do what needs to be done to protect her. To shield her from assholes like Spencer and Logan. To love her so fucking much they'd push her away even when it kills them."

My shoulders drop. If I was a pussy, I'd cry. That heat at the back of your eyes that comes right before tears well up is there.

"Much to my chagrin, that's you." Cross takes his hands out of his pockets. "If you aren't man enough to go after her, then I'll have to rethink everything I thought I knew about you. Set your goddamn pride to the side and do it, Mach. And if you don't do it soon, don't do it at all. Please. Let her go."

Walker's boot shuffles across the gravel. "I don't even know what's happening right now, but I want to go take apart a large piece of machinery to convince myself I still have balls."

"Shut up," Cross says, jabbing Walker in the side.

Walker and Peck walk off, jabbering away about pistons and oil weights. Before I know it, it's just Cross and me.

"Thanks," I say. "I mean, I don't know what to do about any of this, but thanks for what you said."

He grabs my shoulder and shakes it a little as he walks by. "I don't want to have to try to kick your ass, but you're really asking for it."

With a laugh, I follow him to his truck. "Want to give me a ride to my house? I kind of blew the tire out of the car today doing doughnuts out at Bluebird."

"I guess." He grins. "But I'm going to talk the whole way, and you're gonna listen."

For some reason, that doesn't sound as bad as it usually does.

Chapter 33

Hadley

"I know it sounds like a lot, but it's not," Sandy says. "The biggest thing is not to mess with Tom on Fridays. Spending the weekend with his wife stresses him out, so just stay clear."

"Noted." I smile at the woman whose position I'm taking at Boseman. "You've been so helpful this morning—not only with tips about the processes but also with who's who. I appreciate it."

She leans closer. "One more thing. Tricia can be a stick in the mud. So, if you have any of those Not Safe For Work things ..." Her eyes widen. "I had a video my friend Jenn sent of this guy who could bend over and give himself a blow job. Let's just say Tricia didn't find that as interesting as I did."

I laugh. "I kind of want to see that video and kind of don't."

"Email me your phone number, and I'll text it to you." She winks. "Okay. Get settled at your desk. I have a few things I have to wrap up that won't affect you, and then I'll be back to grab you for an afternoon experience of the supply closet."

"Sounds kinky."

Her laughter follows her down the hall.

My desk sits in a little office off the exam rooms. Since I'm new,

I'll spend less time with the dentists and more time doing paperwork, which is fine by me.

The walls are a bright yellow, amplifying the morning sunlight streaming in the windows. A giant toothbrush sits across the front of the desk with a smiley face and a silly grin that reminds me of Peck.

I grab my purse from the chair by the door. My phone is lying on top of my wallet, and I take it out and hit the home key.

My stomach falls to my feet.

One missed call. From Machlan.

It was over an hour ago, and there's no voicemail. When the screen falls asleep, I wake it up to see his name again.

My thumb rests on the screen as if it'll bring me closer to him. That's where I want to be. With him. But as my heart softens to the idea of calling him back, the start of a pimple on my cheek takes the opportunity to burn. It reminds me of crying all day yesterday. Of going to bed without washing my face. Of waking up with pizza sauce in the corner of my mouth and doughnut icing on my shirt.

As much as I want to hear his voice, what I really want is resolution. What I need is to be able to wake up in the morning and start the day without wondering if he'll call.

The chair squeaks as I sit down. My purse hits the floor. I rest my forearms on my desk and open the phone.

I find Machlan's name and let my fingers fly.

Me: Hey, Mach. I saw you called. Look, I'm sorry about everything this weekend. I hate that all that went down, and you got punched. I take responsibility for that. I shouldn't have been there.

> Me: I hope you're good. I hope you're always good. I apologize for trying to give you everything of me before asking if you wanted it. I shouldn't have assumed or hoped or whatever it was. I've tried to hold your hand so many times, and you keep letting go. I get it now.

> Me: I'll be in town to visit Cross and maybe even Nana from time to time, and I hope if we see each other, we can wave and be friendly. I don't hate you. I've loved you too long to ever hate you.

> Me: Take care of yourself. Stop chewing if you can. And don't leave that plug-in turned on if you don't refill the scented oil because it'll burn your house to the ground and that worries the shit out of me.

> Me: Please don't text me back. Don't call. Everything is fine between us. I just can't.

> Me: Xo

I snap my phone shut and put it back in my bag.

Machlan

I am not going to look and see if she called me back.

The grilled cheese grew cold twenty minutes ago, but I take a bite anyway. It's not melty anymore.

"She's probably at work," I tell myself, sliding the sandwich in the trash.

I rinse the plate. In the dishwasher, it goes.

She actually left. I gave her some space before heading to the apartment last night, and when I found it empty, a piece of me died.

My fingers strum against the counter as I look at the doorway leading into the hallway which leads into the bedroom where my phone sits.

Hands in my hair, I pace a circle around the multicolored rug that looks like a kid made it with pieces of rolled-up fabric. Kallie called it a Jelly Roll rug when she was here with Cross. I've spent more time today studying the different colors than any adult should ever spend.

I haven't slept, and that isn't helping anything. There's more coffee in my system than blood. I feel like one of those little dogs that runs laps through your house, sliding around corners and slipping into doors because they can't even slow down to a walk.

It took all day yesterday to concentrate on what Cross had to say. It wasn't until nightfall that I accepted he wouldn't say anything just to make me feel better. That he must have meant what he said. At least to some degree.

And then during the night, after the infomercial about waterproof tape, I was able to mellow out enough to absorb it. And at some point as the sun came up, I realized he was right. Mostly.

I stop walking. There's an itch at the back of my neck, an urgency rushing through my body.

Hadley deserves someone who will fight for her. Cross's words creep through my mind.

I've fought for a lot of things in my life, for Hadley's honor even, but I've never fought *for her.*

I jog down the hallway. My keys are on the table by the door, and I scoop them up. My hands shake, the keys jingling in my palm, as I search for my phone.

She's fought for me her entire life, and I've let her go every damn time.

Except this one.

A zip of fear like I've never felt before swamps me, but it doesn't stop me. It motivates me to hurry. To hustle. To get to her and fix this bullshit before it's too late.

If anyone is going to love Hadley, it might as well be me. I'd die for that girl with no questions asked. I'd rob a bank to make her dreams come true. I'd prune the rose bushes and buy all the fizzy bath shit if it made her smile only for a second.

Hadley loves me. Why, I don't know. How, I'm not sure. But she does. She'd have to if she's still coming around. And even though it terrifies me to think I'll fuck something up with her, I'm already doing that by not just loving her back.

My phone isn't on the couch.

"Damn it," I hiss. Turning around, I jog to my room and swipe the phone from where I tossed it on the bed. It springs to life.

I stop.

I open Hadley's text.

I read the words in her voice—not the one she used last night at Crave, but the one she used when she told me she was leaving. The one she used right before I told her to drive carefully.

"No ..." My head goes side to side as I take in her words, skimming over them on the first read and then starting over again as a form of torture. "Had. No."

She can't mean this. Not now.

Tears wet my eyes as I toss my phone back on the bed. It lands on the spot where she slept, the spot where I laid last night when I tried to sleep. The spot where I held her when she was sleeping and promised her I'd always be here for her.

A lump sits in my throat. My chest burns, the pain encompassing every part of me. I've never felt something this severe, something that literally feels like I'm going to die.

Chapter 34

Machlan

"What the fuck?"

I sit up in my bed.

Bang. Bang. Bang.

Something is pounding somewhere, and I'm not sure if it's just in my head or if I'm really hearing it.

My head is foggy as I try to sort through fact and fiction.

The light coming through the bedroom windows touches the door to the closet, and that only happens when it's after four o'clock this time of year. I know that because I leave for the bar around four. As I'm walking out of my closet after I change into my work clothes, the sun is usually hitting me in the face.

"What time is it?" I ask out loud.

Bang. Bang. Bang.

I stand, my legs heavy, and I glance at the clock. It's 4:16 in the afternoon.

Bang. Bang. Bang.

My phone is lying on the bed, and I grab it. It's dead.

Bang. Bang. Bang.

"Fuck," I hiss.

Running a hand through my hair, trying to figure out how in the hell I'm asleep in the middle of the fucking afternoon, I head down the hallway.

Bang. Bang. Bang.

"Machlan! Open this goddamn door!" Peck's voice is almost shrill. "Fucking hell, Mach! Open up!"

"For fuck's sake." I pull the door open. "What the hell is wrong with you?"

His face is pale. "Mach. It's Nana."

"It's Nana, what?"

"Sienna went by to take her some muffins and found her in her chair." His voice breaks. "Come on. They just took her by ambulance to the hospital."

———

I look at the clock. "You'd think they'd have some information by now."

My entire body hurts. The chairs in the waiting room don't help, but the drain of energy is what kills me. I've paced. I've prayed. I've berated us all for not taking better care of her.

Lance's head hangs. "What are we gonna do if something happens to her?"

"Don't talk like that," Peck says. "She'll be fine." He works his bottom lip between his teeth, an empty coffee cup in his hands. "She has to be."

"Did you call your brother?" Walker looks at Peck. "I know there's nothing he can do, but someone needs to tell him."

Peck nods. "Yeah. I called Vincent on my way to Machlan's. I told him I'd keep him posted." He dangles the cup between his legs. "He was supposed to come home last month. He was gonna bring Sawyer to see Nana and surprise everyone, but Sawyer got sick and then Vincent got busy at work, and he just didn't make it happen."

"He needs to make it happen," I say. "When's the last time he's been here?"

"Christmas. I think," Peck replies. "But it's not easy having a kid and being on your own. He does the best he can."

I nod, looking at the floor. Peck is right. Vincent is a hell of a father to his kid. I'm just pissed off.

We sit quietly, the only sound coming from a cable news program on a television hanging precariously from the ceiling. I studied it earlier in-depth to take my mind off what's happening here.

"Blaire is on her way down," Lance says, looking at his phone. "She just sent me a text."

Walker gets to his feet and heads to the vending machine. He doesn't buy anything. Just looks.

I rest my head against the wall and close my eyes, imagining I'm at home and in bed, and Hadley is there at my side.

There's an unsent text in my phone to Had. I've gone back and forth in the three hours we've been here about calling her or texting her to let her know about Nana. I told Cross in a quick outburst on the way over, but he was a couple of hours away at some boxing clinic and promised he'd come by as soon as he got back to town.

She wanted space. Does this count? Or is this something I should tell her?

My lungs threaten to collapse.

I have no fucking idea, and I have no one to ask. It just feels like bullshit.

I stand but sit again.

I rough my hands down my pants.

I stand again and pace a small circle, ignoring my brothers' sideways glances.

I sit again.

What the fuck do I do?

I want her to want to know. I want her to be here, holding my hand, waiting for the doctor. I want to wipe her tears if she's sad and buy her cookies from the vending machine if she hasn't eaten.

I'm in a room surrounded by my family and a few people who are waiting on people of their own, but I couldn't be more alone. They aren't mine. They have people waiting on them, lives to go to, things to live for. And I don't.

I can't even text her.

I lost her.

I finally fucked up in the greatest way possible.

My hand grips my stomach as pain rips its way through.

"The Gibson family?" A doctor in light blue scrubs and a clipboard stands in the doorway.

We all spring to our feet. Walker walks toward him. "That's us. Do you know anything? How is she?"

"Follow me."

We scurry after him down a long hall and into a room not quite big enough for all of us to fit comfortably. We watch the doctor sit on a stool.

"I'm Dr. Moore," he says. "Mrs. Gibson is your grandmother? Is that correct?"

"Yes," we all say.

"And who might be the decision maker?"

"Blaire," I say. "Our sister. She's on her way from Chicago."

He scribbles on the clipboard. "Very well." He sets the pen down. "Your grandmother has had a myocardial infarction, or a heart attack, as it's commonly called."

"Is she going to be okay?" I ask.

"The blockages appear to be partial, which is a good thing," he says. "She's resting now. We've given her some medications to calm her down, and I expect she'll be out of it for a while, if not most of the night. She took a bit of a beating today."

I sag against the wall. "Can we see her?"

"When she wakes up, you can. But as I said, that likely won't be for a while. In the meantime, we're going to send her charts to a cardiologist and see if we can get him in here first thing in the morning.

He'll take over her case and put together the best game plan going forward."

"But she's going to live, right?" Peck asks.

"Right now, she's stable," the doctor says. "Her vitals are good, and from the information we had on file from Dr. Burns' office, she seems to be fairly healthy. I have hope, but as I tell all my patients, I'm not God. I can't guarantee anything."

Walker stands and extends a hand. "Thank you, Doctor."

"You're welcome. You should get some rest. She's going to be counting on you in the days and weeks ahead. Remember that. This is a marathon, not a sprint."

With a final nod of his head, he's out the door.

A collective exhale rattles the room as we look at each other.

"I'm not leaving," I say. "You guys do what you want, but I'm staying."

"Me too," Peck says quietly.

Walker clamps a hand on Peck's shoulder. "I'll head back to Crank and lock up. I'm not even sure we locked the damn doors." He looks at Lance. "And you look like shit."

"I feel like shit," Lance admits. "I think I got Mariah's flu."

"You go home," Walker commands.

"No. I'm fine. I'm gonna—"

"You're gonna go home." Walker narrows his eyes. "If something happens, someone will call you. But you're doing no one any good sitting around here feeling like crap. Get some rest. Get some food. And when she wakes up, and we can see her, we'll let you know."

Lance looks at the rest of us. "You guys sure?"

"Yeah. Go home," I say.

Peck nods.

Lance stands, still unsure.

"When you come back, bring us some food, okay?" I ask, figuring it'll give him something to focus on. "A burger is fine. Whatever."

"Okay."

Walker guides Lance toward the door. Before he leaves, he stops. "I'll be back soon. Call me if anything happens."

"We will," Peck says. "Hey, make sure I turned off the parts cleaner. I think I left it on." He rubs his forehead. "I'm not sure."

Walker nods and disappears out the door.

I pull out my phone and look at the unsent text to Hadley. My thumb hovers over the green button to send it.

"We probably need to go back to the waiting room," Peck says.

With a final, lingering look at my phone, I shove it back in my pocket. "Yeah. Let's go."

Chapter 35

Machlan

The waiting room on the fifth floor is quiet. An older woman was in here earlier but left a couple of hours ago. Peck sits next to me with his feet straight out and hat over his face.

Walker left around midnight after we promised we'd call for the millionth time. Blaire got stuck in traffic and didn't get in until Walker got home and went there to get a couple of hours sleep. There was nothing she could do here anyway.

I yawn, but sleep won't come. When I try, all I get is nightmares of Nana being alone in her chair having a heart attack or Hadley's voice telling me not to call her again.

I've almost lost them both in the matter of a few hours. My grip on reality wavers.

Someone turned the lights down a while ago. I turned the television off when they started jabbering about politics.

Fuck that.

I yawn again, and this time, I close my eyes. It's Hadley's voice I hear, but I try to imagine her laughter instead. My lips part into a smile. The stress on my shoulders starts to melt away just a little as I live in a fantasy world.

"Gibson family?" The door to the waiting area cracks a little more. A nurse is standing in the stream of light coming from the hall behind her. "Is the Gibson family here?"

"Yeah." I nudge Peck as I sit upright. "That's us."

"She's awake. You aren't really supposed to go in at this hour, as visiting hours were over at eight this evening, but we'll make an exception for a few minutes if you'd like to peek in and say hello."

"We would," Peck says.

We follow her down a long corridor and then through the double doors labeled Intensive Care Unit in bright red letters.

My heart beats so hard I swear Peck can hear it as we walk side by side down the hall. The shuffling of papers and the constant yet inconsistent sound of machines beeping keep the air from feeling as stuffy as it smells.

The nurse sticks her head in the room before motioning for us to go in. I make Peck go first.

"Hey," he says before I can see her. "How ya feeling, Nana?"

I step around the curtain, and my heart sinks.

She's so pale with an oxygen tube under her nose and various monitors attached to her chest and arms. Her eyes show the strain she's under.

I grip the side of her bed. She reaches for my hand but can't move for all the wires, so I reach out and touch hers instead. She squeezes me for all she's worth.

Peck takes her other hand.

"Nana," I say, choking back a sob. "What the fuck?"

She tries to shake my hand in an attempt to quiet me. "Stop that."

Peck and I look at each other and laugh quietly. He brushes away a tear from under his eye.

"If you wanted Blaire to visit, I'm sure you could've called," Peck says. "This was a little dramatic."

Nana furrows a brow. "Blaire? Here?"

"She's at Walker's," I tell her. "They won't let any of us in until morning. Well, they let Peck and me come see you for a few because we're ridiculously handsome ..." I grin as she tries to laugh. "Everyone will be here in the morning. They've all been worried sick about you."

She tries to talk, but her throat is too dry.

"Get her water," Peck says. "Beside you. On the tray."

I grab a pink pitcher and pour some water in a cup. There's a straw on the tray, so I add it. Bringing it to Nana's lips, I help her take a drink.

"Ah," she mumbles, relaxing back against the pillows. "That's better." Her voice is hoarse. "Did you boys have dinner?"

"Will you stop it?" Peck sighs. "You're in the hospital, and you're worrying if we've eaten."

"That's my job," she says. "You're getting a little thin."

"Better get out of here and make me a cheeseball then," he jokes. "How do you feel? Honestly?"

She considers this. "Like I had a heart attack, I reckon." She turns to look at me. "Want to explain why you look like you've been in a fight?"

I hang my head. "Can we do this later?"

Thankfully, the nurse pokes her head around the curtain. "We doing okay in here?"

I nod. I try to smile but can't. I can't find the fucks to pretend everything is fine. It's not.

I want to scream we almost lost our nana. That the fact we're even here means we aren't okay.

"Good," she says. "Can I get one of you to come here for a minute? I need a signature on a couple of forms."

"My sister is the power-of-attorney," I volunteer. "She'll be here in the morning."

"That's fine. If I can get someone to just sign that I gave you these forms, that's all I need tonight."

Peck looks at me. "I'll go." He brings Nana's hand to his lips and presses a kiss on her knuckles. "I love you."

"And I love you, baby. See you in the morning, all right?"

Peck nods. With a look my way, he disappears into the hallway.

"So ..." I blow out a breath. "I'm trying to decide if you're moving in with me or if I'm moving in with you."

She smacks my hand, but it lacks the gusto of her usual admonishments. "You stop that."

"Me stop? You sat in a chair and had a heart attack. You're lucky Sienna stopped by."

She looks at me. "She did? I don't remember that."

"That's what I heard. Peck came and got me." I grab a chair beside her IV pole and pull it to the side of her bed. "Do you remember anything?"

"No. The last thing I remember was watching my soap operas. Skylar just found out Octavia had his babies and fled the country."

"Who's Skylar?"

"On my show," she says. "It's a good one."

"I bet," I say, making a face.

She swats me again. This time, she grabs my hand again and holds it in hers. "I want to talk to you."

The way she says that has my stomach turning inside out. I run my free hand down my pants. "About what?"

"First, we will talk about that black eye." She winces. "You haven't looked like this in a long time."

"Please. Let's not. Another day, we can talk about it, but I can't today."

She looks at me carefully, then nods. "I had a dream the other night," she says. "I was at a wedding. It was beautiful. Pink flowers and green grass—I think it was outside."

"Lance?"

"No. *You*."

My heart sinks. It's salt in a wound, an ass fucking with no lube. It hurts, and it's raw, and if I wasn't in a hospital, I might yelp from the pain of it all.

"Sorry," I say. "Not happening for me anytime soon."

"And why is that?"

I shrug, looking at the window blinds.

"I'm going to tell you something that might make you mad. Or it might upset you, and if it does, I'm sorry, sweet boy. But if I die tonight—"

"Don't say that."

"I'll die at some point, Machlan."

I look at her. "Can you get on with it and leave out the dying shit."

She sighs. "I've let this go as long as I can. And if I don't say something, and God forbid, something happens to me, I'll roll in my grave over and over."

The beeping of the machines pierces the air, suddenly louder than they were before. I watch Nana fight to find the words.

"We can talk about this later," I offer, shifting in my seat.

"No, we can't." She takes a deep breath. "I know you had a baby with Hadley."

My blood runs cold. I try to slip my hand out of hers, but she hangs on for all she's worth.

I shiver, the words resting heavily on my already battered heart. I can't look at her and see the disappointment I know will be there. I can't do it. Not tonight.

"Nana ..."

"Something came in the mail while you were in Ohio. It was during that one month out of your whole life when I couldn't get a hold of you."

I nod, remembering that month specifically. I couldn't call her back. I didn't want to lie to her, and I didn't want her to hear the stress in my voice because she'd know something was wrong.

"Your mail was forwarded to me, and I opened it by accident," she says softly. "I'm sorry, Machlan."

I can't do this. Not today. Not after everything else.

"Nana, I love you, but I can't." My voice is as raw as my insides.

She winces as she moves until she's comfortable. "I can't imagine how hard that was for you."

Staring through the blinds at the lights below, I feel detached from reality. As though this isn't happening. As though I'm going to wake up and the past few days will be a nightmare.

"I'm not gonna lie," she says. "The fact you never told me broke my heart."

I can't look at her. I stare straight ahead and grip the arm of the chair with my left hand while she holds the right.

"Why wouldn't you tell me something like this? Why wouldn't you let me help you?"

I force a swallow. "It wasn't your responsibility."

"No, but that doesn't mean you can't rely on other people to help you. At least help you make the decision." She squeezes my hand again. "The part that kills me the most is thinking of you and Hadley alone. It breaks my heart."

Her body shakes as she cries. I stand and bend over the rail and hug her, her tears pressing into my shirt.

Tears well up in my eyes, too, as I hug her.

"I'm sorry, Nana," I say.

She pats my back and pulls away. I hand her a tissue, and she blots her eyes.

"I called you the night I got that letter," she says quietly. "And there was a resolution in your voice. For the first time, you sounded like a man. And I realized you were going to be okay. And you'd make sure Hadley was too."

Her eyes are crystal clear as she watches me.

"You made the hardest decision a parent can ever make," she says.

"I'm not a parent," I tell her. "I couldn't do it."

"You don't love that baby? Right now, your heart isn't full of love for that child?"

I look at the ground, fighting the bubble of emotion from spilling in the room. "Of course," I say, sounding hoarse. "Of course I love her."

"That's what makes you a parent, Machlan. Your love for that child. A girl?"

I nod.

"I bet she was beautiful," she says, wistfully. "I want you to know something. You didn't think of yourself. You didn't take the easy road out. You put that child and what was best for her over everything else and that's commendable."

"It feels like the easy way out sometimes," I admit.

"Easy? I beg to differ, sweetheart. Most people couldn't do what you and Hadley did. You two loved that baby more than you loved yourselves. A lot of people would've kept the child out of pride or some sense of obligation. You made a very grown-up decision at a time when you weren't one."

Something stirs deep inside my gut, maybe even my soul, as I sit on that plastic hospital chair.

"Where's Hadley now?" Nana asks.

I shake my head.

"I see. You need to fix that," she says.

"What if I can't?"

"You have to. You want to know why?"

"Why?"

"Because you'll never look at another woman like you do her. You look at her like your granddad looked at me. Like Walker looks at Sienna. Like Peck looks at a cheeseball."

I laugh softly, before feeling the heaviness of this again. I look at my grandmother. "She told me not to call her."

"Yeah, I'm sure she did because she's stopped expecting anything different out of you. When's the last time you went after her?"

I shrug, avoiding her gaze.

"She won't come back this time, honey, unless you go get her. She's not a little girl anymore. She's smart as a whip. Strong. A beautiful woman and if you don't give her something to believe in, she'll stop trying to believe in anything at all."

I pull my hand away. "I don't think she'll talk to me."

"On the phone, probably not. And if you let her leave, she

shouldn't answer it." She tries to point her finger at me, but the cords stop it. "Go to her. Now. What time is it?"

"It's late," I say. Even as I say it, I'm math-ing how much time it would take to get to Vigo and what my odds are that she'll call the police. "What if she makes me leave?"

"Play it by ear. But if you don't go, it'll be the first time in your life you've disappointed me."

There are so many more things I want to say. Things I want to ask. Things I want to get to the bottom of. But as I look at her and see the sparkle in her eye, I realize she needs this with Hadley as much as I do.

Or close.

"Nana," I say, leaning over the bedside rail. "I gotta go."

I kiss her cheek. She cups the side of my face and pats it gently.

"Tell her how much you love her," Nana advises. "Give it all you've got. This is your chance. You might not get another one."

"I love you," I tell her. "I love you so goddamn much."

She looks at the ceiling as a machine starts beeping. "Get out of here before you give me another heart attack with that mouth."

I walk backward toward the door. "Not cool, Nana. Not cool."

"Go." She chuckles, shooing me out.

Peck is at the doorway when I turn around. "Go. I got this under control."

"I owe you one."

"Just wipe my tab." He laughs. "Now get to Hadley before Logan does." He holds his hands up. "I'm kidding. I'm kidding."

I'm not.

With a spark in my step, I jog down the hall and through the double doors.

Chapter 36

Hadley

The paragraph starts to blur. Instead of putting the reading device down and turning off the light to try to sleep, I yawn.

Sleep is unattainable. My body refuses to rest, and my brain certainly won't shut off.

I try to re-read the chapter I've been on for over an hour, but it still doesn't make sense. I don't know what's not to understand about a couple having dinner and falling in love, but it's not landing.

Laying the device against my chest, the screen warm against my T-shirt, I close my eyes.

Machlan's smiling face is what I see, the default go-to of my tired brain. There were so many new experiences today at work that I should be focusing on. That I should want to focus on. This is what I've wanted—to start fresh.

But I'm not. I still see him.

I wonder how long it'll take to stop thinking of him every ten seconds. How long does it take to stop a habit you've had for most of your life? Probably longer than two days. Maybe even two years. But at least there's an end in sight.

When I open my eyes, only a minute has passed.

Ripping off the blankets, I swing over the side, and my feet hit the carpeted floor. I pad through the bedroom into the darkened living room. I pause at a window and peer into the starless night sky.

Somewhere out there is Machlan. And with him is a piece of my heart I'll never get back. I don't even want it back. I gave it to him willingly. It belongs with him. I just have to figure out how to live without a whole heart.

"Stop it," I chastise myself.

I step into the kitchen and flip on the light. I'm reminded of the night making grilled cheese with Mach and how he cut them into four little squares like a madman instead of in half diagonally. I can't fight the grin that comes with the memory or the way my heart feels like it bleeds a little.

As I turn to open the fridge, a thud rumbles through the air. It's a low-frequency sound. I almost feel it more than I hear it. My hand freezes midair as I listen.

A neighbor's dog barks, and I'm suddenly hyper-alert. Something jingles. Shoes scrape against the concrete porch. What has to be a flower pot falling from its perch on the little stand by the front door rings out like a bell.

"Oh, my God," I mutter.

I look through the dark living room to my bedroom. My phone is on my bedside table. My heart pounds in my chest, my breathing so quick I'm afraid whoever is lurking around can hear it.

I tiptoe to the doorway. The darkness of the living room sets off a shot of panic as I suddenly feel exposed. It's common knowledge if you stand in the light and someone else is standing in the dark, they can see you, but you can't see them.

I flick the light off.

The only light now comes from the little piece of glass at the top of the front door to my right. It's an orange glow from the streetlight outside. The trees move, casting shadows through the foyer, and I tell myself not to panic. Panicked women die. I also remember vaguely to scream fire and not help because no one will help unless it's a fire. I read that somewhere once.

As soon as my foot hits the floor of the living room, a soft knock raps against the front door. I dash into my bedroom and leap from the doorway onto the bed as if it's a safe zone of some kind.

My heart pounds, white noise rushing by my ears. My body trembles as if I'm cold as I grab my phone off the nightstand. My finger goes to the emergency call when I look at the locked screen.

Machlan: Hey. If you're awake, will you let me in?

Another knock rolls through the house.

My stomach flips.

I can't breathe.

Maybe I read that wrong.

Machlan: It's me. I'm at your front door.

Tears well despite my best efforts tonight to rein them in.

I want to run to the door and rip it open because he came. But, then again, I want to tell him to fuck off and stop this madness.

I can't do that. Even I know that.

Machlan: Please let me in, Had.

There's no way this is real.

I pinch a piece of flesh on the inside of my thigh.

"Shit!" I hiss, shaking my leg.

Machlan: Please.

I climb off the bed. My phone still tucked in my hand, my legs wobbling beneath me, I walk through the house.

An eerie silence settles over me. I don't check my ponytail or look in the mirror for any sleep in my eyes. I just flip on the light in the foyer.

Everything stills inside my body. My hand completely level as I reach for the handle.

"Who is it?" I say, just in case.

"Machlan."

His voice hits me right in the heart. I look at the ceiling as I open the door and will myself to stay strong. When I look down at him, I almost break.

Dark circles make his brown eyes look hollow. His bottom lip is cracked, and a slight bruise sits on top of his cheekbone on the right side. His hair sticks out everywhere, a hat not to be found.

He tries to smile, but it's like he doesn't have the energy for it. "You have other guys coming by this time of night?"

It's an ode to a few days ago when he would come to the apartment above Crave and give me hell. It seems like ages ago.

"What do you want, Mach?"

"Can I come in?"

I lean against the door. It's not a quick drive here, and it's almost three in the morning. It would be rude not to invite him in, but if I do, I'm just screwing myself.

"Why are you here?" I ask. "It's the middle of the night."

"I needed to see you."

My heart skips a beat. "You could've called."

"I did." His smile fades. "You told me not to call you back."

"And that made you think it was okay to show up?"

My hands itch to reach for him, my arms begging to hold him. He looks so tired, so sad, that all I want to do is make him feel better. But if I do that, who is going to put me back together?

I'll just be sucked into a never-ending cycle, and I'm too tired for it. I can't anymore.

"I've had a long day," he says, his voice gruff. He runs his hands down his face, blowing out a breath. When he looks at me again, he's resolved. "I'm sorry."

"For what?" I ask.

"Where do I start?"

"I don't know. You're the one that showed up here." The longer I look at him, the quicker my determination to keep him away melts.

His stomach growls. He frowns. "As I said, it's been a long night."

The neighbor's dog starts barking again, and a light comes on in the house beside me. As much as I know I shouldn't I give in, I can't screw up everyone's night because of this.

"Fine. Come in." I pull open the door and step to the side. Before he can reach for me, which I'm fairly certain he's about to do, I head to the kitchen and flip on a light.

He sits at the table without being asked. His clothes are wrinkled, his shoulders sagging. He looks like hell.

I grab a couple of pieces of pizza from the fridge, pop them on a paper plate, and shove them in the microwave. "What's going on? I have to work in the morning," I say.

He leans forward, his elbows resting on his knees. "There's something I've never said to you that I need to say."

The microwave buzzes. I take out the plate and hand it to him. He sits it on the table without even looking at it.

"I don't want to be nice to you," I say. "I just can't take people being hungry."

He searches my eyes. A small smile touches his slightly swollen lips. "I love you, Hadley."

My insides shake as I stare at him. "No, Mach. Don't do this," I say, backing away. "Please, don't do this."

Tears fill my eyes—years' worth of emotions springing forward. He's a blur in front of me. An unmoving, quiet mess of a vision that I can't deal with right now.

"I'm going to bed," I say. "Let yourself out."

"I'm not leaving."

I look at the ceiling as the tears drip down my face. "Why do you do this to me? Why can't you just let me be?"

"You want to know why? I'll tell you why." He walks across the room until he's in front of me. "I might've thought I fought for you our whole life. Hell, I got into two fights a couple of days ago over you. Both of them," he says, his voice rushed. "But I was wrong, Had."

I look into his face—his handsome, grief-stricken face. My distrust of him is at odds with the earnestness of his voice. I want to believe him. It would be so easy to. And really, he probably means it. But will he mean it tomorrow? Or the day after that? And the day after that?

It takes everything I have to tell him to go. "I need you to leave."

"No. I'm fighting for us now," he says, resting his hand on my arm.

"I've fought for you over and over, and you push me away every time."

He nods. "I know. I'm a fucking idiot."

"Mach ..." My voice is full of tears, both shed and unshed. I don't even try to stop them because it would be futile.

"When I look at you, I don't just see the most beautiful girl I've ever seen. I see the next sixty years of my life."

My breathing hiccups as I try to keep my emotions contained. They spill over my walls like a tropical storm that hits out of nowhere.

My heart breaks from the pain in his face and the loneliness in mine. But if I fix one, it'll only exacerbate the other. If I hold him, it'll hurt that much more tomorrow when he leaves. And if I make him leave, it'll add more pain to him tonight.

For the first time in my life, since the day he walked in while I was sorting clothes, I pick me.

"I'm so glad you've come to this realization, but it's too late," I say, wiping my face with the back of my hand.

"It's never too late."

"Why is this supposed to matter to me now?" I ask, feeling engulfed in a situation I couldn't manage before. "What caused this change of heart?"

A sadness drifts across his eyes. "It doesn't matter."

"No, it does. Because all of a sudden I'm going to be okay and here you are." I shake my head. "I'm out. I've tried. I've fought for you until I can't fight anymore. I don't want to."

"Give me one more chance," he says.

"Why? What will be so different this time?" I throw up my hands. "You're only here because I stopped chasing you. You knew I was serious, so you had to run me down and keep me in the loop."

"You seriously think that?"

"I don't know," I say, my anger getting the best of me. "What will stop you from not telling me about things you tell Navie about? Because you told her about Spencer before you told me, didn't you?"

His face falls.

I laugh at how betrayed I feel. "Just go."

"I'm not leaving."

I'm too tired to fight. Too broken to argue. I have to work in a few hours, and I'll be damned if he's going to ruin that too.

I turn around and head to my bedroom. "If you need to sleep, do it on the sofa. But be gone before I get up."

There's no way I can look at him. So I don't.

Leaving him standing in the middle of the living room, I take my tear-stricken face into my room, close the door, and lock it. I climb into bed, pull the covers up, and cry myself to sleep.

Chapter 37

Machlan

I haven't moved.

The sun started to come up a half hour ago, filling the little living room with a subdued light. It's a cloudy day from the looks of it, and that's fitting.

Her things are scattered around, many of them things I can place. I know where she got the little picture frame that holds a picture of her and Cross on the mantle, and the vase sitting on the little shelf was a Water Festival purchase the year we had our daughter.

I've mostly stared at her bedroom door all night and told myself I can't go in there. I can't bust it down even though I could with probably nothing more than a hard hit of my shoulder. I don't even get up to find the bathroom in case she comes out. I want her to see I'm still here when she does.

I'll be here forever.

Peck has sent me a few texts, letting me know Nana will have more tests today. She fell asleep right after I left, and he sent a few pictures of himself in the waiting room in various precarious positions. It helped what was left of the night pass.

Blowing out a breath, I fight to stay awake. I'm drained. Utterly and completely drained. It would be easy to rest my head against the sequined pillow that spells Hello when you run your hand over it and fall asleep.

But I don't.

A soft rummaging comes from the other side of the six-paneled door. My phone chirps and my attention is pulled between it and Hadley's room.

Taking it out of my pocket, I see a text from Peck.

> Peck: All good here. Lance got here first thing with Blaire. You sure she isn't a doctor?

> Me: Tell her not to piss anyone off until I get there.

> Peck: Too late. LOL

I laugh, shaking my head.

> Me: I'll be there as soon as I can. Keep me posted.

"What's so funny?" Hadley asks.

My head snaps up. I get to my feet like a stumbling idiot.

She looks beautiful with her sleepy eyes and messy hair, despite the glare she's shooting my way. It's a good thing I see through it.

"Good morning," I say.

"Why are you still here?"

"I told you I wasn't leaving." I shrug.

She breezes by me. "I have to work today. Please don't fuck up my head and cost me my job."

I stifle my usual reaction of saying something asshole-ish. She's going to do what she wants. I might as well get used to this since I'm in it for the long haul.

"Go to work," I say, following her. "I'll be here when you get back."

"No, Mach." She spins on her heel. "Why won't you just leave?"

"You wanna know why?" I move across the kitchen until I'm standing in front of her. Her cheeks are tear-stained, her lips plump from crying. She's so goddamn pretty. "I'm not leaving because you never left me."

"Until I did. And now, all of a sudden, you're here. Typical you."

I grab an orange out of a bowl on the table and peel it. She rolls her eyes and starts to make coffee.

I have no idea how this is going to work or what will happen if she does take a long time to give in. She is as stubborn as me. Who will run Crave? I have no clothes. I have to check on Nana.

But as she turns around and puts a hand on her lip, I realize I'll figure it out. She's the top of the totem pole. She's the only thing that really matters right now.

"I'll make dinner while you're at work," I offer. "Want anything in particular?"

The Keurig latch slams in place. "I have dinner plans tonight."

"Oh, really? With who?" I shove two orange segments into my mouth, so I can't say anything stupid because she's about to. I can see it on her face.

"Samuel." She fires a challenge in my direction, and it lands. Hard.

My insides burn as I struggle not to let her see my fury. I chew the fruit slowly, considering my response. By the time I swallow, she's irritated.

"You can bring him by here," I say, the fruit adding to the acid in my stomach. "I'll make enough for all three of us."

"I hate you."

"I don't blame you. I'd hate me if I were you until I realized how much I saw the error of my ways."

She takes her coffee cup from the machine. "You can't see the error of your ways because you're always right. The all-knowing. The one who gets to decide everyone's fate."

I grab her elbow and spin her around. The coffee sloshes around the mug but doesn't spill. She gasps for breath as she looks at me.

"I was wrong. Okay? I thought I was helping you by just taking me off your plate so you could walk away. That's stupid. I see it now."

"Totally stupid."

"I know. And if I'm being honest, I pushed you away for me too. Because if you weren't here and a witness to my failures, then that was a little easier. And it was easier not to have to think I tainted you with my shortcomings."

"You don't think I know your shortcomings?" she asks. "I know your failures better than anyone, Mach. And there are a lot of them. But I have a lot of them too," she adds.

She sets the coffee down but doesn't take her eyes off me.

"We're both imperfect, Mach. We've both made mistakes in our lives. But the thing is, I try not to repeat them. You're hell-bent on doing them over and over."

"Until now."

"Which is a miracle I can't believe." She raises a brow. "Look, Mach—"

"Listen to me," I say, reaching for her hand. I'm surprised she lets me have it. "I love you. I'm so fucking in love with you it scares the shit out of me, okay? What if something happens to you?"

A knowing look flickers through her eyes. "You weren't responsible for what happened to your parents, Machlan."

"I know. I do," I say when I see she's about to argue with me. "I know shit happens. But look at what happened to me in the wake of all that. Do you know what would happen to me if something happened to you? I'd die, Had. I'd fucking die."

My voice wobbles as I hope she gets it.

"Something does happen to me every time you don't love me back. I die." She smiles sadly. "You can't control everything. Being alone doesn't make you impenetrable."

"If I've learned anything over the past few days, it's that I can't control jack shit. Trust me. And half the things I think I know, I don't. The only thing I know for sure is that you love me, and I'm one lucky son-of-a-bitch for that."

I think back to my talk with Nana and the things Cross said. I take Hadley's other hand in mine. The feeling of her palms in mine, the softness of her skin, the fact that she's still here when she shouldn't be has a tear trickling down my cheek.

"You're the smartest person I know. You're the strongest person I know. You're the most patient and kind and thoughtful person I've ever met," I say. "So, I'm going to give you all the facts and let you decide what you want. And whatever that is, I'll respect it."

She seems amused by this, which is fine. I am too.

The truth is, I need her to choose me. I need her to look at me like a baby standing in front of her and still decide I'm the right choice. I need her to choose me and forever with me.

My heart pounds, my palms sweat as I look at her.

"Okay," she says. "Shoot. What are my options?"

Her hands relax, and her fingers lace with mine. I'm not sure she realizes she's doing it.

"I promise not to let my shit get in the way of you and me. And if I start to do it, I want you to call me out on it, which I know you'll hate doing."

She pretends to consider this.

I take a deep, shaky breath.

"I'll just … I'll love you. And I'll take your love, which is hard for me because I start overthinking everything and …"

She places a hand over my mouth and takes a step toward me. The jade flecks shine like the stars on a clear night, and I want to kiss her like she needs to be kissed. But I can't. Not yet.

I'm going to spell it out, bare it all, and if she says yes, I'm all in. I'll be in so far she won't know what hit her.

"I want to grow old with you," I whisper as she drops her hands. "I want to fall asleep next to you and wake up with you curled up against me, making me too hot. I want to fix you grilled cheese when I come home from the bar and hold you when you have a bad day."

"I want you to hold me when I have good days, too."

My heart beats a mile a minute. "I love you more, Hadley. Not more than you love me, but more than all our fights and disagreements. I love you more than the bad days and the bullshit we'll have to go through in life. Because if I have to go through it, I don't want to do it without you."

"Oh, Mach ..."

Her voice cracks as she wraps her arms around my waist. She buries her head in my chest, and I hold her so tight I think I might break her.

"All I can promise you is you'll never find someone to love you more than me," I say, kissing the top of her head.

She pulls back and looks up at me. "You know if you would've done this a long time ago, it would've stopped a lot of problems, right?"

"Yeah."

She bites her lip. "You're serious. Right? Like you won't leave or second-guess this or back away once reality hits you."

"No."

"I swear on my life, if you pull that shit again, I won't come back, and I'll find the one guy in the world who will drive you absolutely crazy and marry him on the spot."

"You're pushing it." I give her a look.

"I mean it. I'll marry Logan just to spite you."

She laughs.

As the sound washes over my ears, I think back to what Lance said about getting married. And then I think about Nana lying in the hospital bed, the wedding ring on her finger from a man who's been dead for years.

Looking at Hadley, I kick myself for all the years we've wasted because of me. Letting another day go by seems like such a waste of a life. Too many days have come and gone to forfeit another.

I suck in a breath, my head spinning, but I've never felt more confident in a decision than this one.

"You've never really been mine but have always been mine," I say.

"Your fault."

"Yes. My fault," I agree. "I don't have a ring because I didn't think this out, but thinking gets me in trouble sometimes, and I'm really trying to just go with the flow here and do what's right and ..." I take a deep breath, bending on one knee. "Will you marry me, Hadley Jacobs?"

She jerks her hands out of mine and covers her mouth. Tears stream, her body shaking so hard I can't quite figure out if this is good or bad.

"Only you," she says, laughing through the tears. "Only you can go from one to one thousand in half a second."

"I'm doing what feels right," I say, a nervous wobble to my voice.

"And you want to propose?"

"Even if you say no, I'll love you and I'll convince you that—"

She hits me in the chest before propelling herself at me. I fall backward, holding her as I land on the floor.

She continues to cry, but now, it's intermixed with crazy, wild laughter. I just keep my arms around her and hope for the best.

Because that's all I can do.

Hope for the best and love her until the day I die.

Chapter 38

Machlan

"I should've driven my car." Hadley leans against my shoulder and pops a Swedish Fish in her mouth.

"It was your choice."

She taps me with the side of her head. "Stop saying that."

"Everything is your choice. The candy at the gas station. Whether you go to work or quit your brand-new job. Whether you move in with me."

"I just accepted a marriage proposal." She sits up and laughs. "Should I not move in with you?"

"It's your choice." I smirk, reaching over and grabbing her thigh. "Whatever you want."

"If you say that again, I'm gonna kill you." She pops another candy in her mouth. "What am I going to do now? I just quit a job I had for a day." She makes a face while she chews. "I don't think I would've liked it anyway."

As I glance at her out of the corner of my eye, a spark of anxiety flickers in my gut. "You aren't having second thoughts, are you?"

She grins slowly, another red candy sliding past her lips.

"Can you not fuck with me right now?" I ask. "I'm trying to be this nice, good guy and back off and let you do your thing, but when you look at me like that when I ask you something this fucking serious, it makes me wanna—"

"What? What's it make you wanna do, Mach?"

I study her for a long second. "It makes me want to turn the truck down one of these side roads and pull you on my lap and have you ride me until I come in your pussy."

"Do it." She gulps.

I snicker.

"Come on," she says, reaching across the truck and grabbing the crotch of my pants. I groan, thrusting my hips toward her. "Chicken."

"I can't. I have somewhere to be."

"Oh, you do, do you?" She settles back in her seat. "And where might that be?"

"I need to get to the hospital."

"The hospital? Why?"

My foot eases up on the accelerator. Peck said she's fine in a text he sent right before we left Hadley's. Still, I haven't told Hadley, and I'm not sure how she'll take me not telling her until now.

"Nana is in the intensive care unit," I say carefully.

"What?" The candy flies off her lap as she twists to look at me. "What are you talking about?"

"She had a heart attack yesterday."

"And you didn't tell me?" Her jaw drops. "You were at my house when she was in the hospital? Machlan!"

I take my hand off her leg. "Trust me. She was fine with it." I rough my hand over my chin. "We were there all afternoon yesterday until, well, whatever time I showed up last night."

"And you didn't tell me? Is she okay?"

Looking at her, I let her see the somberness in my features. "I didn't tell you because I didn't want it to be about that. I want this moment to be about us. I didn't want you to think I showed up at your house because of that. I didn't."

She nods, mulling that over. "But ... is she okay?" she asks softly.

"She's okay. Peck has been texting me. Everyone is there. Even Blaire." I catch a look of concern on her face. "I know Blaire can be scary, but she'll love you."

"She's so not like me, Mach," she says warily. "She's ... extra."

"Extra?" I burst out laughing. "That's a good way to put it. Extra. I'll tell her that."

"Don't you dare," she warns. "She'll kill me with one look. I've never been terrified of someone my entire life except Blaire."

"Chicken," I tease.

"Damn right. Now, back to Nana."

"Anyway," I say, "they're running tests today to see how bad it was. I talked to her for a long time last night, and she sounded strong."

Hadley rests her head on my shoulder again. "I can't believe you left her, though. She wasn't alone, was she?"

"She had Peck. He was convincing her to get better to make cheeseballs. Trust me, they're fine." I kiss the side of her head. "She told me to leave, actually."

"Why?"

"She told me to go get you." I extend my arm toward her. "She pointed out a lot of good things, some of them we'll talk about someday, and made me realize I'd never get over you. So I might as well go get you."

She wraps an arm around my middle. The cab of the truck is warm. Soft country music plays on the stereo, and Hadley hums along as we go down the road.

I think about Nana and all the things she said. And about my parents and how my mother always said to find our blessings.

That's been a hard one for me over the years—to find my blessings. A lot of my life felt as if I'd been robbed of most of them. But right now, sitting here with Hadley, going to see my Nana and getting to see my extra sister that doesn't come home nearly enough, I feel pretty fucking blessed.

Mom used to say blessings weren't always pretty. That sometimes they came hidden, and you had to pluck them out of the ugly and use them.

Maybe a blessing was Hadley finally getting fed up with my shit. Maybe a blessing was Nana getting shook up enough to have a conversation that wasn't easy for either of us. If those things are true, I have to use them. Otherwise, they'll go to waste.

"Can I ask you something?" I ask.

"You just did."

"Ha. Ha. Ha." I bend my arm around her back and snuggle her closer to my side. "It's your choice, but—"

"Fucking stop it." She laughs. "You're going to run this in the ground, aren't you?"

I chuckle. "Seriously. I would like to get married sooner than later."

"I don't know ..." She tries to pull away, but I don't let her. I need her close, touching me, while she thinks about what I've said.

My stomach swirls with apprehension as she quiets. Maybe I shouldn't have brought it up, but I had to. It's the right call.

"I do know."

"You're sure?" she asks. "You don't have to rush this, Mach."

"I don't *have* to do anything. But I *want* to marry you as soon as possible."

She tries to rise up again. This time, I let her go.

"Why?" she asks, her eyes full of concern.

"When you know, you know." I shrug. "And I'd like Nana to be there when it happens. And I'd like to stop wasting fucking time pretending it isn't going to happen because we've done that for long enough."

She doesn't answer. As I turn my head to try to get a hold of her reaction, she scoots all the way next to me.

"This has nothing to do with anything but me and you," I tell her. "Whatever comes our way, we'll figure it out together. I mean, can you imagine us fighting on the same side for once?"

Her mouth covers mine. I laugh against her lips, trying to see over her head so we don't wreck. "Had," I mumble. "I can't see."

She pulls back, smiling wickedly. "Don't worry." Her hands go to the button of my jeans.

I gasp as she undoes the button. The zipper cracks through the air.

"You'll be able to see over me from here," she says.

"Oh, God," I mutter through clenched teeth as she licks the top of my cock.

My phone buzzes from the holder by the radio, and I see a text from Peck.

Peck: Taking her back for tests. Will be a couple of hours. Don't rush. Everything is fine.

I take a quick right onto a dirt road. The abrupt motion makes her grip my thighs so she doesn't fall to the floor.

"Where are we going?" she asks as she sits up and looks around.

"I'm trying something new today."

"You aren't trusting your phone for directions, are you? Mine almost ran me off a bridge the other day."

I laugh. "No. Not that."

"Then what?"

"We're going to go to the hospital in a minute. I'm going to be there for my family. But starting today, you come first."

I pull off the road behind a little-abandoned shed. I kill the engine and look at her.

Hadley grins. "I hope that has a double meaning."

I grab her, making her squeal, as I pull her on my lap. "Whatever you want."

She smacks my chest, starting to tear into me, but I smother her with kisses.

Epilogue

Hadley

"Yours looks better than mine." Sienna makes a face, holding up a bowl of scalloped potatoes. "Are they supposed to look like this?"

I shrug. "I don't know. But they look a little dark."

"Is that a nice way to say burnt?" Sienna laughs. "I should've ordered this at Peaches, put it in a dish at home, and brought it over. My mom does that sometimes."

Mariah laughs. "Well, the baked beans are stuck to the bottom of the kettle, so there's that."

"We're a mess, girls." Sienna shrugs. "None of this may be edible."

"Peck will eat it," I say, leading everyone to the table. "If nothing else, we'll send it all home with him."

We enter Nana's dining room to see our men all settled around the table. Nana is at the head, the color in her face a little rosier than it has been. I get why. It would be hard to feel like crap surrounded by the Gibson boys.

Peck takes the bowl of potatoes from Sienna and doesn't comment a bit about how black the top is. Walker and Lance discuss one of the Landry businesses Sienna's family runs as I sit next to Machlan.

It's been a week since Nana was released from the hospital. The ten days she was admitted was one of the most interesting experiences of my life. I've never seen anything like it.

One of her grandchildren was always with her. No one complained or couldn't make it, not one of them ever bailed. The four of them traded off with the expertise of a well-oiled machine with this woman in the center.

Mariah, Sienna, and I stayed too when Blaire left. She had a big case in Chicago and had to leave after a couple of days. Seeing Blaire, this gorgeous, powerful woman, break down in tears beside Nana's bed was a scene I'll never forget. The love and acceptance are something I've always wanted, the feeling of being together through thick and thin. Having them accept me into the fold makes me feel like I'm walking in the clouds.

"Peck, will you say grace?" Nana asks.

Machlan takes my hand and holds it under the table as Peck says grace. I watch him out of the corner of my eye during the prayer. His eyes are closed, a silent prayer of his own going up to the man upstairs. It fills me with a warmth I can't explain.

Hands reach for spoons, Nana dishing out instructions to add more butter here and to give the baked beans a final stir.

I catch Machlan watching me. He raises a brow, and I nod.

"Hey," he says over the chaos of the table. "Had and I have something we want to say."

Everything quiets. All eyes shift to Mach.

"Hadley and I have decided something," he says. He nudges me with a mischievous grin. "You tell them."

"We're getting married," I say.

I bow my head as everyone celebrates, a mixture of clapping and cheering with a few jabs thrown in from Peck. My heart threatens to explode at the happiness everyone shows for us. When I finally look up, I see Nana.

She's wiping her eyes with a napkin, wearing the sweetest, softest grin on her face. She reaches for Machlan, and he takes her hand.

"Hadley, sweetheart, I can't tell you how happy this makes this old lady," Nana says. "I love you, little girl."

"I love you, Nana," I say.

This shouldn't make me want to cry, but it does. No one has said they love me except my brother, and Machlan as of late, since I was in high school. To hear her say it makes my lips tremble.

"We're going to elope," Machlan jokes to take the attention off me.

Nana taps the top of his hand and gives him a no-nonsense look. "I'll hear none of that," she says. "I've put up with you all these years, and you aren't cutting me out of the good part now."

"He's kidding, Nana," I say.

"Good. Because if you let them elope, we're eloping," Lance says. "I mean, we even have a good excuse."

There's something about the way he says it that has everyone looking at him.

Mariah smacks Lance's shoulder. He must've put his foot in his mouth because his eyes go wide. Mariah casts him a glare that really doesn't look mean before setting her fork next to her plate.

"Everyone," Mariah says, clearing her throat. "We're going to adopt a baby."

"Oh, dear sweet Jesus," Nana says, clutching her chest. "Are you really?"

"We are," Lance says. "We've been going through the process for a while. It'll help things if we're married, which is why we floated the idea of eloping."

"I still don't like it," Nana says, "but if it speeds things up, maybe we can do something here. Would you be up for that?"

Mariah beams. "Nana, I just want to be his wife. We can do it in your kitchen if that works. It doesn't matter to me."

"You come here and hug me," Nana says.

"I really hope you and Sienna will help me get a nursery together, Hadley. I have no idea what I'm doing, and I need some help." She smiles at me across the table. "I don't know the first thing about this, and I'm so nervous."

"Of course," I say. "I'd love to."

Sienna carries on about a designer she knows. Machlan wraps an arm around my shoulders.

"You okay?" he whispers. "With the nursery thing?"

I nod, looking into his eyes. "I am. I'm really happy for them."

Nana sniffles. "You kids are gonna make sure I have another heart attack, aren't you?"

"Not funny," Walker and Machlan say at the same time.

She dabs at her eyes again. "Two weddings and a baby. Walker, what do you have for me?"

"Oh, that's not putting him on the spot." Peck snorts.

Walker's chest puffs out like a peacock. "Well, since you asked so nicely." He grins. "Sienna just got a huge contract for designing gowns for a bridal company."

"That's amazing," I say. "I didn't know you did that!"

"She can design anything," Walker beams.

Sienna's smile lights up the room. "I got the contract a while ago, but with Nana being sick and then I had the flu ..." She fires a look at Lance. "I know I got it from you."

"How'd you get it from me?" he asks.

"You came over that day to get the soup I made for Mariah and left your germs."

"That soup was excellent, by the way," Mariah tosses in.

"You made soup, and I didn't get any?" Peck asks. "Sienna. I'm hurt."

Walker sighs. "She's my girlfriend. Not yours. How many goddamn times do I have to tell you that?"

Sienna laughs, resting her head on Walker's shoulder. "I'll make you some tomorrow, Peck."

"Thanks." He smiles smugly at Walker. "And since everyone is listening to me for a change, I have some news of my own."

"They aren't going to like it," I tell him.

He and I exchange a look at the news he shared with me last night. I want to be excited for him. I want to encourage him and be happy for him, but I'm not. And they won't be either.

"I don't care if they like it or not," he tells me

"Just prepare yourself," I say.

"Will someone tell the rest of us?" Machlan asks. "And I don't like you two having secrets."

"Watch him," Walker says, taking a bite of beans. "He'll try to steal your woman."

Peck glares at Walker and then at Machlan.

He fills his fork full of scalloped potatoes and takes a bite. He winces as he swallows the burnt potatoes but doesn't say a word about it. He just washes it down with a drink of iced tea.

"Any day now, asshole," Machlan says, getting a look from Nana.

"I have a date." Peck sits up, shoulders back, and grins.

"Navie?" Machlan asks.

"Nope. Molly."

"What the fuck?" Machlan asks.

"Machlan Daniel. Enough," Nana says.

"I told you," I tell Peck.

"Oh, wait till you meet her," Lance tells Nana. "You'll be 'What the fuck-ing' along with the rest of us."

Peck's face falls. "Guys, be nice. I don't give you hell."

"Yes, you do," they say in unison, making everyone, even Nana, laugh.

"I'm sure she's a nice girl if Peck likes her," Nana offers.

"That's one way to put it," Walker mumbles. "She's nice to everyone, if you catch my drift."

Peck shrugs and goes back to his meal. "Well, I'm looking forward to it. Things are starting to come around."

The table breaks out into chatter again, everyone sparring back and forth in typical Gibson fashion. Machlan takes my hand again and holds it while we eat.

I take my time, eating slowly and taking in the love and family around me. I've wanted this my entire life. For a while, I didn't think I'd ever have it.

But as I sit at Nana's table, listening to Peck give Walker crap about a tractor at Crank and watching Machlan dote on his grandmother, I realize something: things like this, like what's sitting around this table, don't happen overnight. You can't force them to happen. You can't make them *not* happen. You just have to water them with love and give them room to breathe and enough support to anchor the roots into the foundation of something good.

If Machlan and I had tried to stay together years ago, our roots weren't planted yet. They would've given in to the weight of the world and we wouldn't fallen on our faces.

All those years of not being together weren't in vain. They weren't a waste, like Machlan thinks. They were a way to build us up to this point so we can enjoy it now.

I look at the little tattoo on my wrist. Machlan catches me looking at it and lifts my arm to his lips. He presses a kiss where the wings meet, letting his lips linger on my skin for a long moment.

"I love you," I whisper.

He smiles my favorite smile. The one that's just for me. "I love you too."

The End

CRAZY, Peck's story is live now on Amazon, Audible, and is in Kindle Unlimited. Continue reading for Chapter One ...

Meet Peck Ward

Peck

"It's *you.*"

A pair of red flip-flops come to a stop next to the truck. Dust billows from the harder-than-necessary halt to movement and flows under the truck and right into my face. I wave my hand in front of me and cough.

"Yeah?" I ask. "What's your point?"

Toenails painted the color of grass on a spring day tap against the gravel. A thin gold ring adorns the second toe.

"Are you proud of yourself?" she asks.

The tone she's using nixes any ideas I may have had to scoot out from underneath this vehicle. It has that flair to it, that you've-done-and-gone-screwed-up-but-I'm-going-to-make-you-wallow-a-while thing that turns men's blood to ice.

The only problem is that I can't figure out what I've done. Or who she is.

I drop the wrench in my hand and study the tanned legs visible from my disadvantageous position. They're short and tanned, the muscles in her calves flexing as she pops one foot up on her toe.

The voice—one that's clearly annoyed with me for some reason—isn't familiar, nor are the legs. A quick scan of recent activity doesn't unearth a woman who should be pissed. Not that a woman needs a reason to be pissed, but still.

"Well," I say, "it depends on why you're asking."

"What's that supposed to mean?"

"It means that if you're asking if I'm proud of the fact that I diagnosed and will have Dave's truck fixed in under an hour—minus the time I spend in this conversation with you—then yes. I am. Or if you're asking about the black lines down the middle of Main Street, I'm proud of that too. I—"

"That's not what I mean, and you know it."

"Do I?" I scratch the top of my head.

Staring at the undercarriage, I attempt to figure out what the heck is happening here. The day has been a doozy already. Between Nana calling me at four in the morning because she couldn't get out of bed and my cousin Walker's pissy mood when I got to work at his mechanic's shop, Crank, I should've just called in sick. I should've stayed in bed instead of trying to make the best out of the day.

Sometimes, you just know better. I knew better this morning. I'm just not smart enough to listen to myself.

"You're a jerk, you know that?" she says with a huff. She shifts her weight from one foot to the other. "No, I take that back. You're more than that. You're a jackass."

"What in the world are you talking about?"

"You know what I'm talking about."

"Um, nope. I really don't."

"Yes, you do. Now come out here and face me like a man."

"If you insist," I mutter.

Pressing my heels into the gravel, I roll myself out from under the truck. The sun is bright, almost blinding me with its early afternoon rays. I shield my eyes and look up into the face of a woman who looks like she wants to kill me.

Her bright green eyes widen just a bit before resuming their narrowed position. A set of full lips are pressed together in a hard line. Her face is framed by a couple of unruly strands of sandy brown hair that's fallen from a lopsided ponytail.

I bite back a smile. I'm one hundred percent certain I'm supposed to be intimidated and not entertained right now, but I can't help it. She's fucking adorable.

"Well, here I am," I say.

She takes a step back. Her eyes release from mine and drag down the length of my body. When they return to my face, she narrows them again. "You're a jackass."

"You've said that." I get to my feet and brush off my hands. "Look, do I know you? Not that I don't love being yelled at by a stranger ..."

"You are incredible," she says, dropping those pretty little lips of hers open.

"Thanks." I smile. The gesture does not get returned. "If you're Tad's daughter or something, tell him I put the gas cans back. It was an emergency. I swear. Just tell him they're behind the shovels in the barn, and I'll pay him back. Okay?"

She cocks a brow. "And you steal gas too. Wow. What a winner."

"You're awfully judgy for someone who doesn't even know me."

"I know all I want to know about you."

"That's a shame," I say, sliding my hands down my jeans.

A gasp sneaks through the air as her hands fall to her sides in exasperation. I take a step back for self-preservation. Just in case.

"Are you hitting on me?" She blinks once, then twice.

"No," I say. "I mean, if you want me to, I'd—"

She throws her hands up in the air. "She said you worked fast and would move on without thinking twice about it, but I had hoped that she'd be wrong."

"Who? Who said that? I have no clue what you're talking about."

She lets out a little laugh that's anything but funny. I wait for steam to come out of her ears, but the only thing rolling off her is the scent of oranges.

I glance around for cameras because this has to be a joke. Surely, one of my cousins is setting me up. But the longer I look, the more it becomes apparent: she's as serious as a heart attack.

"You're exactly like she said you'd be," she says.

I rub my forehead, wishing once again I'd have stayed home. I have a good twenty minutes left on this truck and then a fifteen-minute drive back to Crank to clock out. Then I need to check on Nana and make sure she got lunch before I can go home and get a shower and close my damn eyes. But before any of that can happen, I have to figure out what the hell this girl is talking about.

Blowing out a breath, I focus.

"Let's just restart this whole thing," I say. "What's your name?"

"We're really doing this?"

"Doing what?" I hold my hands in front of me. "What are we really doing? I don't get it."

She flashes me a disapproving look. "You're really asking my name?"

"That's what ya do when you don't know somebody. At least it is around here."

"Fine. I'll play along. I'm Dylan," she says as if she's talking to a baby. "And we talked last week about how much you love my best friend."

The last part of that gets loud. Really, really loud. She takes my cringing as a sign of weakness.

She moves toward me, her eyes flashing her fury at me like bolts of lightning. Her finger jabs me in the chest.

"You better be scared of me," she says. "Thinking you're gonna ghost her like some careless asshole after she opens up to you about—"

"Whoa, wait—"

"No, I'm not gonna wait." She jabs me again, harder this time. Her face twists when I don't budge. "I shouldn't have even shown up out here because that probably will make your ego explode."

My brain scrambles with her accusation but gets even more fogged up with the look in her eyes. Worry is etched on her face.

"Listen, I'm sorry about your friend. Honest. But—"

"I highly doubt that." She takes a deep breath, the passion starting to wane as she thinks her point has been delivered. "You better stay away from her. Do you hear me?"

I have no idea what we're doing here, but I feel bad for Dylan. And her friend. And for the guy who ghosted her friend if Dylan ever catches up with him.

A part of me wants to maintain my innocence, but I'm not sure it matters.

"I get it," I tell her. "Your friend is hurting, and you're ready to go to battle. I respect that. Lord knows the battles my family has gotten me in. But I ..."

This placates her a little. She opens her mouth, but no words come out. Another deep breath is taken, causing the tiny chip of diamond in her nose to shine.

She's pretty. This girl with her golden-brown skin and long

eyelashes and personality for days would have me chasing after her if I didn't want to run out of fear for my life.

The venom in her eyes subsides. She reaches up and brushes back a strand of hair that came out as she railed me, and I see a tattoo on her wrist. It's the word *family* written in a delicate script. I think about my brother, Vincent, and how many times I've gone to war for him or my cousins.

I consider telling her I'm not who she thinks I am. But if I do that, she's going to start shouting again, which means I'll just be here longer fixing this damn truck. Besides, I did nothing wrong, so maybe I'll let it go. Let Dylan get it off her chest and move on. I have broad shoulders. Besides, the guy, whomever he is, probably wouldn't give a shit anyway from how it sounds. It'll probably make her feel better to think the guy feels bad—at least a little.

"I'm sorry," I say. "Is there anything I can do to make this better?"

"Stay away from her."

"I will. Promise. Cross my heart," I say, acting out the gesture in front of her. "Anything else?"

She nods, looking around Dave's front yard. "Well, you could bring her pots and pans back. They were the first nice thing she ever bought for herself, and it makes it easier to save money if you can cook at home. I'm sure she'd like to have them returned."

"Okay," I say, wondering why some dude would take a woman's kitchen equipment. "I'll see what I can do."

I bite my bottom lip, trying to figure out how to get a set of pans back from a guy I don't even know. Dylan scrutinizes every move I make. Finally, she shakes her head.

"You pawned them, didn't you?"

"No," I insist, slightly offended. "I wouldn't pawn someone's pots and pans. Who do you think I am?"

"A jackass."

I roll my eyes. "Right. I forgot."

"And you could bring me a bottle of Jack. After all, I'm helping her pick up all the pieces of her heart that you so thoughtlessly threw against the wall. So thanks for that."

"You're welcome."

She scowls. "Really?"

"Look, I'm doing my best here," I say with a chuckle. "Give me some credit."

Her arms cross over her chest as she considers this. "Fine. I'll give you *some* credit for at least *sort of* taking responsibility. That's it. That's all you get."

"Good enough, I guess."

With a satisfied nod of her head, she starts to turn away, but then she stops before she gets too far. "One more thing," she says, looking at me over her shoulder. "Don't tell Navie I was here."

I blink once. Twice. Three times.

Navie? Bartender Navie? Navie-Who-Works-At-My-Cousin's-Bar Navie?

My friend Navie?

Navie knows Dylan? And Dylan doesn't know me?

Am I being set up here?

I grab at my temple with my right hand.

"You won't, right?" Dylan asks when I fail to answer.

"Yeah. Sure. I, um, I won't say a word," I say, trying to piece all this together.

Her shoulders relax, the V-neck dropping low enough to see the cleavage that I would enjoy any other time except right now when I'm mentally marinating Navie knowing Dylan and Dylan thinking I'm some other guy.

I run a hand down my face and, once again, regret not going back to bed.

"It's a shame you're such a jackass," she says.

I drop my hands. "Well, thanks. But I'm not one really."

"I beg to differ."

"Suit yourself," I say. "But tell Navie that if she needs to talk—"

"Nope. If you want to talk to her, you do it. Be a man. Prove me wrong." She walks toward her car again. "And bring back her pots and pans. Do you hear me?"

"If I can find them."

She stops at her car and flings open the door. Her eyes narrow again. She's so damn cute, and this entire thing is so bizarre that I can't take it. I laugh.

"If you don't find them, I'll come find you," she says.

"Could you warn me first? And let me schedule that into my day because I'm running about a half hour behind right now."

She fights a smile as she climbs into her car. She pulls away just as quickly as she arrived, and I'm left standing next to Old Man Dave's truck, wondering what the hell just happened.

Crazy is now available on Amazon, Audible, and is in Kindle Unlimited.

About the Author

Adriana Locke is a USA Today and Amazon Charts Bestselling author with a knack for writing swoony, unforgettable contemporary romances. At nineteen, she traded her small-town roots for big-city life, only to realize her heart beats for quiet mornings and cozy chaos. These days, she's living her happily-ever-after in Ohio with Mr. Locke—her high school sweetheart—four lively sons, and two hilariously hyper Jack Russell terriers.

When she's not penning love stories that will leave you laughing and sighing, Adriana is battling the epic quest of missing silverware, "gardening" (a.k.a. chatting with her plants), or leaving her grocery list on the counter as she heads to the store. Grab a cup of coffee, settle in, and let her books whisk you away to a world of heartwarming romance and irresistible heroes.

Join her reader group and talk all the bookish things by clicking here.

www.adrianalocke.com

Acknowledgments

As always, first and foremost, thank you to the Creator for everything in my life. Even the difficult times are a blessing and I'm forever grateful.

So much love to Mr. Locke and our four sons. Your support, love, and cheerleading fills my heart. You are the greatest part of my life.

My mom is "that mom". The one that hands out her daughter's pens and Amazon link to everyone she meets. She's also the best mom in the whole wide world. Thank you for being the role model every little girl should have.

My mother-in-law makes the best butterscotch pie ever. (Hint, hint, Peggy.) And even though Rob has sketchy sports team preferences, he's still pretty special. I love you both.

My team is the best. Plain and simple. Kari March, Tiffany Remy, Kim Cermak, Jen Costa, Susan Rayner, Carleen Riffle, Michele Ficht, Candace Fleming— thank you doesn't come close. Not only do you give so much to my books, but you give so much to me. You're some of the best people I know and I adore you all. So very much.

Mandi Beck is the ying to my yang. (Or is it the other way around?)

Without the ten calls a day to S.L. Scott, I don't think I'd make it. (But I could forgo all the stock image searches. Ha!)

Becca Mysoor is everything. More than a developmental editor, more than a set of eyes on a book, she brings joy and light and honesty to every project. I love working with you, sweet friend.

Jenny Sims took me on last minute and did an impeccable job editing this book. Girl, I'm so glad I found you. I'm even happier you can deal with my madness! Thank you for working with me. I'm honored.

Ebbie Moresco keeps Books by Adriana Locke moving (literally!) and Kaitie Reister is the admin-in-chief of All Locked UP. You two do such an amazing job. I could never thank you enough.

I would like to take a second to thank all the bloggers that work so tirelessly to bring book love to the world. I see you. I appreciate you. You are loved!

Books by Adriana Locke is my Facebook group and also my happy place. Filled with the most amazing women (and a few men), it's a concentration of laughs, support, and love. Thank you for being just as an important member of my team as anyone.

And you, the person reading this—thank you. I appreciate your willingness to try Crave. I hope you enjoyed it.

Xo, Adriana

www.ingramcontent.com/pod-product-compliance
Lightning Source LLC
Chambersburg PA
CBHW011139310726

48972CB00009B/2771